PENGUIN BOOKS

OUTSIDE IRELAND: SELECTED STORIES

William Trevor was born in Mitchelstown, Co. Cork, in 1928, and spent his childhood in provincial Ireland. He attended a number of Irish schools and later Trinity College, Dublin. He is a member of the Irish Academy of Letters.

Among his books are *The Old Boys* (1964), winner of the Hawthornden Prize, *The Boarding House* (1965), *The Love Department* (1966), *Mrs Eckdorf in O'Neill's Hotel* (1969), *Miss Gomez and the Brethren* (1971), *Elizabeth Alone* (1973), *The Children of Dynmouth* (1976), winner of the Whitbread Award, *Other People's Worlds* (1980), *Fools of Fortune* (1983), winner of the Whitbread Award, *A Writer's Ireland* (1984), *The Silence in the Garden* (1988), winner of the *Yorkshire Post* Book of the Year Award, and *Two Lives* (1991), which was short listed for the *Sunday Express* Book of the Year Award and includes the Booker-shortlisted novella *Reading Turgenev*. His latest novel, *Felicia's Journey*, was published by Viking in 1994 and is forthcoming in Penguin. His seven volumes of previously published short stories, together with four new stories, were brought together as the *Collected Stories of William Trevor* (1992). A collection of his autobiographical essays entitled *Excursions in the Real World* appeared in 1993. Many of his books are published by Penguin. He is also the editor of *The Oxford Book of Irish Short Stories* (1989) and has written plays for the stage and for radio and television. Several of his television plays have been based on his short stories. In 1976 William Trevor received the Allied Irish Banks' Prize and in 1977 was awarded an honorary CBE in recognition of his valuable services to literature. In 1992 he received the *Sunday Times* Award for Literary Excellence.

Penguin also publish a companion volume of short stories entitled *Ireland: Selected Stories*.

WILLIAM TREVOR

OUTSIDE IRELAND: SELECTED STORIES

PENGUIN BOOKS

PENGUIN BOOKS

Published by the Penguin Group
Penguin Books Ltd, 27 Wrights Lane, London W8 5TZ, England
Penguin Books USA Inc., 375 Hudson Street, New York, New York 10014, USA
Penguin Books Australia Ltd, Ringwood, Victoria, Australia
Penguin Books Canada Ltd, 10 Alcorn Avenue, Toronto, Ontario, Canada M4V 3B2
Penguin Books (NZ) Ltd, 182–190 Wairau Road, Auckland 10, New Zealand

Penguin Books Ltd, Registered Offices: Harmondsworth, Middlesex, England

William Trevor: The Collected Stories first published by Viking 1992
This selection published in Penguin Books 1995
3 5 7 9 10 8 6 4 2

'The General's Day', 'The Penthouse Apartment' and 'Raymond Bamber and Mrs Fitch'
from *The Day We Got Drunk On Cake and Other Stories*, Bodley Head 1967
Published in Penguin Books 1969

'Access to the Children', 'Going Home' and 'O, Fat White Women' from
The Ballroom of Romance and Other Stories, Bodley Head 1972
Published in Penguin Books 1976

'Broken Homes', 'Torridge' and 'Lovers of their Time' from
Lovers of their Time and Other Stories, Bodley Head 1978
Published in Penguin Books 1980

'On the Zattere', 'Running Away', 'Cocktails at Doney's' and 'Lunch in Winter' from
The News from Ireland and Other Stories, Bodley Head 1986
Published in Penguin Books 1987

'A Trinity', 'The Printmaker' and 'Coffee with Oliver' from
Family Sins and Other Stories, Bodley Head 1990
Published in Penguin Books 1991

'The Smoke Trees of San Pietro' first appeared in *William Trevor: The Collected Stories*
First published by Viking 1992

Printed in England by Clays Ltd, St Ives plc

CONTENTS

Author's Note

This selection of stories has been made from the Viking and Penguin edition of my *Collected Stories*. It is representative of this larger collection as a whole rather than being a personal choice of those stories which I consider to be the best.

Access to the Children

Malcolmson, a fair, tallish man in a green tweed suit that required pressing, banged the driver's door of his ten-year-old Volvo and walked quickly away from the car, jangling the keys. He entered a block of flats that was titled – gold engraved letters on a granite slab – The Quadrant.

It was a Sunday afternoon in late October. Yellow-brown leaves patterned grass that was not for walking on. Some scurried on the steps that led to the building's glass entrance doors. Rain was about, Malcolmson considered.

At three o'clock precisely he rang the bell of his ex-wife's flat on the third floor. In response he heard at once the voices of his children and the sound of their running in the hall. 'Hullo,' he said when one of them, Deirdre, opened the door. 'Ready?'

They went with him, two little girls, Deirdre seven and Susie five. In the lift they told him that a foreign person, the day before, had been trapped in the lift from eleven o'clock in the morning until teatime. Food and cups of tea had been poked through a grating to this person, a Japanese businessman who occupied a flat at the top of the block. 'He didn't get the hang of an English lift,' said Deirdre. 'He could have died there,' said Susie.

In the Volvo he asked them if they'd like to go to the Zoo and they shook their heads firmly. On the last two Sundays he'd taken them to the Zoo, Susie reminded him in her specially polite, very quiet voice: you got tired of the Zoo, walking round and round, looking at all the same animals. She smiled at him to show she wasn't being ungrateful. She suggested that in a little while, after a month or so, they could go to the Zoo again, because there might be some new animals. Deirdre said that there wouldn't be, not after a month or so: why should there be? 'Some old animals might have died,' said Susie.

Malcolmson drove down the Edgware Road, with Hyde Park in mind.

'What have you done?' he asked.

'Only school,' said Susie.

'And the news cinema,' said Deirdre. 'Mummy took us to a news cinema. We saw a film about how they make wire.'

'A man kept talking to Mummy. He said she had nice hair.'

'The usherette told him to be quiet. He bought us ice-creams, but Mummy said we couldn't accept them.'

'He wanted to take Mummy to a dance.'

'We had to move to other seats.'

'What else have you done?'

'Only school,' said Susie. 'A boy was sick on Miss Bawden's desk.'

'After school stew.'

'It's raining,' said Susie.

He turned the windscreen-wipers on. He wondered if he should simply bring the girls to his flat and spend the afternoon watching television. He tried to remember what the Sunday film was. There often was something suitable for children on Sunday afternoons, old films with Deanna Durbin or Nelson Eddy and Jeanette MacDonald.

'Where're we going?' Susie asked.

'Where d'you want to go?'

'*A Hundred and One Dalmatians*.'

'Oh, please,' said Susie.

'But we've seen it. We've seen it five times.'

'Please, Daddy.'

He stopped the Volvo and bought a *What's On*. While he leafed through it they sat quietly, willing him to discover a cinema, anywhere in London, that was showing the film. He shook his head and started the Volvo again.

'Nothing else?' Deirdre asked.

'Nothing suitable.'

At Speakers' Corner they listened to a Jehovah's Witness and then to a woman talking about vivisection. 'How horrid,' said Deirdre. 'Is that true, Daddy?' He made a face. 'I suppose so,' he said.

In the drizzle they played a game among the trees, hiding and chasing one another. Once when they'd been playing this game a woman had brought a policeman up to him. She'd seen him approaching the girls, she said; the girls had been playing alone and he'd joined in. 'He's our daddy,' Susie had said, but the woman had still argued, claiming that he'd given them sweets so that they'd say that. 'Look at him,' the woman had insultingly said. 'He needs a shave.' Then she'd gone away, and the policeman had apologized.

'The boy who was sick was Nicholas Barnet,' Susie said. 'I think he could have died.'

A year and a half ago Malcolmson's wife, Elizabeth, had said he must choose between her and Diana. For weeks they had talked about it; she knowing that he was in love with Diana and was having some kind of an affair with her, he caught between the two of them, attempting the impossible in his effort not to hurt anyone. She had given him a chance to get over Diana, as she put it, but she couldn't go on for ever giving him a chance, no woman could. In the end, after the shock and the tears and the period of reasonableness, she became bitter. He didn't blame her: they'd been in the middle of a happy marriage, nothing was wrong, nothing was lacking.

He'd met Diana on a train; he'd sat with her, talking for a long time, and after that his marriage didn't seem the same. In her bitterness Elizabeth said he was stupidly infatuated: he was behaving like a murderer: there was neither dignity nor humanity left in him. Diana she described as a flat-chested American nymphomaniac and predator, the worst type of woman in the world. She was beautiful herself, more beautiful than Diana, more gracious, warmer, and funnier: there was a sting of truth in what she said; he couldn't understand himself. In the very end, after they'd been morosely drinking gin and lime-juice, she'd suddenly shouted at him that he'd better pack his bags. He sat unhappily, gazing at the green bottle of Gordon's gin on the carpet between his chair and hers. She screamed; tears poured in a torrent from her eyes. 'For God's sake go away!' she cried, on her feet, turning away from him. She shook her head in a wild gesture, causing her long fair hair to move like a horse's mane. Her hands, clenched into fists, beat at his cheeks, making bruises that Diana afterwards tended.

For months after that he saw neither Elizabeth nor his children. He tried not to think about them. He and Diana took a flat in Barnes, near the river, and in time he became used to the absence of the children's noise in the mornings, and to Diana's cooking and her quick efficiency in little things, and the way she always remembered to pass on telephone messages, which was something that Elizabeth had always forgotten to do.

Then one day, a week or so before the divorce was due, Diana said she didn't think there was anything left between them. It hadn't worked, she said; nothing was quite right. Amazed and bewildered, he argued with her. He frowned at her, his eyes screwed up as though he couldn't properly see her. She was very poised, in a black dress, with a necklace at her throat, her hair pulled smooth and neatly tied. She'd met a man called Abbotforth, she said, and she went on talking about that, still standing.

'We could go to the Natural History Museum,' Deirdre said.

'Would you like to, Susie?'

'Certainly not,' said Susie.

They were sitting on a bench, watching a bird that Susie said was a yellow-hammer. Deirdre disagreed: at this time of year, she said, there were no yellow-hammers in England, she'd read it in a book. 'It's a little baby yellow-hammer,' said Susie. 'Miss Bawden said you see lots of them.'

The bird flew away. A man in a raincoat was approaching them, singing quietly. They began to giggle. *'Sure, maybe some day I'll go back to Ireland,'* sang the man, *'if it's only at the closing of my day.'* He stopped, noticing that they were watching him.

'Were you ever in Ireland?' he asked. The girls, still giggling, shook their heads. 'It's a great place,' said the man. He took a bottle of VP wine from his raincoat pocket and drank from it.

'Would you care for a swig, sir?' he said to Malcolmson, and Malcolmson thanked him and said he wouldn't. 'It would do the little misses no harm,' suggested the man. 'It's good, pure stuff.' Malcolmson shook his head. 'I was born in County Clare,' said the man, 'in 1928, the year of the Big Strike.' The girls, red in the face from containing their laughter, poked at one another with their elbows. 'Aren't they the great little misses?' said the man. 'Aren't they the fine credit to you, sir?'

In the Volvo on the way to Barnes they kept repeating that he was the funniest man they'd ever met. He was nicer than the man in the news cinema, Susie said. He was quite like him, though, Deirdre maintained: he was looking for company in just the same way, you could see it in his eyes. 'He was staggering,' Susie said. 'I thought he was going to die.'

Before the divorce he had telephoned Elizabeth, telling her that Diana had gone. She hadn't said anything, and she'd put the receiver down before he could say anything else. Then the divorce came through and the arrangement was that the children should remain with Elizabeth and that he should have reasonable access to them. It was an extraordinary expression, he considered: reasonable access.

The Sunday afternoons had begun then, the ringing of a doorbell that had once been his own doorbell, the children in the hall, the lift, the Volvo, tea in the flat where he and Diana had lived and where now he lived on his own. Sometimes, when he was collecting them, Elizabeth spoke to him, saying in a matter-of-fact way that Susie had a cold and should not be outside too much, or that Deirdre was being bad about practising her clarinet and would he please speak to her. He loved Elizabeth again; he said to himself that he had never not loved her; he wanted to say to her that she'd been right about Diana. But he didn't say anything, knowing that wounds had to heal.

Every week he longed more for Sunday to arrive. Occasionally he invented reasons for talking to her at the door of the flat, after the children had gone in. He asked questions about their progress at school, he wondered if there were ways in which he could help. It seemed unfair, he said, that she should have to bring them up single-handed like this; he made her promise to telephone him if a difficulty arose; and if ever she wanted to go out in the evenings and couldn't find a babysitter, he'd willingly drive over. He always hoped that if he talked for long enough the girls would become so noisy in their room that she'd be forced to ask him in so that she could quieten them, but the ploy never worked.

In the lift on the way down every Sunday evening he thought she was more beautiful than any woman he'd ever seen, and he thought it was amazing that once she should have been his wife and should have borne him children, that once they had lain together and loved, and that he had let her go. Three weeks ago she had smiled at him in a way that was like the old way. He'd been sure of it, positive, in the lift on the way down.

He drove over Hammersmith Bridge, along Castelnau and into Barnes High Street. No one was about on the pavements; buses crept sluggishly through the damp afternoon.

'Miss Bawden's got a black boyfriend,' Susie said, 'called Eric Mantilla.'

'You should see Miss Bawden,' murmured Deirdre. 'She hasn't any breasts.'

'She has lovely breasts,' shouted Susie, 'and lovely jumpers and lovely skirts. She has a pair of earrings that once belonged to an Egyptian empress.'

'Flat as a pancake,' said Deirdre.

After Diana had gone he'd found it hard to concentrate. The managing director of the firm where he worked, a man with a stout red face called Sir Gerald Travers, had been sympathetic. He'd told him not to worry. Personal troubles, Sir Gerald had said, must naturally affect professional life; no one would be human if that didn't happen. But six months later, to Malcolmson's surprise, Sir Gerald had suddenly suggested to him that perhaps it would be better if he made a move. 'It's often so,' Sir Gerald had said, a soft smile gleaming between chubby cheeks. 'Professional life can be affected by the private side of things. You understand me, Malcolmson?' They valued him immensely, Sir Gerald said, and they'd be generous when the moment of departure came. A change was a tonic; Sir Gerald advised a little jaunt somewhere.

In reply to all that Malcolmson said that the upset in his private life was now over; nor did he feel, he added, in need of recuperation. 'You'll easily find another berth,' Sir Gerald Travers replied, with a wide, confident smile. 'I think it would be better.'

Malcolmson had sought about for another job, but had not been immediately successful: there was a recession, people said. Soon it would be better, they added, and because of Sir Gerald's promised generosity Malcolmson found himself in a position to wait until things seemed brighter. It was always better, in any case, not to seem in a hurry.

He spent the mornings in the Red Lion, in Barnes, playing dominoes with an old-age pensioner, and when the pensioner didn't turn up owing to bronchial trouble Malcolmson would borrow a newspaper from the landlord. He slept in the afternoons and returned to the Red Lion later. Occasionally when he'd had a few drinks he'd find himself thinking about his children and their mother. He always found it pleasant then, thinking of them with a couple of drinks inside him.

'It's *The Last of the Mohicans*,' said Deirdre in the flat, and he guessed that she must have looked at the *Radio Times* earlier in the day. She'd known they'd end up like that, watching television. Were they bored on Sundays? he often wondered.

'Can't we have *The Golden Shot*?' demanded Susie, and Deirdre pointed out that it wasn't on yet. He left them watching Randolph Scott and Binnie Barnes, and went to prepare their tea in the kitchen.

On Saturdays he bought meringues and brandy-snaps in Frith's Patisserie. The elderly assistant smiled at him in a way that made him wonder if she knew what he wanted them for; it occurred to him once that she felt sorry for him. On Sunday mornings, listening to the omnibus edition of *The Archers*, he made Marmite sandwiches with brown bread and tomato sandwiches with white. They loved sandwiches, which was something he remembered from the past. He remembered parties, Deirdre's friends sitting around a table, small and silent, eating crisps and cheese puffs and leaving all the cake.

When *The Last of the Mohicans* came to an end they watched *Going for a Song* for five minutes before changing the channel for *The Golden Shot*. Then Deirdre turned the television off and they went to the kitchen to have tea. 'Wash your hands,' said Susie, and he heard her add that if a germ got into your food you could easily die. 'She kept referring to death,' he would say to Elizabeth when he left them back. 'D'you think she's worried about anything?' He imagined Elizabeth giving the smile she had given three weeks ago and then saying he'd better come in to discuss the matter.

'Goody,' said Susie, sitting down.

'I'd like to marry a man like that man in the park,' said Deirdre. 'It'd be much more interesting, married to a bloke like that.'

'He'd be always drunk.'

'He wasn't drunk, Susie. That's not being drunk.'

'He was drinking out of a bottle –'

'He was putting on a bit of flash, drinking out of a bottle and singing his little song. No harm in that, Susie.'

'I'd like to be married to Daddy.'

'You couldn't be married to Daddy.'

'Well, Richard then.'

'Ribena, Daddy. Please.'

He poured drops of Ribena into two mugs and filled them up with warm water. He had a definite feeling that today she'd ask him in, both of them pretending a worry over Susie's obsession with death. They'd sit together while the children splashed about in the bathroom; she'd offer him gin and lime-juice, their favourite drink, a drink known as a Gimlet, as once he'd told her. They'd drink it out of the green glasses they'd bought, years ago, in Italy. The girls would dry themselves and come to say good-night. They'd go to bed. He might tell them a story, or she would. 'Stay to supper,' she would say, and while she made risotto he would go to her and kiss her hair.

'I like his eyes,' said Susie. 'One's higher than another.'

'It couldn't be.'

'It is.'

'He couldn't see, Susie, if his eyes were like that. Everyone's eyes are –'

'He isn't always drunk like the man in the park.'

'Who?' he asked.

'Richard,' they said together, and Susie added: 'Irishmen are always drunk.'

'Daddy's an Irishman and Daddy's not always –'

'Who's Richard?'

'He's Susie's boyfriend.'

'I don't mind,' said Susie. 'I like him.'

'If he's there tonight, Susie, you're not to climb all over him.'

He left the kitchen and in the sitting-room he poured himself some whisky. He sat with the glass cold between his hands, staring at the grey television screen. 'Sure, maybe some day I'll go back to Ireland,' Deirdre sang in the kitchen, and Susie laughed shrilly.

He imagined a dark-haired man, a cheerful man, intelligent and subtle, a man who came often to the flat, whom his children knew well and were already fond of. He imagined him as he had imagined himself ten minutes before, sitting with Elizabeth, drinking Gimlets from the green Italian glasses. 'Say good-night to Richard,' Elizabeth would say, and the girls would go to him and kiss him good-night.

'Who's Richard?' he asked, standing in the kitchen doorway.

'A friend,' said Deirdre, 'of Mummy's.'

'A nice friend?'

'Oh, yes.'

'I love him,' said Susie.

He returned to the sitting-room and quickly poured himself more whisky. Both of his hands were shaking. He drank quickly, and then poured and drank some more. On the pale carpet, close to the television set, there was a stain where Diana had spilt a cup of coffee. He hated now this memory of her, he hated her voice when it came back to him, and the memory of her body and her mind. And yet once he had been rendered lunatic with the passion of his love for her. He had loved her more than Elizabeth, and in his madness he had spoilt everything.

'Wash your hands,' said Susie, close to him. He hadn't heard them come into the room. He asked them, mechanically, if they'd had enough to eat. 'She hasn't washed her hands,' Susie said. 'I washed mine in the sink.'

He turned the television on. It was the girl ventriloquist Shari Lewis, with Lamb Chop and Charley Horse.

Well, he thought under the influence of the whisky, he had had his fling. He had played the pins with a flat-chested American nymphomaniac and predator, and he had lost all there was to lose. Now it was Elizabeth's turn: why shouldn't she have, for a time, the dark-haired Richard who took another man's children on to his knee and kissed them good-night? Wasn't it better that the score should be even before they all came together again?

He sat on the floor with his daughters on either side of him, his arms about them. In front of him was his glass of whisky. They laughed at Lamb Chop and Charley Horse, and when the programme came to an end and the news came on he didn't want to let his daughters go. An electric fire glowed cosily. Wind blew the rain against the windows, the autumn evening was dark already.

He turned the television off. He finished the whisky in his glass and poured some more. 'Shall I tell you,' he said, 'about when Mummy and I were married?'

They listened while he did so. He told them about meeting Elizabeth in the first place, at somebody else's wedding, and of the days they had spent walking about together, and about the wet, cold afternoon on which they'd been married.

'February the 24th,' Deirdre said.

'Yes.'

'I'm going to be married in summer-time,' Susie said, 'when the roses are out.'

His birthday and Elizabeth's were on the same day, April 21st. He reminded the girls of that; he told them of the time he and Elizabeth had discovered they shared the date, a date shared also with Hitler and the Queen. They listened quite politely, but somehow didn't seem much interested.

They watched *What's in a Game*? He drank a little more. He wouldn't be able to drive them back. He'd pretend he couldn't start the Volvo and then he'd telephone for a taxi. It had happened once before that in a depression he'd begun to drink when they were with him on a Sunday afternoon. They'd been to Madame Tussaud's and the Planetarium, which Susie had said frightened her. In the flat, just as this time, while they were eating their sandwiches, he'd been overcome with the longing that they should all be together again. He'd begun to drink and in the end, while they watched television, he'd drunk quite a lot. When the time came to go he'd said that he couldn't find the keys of the Volvo and that they'd have to have a taxi. He'd spent five minutes brushing his teeth so that Elizabeth wouldn't smell the alcohol when she opened the door. He'd smiled at her with his well-brushed teeth but she, not then being over her bitterness, hadn't smiled back.

The girls put their coats on. Deirdre drank some Ribena; he had another small tot of whisky. And then, as they were leaving the flat, he suddenly felt he couldn't go through the farce of walking to the Volvo, putting the girls into it and then pretending he couldn't start it. 'I'm tired,' he said instead. 'Let's have a taxi.'

They watched the Penrhyn Male Voice Choir in *Songs of Praise* while they waited for it to arrive. He poured himself another drink, drank it slowly, and then went to the bathroom to brush his teeth. He remembered the time Deirdre had been born, in a maternity home in the country because they'd lived in the country then. Elizabeth had been concerned because she'd thought one of Deirdre's fingers was bent and had kept showing it to nurses who said they couldn't see anything the matter. He hadn't been able to see anything the matter either, nor had the doctor. 'She'll never be as beautiful as you,' he'd said and quite soon after that she'd stopped talking about the finger and had said he was nice to her. Susie had been born at home, very quickly, very easily.

The taxi arrived. 'Soon be Christmas,' said the taxi man. 'You chaps looking forward to Santa Claus?' They giggled because he had called them chaps. 'Fifty-six more days,' said Susie.

He imagined them on Christmas Day, with the dark-haired Richard explaining the rules of a game he'd bought them. He imagined all four of them sitting down at Christmas dinner, and Richard asking the girls which they liked, the white or the brown of the turkey, and then cutting them small slices. He'd have brought, perhaps, champagne, because he was that kind of person. Deirdre would sip from his glass, not liking the taste. Susie would love it.

He counted in his mind: if Richard had been visiting the flat for, say, six weeks already and assuming that his love affair with Elizabeth had begun two weeks before his first visit, that left another four months to go, allowing the affair ran an average course of six months. It would therefore come to an end at the beginning of March. His own affair with Diana had lasted from April until September. 'Oh darling,' said Diana, suddenly in his mind, and his own voice replied to her, caressing her with words. He remembered the first time they had made love and the guilt that had hammered at him and the passion there had been between them. He imagined Elizabeth naked in Richard's naked arms, her eyes open, looking at him, her fingers touching the side of his face, her lips slightly smiling. He reached forward and pulled down the glass shutter. 'I need cigarettes,' he said. 'There's a pub in Shepherd's Bush Road, the Laurie Arms.'

He drank two large measures of whisky. He bought cigarettes and lit one, rolling the smoke around in his mouth to disguise the smell of the alcohol. As he returned to the taxi, he slipped on the wet pavement and almost lost his balance. He felt very drunk all of a sudden. Deirdre and Susie were telling the taxi man about the man in Hyde Park.

He was aware that he walked unsteadily when they left the taxi and moved across the forecourt of the block of flats. In the hall, before they got into the lift, he lit another cigarette, rolling the smoke about his mouth. 'That poor Japanese man,' said Deirdre.

He rang the bell, and when Elizabeth opened the door the girls turned to him and thanked him. He took the cigarette from his mouth and kissed them. Elizabeth was smiling: if only she'd ask him in and give him a drink he wouldn't have to worry about the alcohol on his breath. He swore to himself that she was smiling as she'd smiled three weeks ago. 'Can I come in?' he asked, unable to keep the words back.

'In?' The smile was still there. She was looking at him quite closely. He released the smoke from his mouth. He tried to remember what it was he'd planned to say, and then it came to him.

'I'm worried about Susie,' he said in a quiet voice. 'She talked about death all the time.'

'Death?'

'Yes.'

'There's someone here actually,' she said, stepping back into the hall. 'But come in, certainly.'

In the sitting-room she introduced him to Richard who was, as he'd imagined, a dark-haired man. The sitting-room was much the same as it always had been. 'Have a drink,' Richard offered.

'D'you mind if we talk about Susie?' Elizabeth asked Richard. He said he'd put them to bed if she liked. She nodded. Richard went away.

'Well?'

He stood with the familiar green glass in his hand, gazing at her. He said:

'I haven't had gin and lime-juice since –'

'Yes. Look, I shouldn't worry about Susie. Children of that age often say odd things, you know –'

'I don't mind about Richard, Elizabeth, I think it's your due. I worked it out in the taxi. It's the end of October now –'

'My due?'

'Assuming your affair has been going on already for six weeks –'

'You're drunk.'

He closed one eye, focusing. He felt his body swaying and he said to himself that he must not fall now, that no matter what his body did his feet must remain firm on the carpet. He sipped from the green glass. She wasn't, he noticed, smiling any more.

'I'm actually not drunk,' he said. 'I'm actually sober. By the time our birthday comes round, Elizabeth, it'll all be over. On April the 21st we could have family tea.'

'What the hell are you talking about?'

'The future, Elizabeth. Of you and me and our children.'

'How much have you had to drink?'

'We tried to go to *A Hundred and One Dalmatians*, but it wasn't on anywhere.'

'So you drank instead. While the children –'

'We came here in a taxi-cab. They've had their usual tea, they've watched a bit of *The Last of the Mohicans* and a bit of *Going for a Song* and all of *The Golden Shot* and *The Shari Lewis Show* and –'

'You see them for a few hours and you have to go and get drunk –'

'I am not drunk, Elizabeth.'

He crossed the room as steadily as he could. He looked aggressively at her. He poured gin and lime-juice. He said:

'You have a right to your affair with Richard, I recognize that.'

'A *right*?'

'I love you, Elizabeth.'

'You loved Diana.'

'I have never not loved you. Diana was nothing – nothing, nothing at all.'

'She broke our marriage up.'

'No.'

'We're divorced.'

'I love you, Elizabeth.'

'Now listen to me –'

'I live from Sunday to Sunday. We're a family, Elizabeth; you and me and them. It's ridiculous, all this. It's ridiculous making Marmite sandwiches with brown bread and tomato sandwiches with white. It's ridiculous buying meringues and going five times to *A Hundred and One Dalmatians* and going up the Post Office Tower until we're sick of the sight of it, and watching drunks in Hyde Park and poking about at the Zoo –'

'You have reasonable access –'

'Reasonable access, my God!' His voice rose. He felt sweat on his forehead. Reasonable access, he shouted, was utterly no good to him; reasonable access was meaningless and stupid; a day would come when they wouldn't want to go with him on Sunday afternoons, when there was nowhere left in London that wasn't an unholy bore. What about reasonable access then?

'Please be quiet.'

He sat down in the armchair that he had always sat in. She said:

'You might marry again. And have other children.'

'I don't want other children. I have children already. I want us all to live together as we used to –'

'Please listen to me –'

'I get a pain in my stomach in the middle of the night. Then I wake up and can't go back to sleep. The children will grow up and I'll grow old. I couldn't begin a whole new thing all over again: I haven't the courage. Not after Diana. A mistake like that alters everything.'

'I'm going to marry Richard.'

'Three weeks ago,' he said, as though he hadn't heard her, 'you smiled at me.'

'Smiled?'

'Like you used to, Elizabeth. Before –'

'You made a mistake,' she said, softly. 'I'm sorry.'

'I'm not saying don't go on with your affair with this man. I'm not saying that, because I think in the circumstances it'd be a cheek. D'you understand me, Elizabeth?'

'Yes, I do. And I think you and I can be perfectly good friends. I don't feel sour about it any more: perhaps that's what you saw in my smile.'

'Have a six-month affair –'

'I'm in love with Richard.'

'That'll all pass into the atmosphere. It'll be nothing at all in a year's time –'

'No.'

'I love you, Elizabeth.'

They stood facing one another, not close. His body was still swaying. The liquid in his glass moved gently, slopping to the rim and then settling back again. Her eyes were on his face: it was thinner, she was thinking. Her fingers played with the edge of a cushion on the back of the sofa.

'On Saturdays,' he said, 'I buy the meringues and the brandy-snaps in Frith's Patisserie. On Sunday morning I make the sandwiches. Then I cook sausages and potatoes for my lunch, and after that I come over here.'

'Yes, yes –'

'I look forward all week to Sunday.'

'The children enjoy their outings, too.'

'Will you think about it?'

'About what?'

'About all being together again.'

'Oh, for heaven's sake!' She turned away from him. 'I wish you'd go now,' she said.

'Will you come out with me on our birthday?'

'I've told you.' Her voice was loud and angry, her cheeks were flushed. 'Can't you understand? I'm going to marry Richard. We'll be married within a month, when the girls have had time to get to know him a little better. By Christmas we'll be married.'

He shook his head in a way that annoyed her, seeming in his drunkenness to deny the truth of what she was saying. He tried to light a cigarette; matches dropped to the floor at his feet. He left them there.

It enraged her that he was sitting in an armchair in her flat with his eyelids drooping through drink and an unlighted cigarette in his hand and his matches spilt all over the floor. They were his children, but she wasn't his wife: he'd destroyed her as a wife, he'd insulted her, he'd left her to bleed and she had called him a murderer.

'Our birthday,' he said, smiling at her as though already she had agreed to join him on that day. 'And Hitler's and the Queen's.'

'On our birthday if I go out with anyone it'll be Richard.'

'Our birthday is beyond the time –'

'For God's sake, there is no beyond the time. I'm in love with another man –'

'No.'

'On our birthday,' she shouted at him, 'on the night of our birthday

Richard will make love to me in the bed you slept in for nine years. You have access to the children. You can demand no more.'

He bent down and picked up a match. He struck it on the side of the empty box. The cigarette was bent. He lit it with a wobbling flame and dropped the used match on to the carpet. The dark-haired man, he saw, was in the room again. He'd come in, hearing her shouting like that. He was asking her if she was all right. She told him to go away. Her face was hard; bitterness was there again. She said, not looking at him:

'Everything was so happy. We had a happy marriage. For nine years we had a perfectly happy marriage.'

'We could –'

'Not ever.'

Again he shook his head in disagreement. Cigarette ash fell on to the green tweed of his suit. His eyes were narrowed, watching her, seemingly suspicious.

'We had a happy marriage,' she repeated, whispering the words, speaking to herself, still not looking at him. 'You met a woman on a train and that was that: you murdered our marriage. You left me to plead, as I am leaving you to now. You have your Sunday access. There is that legality between us. Nothing more.'

'Please, Elizabeth –'

'Oh for God's sake, stop.' Her rage was all in her face now. Her lips quivered as though in an effort to hold back words that would not be denied. They came from her, more quietly but with greater bitterness. Her eyes roved over the green tweed suit of the man who once had been her husband, over his thin face and his hair that seemed, that day, not to have been brushed.

'You've gone to seed,' she said, hating herself for saying that, unable to prevent herself. 'You've gone to seed because you've lost your self-respect. I've watched you, week by week. The woman you met on a train took her toll of you and now in your seediness you want to creep back. Don't you know you're not the man I married?'

'Elizabeth –'

'You didn't have cigarette burns all over your clothes. You didn't smell of toothpaste when you should have smelt of drink. You stand there, pathetically, Sunday after Sunday, trying to keep a conversation going. D'you know what I feel?'

'I love –'

'I feel sorry for you.'

He shook his head. There was no need to feel sorry for him, he said, remembering suddenly the elderly assistant in Frith's Patisserie and remembering also, for some reason, the woman in Hyde Park who peculiarly had said that he wasn't shaved. He looked down at his clothes and saw the burn marks she had mentioned. 'We think it would be better', said the voice of Sir Gerald Travers unexpectedly in his mind.

'I'll make some coffee,' said Elizabeth.

She left him. He had been cruel, and then Diana had been cruel, and now Elizabeth was cruel because it was her right and her instinct to be so. He recalled with vividness Diana's face in those first moments on the train, her eyes looking at him, her voice. 'You have lost all dignity,' Elizabeth had whispered, in the darkness, at night. 'I despise you for that.' He tried to stand up but found the effort beyond him. He raised the green glass to his lips. His eyes closed and when he opened them again he thought for a drunken moment that he was back in the past, in the middle of his happy marriage. He wiped at his face with a handkerchief.

He saw across the room the bottle of Gordon's gin so nicely matching the green glasses, and the lime-juice, a lighter shade of green. He made the journey, his legs striking the arms of chairs. There wasn't much gin in the bottle. He poured it all out; he added lime-juice, and drank it.

In the hall he could hear voices, his children's voices in the bathroom, Elizabeth and the man speaking quietly in the kitchen. 'Poor wretch,' Elizabeth was saying. He left the flat and descended to the ground floor.

The rain was falling heavily. He walked through it, thinking that it was better to go, quietly and without fuss. It would all work out; he knew it; he felt it definitely in his bones. He'd arrive on Sunday, a month or so before their birthday, and something in Elizabeth's face would tell him that the dark-haired man had gone for ever, as Diana had gone. By then he'd be established again, with better prospects than the red-faced Sir Gerald Travers had ever offered him. On their birthday they'd both apologize to one another, wiping the slate clean: they'd start again. As he crossed the Edgware Road to the public house in which he always spent an hour or so on Sunday nights, he heard his own voice murmuring that it was understandable that she should have taken it out on him, that she should have tried to hurt him by saying he'd gone to seed. Naturally, she'd say a thing like that; who could blame her after all she'd been through? At night in the flat in Barnes he watched television until the programmes closed down. He usually had a few drinks, and as often as not he dropped off to sleep with a cigarette between his fingers: that was how the burns occurred on his clothes.

He nodded to himself as he entered the saloon bar, thinking he'd been wise not to mention any of that to Elizabeth. It would only have annoyed her, having to listen to a lot of stuff about late-night television and cigarettes. Monday, Tuesday, Wednesday, he thought, Thursday, Friday. On Saturday he'd buy the meringues and brandy-snaps, and then it would be Sunday. He'd make the sandwiches listening to *The Archers*, and at three o'clock he'd ring the bell of the flat. He smiled in the saloon bar, thinking of that, seeing in his mind the faces of his children and the beautiful face of their mother. He'd planted an idea in Elizabeth's mind and even though she'd been a bit shirty she'd see when she thought about it that it was what she wanted, too.

He went on drinking gin and lime-juice, quietly laughing over being so upset when the children had first mentioned the dark-haired man who took them on to his knee. Gin and lime-juice was a Gimlet, he told the barmaid. She smiled at him. He was celebrating, he said, a day that was to come. It was ridiculous, he told her, that a woman casually met on a train should have created havoc, that now, at the end of it all, he should week by week butter bread for Marmite and tomato sandwiches. 'D'you understand me?' he drunkenly asked the barmaid. 'It's *too* ridiculous to be true – that man will go because none of it makes sense the way it is.' The barmaid smiled again and nodded. He bought her a glass of beer, which was something he did every Sunday night. He wept as he paid for it, and touched his cheeks with the tips of his fingers to wipe away the tears. Every Sunday he wept, at the end of the day, after he'd had his access. The barmaid raised her glass, as always she did. They drank to the day that was to come, when the error he had made would be wiped away, when the happy marriage could continue. 'Ridiculous,' he said. 'Of course it is.'

The General's Day

General Suffolk pulled on two grey knitted socks and stood upright. Humming a marching air, he walked to the bathroom, intent upon his morning shave. The grey socks were his only apparel and he noticed as he passed the mirror of his wardrobe the white spare body of an elderly man reflected without flattery. He voiced no comment nor did he ponder, even in passing, upon this pictured nakedness. He was used to the sight; and had, over the years, accepted the changes as they came. Still humming, he half filled the wash-basin with water. It felt keenly warm on his fingers, a circumstance he inwardly congratulated himself on.

With deft strokes the General cleared his face of lather and whisker, savouring the crisp rasp of razor upon flesh. He used a cut-throat article and when shorn to his satisfaction wiped it on a small absorbent pad, one of a series he had collected from the bedrooms of foreign hotels. He washed, dressed, set his moustache as he liked to sport it, and descended to his kitchen.

The General's breakfast was simple: an egg poached lightly, two slices of toast and a pot of tea. It took him ten minutes to prepare and ten to consume. As he finished he heard the footsteps of the woman who daily came to work for him. They were slow, dragging footsteps implying the bulk they gracelessly shifted. The latch of the door rose and fell and Mrs Hinch, string bags and hairnet, cigarette cocked from the corner of her mouth, stood grinning before him. 'Hullo,' this woman said, adding as she often did, 'my dear.'

'Good morning, Mrs Hinch.'

Mrs Hinch stripped herself of bags, coat and cigarette with a single complicated gesture. She grinned again at the General, replaced her cigarette and set to clearing the table.

'I shall walk to the village this morning,' General Suffolk informed her. 'It seems a pleasant morning to dawdle through. I shall take coffee at the brown café and try my luck at picking up some suitable matron.'

Mrs Hinch was accustomed to her employer's turn of speech. She laughed shrilly at this sally, pleased that the man would be away for the morning. 'Ah, General, you'll be the death of us,' she cried; and planned for his absence a number of trunk calls on his telephone, a leisurely bath and the imbibing of as much South African sherry as she considered discreet.

'It is Saturday if I am not mistaken,' the General went on. 'A good morning for my plans. Is it not a fact that there are stout matrons in and out of the brown café by the score on a Saturday morning?'

'Why, sure, General,' said Mrs Hinch, anxious to place no barrier in his way. 'Why, half the county goes to the brown café of a Saturday morning. You are certain to be successful this time.'

'Cheering words, Mrs Hinch, cheering words. It is one thing to walk through the campion-clad lanes on a June morning, but quite another to do so with an objective one is sanguine of achieving.'

'This is your day, General. I feel it in my bones. I said it to Hobson as I left. "This is a day for the General," I said. "The General will do well today," I said.'

'And Hobson, Mrs Hinch? Hobson replied?'

Again Mrs Hinch, like a child's toy designed for the purpose, shrilled her merriment.

'General, General, Hobson's my little bird.'

The General, rising from the table, frowned. 'Do you imagine I am unaware of that? Since for six years you have daily informed me of the fact. And why, pray, since the bird is a parrot, should the powers of speech be beyond it? It is not so with other parrots.'

'Hobson's silent, General. You know Hobson's silent.'

'Due to your lethargy, Mrs Hinch. No bird of his nature need be silent: God does not intend it. He has taken some pains to equip the parrot with the instruments of speech. It is up to you to pursue the matter in a practical way by training the animal. A child, Mrs Hinch, does not remain ignorant of self-expression. Nor of the ability to feed and clean itself. The mother teaches, Mrs Hinch. It is part of nature. So with your parrot.'

Enthusiastic in her own defence, Mrs Hinch said: 'I have brought up seven children. Four girls and three boys.'

'Maybe. Maybe. I am in no position to question this. But indubitably with your parrot you are flying in the face of nature.'

'Oh, General, never. Hobson's silent and that's that.'

The General regarded his adversary closely. 'You miss my point,' he said drily; and repeating the remark twice he left the room.

In his time General Suffolk had been a man of more than ordinary importance. As a leader and a strategist in two great wars he had risen rapidly to the heights implied by the title he bore. He had held in his hands the lives of many thousands of men; his decisions had more than once set the boundaries of nations. Steely intelligence and physical prowess had led him, in their different ways, to glories that few experience at Roeux; and at Monchy-le-Preux he had come close to death. Besides all that, there was about the General a quality that is rare in the ultimate leaders of his army: he was to the last a rake, and for this humanity a popular figure. He had cared for women, for money, for alcohol of every sort; but in the end he had found himself with none of these commodities. In his modest cottage he was an elderly man with a violent past; with neither wife nor riches nor cellar to help him on his way.

Mrs Hinch had said he would thrive today. That the day should be agreeable was all he asked. He did not seek merriness or reality or some moment of truth. He had lived for long enough to forgo excitement; he had had his share; he wished only that the day, and his life in it, should go the way he wished.

In the kitchen Mrs Hinch scoured the dishes briskly. She was not one to do things by halves; hot water and detergent in generous quantities was her way.

'Careful with the cup handles,' the General admonished her. 'Adhesive for the repair of such a fracture has apparently not yet been perfected. And the cups themselves are valuable.'

'Oh they're flimsy, General. So flimsy you can't watch them. Declare to God, I shall be glad to see the last of them!'

'But not I, Mrs Hinch. I like those cups. Tea tastes better from fine china. I would take it kindly if you washed and dried with care.'

'Hoity-toity, General! Your beauties are safe with me. I treat them as babies.'

'Babies? Hardly a happy analogy, Mrs Hinch – since five of the set are lost for ever.'

'Six,' said Mrs Hinch, snapping beneath the water the handle from the cup. 'You are better without the bother of them. I shall bring you a coronation mug.'

'You fat old bitch,' shouted the General. 'Six makes the set. It was my last remaining link with the gracious life.'

Mrs Hinch, understanding and wishing to spite the General further, laughed. 'Cheery-bye, General,' she called as she heard him rattling among his walking sticks. He banged the front door and stepped out into the heat of the day. Mrs Hinch turned on the wireless.

'*I walked entranced*,' intoned the General, '*through a land of morn. The sun in wondrous excess of light* ...' He was seventy-eight: his memory faltered over the quotation. His stick, weapon of his irritation, thrashed through the campions, covering the road with broken blooms. Grasshoppers clicked; bees darted, paused, humming in flight, silent in labour.

The road was brown with dust, dry and hot in the sunlight. It was a day, thought the General, to be successfully in love; and he mourned that the ecstasy of love on a hot summer's day was so far behind him. Not that he had gone without it; which gave him his yardstick and saddened him the more.

Early in his retirement General Suffolk had tried his hand in many directions. He had been, to start with, the secretary of a golf club; though in a matter of months his temper relieved him of the task. He was given to disagreement and did not bandy words. He strode away from the golf club, red in the face, the air behind him stinging with insults. He lent his talents to the business world and to a military academy: both were dull and in both he failed. He bought his cottage, agreeing with himself that retirement was retirement and meant what it suggested. Only once since moving to the country had he involved himself with salaried work: as a tennis coach in a girls' school. Despite his age he was active still on his legs and managed well enough. Too well, his grim and beady-eyed headmistress avowed, objecting to his method of instructing her virgins in the various stances by which they might achieve success with the serve. The General paused only to level at the headmistress a battery of expressions well known to him but new to her. He went on his way, his cheque in his wallet, his pockets bulging with small articles from her study. The girls he had taught pursued him, pressing upon him packets of cheap cigarettes, sweets and flowers.

The General walked on, his thoughts rambling. He thought of the past; of specific days, of moments of shame or pride in his life. The past was his hunting ground; from it came his pleasure and a good deal of everything else. Yet he was not proof against the moment he lived in. The present could snarl at him; could drown his memories so completely that when they surfaced again they were like the burnt tips of matches floating on a puddle, finished and done with. He walked through the summery day, puzzled that all this should be so.

The brown café, called 'The Cuppa', was, as General Suffolk and Mrs Hinch had anticipated, bustling with mid-morning traffic. Old men and their wives sat listening to the talk about them, exchanging by the way a hard comment on their fellows. Middle-aged women, outsize in linen dresses, were huddled three or four to a table, their great legs battling for room in inadequate space, their feet hot and unhappy in unwise shoes. Mothers passed unsuitable edibles towards the searching mouths of their young. Men with girls sipped at the pale creamy coffee, thinking only of the girls. Crumbs were everywhere; and the babel buzzed like a clockwork wind.

The General entered, surveyed the scene with distaste, and sat at a table already occupied by a youth engrossed in a weekly magazine. The youth, a fat bespotted lad, looked up and immediately grinned. General Suffolk replied in kind, stretching the flesh of his face to display his teeth in a smile designed to promote goodwill between them, for the pair were old friends.

'Good morning, Basil. And how is youth and vigour today?'

'Oh well, not so bad, General. My mum's in the family way again.'

'A cause for joy,' murmured General Suffolk, ordering coffee with Devonshire cream and the fruit pie he favoured. 'Your mother is a great one for babies, is she not?'

'My dad says the same. He don't understand it neither. Worried, is Dad. Anyone can see that.'

'I see.'

'Well, it is a bit fishy, General. Dad's not the man to be careless. It's just about as fishy as hell.'

'Basil, your mother needs all the support she can get at a time like this. Talk about fishiness is scarcely going to help her in her ordeal.'

'Mum's had five. Drops 'em like hot bricks so she says. Thing is, if this one's fishy what about the others?'

The General placed a portion of pie in his mouth. Crumbs of pastry and other matter lingered on his moustache. 'You are thinking of yourself, Basil.'

'Wouldn't you? I mean to say.'

'I would attach no importance to such a doubt, I do assure you. Basil, what do you say we spend this afternoon at some local fête? It is just an afternoon for a fête. I will stand you lunch.'

The plumpness of Basil's face sharpened into suspicion. He moved his large hams uneasily on his chair and avoided his companion's gaze. 'It's Mum really, General. I've got to tend her a bit, like you say it's a hard time for her. And with Dad so snappish and the kids all over the place I don't think she'd take it kindly if I was to go going off to fêtes and that. Not at a time like this like.'

'Ah, filial duty. I trust your mother appreciates your sacrifices.'

But Basil, not anxious to prolong the conversation in this direction, was on his feet, his right hand hovering for the General's grasp. And then, the handshake completed, he moved himself clumsily between the tables and passed through the open doorway.

General Suffolk stirred sugar into his coffee and looked about him. A lanky schoolmistress from the school he had taught tennis at sat alone at a corner table. She was a woman of forty or so, the General imagined; and he recalled having seen her by chance once, through an open window, in her underclothes. Since then he had often considered her in terms of sex, though now, when he might have explored the possibility, he found himself unable to remember her name. He watched her, trying to catch her glance, but either she did not recognize him or did not wish to associate with so reprobate a character. He dismissed her mentally and surveyed the room again. There was no one with whom he could fall into casual conversation, except perhaps a certain Mrs Consitine, known in her youth as Jumbo Consitine because of her size, and whose freakish appearance repelled him always to the point of physical sickness. He dodged the lady's predatory stare and left the café.

It was a quarter to twelve. If the General walked through the village he would be just in time for a morning drink with Frobisher. Frobisher always drank – sometimes considerably – before lunch. On a day like this a drink was emphatically in order.

Mrs Hinch, the General reflected, would be settling down to his South African sherry about now. 'You thieving old bitch,' he said aloud. 'Fifty years in Their Majesties' service and I end up with Mrs bloody Hinch.' A man carrying a coil of garden hose tripped and fell across his path. This man, a weekend visitor to the district, known to the General by sight and disliked by him, uttered as he dropped to the ground a series of expletives of a blasphemous and violent nature. The General, since the man's weight lay on his shoes, stooped to assist him. 'Oh, buzz off,' ordered the man, his face close to the General's. So the General left him, conscious not so much of his dismissal as of the form of words it had taken. The sun warmed his forehead and drops of sweat glistened on his nose and chin.

The Frobishers' house was small and vaguely Georgian. From the outside it had the feeling of a town house placed by some error in the country. There were pillars on either side of the front door, which was itself dressed in a grey and white canvas cover as a protection against the sun. Door and cover swung inwards and Mrs Frobisher, squat and old, spoke from the hall.

'It's General Suffolk,' she said.

'Yes,' said the General. 'That old soldier.'

'You've come to see Frob. Come in a minute and I'll fetch him. What a lovely day.'

The General stepped into the hall. It was cool and smelt rather pleasantly of floor polish. Daggers, swords, Eastern rugs, knick-knacks and novelties hung in profusion everywhere. 'Frob! Frob!' Mrs Frobisher called, climbing the stairs. There had been a day, a terrible sultry day in India all of fifty years ago, when the General – though then not yet a general – had fought a duel with a certain Major Service. They had walked together quietly to a selected spot, their seconds, carrying a pair of *kukris*, trailing behind them. It had been a quarrel that involved, surprisingly, neither man's honour. In retrospect General Suffolk could scarcely remember the cause: some insult directed against some woman, though by whom and in what manner escaped him. He had struck Major Service on the left forearm, drawing a considerable quantity of blood, and the duel was reckoned complete. An excuse was made for the wound sustained by the Major and the affair was successfully hushed up. It was the nearest that General Suffolk had ever come to being court-martialled. He was put in mind of the occasion by the presence of a *kukri* on the Frobishers' wall. A nasty weapon, he reflected, and considered it odd that he should once have wielded one so casually. After all, Major Service might easily have lost his arm or, come to that, his life.

'Frob! Frob! Where are you?' cried Mrs Frobisher. 'General Suffolk's here to see you.'

'Suffolk?' Frobisher's voice called from another direction. 'Oh my dear, can't you tell him I'm out?'

The General, hearing the words, left the house.

In the saloon bar of the public house General Suffolk asked the barman about the local fêtes.

'Don't think so, sir. Not today. Not that I've heard of.'

'There's a fête at Marmount,' a man at the bar said. 'Conservative fête, same Saturday every year.'

'Ah certainly,' said the barman, 'but Marmount's fifteen miles away. General Suffolk means a *local* fête. The General doesn't have a car.'

'Of course, of course,' said the man. 'Marmount's not an easy spot to reach. Even if you did have a car, sir.'

'I will have a sandwich, Jock,' said General Suffolk. 'Chop me a cheese sandwich like a good man.' He was beginning to feel low; the day was not good; the day was getting out of control. Fear filled his mind and the tepid beer was no comfort. He began to pray inwardly, but he had little faith now in this communication. 'Never mind,' he said aloud. 'It is just that it seems like a day for a fête. I won a half guinea at a summer fête last year. One never knows one's luck.' He caught sight of a card advertising the weekly films at the cinema of the nearby town.

'Have you seen *The Guns of Navarone*?' he questioned the barman.

'I have, sir, and very good it is.'

The General nodded. 'A powerful epic by the sound of it.'

'That's the word, General. As the saying goes, it had me riveted.'

'Well, hurry the sandwiches then. I can catch the one-ten bus and achieve the first performance.'

'Funny thing, sir,' said the barman. 'I can never take the cinema of an afternoon. Not that it isn't a time that suits me, the hours being what they are. No, I go generally on my night off. Can't seem to settle down in the afternoon or something. Specially in the good weather. To me, sir, it seems unnatural.'

'That is an interesting point of view, Jock. It is indeed. And may well be shared by many – for I have noticed that the cinemas are often almost empty in the afternoon.'

'I like to be outside on a good afternoon. Taking a stroll by a trout stream or in a copse.'

'A change is as good as a cure, or whatever the adage is. After all, you are inside a good deal in your work. To be alone must be quite delightful after the idle chatter you have to endure.'

'If you don't mind my saying it, General, I don't know how you do it. It would kill me to sit at the pictures on an afternoon like this. I would feel – as it were, sir – guilty.'

'Guilty, Jock?'

'Looking the Great Gift Horse in the mouth, sir.'

'The –? Are you referring to the Deity, Jock?'

'Surely, sir. I would feel it like an unclean action.'

'Maybe, Jock. Though I doubt that God would care to hear you describe Him as a horse.'

'Oh but, General –'

'You mean no disrespect. It is taken as read, Jock. But you cannot be too careful.'

'Guilt is my problem, sir.'

'I am sorry to hear it. Guilt can often be quite a burden.'

'I am never free of it, sir. If it's not one thing it's another.'

'I know too well, Jock.'

'It was not presumptuous of me to mention that thing about the cinema? I was casting no stone at you, sir.'

'Quite, quite. It may even be that I would prefer to attend an evening house. But beggars, you know, cannot be choosers.'

'I would not like to offend you, General.'

'Good boy, Jock. In any case I am not offended. I enjoy a chat.'

'Thank you, sir.'

'Not at all. But now I must be on my way. Consider your problem closely: you may discover some simple solution. There are uncharted regions in the human mind.'

'Sir?'

'You are a good fellow, Jock. We old soldiers must stick together.'

'Ha, ha,' said Jock, taking the remark as a joke, since he was in the first place a young man still, and had never been in the army.

'Well, cheerio then.'

'Cheerio, sir.'

How extraordinary, thought the General, that the man should feel like that: guilty about daytime cinema attendance. As Mrs Hinch would have it, it takes all sorts.

The thought of Mrs Hinch depressed the General further and drove him straight to a telephone booth. He often telephoned his cottage at this time of day as a check on her time-keeping. She was due to remain at work for a further hour, but generally the telephone rang unanswered. Today he got the engaged signal. As he boarded his bus, he wondered how much it was costing him.

Taurus. 21 April to 20 May. Financial affairs straighten themselves out. Do not make decisions this afternoon: your judgement is not at its best.

The General peeped around the edge of the newspaper at the woman who shared his table. She was a thin, middle-aged person with a face like a faded photograph. Her hair was inadequately dyed a shade of brown, her face touched briefly with lipstick and powder. She wore a cream-coloured blouse and a small string of green beads which the General assumed, correctly, to be jade. Her skirt, which the General could not see, was of fine tweed.

'How thoughtless of me,' said the General. 'I have picked up your paper. It was on the chair and I did it quite automatically. I am so sorry.'

He knew the newspaper was not hers. No one places a newspaper on the other chair at a café table when the other chair is so well out of reach. Unless, that is, one wishes to reserve the place, which the lady, since she made no protest at his occupying it, was clearly not interested in doing. He made the pretence of offering the paper across the tea-table, leaning forward and sideways to catch a glimpse of her legs.

'Oh but,' said the lady, 'it is not my newspaper at all.'

Beautiful legs. Really beautiful legs. Shimmering in silk or nylon, with fine firm knees and intoxicating calves.

'Are you sure? In that case it must have been left by the last people. I was reading the stars. I am to have an indecisive afternoon.' She belongs to the upper classes, General Suffolk said to himself; the upper classes are still well-bred in the leg.

The lady tinkled with laughter. I am away, the General thought. 'When is your birthday?' he asked daringly. 'And I will tell you what to expect for the rest of today.'

'Oh, I'm Libra, I think.'

'It is a good moment for fresh associations,' lied the General, pretending to read from the paper. 'A new regime is on its way.'

'You can't believe a thing they say.'

'Fighting words,' said the General, and they laughed and changed the subject of conversation.

In the interval at the cinema, when the lights had gone up and the girls with ice-cream began their sales stroll, the General had seen, two or three rows from the screen, the fat unhealthy figure of his friend Basil. The youth was accompanied by a girl, and it distressed General Suffolk that Basil should have made so feeble an excuse when earlier he had proposed an excursion to a fête. The explanation that Basil wished to indulge in carnal pleasures in the gloom of a picture house would naturally have touched the General's sympathy. Basil was an untrustworthy lad. It was odd, the General reflected, that some people are like that: so addicted to the lie that to avoid one, when the truth is in order, seems almost a sin.

'General Suffolk,' explained the General. 'Retired, of course.'

'We live in Bradoak,' said the lady. 'My name actually is Mrs Hope-Kingley.'

'Retired?'

'Ha, ha. Though in a way it's true. My husband is not alive now.'

'Ah,' said the General, delighted. 'I'm sorry.'

'I am quite over it, thank you. It is all of fifteen years since last I saw him. We had been divorced some time before his death.'

'Divorce and death, divorce and death. You hear it all the time. May I be personal now and say I am surprised you did not remarry?'

'Oh, General Suffolk, Mr Right never came along!'

'*Attention! Les étoiles!*'

'Ha, ha.' And to her own surprise, Mrs Hope-Kingley proceeded to reveal to this elderly stranger the story of her marriage.

As he listened, General Suffolk considered how best to play his cards. It was a situation he had found himself in many times before, but as always the game must vary in detail. He felt mentally a little tired as he thought about it; and the fear that, in this, as in almost everything else, age had taken too great a toll struck at him with familiar ruthlessness. In his thirties he had played superbly, as good at love as he was at tennis. Now arrogant, now innocent, he had swooped and struck, captured and killed; and smiled over many a breakfast at the beauty that had been his prize.

They finished their tea. 'I am slipping along to the County for a drink,' said the General. 'Do join me for a quick one.'

'How kind of you. I must not delay though. My sister will expect me.' And they climbed into Mrs Hope-Kingley's small car and drove to the hotel. Over their gins the General spoke of his early days in the army and touched upon his present life, naming Mrs Hinch.

'What a frightful woman! You must sack her.'

'But who would do for me? I need my bed made and the place kept clean. Women are not easy to find in the country.'

'I know a Mrs Gall who lives in your district. She has the reputation of being particularly reliable. My friends the Boddingtons use her.'

'Well, that is certainly a thought. D'you know, I had become quite reconciled to Hinch. I never thought to change her really. What a breath of life you are!'

After three double gins Mrs Hope-Kingley was slightly drunk. Her face flushed with pleasure. Compliments do not come your way too often these days, thought the General; and he ambled off to the bar to clinch the matter with a further drink. How absurd to be upset by the passing details of the day! What did it all matter, now that he had found this promising lady? The day and its people, so directed against him, were balanced surely by this meeting? With her there was strength; from her side he might look out on the world with power and with confidence. In a panic of enthusiasm he almost suggested marriage. His hands were shaking and he felt again a surge of the old arrogance. There is life in the old dog yet, he thought. Handing her her drink, he smiled and winked.

'After this I must go,' the lady said.

'Come, come, the night is younger than we are. It is not every day I can pick up a bundle of charms in a teashop.'

'Ha, ha, ha.' Mrs Hope-Kingley purred, thinking that for once her sister would simply have to wait, and wondering if she should dare to tell her that she had been drinking with an elderly soldier.

They were sitting at a small table in a corner. Now and again, it could have been an accident, the General's knee touched hers. He watched the level of gin lower in her glass. 'You are a pretty lady,' murmured the General, and beneath the table his hand stroked her stockinged knee and ventured a little beyond it.

'My God!' said Mrs Hope-Kingley, her face like a beetroot. The General lowered his head. He heard her snatch her handbag from the seat beside him. When he looked up she was gone.

*

'When were you born?' General Suffolk asked the man in the bus.

The man seemed startled. 'Well,' he said, 'nineteen-oh-three actually.'

'No, no, no. What month? When does your birthday fall?'

'Well, October the 21st actually.'

'Libra by a day,' the General informed him, consulting his newspaper as he spoke. 'For tomorrow, there are to be perfect conditions for enjoying yourself; though it may be a little expensive. Don't gamble.'

'I see,' said the man, glancing in embarrassment through the window.

'Patrelli is usually reliable.'

The man nodded, thinking: The old fellow is drunk. He was right: the General was drunk.

'I do not read the stars every day,' General Suffolk explained. 'It is only when I happen upon an evening paper. I must say I find Patrelli the finest augur of the lot. Do you not agree?'

The man made an effort to smile, muttering something incomprehensible.

'What's that, what's that? I cannot hear you.'

'I don't know at all. I don't know about such matters.'

'You are not interested in the stars?'

The man shook his head.

'In that case, I have been boring you.'

'No, no –'

'If you were not interested in my conversation you should have said so. It is quite simple to say it. I cannot understand you.'

'I'm sorry –'

'I do not like to offend people. I do not like to be a nuisance. You should have stopped me, sir.'

The man made a gesture vague in its meaning.

'You have taken advantage of an old warrior.'

'I cannot see –'

'You should have halted me. It costs nothing to speak.'

'I'm sorry.'

'Think nothing of it. Think nothing of it at all. Here is my village. If you are dismounting, would you care to join me in a drink?'

'Thank you, no. I am –'

'I swear not to speak of the stars.'

'I go on a bit. This is not my stop.'

The General shook his head, as though doubting this statement. The bus stopped and, aided by the conductor, he left it.

'Did you see *The Guns*, General?' Jock shouted across the bar.

Not hearing, but understanding that the barman was addressing him, General Suffolk waved breezily. 'A large whisky, Jock. And a drop of beer for yourself.'

'Did you see *The Guns* then?'

'The guns?'

'The pictures, General. *The Guns of Navarone*.'

'That is very kind of you, Jock. But we must make it some other time. I saw that very film this afternoon.'

'General, did you like it?'

'Certainly, Jock. Certainly I liked it. It was very well done. I thought it was done very well indeed.'

'Two gins and split a bottle of tonic,' a man called out.

'I beg your pardon,' said the General, 'I think I am in your way.'

'Two gins and a split tonic,' repeated Jock.

'And something for our friend,' the man added, indicating the General.

'That is kind of you. Everyone is kind tonight. Jock here has just invited me to accompany him to the pictures. Unfortunately I have seen the film. But there will be other occasions. We shall go together again. May I ask you when you were born, the month I mean?'

The man, whose attention was taken up with the purchasing and transportation of his drinks, said: 'Some time in May, I think.'

'But exactly? When is your birthday, for instance?' But the man had returned to a small table against the wall, where a girl and several packets of unopened crisps awaited him.

'Jock, do you follow the stars?'

'D'you mean telescopes and that?'

'No, no, my boy.' The General swayed, catching at the bar to balance himself. He had had very little to eat all day: the old, he maintained, did not need it. 'No, no, I mean the augurs. Capricorn, Scorpio, Gemini, you know what I mean.'

'Lord Luck in the *Daily Express*?'

'That's it. That's the kind of thing. D'you take an interest at all?'

'Well, General, now, I don't.'

'When's your birthday, Jock?'

'August the 15th.'

'A Leo, by Harry! It is quite something to be a Leo, Jock. I would never have guessed it.'

Jock laughed loudly. 'After all, General, it is not my doing.'

'Fill up our glasses. Let me see what tomorrow holds for you.' But examining the paper, he found it difficult to focus. 'Here Jock, read it yourself.'

And Jock read aloud:

'*You will gain a lot by mingling with friends old and new. Late evening particularly favours entry into new social circles.*'

'Hark at that then! Remember the words, my friend. Patrelli is rarely wrong. The best augur of the bunch.' The General had become dishevelled. His face was flushed and his eyelids drooped intermittently and uncontrollably. He fidgeted with his clothes, as though nervous about the positioning of his hands. 'A final whisky, Jock boy; and a half bottle to carry home.'

On the road from the village to his cottage the General felt very drunk indeed. He lurched from one grass verge to the other, grasping his half bottle of whisky and singing gently under his breath. He knocked on the Frobishers' door with his stick, and scarcely waiting for a reply knocked loudly again.

'For God's sake, man,' Frobisher demanded, 'what's the matter with you?'

'A little drink,' explained General Suffolk. 'You and me and Mrs Frob, a little drink together. I have brought some with me. In case you had run out.'

Frobisher glared at him. 'You're drunk, Suffolk. You're bloody well drunk.'

General Suffolk loosed a peal of laughter. 'Ha, ha, the old man's drunk. Let me in, Frob, and so shall you be.'

Frobisher attempted to close the door, but the General inserted his stick.

He laughed again, and then was silent. When he spoke his voice was pleading.

'One drink, Frob. Just one for you and me. Frob, when were you born?'

Frobisher began to snort with anger: he was a short-tempered man, he saw no reason to humour this unwelcome guest. He kicked sharply at the General's stick, then opening the door widely he shouted into his face: 'Get the hell off my premises, you bloody old fool! Go on, Suffolk, hop it!'

The General did not appear to understand. He smiled at Frobisher. 'Tell me the month of your birth and I shall tell you in return what the morrow holds –'

'God damn it, Suffolk –'

'One little drink, and we'll consult the stars together. They may well be of interest to Mrs –'

'Get off my premises, you fool! You've damaged my door with your damned stick. You'll pay for that, Suffolk. You'll hear from my solicitors. I promise you, if you don't go immediately I won't hesitate to call for the police.'

'One drink, Frob. Look, I'm a little lonely –'

Frobisher banged the door. 'Frob, Frob,' General Suffolk called, striking the door with his stick. 'A nightcap, my old friend. Don't refuse a drink now.' But the door remained closed against him. He spoke for a while to himself, then made his way unsteadily homewards.

'General Suffolk, are you ill?'

The General narrowed his eyes, focusing on the couple who stood before him; he did not recognize them; he was aware of feeling guilty because of it.

'We are returning home from a game of cards,' the woman of the two told him. 'It is a balmy evening for a stroll.'

The General tried to smile. Since leaving the Frobishers' house he had drunk most of the whisky. The people danced a bit before him, like outsize puppets. They moved up and down, and from side to side. They walked rapidly, silently, backwards. 'Ha, ha, ha,' laughed the General. 'What can I do for you?'

'Are you ill? You don't seem yourself.'

The General smiled at some little joke. 'I have not been myself for many years. Today is just another day.'

The people were moving away. He could hear them murmuring to each other.

'You have not asked me about the stars,' he shouted after them. 'I could tell you if you asked.' But they were already gone, and uncorking the bottle he drained the remains and threw it into a ditch.

As he passed Mrs Hinch's cottage he decided to call on her. He had it on his mind to play some joke on the woman, to say that she need not again attend to his household needs. He banged powerfully on the door and in a moment Mrs Hinch's head, rich in curling pins, appeared at a window to his right.

'Why, General dear,' said Mrs Hinch, recognizing immediately his condition. 'You've been on the razzle.'

'Mrs Hinch, when is your birthday?'

'Why, my dear? Have you a present for little Hinchie?'

'Give me the information and I will let you know what tomorrow brings.'

'May the 3rd. I was born at two o'clock in the morning.'

But in his walk he had somewhere mislaid the newspaper and could tell her nothing. He gripped the doorstep and seemed about to fall.

'Steady now,' said Mrs Hinch. 'I'll dress myself and help you home.' The head was withdrawn and the General waited for the company of his unreliable servant.

She, in the room, slipped out of her nightdress and buttoned about her her everyday clothes. This would last her for months. 'Ho ho, my dear,' she would say, 'remember that night? Worse for wear you were. Whatever would you have done without your little Hinchie?' Chortling and crowing, she hitched up her skirts and paraded forth to meet him.

'Oh General, you're naughty! You shouldn't be allowed out.'

The General laughed. Clumsily he slapped her broad buttocks. She screamed shrilly, enjoying again the position she now held over him. 'Dirty old General! Hinchie won't carry her beauty home unless he's a good boy tonight.' She laughed her cackling laugh and the General joined in it. He dawdled a bit, and losing her patience Mrs Hinch pushed him roughly in front of her. He fell, and in picking him up she came upon his wallet and skilfully extracted two pounds ten. 'General would fancy his Hinchie tonight,' she said, shrieking merrily at the thought. But the General was silent now, seeming almost asleep as he walked. His face was gaunt and thin, with little patches of red. 'I could live for twenty years,' he whispered. 'My God Almighty, I could live for twenty years.' Tears spread on his cheeks. 'Lor' love a duck!' cried Mrs Hinch; and leaning on the arm of this stout woman the hero of Roeux and Monchy-le-Preux stumbled the last few yards to his cottage.

The Smoke Trees of San Pietro

My father was a great horseman. My mother was the most beautiful woman I have ever seen. I was taken to watch my father jumping as a member of the military team in Linvik when I was five years old. The team did not win that afternoon but my father's performance was faultless and he himself received a personal award. I remember the applause and his saluting, and my mother's fingers tightening on my arm. 'Oh, how deserved that is!' she whispered, and when my father joined us later you could see that he was proud. He smelt of horses and of leather, as he always did when he'd been jumping: to this day, I can evoke that smell at will.

That is the most vivid memory of that early time in my childhood. We drove away from the stadium and then there was my first dinner in a restaurant, my mother and father on either side of me, red roses in a vase, a candle burning in a wooden candlestick that was painted blue and green. 'One day,' my father predicted, anticipating that in time I, too, would be a member of the military team. Already I was promising: so he insisted when he watched me cantering with my mother along the grassy path beside the birch woods. In the restaurant they touched their wine-glasses and my father requested the waiter to pour me just a little wine so that on this particular occasion I might have my first taste of it. Johan my father called the waiter, while I wondered which feature it was that in particular made my mother's beauty so remarkable. One moment it seemed to be the candlelight gleaming on her pale hair, the next the blue of her eyes, and then her lips and the tiny wrinkle on her forehead, and then the graceful way she held her head. My father's hand reached across the tablecloth for one of hers, and there that memory ceases.

There is another one. In his surgery Dr Edlund probed my eyes with the beam of a torch that was as slim as a pencil. The disc of his stethoscope lingered on my back and chest, my reflexes were tested, my throat examined, my blood gathered in a capsule, the cavities of my body sounded. And afterwards, when weeks had passed, it was declared that I was not strong. Tiredness in future was to be avoided; I must canter more gently; becoming hot was not good. 'He will be different from what we imagined,' my father said. 'That is all.' I did not, then, sense the disappointment in his voice.

It was because of my delicate constitution that my mother first took me to San Pietro al Mare, initiating a summer regime that was to continue throughout my childhood. We went by train and because of my delicate constitution more time was devoted to the journey than might otherwise have been considered necessary. A night was spent in Hamburg, at the Hotel Kronberg, then by day and night we went slowly on, the air noticeably warmer each time we stopped at a station. A final night was spent at Milan, at the Hotel Belvedere. We arrived at San Pietro al Mare in the early afternoon.

I think, that first evening, my mother was a little nervous. She addressed the hotel staff in English and was apprehensive lest she was not correctly understood. In the restaurant, at dinner, she spoke very slowly to the waiter and I did not entirely follow what was said because I did not yet understand much English. But the waiter, who was extremely rapid in all he did – flicking open our napkins and expertly covering our knees with them, running his finger down the menu to make a suggestion, noting my mother's order on his pad – did not once request her to repeat a word. When he had gone my mother asked me if I felt tired, but I was not in the least. From the moment the train had begun to slow down for San Pietro I'd felt exhilarated. I was supposed not to carry heavy luggage but I had done so none the less, assisting the porter at the station to pack our suitcases into the taxi while my mother was at the *Cambio*. We had driven by palm trees – the first time I had ever seen such trees – and beyond them the sea was a shimmer of blue, just like the sky. Then the taxi turned abruptly, leaving behind the strolling couples on the promenade – the men in white suits, women in beach dresses – and the coloured umbrellas that offered each café table a pool of shade. For a very short time, no more than half a minute perhaps, the taxi climbed a hill which became quite steep and then drew up at the Villa Parco. The palm trees and the promenade were far below, the limpid sea appeared to stretch for ever.

At dinner I said I had never been in such an exotic place. The dining-room where we sat was more elegant and gracious, and a great deal larger, than the restaurant my father had taken us to on the evening of his triumph with the military team. I had never before seen so many people dining at the same time, many of them in evening dress. Spirit stoves burned at each table. Glass doors which stretched from the ceiling to the floor were thrown wide open to a terrace with a decorated balustrade – coloured medallions set among its brief, grey pillars. Beyond that the garden of the Villa Parco was spread with flowers that were quite unfamiliar to me: burgeoning shrubs of oleander and bougainvillaea, and trees called smoke trees, so my mother said. In the hotel I loved the sound of Italian, the mysterious words and phrases the chambermaids and the waiters called out to one another. And I loved the hesitant English of my mother.

The next morning – and every morning after that – my mother and I bathed among the rocks because Dr Edlund had prescribed as advantageous the exercise of unhurried swimming. We took the lift that descended to the bathing place from the hotel garden and afterwards we lay for a short time in the sun, covered with protecting creams, before walking to a café for an *albicocca*. We watched the people sauntering by, remarking on them when they were unusual. In this connection my mother taught me English words: 'haughty', 'wan', 'abstracted', and made me say in English, 'Thank you very much', when the waitress brought our *albicocca*. Then we would return to the hotel garden where, until lunchtime, my mother read to me from *Kidnapped*. I drew the faces of the waiters and the hall-porters, and the façade of the Villa Parco, and the white-painted chairs among the smoke trees. A visitor at the hotel would take one of these iron chairs and carry it to a secluded place and later idly leave it there. Or a tête-à-tête would occur, two of the chairs drawn away in the same manner and then vacated, two empty glasses left on a table. After lunch we rested, then swam again, and again visited the town. 'We must complete our postcard,' my mother would say on the way in to dinner or during the meal itself, and afterwards we would do so before dropping the postcard into the letter-box in the hall. Sometimes I made a drawing on it for my father, a caricature of a face or the outline of a shell we'd found, and from my mother there would always be a reference to my health.

That pattern of our holiday, established during our first summer at San Pietro, remained to influence the subsequent years. We always left Linvik on a Tuesday and stayed, *en route*, at the Hotel Kronberg in Hamburg and the Belvedere in Milan: we always remained for July and August at San Pietro. But on the later occasions there were differences also: my mother was no longer nervous about her English; the staff at the Villa Parco remembered us and welcomed us with increasing warmth; some of the other visitors, familiar from previous years, would greet us when we arrived. This pleased my mother but, for myself, I preferred the novelty of strangers. I liked to watch the laden taxis draw up, the emergence of a man and woman or a family, an elderly person of either sex issuing orders to a younger companion, or the arrival of a solitary figure, always the most interesting from the point of view of speculation. Monsieur Paillez was one of these: he appeared at the Villa Parco for the first time during our third summer, to be assessed by us, and no doubt by other regulars as well, when he strolled down the terrace steps late one afternoon, a thin, tall, dark-haired man in a linen suit. He sat not far from where we were and a moment later a waiter brought him a tray of tea. He smoked while he drank it, taking no interest either in his surroundings or the other people in the garden.

'A town called Linvik,' my mother said, and two ladies in the garden listened while she described it. The ladies were Italian, Signora Binelli and her daughter Claudia. They came from Genoa, they told my mother, which was a city renowned for its trade associations and its cuisine. They spoke of formidable grey stone and formidable palaces, stirring in the false impression that the palaces had been carved out of the side of an immense grey mountain. A passenger lift went up and down all day long between the heights of Genoa and its depths, making its passage through the mountain rock. This information the Italian ladies repeated, remarking that the lift was a great deal larger and more powerful than the one that conveyed us from the garden of the Villa Parco to the bathing place. The palaces of Genoa were built of rectangular blocks and decoratively finished, they said, and the earlier imprecision was adjusted in my mind.

Signora Binelli was very stout. She had smooth white skin, very tight, that seemed to labour under as much strain as her silk dresses did. She knew, my mother murmured once as we walked away from the two Italian ladies, not to wear over-bright clothes. There was always some black in them – in the oak leaves that patterned dark maroon or green, behind swirls of blue or brown. The Italians knew about being fat, my mother said.

Signora Binelli's daughter, Claudia, was not at all like that. She was a film star we were told, and certainly she presented that appearance, many of her fingers displaying jewelled rings, her huge red lips perpetually parted to display a glistening flash of snowy teeth. Her eyes were huge also, shown off to best effect by the dark saucers beneath them. Her clothes were more colourful than Signora Binelli's, but discreetly so. My mother said Claudia had taste.

'*Buon giorno*,' Monsieur Paillez greeted my mother and these ladies one morning in the garden, inclining his head as he went on his way to the lift. We sat at one of the tables, shaded by its vast blue-and-grey umbrella. Claudia's swimming bag hung from the arm of her chair; sunglasses obscured her magnificent eyes. A yellow-backed book, *Itinerario Svizzero*, was on the table beside the ashtray; she smoked a cigarette. Signora Binelli wore a wide-brimmed white hat that protected the skin of her face from the sunshine. The sleeves of her dark dress were buttoned at her wrists; her shoulders and much of her neck were covered.

'Paillez,' Signora Binelli said. 'Is it in France a name to know? Count Paillez?' Bewildered by these questions, my mother only smiled in reply.

Claudia removed the cigarette from between her lips. She did not think Monsieur Paillez was a count, she said. She had not heard that in the hotel.

'We do not have counts in my country,' my mother contributed.

'In Italian we say *conte*,' Signora Binelli explained. 'So also *contessa*.'

'I take my swim,' Claudia said.

My mother said we would take ours soon. In prescribing this form of exercise for me Dr Edlund had reminded my mother that it must not be indulged in while food was in the early stages of digestion: we always permitted two hours at least for my breakfast of tea and brioche to settle itself before I entered the sea. Others, I noticed, were not so meticulous about such matters, but I had become used to being different where health was concerned. A day would come, Dr Edlund had confidently assured me, when I would look back on all this mollycoddling with amusement – and with gratitude also, he hastily added, for I would be the stronger for it. He was not telling the truth, as doctors sometimes cannot. My life was confined to childhood, was what he'd told my mother and my father: it would not reach beyond it. 'We do not speak much of this,' my father had said in a moment when he did not know I could hear. My grandmother had come to Linvik for a few days: it was she he told, and he'd been wise enough to keep the news from her until her departure was quite imminent. Care and attention saw to it that my childhood continued to advance without mishap, my father said, but even so my grandmother hugged me tearfully before she went, pressing me so tightly into her arms that I thought my end would come there and then. That was some time before my mother and I spent our first summer at San Pietro al Mare. I was eleven the summer Monsieur Paillez arrived at the Villa Parco.

'Well, we might go now,' my mother said, and we gathered up our things and descended the slope of the lawn to the lift that took us to the bathing place. Signora Binelli, in search of deeper shade, had moved to a table beneath the trees.

There is very little I have since liked better than swimming among the rocks at San Pietro. The water was of a tranquillity and a clear blueness that made it seem more like a lake than the sea. The rocks were washed white, like smooth, curved bones that blissfully held your body when you lay on them. Two small bathing huts – in blue-and-grey canvas similar to the lawn umbrellas – became a world, my mother's and mine, safely holding our belongings while we swam or floated.

'*T'amuses-tu?*' Monsieur Paillez slipped by me, his overarm strokes hardly rippling the surface. '*Ti diverti?*' And finally translating into the language I had become familiar with: 'You enjoy yourself?'

'Oh yes, of course. Yes, thank you.'

'*C'est bon,*' he called back, over his shoulder. 'We are here to enjoy ourselves, eh?'

An attendant supplied my mother with inflated cushions to lie on, but I myself preferred the bonelike rock. Claudia had made a personal territory of a narrow little cape, spreading on it her towels and various possessions from her bathing bag, then stretching herself prone, and slumbering. The other bathers disposed themselves in similar ways, oiling the skin of their legs and backs. Monsieur Paillez briskly dried himself and went away.

That same day, an hour before dinner, my mother and I were returning from our evening walk around the town when a taxi drew up beside us and Monsieur Paillez said:

'May I offer you a lift?'

When my mother explained that our walk was taken for pleasure the Frenchman paid the driver and fell into step with us. This was a considerable surprise. ('I was quite astounded,' my mother remarked later, as we went over the incident during dinner.)

'I have a little business to conduct in Triora,' Monsieur Paillez said. 'How cool it is now!'

It had been oppressive in Triora, he said. How pleasant it always was to return to San Pietro! 'I greatly admire the smoke trees of San Pietro. Do you not also, madame?'

My mother said she did, and a conversation ensued between them concerning shrubs and horticulture. After that my mother revealed that she and I had been coming to San Pietro al Mare for three years, and Monsieur Paillez confessed that he did not know it as well as we did, this being his first visit. He had decided he might prefer the sea and a good hotel to what Triora had to offer. Triora he knew particularly well.

'We have always been happy at the Villa Parco,' my mother said.

Monsieur Paillez asked questions in a polite manner: if our journey to San Pietro was a long one, how we made it, where we stayed *en route*. My mother answered, equally politely.

'You have travelled from Paris, Monsieur Paillez?'

'Ah, no. Not Paris. I travel from Lille. Have you by chance heard of Lille?'

My mother had and when he questioned her again she mentioned Linvik, repeating the name because Monsieur Paillez had difficulty in understanding it at first. He had not known of our town's existence.

'Well, quite like Lille maybe,' my mother said. 'With manufacturing interests.'

'Though less extensive in size I would suggest?'

'Oh yes, much less extensive.'

'The scent in the air is the evening scent of the smoke trees,' Monsieur Paillez said. (Afterwards – over dinner – my mother confessed to me that she had only been aware of the familiar scent of bougainvillaea, and had never before heard that smoke trees gave off a perfume of any kind.)

'Such a place!' Monsieur Paillez enthused as we passed through the gardens of the hotel. 'Such a place!'

That was the beginning of Monsieur Paillez's friendship with my mother. The following morning, when we were resting after breakfast on the lawn, he did not pass our table by but again dropped into conversation and then inquired if he might sit down. Signora Binelli and Claudia, emerging from the hotel ten minutes later and about to join us, as on other days, did not do so. Signora Binelli settled herself beneath the smoke trees, Claudia went straight to the lift. It was clear to me – though possibly not to my mother and Monsieur Paillez, who by now were exchanging views on Mozart's operas – that the Italian ladies were displeased.

'What fun *Così fan Tutte* is!' Monsieur Paillez later exclaimed in the lift. 'It is the fun of it I love.'

The excursion to the bathing place, and the routine that followed it, did not vary from day to day. Everything was the same: my mother and I swimming for twenty minutes or so, then lying in the sunshine before swimming again, Claudia claiming her private territory, other swimmers occupying their places of the day before, Monsieur Paillez briskly drying himself and going away, as if suddenly in a hurry.

'Business in Triora!' Signora Binelli remarked one evening when he did not return to the hotel at his usual time. It was not yet too cool for me to be permitted to remain on the terrace with my mother while she took her aperitif. Signora Binelli and Claudia occupied the table next to ours, as always they did. Since the evening Monsieur Paillez had halted his taxi it had become his habit to join my mother while she had her aperitif and he his. A general conversation then took place, the Binellis drawn into it because it was natural that they should be, I the only silent one.

'There is not much business, I would have thought, in Triora,' Claudia said, placing her cigarette on the table's ashtray in order to select an olive. 'Not business to attract a Frenchman.'

'Monsieur Paillez visits his wife,' my mother said. 'It is his manner of speech to call it business.'

'Wife!' Signora Binelli repeated sharply. '*Moglie,*' she translated, visibly annoying her daughter.

'I am not uneducated,' Claudia retorted. 'So Monsieur Paillez is married, *signora*?'

'His wife is an Italian lady.' My mother paused. 'She is in the care of nuns.'

'*Le suore,*' Signora Binelli supplied, and Claudia crossly sighed.

'An asylum for the afflicted in Triora,' my mother said. 'She being of Triora originally. I think aristocratic.'

Abruptly Signora Binelli changed the subject. She did so in a manner that suggested the one engaging our attention required thinking about before it might profitably be continued. 'Claudia is to have a part,' she announced. 'We hear today. A fine part, in *Il Marito in Collegio*.'

'It's just a possibility,' Claudia corrected, retaining the crossness in her voice. 'First the film must be financed.'

Monsieur Paillez did not join us that evening, nor did he appear in the dining-room. My mother did not remark on this, but when we left our table we had to pass close to the Binellis'. 'He would not surely have gone without saying goodbye?' Signora Binelli said. With small, beady eyes she peered from the fatness of her face, searching my mother's expression for the explanation she clearly believed her to possess. 'Monsieur Paillez said nothing to me,' my mother replied, but when we had reached my room she quietly murmured, almost to herself: 'His wife has not been well today.'

After breakfast the next morning he did not join us, nor did he arrive at the bathing place. My mother, I thought, became a little disconsolate, as if some flickering of doubt had crept into her mind, as if she'd begun to imagine that she was wrong in the explanation that had occurred to her. But if this doubt had indeed begun to haunt her it was soon dissipated.

'This has been a sorrowful time for me,' Monsieur Paillez said in the town that evening, appearing suddenly beside us as we left the pharmacy where one of my prescriptions had been renewed. 'Since yesterday at midday it has been unhappy.'

'Oh, I'm sorry.'

'From time to time this has to be.'

Monsieur Paillez had a mobile face. His expressions changed rapidly, his dark eyes conveying the mood that possessed him, even before the line of his lips did. His wife was mad, my mother had told me when I'd asked her the evening before, not quite understanding the exchanges with Signora Binelli. It was not easy for Monsieur Paillez, my mother had added.

He walked with us back to the hotel and then sat on the terrace, ordering the aperitifs for my mother and himself and an *albicocca* for me. He had bought a linen hat in Triora, to match his suit. The sun was always fierce in Triora, he said.

'You have returned to us!' Signora Binelli cried as soon as she saw him sitting there.

'Ah, *oui*,' he replied. 'I have returned.'

In English he had difficulty with his h's, but only when they came at the beginning of a word. Sometimes he repeated what he'd just said, in order to set that right. He nodded after he'd agreed he had returned. He listened while Signora Binelli said everyone had missed him.

'Monsieur Paillez is safely here again,' she pointed out to her daughter when she arrived on the terrace. 'He has not gone without farewells.'

'Never,' Monsieur Paillez protested. 'Never would I be guilty.'

That evening – no doubt because of his low spirits – Monsieur Paillez sat with us for dinner. 'I do not intrude?' he said. 'I would not wish to.' My mother assured him he did not, and I do not believe she once observed the staring of Signora Binelli across the crowded dining-room, or Claudia's pretence that she had not noticed.

'Tell me what you like best to draw,' Monsieur Paillez invited me, 'here in San Pietro.'

I could not think what to reply – the rocks where we bathed? the waiters? the promenade when we sat outside a café? Claudia or Signora Binelli? So I said:

'The smoke trees because they are so difficult.' It was true. Try as I would, I could not adequately represent the misty foliage or catch the subtlety of its colours.

'And no drawing of course,' my mother said, 'could ever convey the smoke trees' evening scent.'

She laughed, and Monsieur Paillez laughed: at some time or another, although I could not guess when, his error in imagining that the smoke trees gave off a night-time perfume had become a joke between them. Sitting there not saying anything further, I received the impression that my mother had come to know Monsieur Paillez better than the moments after breakfast on the lawn, and the whiling away of their aperitifs, allowed. I experienced the bewildering feeling that their exchanges – even those in which I had taken part – conveyed more than the words were called upon to communicate.

'My dear, go up,' my mother said. 'I'll follow in a moment.'

I was a little shy, having to leave the dining-room on my own, which I had never done before. People always looked at my mother and myself when we did so together, some of them inclining their heads as a way of bidding us good-night, others actually saying *'Buona notte'* or *'Bon nuit'*. No one bothered with me on my own, except of course Signora Binelli, who remarked: 'So they have packed you off!'

'Buona notte, signora.'

Claudia clapped together the tips of her fingers, pleased that I spoke in Italian because she had taught me a few phrases. I had said good evening beautifully, she complimented, calling after me that certainly I had an ear.

'That poor child,' her mother tartly deplored as I pushed at the dining-room's swing-doors. 'What a thing for a child!'

That night I had a nightmare. My father and I were in the rector's house in Linvik. The purpose of our being there was mysterious, but having eaten something with the rector we were taken to a small room which was full of the clocks he collected and repaired as a pastime. Here, while he and my father were in conversation, I stole a clock face, attempting to secrete it in my clothes. Then it seemed that I had stolen more than that: springs and cogs and wheels and hands had been lifted from the blue baize of the table and filled all my pockets. 'I insist on the police,' the rector said, and I was made to sit down on a chair to which my father tied me with a rope. But it was not the police who came, only the old man who delivered firewood to us. 'This is a new treatment,' he said, taking from the blue baize cover on the table the minute hand of a grandfather clock and inserting its point beneath one of my eyelids.

'Now, now,' my mother said. 'It's only a nightmare.'

Her embrace protected me; her lips were cool on my cheek. The garlic in the veal escalope had made it rich, she said, and begged me to tell her the dream. But already it seemed silly to have been frightened by such absurdity, and although I told her about the woodseller's punishment I was ashamed that in my dream I had not been able to recognize this for what it was.

Behind my mother as she bent over me there was an upright rectangle of light. It came from the open doorway of her bedroom: because of my delicate constitution we always had adjoining rooms in the hotels where we stayed. 'Shall we have it like that tonight?' she suggested, but I shook my head, and rejected also her suggestion that my bedside light should be left burning. It was cowardly to capitulate to the threat of fantasies: my father may once have said so, although if he had he would not have said it harshly, for that was not my father's way.

I believe I slept for a while, impossible to gauge how long. I awoke abruptly and recalled at once the rector's clock-room and the fear that had possessed me. Without my mother's consoling presence, I did not wish to return to sleep, cowardice notwithstanding, and was immediately more wide awake than I had been when she'd come to put her arms around me. I lay in the darkness, fearful only of closing my eyes.

I heard the murmur of voices. A crack of light showed beneath the door that led to my mother's room. I stared at it and listened: my mother was speaking to someone, and being spoken to in return. There would be a silence for a while and then the murmur would begin again.

When the door unexpectedly opened I closed my eyes, not wishing my mother to know I was frightened of sleeping. She came softly to my bedside, stood still, and then re-crossed the room. Before she closed the door she said: 'He is sleeping.' Monsieur Paillez's voice replied that that was good.

Their quiet exchanges began again. What did they say to one another? I wondered. Had she told him about my delicate constitution? Had she said that in spite of Dr Edlund's bluff pretence it was accepted by everyone that I would not live beyond my childhood? I imagined her telling him, and Monsieur Paillez commiserating, as my mother would have over his mad Italian wife. I was glad for her that she had found such a friend at San Pietro, for she was so very kind to me, travelling this great distance down through Europe just for my sake, with nothing much to do when she arrived except to read and swim and exchange politenesses. I was aware that it had not been possible for my mother to have other children, for once I had asked her about the brothers and sisters who were not there. I was aware that sacrifices had been made for me, and of the sadness there would one day be for both my mother and my father, when my life came to an end. I should feel no sadness myself, since of course I should not know; I expected nothing more, beyond what I'd been promised.

I slept and dreamed again, but this time pleasantly: my mother and father and I were in the restaurant I had been taken to after my father's success in the jumping ring. Around us people were laughing and talking, and so were my mother and father. There was no more to the dream, but I felt happy when I remembered it in the morning.

'There is a fine Deposition in Triora,' Monsieur Paillez said on the lawn after breakfast. 'You might find it worth the journey.'

My mother answered as though she'd been expecting the suggestion. She answered quickly, almost before Monsieur Paillez had ceased to speak, and then she turned to me to say a visit to Triora might make an outing.

'There is a pretty trattoria not far from that church,' Monsieur Paillez said. 'Its terrace is shaded by a vine. Once or twice I have had lunch there.'

And so, after our swim that day, my mother did not lie on the inflated cushions nor I on the white rock I had made my own, but dressed ourselves and were as swift as Monsieur Paillez about it. The taxi he took every day to Triora was waiting outside the hotel.

I enjoyed the change in our routine, though not the Deposition, nor the church which housed it. We didn't spend long there, hardly more than a minute, finding instead a café where we wrote our daily postcard to my father. *We have come today to Triora*, I wrote, *with Monsieur Paillez*, *who is visiting his mad Italian wife. We have seen a picture in a church.* At last there was something different to write and for once the words came easily. I was smiling when I handed the postcard to my mother, anticipating her surprise that I had completed my message so quickly. She read it carefully, but did not immediately add her own few sentences. She would do that later, she said, placing the postcard in her handbag. (I afterwards found it, torn into little pieces, in the wastepaper basket in her room.)

'At peace today,' Monsieur Paillez reported in the trattoria with the vine. 'Yes, more at peace today.'

It was usually so, he explained: when his wife had had a bad spell there was often a period of tranquillity. Because of it he did not visit the asylum in the afternoon, but returned with us to the Villa Parco and joined us when we swam again.

'It is almost certain that Claudia has secured the part,' Signora Binelli announced on the terrace before dinner. 'All day long the telephone has been ringing for her.'

My mother and Monsieur Paillez smiled, though without exchanging a look. Claudia, arriving on the terrace, said the part in *Il Marito in Collegio* was far from certain. The telephone ringing was always a bad sign, implying indecision.

Just for a moment on the way in to dinner Monsieur Paillez's hand gently cupped my mother's elbow. Tonight he sat with us also, even though his spirits were no longer low, and as he and my mother conversed I again felt happy that she had a friend in San Pietro, one who could be called that more than the Binellis or any of the other guests could. That night I woke up once, and listened, and heard the murmuring.

On the way back to Linvik – in Hamburg, I believe it was – my mother said:

'Let's forget about that day we went to Triora.'

'Forget it?'

'Well, I mean, let's have it as a secret.'

I asked her why we should do that. She did not hesitate but said that on that day, passing a shop window, she had seen in it what she wished to buy my father for Christmas. She had not bought it at the time, but had asked Monsieur Paillez to do so when he was next in Triora.

'And did he?'

'Yes, he did.'

Monsieur Paillez was just my father's size, she said: whatever the garment was (my mother didn't identify it), he had kindly tried it on. 'I shall not say much about Monsieur Paillez,' my mother said, 'in case I stupidly divulge that little secret. When you talk about a person you sometimes do so without thinking. So perhaps we should neither of us much mention Monsieur Paillez.'

As I listened, I knew that I had never before heard my mother say anything as silly. Every evening after the day of our excursion to Triora Monsieur Paillez had stepped out of his taxi in front of the hotel and had joined us on the terrace. On none of these occasions had he carried a parcel, let alone handed one to my mother. In Triora I could not recollect her pausing even once by a shop window that contained men's clothes.

'Yes, all right,' I said.

That was the moment my childhood ended. It is the most devious irony that Dr Edlund's bluff assurances – certainly not believed by him – anticipated the circumstance that allows me now to look back to those summers in San Pietro al Mare, and to that summer in particular. It is, of course, the same circumstance that allows me to remember the rest of each year in Linvik. I did not know in my childhood that my mother and father had ceased to love one another. I did not know that it was my delicate constitution that kept them tied to one another; a child who had not long to live should not, in fairness, have to tolerate a family's disruption as well as everything else.

At the Villa Parco, when we returned the following summer, Monsieur Paillez was already there, visiting his mad Italian wife. The very first night he shared our table, and after that we did everything together. Signora Binelli and her daughter were not at the hotel that year. (Nor were they again at the Villa Parco when we were. My mother and Monsieur Paillez were relieved about that, I think, although they often mentioned Signora Binelli and her daughter and seemed amused by the memory of them.)

'We had snow in Lille as early as October,' Monsieur Paillez said, and so the conversation was on this night, and on other nights – conducted in such a manner because my presence demanded it. Later my mother did not say that we should avoid mentioning Monsieur Paillez when we returned to Linvik. She knew it was not necessary to go through another palaver of silliness.

When I was sixteen and seventeen we still returned to San Pietro. What had begun for my mother as a duty, taking her weakling child down through Europe to the sun, became the very breath of her life. Long after it was necessary to do so we continued to make the journey, our roles reversed, I now being the one inspired by compassion. The mad wife of Monsieur Paillez, once visited in compassion, died; but Monsieur Paillez did not cease to return to the Villa Parco. In the dining-room I sometimes observed the waiters repeating what there was to repeat to younger waiters, newly arrived at the hotel. As I grew older, my mother and I no longer had adjoining rooms.

In Linvik my father had other women. After my childhood ended I noticed that sometimes in the evenings he was drunk. It won't be long, he and my mother must have so often thought, but they were steadfast in their honourable resolve.

Slow years of wondering washed the magic from my childhood recollections and left them ordinary, like pallid photographs that gracelessly record the facts. Yet what a memory it was for a while, his hand reaching across the tablecloth, the candlelight on her hair. What a memory the smoke trees were, and Signora Binelli, and Claudia, and the sea as blue as the sky! My father was a great horseman, my mother the most beautiful woman I have ever seen. *'Ti diverti?'* Monsieur Paillez's voice was hardly raised as he swam by: how pleased I was that he had chosen to address me!

In my borrowed time I take from an ebony box my smudged attempts to draw the smoke trees of San Pietro and reflect that my talent did not amount to much. Silly, it seems now, to have tried so hard to capture the elusive character of that extraordinary foliage.

Broken Homes

'I really think you're marvellous,' the man said.

He was small and plump, with a plump face that had a greyness about it where he shaved; his hair was grey also, falling into a fringe on his forehead. He was untidily dressed, a turtlenecked red jersey beneath a jacket that had a ballpoint pen and a pencil sticking out of the breast pocket. When he stood up his black corduroy trousers developed concertina creases. Nowadays you saw a lot of men like this, Mrs Malby said to herself.

'We're trying to help them,' he said, 'and of course we're trying to help you. The policy is to foster a deeper understanding.' He smiled, displaying small, evenly arranged teeth. 'Between the generations,' he added.

'Well, of course it's very kind,' Mrs Malby said.

He shook his head. He sipped the instant coffee she'd made for him and nibbled the edge of a pink wafer biscuit. As if driven by a compulsion, he dipped the biscuit into the coffee. He said:

'What age actually are you, Mrs Malby?'

'I'm eighty-seven.'

'You really are splendid for eighty-seven.'

He went on talking. He said he hoped he'd be as good himself at eighty-seven. He hoped he'd even be in the land of the living. 'Which I doubt,' he said with a laugh. 'Knowing me.'

Mrs Malby didn't know what he meant by that. She was sure she'd heard him quite correctly, but she could recall nothing he'd previously stated which indicated ill-health. She thought carefully while he continued to sip at his coffee and attend to the mush of biscuit. What he had said suggested that a knowledge of him would cause you to doubt that he'd live to old age. Had he already supplied further knowledge of himself which, due to her slight deafness, she had not heard? If he hadn't, why had he left everything hanging in the air like that? It was difficult to know how best to react, whether to smile or to display concern.

'So what I thought,' he said, 'was that we could send the kids on Tuesday. Say start the job Tuesday morning, eh, Mrs Malby?'

'It's extremely kind of you.'

'They're good kids.'

He stood up. He remarked on her two budgerigars and the geraniums on her window-sill. Her sitting-room was as warm as toast, he said; it was freezing outside.

'It's just that I wondered,' she said, having made up her mind to say it, 'if you could possibly have come to the wrong house?'

'Wrong? *Wrong*? You're Mrs Malby, aren't you?' He raised his voice. 'You're Mrs Malby, love?'

'Oh, yes, it's just that my kitchen isn't really in need of decoration.'

He nodded. His head moved slowly and when it stopped his dark eyes stared at her from beneath his grey fringe. He said, quite softly, what she'd dreaded he might say: that she hadn't understood.

'I'm thinking of the community, Mrs Malby. I'm thinking of you here on your own above a greengrocer's shop with your two budgies. You can benefit my kids, Mrs Malby; they can benefit you. There's no charge of any kind whatsoever. Put it like this, Mrs Malby: it's an experiment in community relations.' He paused. He reminded her of a picture there'd been in a history book, a long time ago, History with Miss Deacon, a picture of a Roundhead. 'So you see, Mrs Malby,' he said, having said something else while he was reminding her of a Roundhead.

'It's just that my kitchen is really quite nice.'

'Let's have a little look, shall we?'

She led the way. He glanced at the kitchen's shell-pink walls, and at the white paintwork. It would cost her nearly a hundred pounds to have it done, he said; and then, to her horror, he began all over again, as if she hadn't heard a thing he'd been saying. He repeated that he was a teacher, from the school called the Tite Comprehensive. He appeared to assume that she wouldn't know the Tite Comprehensive, but she did: an ugly sprawl of glass-and-concrete buildings, children swinging along the pavements, shouting obscenities. The man repeated what he had said before about these children: that some of them came from broken homes. The ones he wished to send to her on Tuesday morning came from broken homes, which was no joke for them. He felt, he repeated, that we all had a special duty where such children were concerned.

Mrs Malby again agreed that broken homes were to be deplored. It was just, she explained, that she was thinking of the cost of decorating a kitchen which didn't need decorating. Paint and brushes were expensive, she pointed out.

'Freshen it over for you,' the man said, raising his voice. 'First thing Tuesday, Mrs Malby.'

He went away, and she realized that he hadn't told her his name. Thinking she might be wrong about that, she went over their encounter in her mind, going back to the moment when her doorbell had sounded. 'I'm from Tite Comprehensive,' was what he'd said. No name had been mentioned, of that she was positive.

In her elderliness Mrs Malby liked to be sure of such details. You had to work quite hard sometimes at eighty-seven, straining to hear, concentrating carefully in order to be sure of things. You had to make it clear you understood because people often imagined you didn't. Communication was what it was called nowadays, rather than conversation.

Mrs Malby was wearing a blue dress with a pattern of darker blue flowers on it. She was a woman who had been tall but had shrunk a little with age and had become slightly bent. Scant white hair crowned a face that was touched with elderly freckling. Large brown eyes, once her most striking feature, were quieter than they had been, tired behind spectacles now. Her husband, Ernest, the owner of the greengrocer's shop over which she lived, had died five years ago; her two sons, Derek and Roy, had been killed in the same month – June 1942 – in the same desert retreat.

The greengrocer's shop was unpretentious, in an unpretentious street in Fulham called Catherine Street. The people who owned it now, Jewish people called King, kept an eye on Mrs Malby. They watched for her coming and going and if they missed her one day they'd ring her doorbell to see that she was all right. She had a niece in Ealing who looked in twice a year, and another niece in Islington, who was crippled with arthritis. Once a week Mrs Grove and Mrs Halbert came round with Meals on Wheels. A social worker, Miss Tingle, called; and the Reverend Bush called. Men came to read the meters.

In her elderliness, living where she'd lived since her marriage in 1920, Mrs Malby was happy. The tragedy in her life – the death of her sons – was no longer a nightmare, and the time that had passed since her husband's death had allowed her to come to terms with being on her own. All she wished for was to continue in these same circumstances until she died, and she did not fear death. She did not believe she would be reunited with her sons and her husband, not at least in a specific sense, but she could not believe, either, that she would entirely cease to exist the moment she ceased to breathe. Having thought about death, it seemed likely to Mrs Malby that after it came she'd dream, as in sleep. Heaven and hell were surely no more than flickers of such pleasant dreaming, or flickers of a nightmare from which there was no waking release. No loving omnipotent God, in Mrs Malby's view, doled out punishments and reward: human conscience, the last survivor, did that. The idea of a God, which had puzzled Mrs Malby for most of her life, made sense when she thought of it in terms like these, when she forgot about the mystic qualities claimed for a Church and for Jesus Christ. Yet fearful of offending the Reverend Bush, she kept such conclusions to herself when he came to see her.

All Mrs Malby dreaded now was becoming senile and being forced to enter the Sunset Home in Richmond, of which the Reverend Bush and Miss Tingle warmly spoke. The thought of a communal existence, surrounded by other elderly people, with sing-songs and card-games, was anathema to her. All her life she had hated anything that smacked of communal jolliness, refusing even to go on coach trips. She loved the house above the greengrocer's shop. She loved walking down the stairs and out on to the street, nodding at the Kings as she went by the shop, buying birdseed and eggs and fire-lighters, and fresh bread from Bob Skipps, a man of sixty-two whom she'd remembered being born.

The dread of having to leave Catherine Street ordered her life. With all her visitors she was careful, constantly on the lookout for signs in their eyes which might mean they were diagnosing her as senile. It was for this reason that she listened so intently to all that was said to her, that she concentrated, determined to let nothing slip by. It was for this reason that she smiled and endeavoured to appear agreeable and cooperative at all times. She was well aware that it wasn't going to be up to her to state that she was senile, or to argue that she wasn't, when the moment came.

After the teacher from Tite Comprehensive School had left, Mrs Malby continued to worry. The visit from this grey-haired man had bewildered her from the start. There was the oddity of his not giving his name, and then the way he'd placed a cigarette in his mouth and had taken it out again, putting it back in the packet. Had he imagined cigarette smoke would offend her? He could have asked, but in fact he hadn't even referred to the cigarette. Nor had he said where he'd heard about her: he hadn't mentioned the Reverend Bush, for instance, or Mrs Grove and Mrs Halbert, or Miss Tingle. He might have been a customer in the greengrocer's shop, but he hadn't given any indication that that was so. Added to which, and most of all, there was the consideration that her kitchen wasn't in the least in need of attention. She went to look at it again, beginning to wonder if there were things about it she couldn't see. She went over in her mind what the man had said about community relations. It was difficult to resist men like that, you had to go on repeating yourself and after a while you had to assess if you were sounding senile or not. There was also the consideration that the man was trying to do good, helping children from broken homes.

'Hi,' a boy with long blond hair said to her on the Tuesday morning. There were two other boys with him, one with a fuzz of dark curls all round his head, the other red-haired, a greased shock that hung to his shoulders. There was a girl as well, thin and beaky-faced, chewing something. Between them they carried tins of paint, brushes, cloths, a blue plastic bucket and a transistor radio. 'We come to do your kitchen out,' the blond boy said. 'You Mrs Wheeler then?'

'No, no. I'm Mrs Malby.'

'That's right, Billo,' the girl said. 'Malby.'

'I thought he says Wheeler.'

'Wheeler's the geyser in the paint shop,' the fuzzy-haired boy said.

'Typical Billo,' the girl said.

She let them in, saying it was very kind of them. She led them to the kitchen, remarking on the way that strictly speaking it wasn't in need of decoration, as they could see for themselves. She'd been thinking it over, she added: she wondered if they'd just like to wash the walls down, which was a task she found difficult to do herself?

They'd do whatever she wanted, they said, no problem. They put their paint tins on the table. The red-haired boy turned on the radio. 'Welcome back to Open House', a cheery voice said and then reminded its listeners that it was the voice of Pete Murray. It said that a record was about to be played for someone in Upminster.

'Would you like some coffee?' Mrs Malby suggested above the noise of the transistor.

'Great,' the blond boy said.

They all wore blue jeans with patches on them. The girl had a T-shirt with the words *I Lay Down With Jesus* on it. The others wore T-shirts of different colours, the blond boy's orange, the fuzzy one's light blue, the red-haired one's red. *Hot Jam-roll* a badge on the chest of the blond boy said; *Jaws* and *Bay City Rollers* other badges said.

Mrs Malby made them Nescafé while they listened to the music. They lit cigarettes, leaning about against the electric stove and against the edge of the table and against a wall. They didn't say anything because they were listening. 'That's a load of crap,' the red-haired boy pronounced eventually, and the others agreed. Even so they went on listening. 'Pete Murray's crappy,' the girl said.

Mrs Malby handed them the cups of coffee, drawing their attention to the sugar she'd put out for them on the table, and to the milk. She smiled at the girl. She said again that it was a job she couldn't manage any more, washing walls.

'Get that, Billo?' the fuzzy-haired boy said. 'Washing walls.'

'Who loves ya, baby?' Billo replied.

Mrs Malby closed the kitchen door on them, hoping they wouldn't take too long because the noise of the transistor was so loud. She listened to it for a quarter of an hour and then she decided to go out and do her shopping.

In Bob Skipps' she said that four children from the Tite Comprehensive had arrived in her house and were at present washing her kitchen walls. She said it again to the man in the fish shop and the man was surprised. It suddenly occurred to her that of course they couldn't have done any painting because she hadn't discussed colours with the teacher. She thought it odd that the teacher hadn't mentioned colours and wondered what colour the paint tins contained. It worried her a little that all that hadn't occurred to her before.

'Hi, Mrs Wheeler,' the boy called Billo said to her in her hall. He was standing there combing his hair, looking at himself in the mirror of the hall-stand. Music was coming from upstairs.

There were yellowish smears on the stair-carpet, which upset Mrs Malby very much. There were similar smears on the landing carpet. 'Oh, but please,' Mrs Malby cried, standing in the kitchen doorway. 'Oh, please, no!' she cried.

Yellow emulsion paint partially covered the shell-pink of one wall. Some had spilt from the tin on to the black-and-white vinyl of the floor and had been walked through. The boy with fuzzy hair was standing on a draining board applying the same paint to the ceiling. He was the only person in the kitchen.

He smiled at Mrs Malby, looking down at her. 'Hi, Mrs Wheeler,' he said.

'But I said only to wash them,' she cried.

She felt tired, saying that. The upset of finding the smears on the carpets and of seeing the hideous yellow plastered over the quiet shell-pink had already taken a toll. Her emotional outburst had caused her face and neck to become warm. She felt she'd like to lie down.

'Eh, Mrs Wheeler?' The boy smiled at her again, continuing to slap paint on to the ceiling. A lot of it dripped back on top of him, on to the draining board and on to cups and saucers and cutlery, and on to the floor. 'D'you fancy the colour, Mrs Wheeler?' he asked her.

All the time the transistor continued to blare, a voice inexpertly singing, a tuneless twanging. The boy referred to this sound, pointing at the transistor with his paintbrush, saying it was great. Unsteadily she crossed the kitchen and turned the transistor off. 'Hey, sod it, missus,' the boy protested angrily.

'I said to wash the walls. I didn't even choose that colour.'

The boy, still annoyed because she'd turned off the radio, was gesturing crossly with the brush. There was paint in the fuzz of his hair and on his

T-shirt and his face. Every time he moved the brush about paint flew off it. It speckled the windows, and the small dresser, and the electric stove and the taps and the sink.

'Where's the sound gone?' the boy called Billo demanded, coming into the kitchen and going straight to the transistor.

'I didn't want the kitchen painted,' Mrs Malby said again. 'I told you.'

The singing from the transistor recommenced, louder than before. On the draining board the fuzzy-haired boy began to sway, throwing his body and his head about.

'Please stop him painting,' Mrs Malby shouted as shrilly as she could.

'Here,' the boy called Billo said, bundling her out on to the landing and closing the kitchen door. 'Can't hear myself think in there.'

'I don't want it painted.'

'What's that, Mrs Wheeler?'

'My name isn't Wheeler. I don't want my kitchen painted. I told you.'

'Are we in the wrong house? Only we was told –'

'Will you please wash that paint off?'

'If we come to the wrong house –'

'You haven't come to the wrong house. Please tell that boy to wash off the paint he's put on.'

'Did a bloke from the Comp come in to see you, Mrs Wheeler? Fat bloke?'

'Yes, yes, he did.'

'Only he give instructions –'

'Please would you tell that boy?'

'Whatever you say, Mrs Wheeler.'

'And wipe up the paint where it's spilt on the floor. It's been trampled out, all over my carpets.'

'No problem, Mrs Wheeler.'

Not wishing to return to the kitchen herself, she ran the hot tap in the bathroom on to the sponge-cloth she kept for cleaning the bath. She found that if she rubbed hard enough at the paint on the stair-carpet and on the landing carpet it began to disappear. But the rubbing tired her. As she put away the sponge-cloth, Mrs Malby had a feeling of not quite knowing what was what. Everything that had happened in the last few hours felt like a dream; it also had the feeling of plays she had seen on television; the one thing it wasn't like was reality. As she paused in her bathroom, having placed the sponge-cloth on a ledge under the hand-basin, Mrs Malby saw herself standing there, as she often did in a dream: she saw her body hunched within the same blue dress she'd been wearing when the teacher called, and two touches of red in her pale face, and her white hair tidy on her head, and her fingers seeming fragile. In a dream anything could happen next: she might suddenly find herself forty years younger, Derek and Roy might be alive. She might be even younger; Dr Ramsey might be telling her she was pregnant. In a television play it would be different: the children who had come to her house might kill her. What she hoped for from reality was that order would be restored in her kitchen, that all the paint would be washed away from her walls as she had wiped it from her carpets, that the misunderstanding would be over. For an instant she saw herself in her kitchen, making tea for the children, saying it didn't matter. She even heard herself adding that in a life as long as hers you became used to everything.

She left the bathroom; the blare of the transistor still persisted. She didn't want to sit in her sitting-room, having to listen to it. She climbed the stairs to her bedroom, imagining the coolness there, and the quietness.

'Hey,' the girl protested when Mrs Malby opened her bedroom door.

'Sod off, you guys,' the boy with the red hair ordered.

They were in her bed. Their clothes were all over the floor. Her two budgerigars were flying about the room. Protruding from sheets and blankets she could see the boy's naked shoulders and the back of his head. The girl poked her face up from under him. She gazed at Mrs Malby. 'It's not them,' she whispered to the boy. 'It's the woman.'

'Hi there, missus.' The boy twisted his head round. From the kitchen, still loudly, came the noise of the transistor.

'Sorry,' the girl said.

'Why are they up here? Why have you let my birds out? You've no right to behave like this.'

'We needed sex,' the girl explained.

The budgerigars were perched on the looking-glass on the dressing-table, beadily surveying the scene.

'They're really great, them budgies,' the boy said.

Mrs Malby stepped through their garments. The budgerigars remained where they were. They fluttered when she seized them but they didn't offer any resistance. She returned with them to the door.

'You had no right,' she began to say to the two in her bed, but her voice had become weak. It quivered into a useless whisper, and once more she thought that what was happening couldn't be happening. She saw herself again, standing unhappily with the budgerigars.

In her sitting-room she wept. She returned the budgerigars to their cage and sat in an armchair by the window that looked out over Catherine Street. She sat in sunshine, feeling its warmth but not, as she might have done, delighting in it. She wept because she had intensely disliked finding the boy and girl in her bed. Images from the bedroom remained vivid in her mind. On the floor the boy's boots were heavy and black, composed of leather that did not shine. The girl's shoes were green, with huge heels and soles. The girl's underclothes were purple, the boy's dirty. There'd been an unpleasant smell of sweat in her bedroom.

Mrs Malby waited, her head beginning to ache. She dried away her tears, wiping at her eyes and cheeks with a handkerchief. In Catherine Street people passed by on bicycles, girls from the polish factory returning home to lunch, men from the brickworks. People came out of the greengrocer's with leeks and cabbages in baskets, some carrying paper bags. Watching these people in Catherine Street made her feel better, even though her headache was becoming worse. She felt more composed, and more in control of herself.

'We're sorry,' the girl said again, suddenly appearing, teetering on her clumsy shoes. 'We didn't think you'd come up to the bedroom.'

She tried to smile at the girl, but found it hard to do so. She nodded instead.

'The others put the birds in,' the girl said. 'Meant to be a joke, that was.'

She nodded again. She couldn't see how it could be a joke to take two budgerigars from their cage, but she didn't say that.

'We're getting on with the painting now,' the girl said. 'Sorry about that.'

She went away and Mrs Malby continued to watch the people in Catherine Street. The girl had made a mistake when she'd said they were getting on with the painting: what she'd meant was that they were getting on with washing it off. The girl had come straight downstairs to say she was sorry; she hadn't been told by the boys in the kitchen that the paint had been applied in error. When they'd gone, Mrs Malby said to herself, she'd open her bedroom window wide in order to get rid of the odour of sweat. She'd put clean sheets on her bed.

From the kitchen, above the noise of the transistor, came the clatter of raised voices. There was laughter and a crash, and then louder laughter. Singing began, attaching itself to the singing from the transistor.

She sat for twenty minutes and then she went and knocked on the kitchen door, not wishing to push the door open in case it knocked someone off a chair. There was no reply. She opened the door gingerly.

More yellow paint had been applied. The whole wall around the window was covered with it, and most of the wall behind the sink. Half of the ceiling had it on it; the woodwork that had been white was now a glossy dark blue. All four of the children were working with brushes. A tin of paint had been upset on the floor.

She wept again, standing there watching them, unable to prevent her tears. She felt them running warmly on her cheeks and then becoming cold. It was in this kitchen that she had cried first of all when the two telegrams had come in 1942, believing when the second one arrived that she would never cease to cry. It would have seemed ridiculous at the time, to cry just because her kitchen was all yellow.

They didn't see her standing there. They went on singing, slapping the paintbrushes back and forth. There'd been neat straight lines where the shell-pink met the white of the woodwork, but now the lines were any old how. The boy with the red hair was applying the dark-blue gloss.

Again the feeling that it wasn't happening possessed Mrs Malby. She'd had a dream a week ago, a particularly vivid dream in which the Prime Minister had stated on television that the Germans had been invited to invade England since England couldn't manage to look after herself any more. That dream had been most troublesome because when she'd woken up in the morning she'd thought it was something she'd seen on television, that she'd actually been sitting in her sitting-room the night before listening to the Prime Minister saying that he and the Leader of the Opposition had decided the best for Britain was invasion. After thinking about it, she'd established that of course it hadn't been true; but even so she'd glanced at the headlines of newspapers when she went out shopping.

'How d'you fancy it?' the boy called Billo called out to her, smiling across the kitchen at her, not noticing that she was upset. 'Neat, Mrs Wheeler?'

She didn't answer. She went downstairs and walked out of her hall door, into Catherine Street and into the greengrocer's that had been her husband's. It never closed in the middle of the day; it never had. She waited and Mr King appeared, wiping his mouth. 'Well then, Mrs Malby?' he said.

He was a big man with a well-kept black moustache and Jewish eyes. He didn't smile much because smiling wasn't his way, but he was in no way morose, rather the opposite.

'So what can I do for you?' he said.

She told him. He shook his head and repeatedly frowned as he listened. His expressive eyes widened. He called his wife.

While the three of them hurried along the pavement to Mrs Malby's open hall door it seemed to her that the Kings doubted her. She could feel them thinking that she must have got it all wrong, that she'd somehow imagined all this stuff about yellow paint and pop music on a radio, and her birds flying around her bedroom while two children were lying in her bed. She didn't blame them; she knew exactly how they felt. But when they entered her house the noise from the transistor could at once be heard.

The carpet of the landing was smeared again with the paint. Yellow footprints led to her sitting-room and out again, back to the kitchen.

'You bloody young hooligans,' Mr King shouted at them. He snapped the switch on the transistor. He told them to stop applying the paint immediately. 'What the hell d'you think you're up to?' he demanded furiously.

'We come to paint out the old ma's kitchen,' the boy called Billo explained, unruffled by Mr King's tone. 'We was carrying out instructions, mister.'

'So it was instructions to spill the blooming paint all over the floor? So it was instructions to cover the windows with it and every knife and fork in the place? So it was instructions to frighten the life out of a poor woman by messing about in her bedroom?'

'No one frightens her, mister.'

'You know what I mean, son.'

Mrs Malby returned with Mrs King and sat in the cubbyhole behind the shop, leaving Mr King to do his best. At three o'clock he arrived back, saying that the children had gone. He telephoned the school and after a delay was put in touch with the teacher who'd been to see Mrs Malby. He made this telephone call in the shop but Mrs Malby could hear him saying that what had happened was a disgrace. 'A woman of eighty-seven,' Mr King protested, 'thrown into a state of misery. There'll be something to pay on this, you know.'

There was some further discussion on the telephone, and then Mr King replaced the receiver. He put his head into the cubbyhole and announced that the teacher was coming round immediately to inspect the damage. 'What can I entice you to?' Mrs Malby heard him asking a customer, and a woman's voice replied that she needed tomatoes, a cauliflower, potatoes and Bramleys. She heard Mr King telling the woman what had happened, saying that it had wasted two hours of his time.

She drank the sweet milky tea which Mrs King had poured her. She tried not to think of the yellow paint and the dark-blue gloss. She tried not to remember the scene in the bedroom and the smell there'd been, and the new marks that had appeared on her carpets after she'd wiped off the original ones. She wanted to ask Mr King if these marks had been washed out before the paint had had a chance to dry, but she didn't like to ask this because Mr King had been so kind and it might seem like pressing him.

'Kids nowadays,' Mrs King said. 'I just don't know.'

'Birched they should be,' Mr King said, coming into the cubbyhole and picking up a mug of the milky tea. 'I'd birch the bottoms off them.'

Someone arrived in the shop, Mr King hastened from the cubbyhole. 'What can I entice you to, sir?' Mrs Malby heard him politely inquiring and the voice of the teacher who'd been to see her replied. He said who he was and Mr King wasn't polite any more. An experience like that, Mr King declared thunderously, could have killed an eighty-seven-year-old stone dead.

Mrs Malby stood up and Mrs King came promptly forward to place a hand under her elbow. They went into the shop like that. 'Three and a half p,' Mr King was saying to a woman who'd asked the price of oranges. 'The larger ones at four.'

Mr King gave the woman four of the smaller size and accepted her money. He called out to a youth who was passing by on a bicycle, about to start an afternoon paper round. He was a youth who occasionally assisted him on Saturday mornings: Mr King asked him now if he would mind the shop for ten minutes since an emergency had arisen. Just for once, Mr King argued, it wouldn't matter if the evening papers were a little late.

'Well, you can't say they haven't brightened the place up, Mrs Malby,' the teacher said in her kitchen. He regarded her from beneath his grey fringe. He touched one of the walls with the tip of a finger. He nodded to himself, appearing to be satisfied.

The painting had been completed, the yellow and the dark-blue gloss. Where the colours met there were untidily jagged lines. All the paint that had been spilt on the floor had been wiped away, but the black-and-white vinyl had become dull and grubby in the process. The paint had also been wiped from the windows and from other surfaces, leaving them smeared. The dresser had been wiped down and was smeary also. The cutlery and the taps and the cups and saucers had all been washed or wiped.

'Well, you wouldn't believe it!' Mrs King exclaimed. She turned to her husband. However had he managed it all? she asked him. 'You should have seen the place!' she said to the teacher.

'It's just the carpets,' Mr King said. He led the way from the kitchen to the sitting-room, pointing at the yellow on the landing carpet and on the sitting-room one. 'The blooming stuff dried,' he explained, 'before we could get to it. That's where compensation comes in.' He spoke sternly, addressing the teacher. 'I'd say she has a bob or two owing.'

Mrs King nudged Mrs Malby, drawing attention to the fact that Mr King was doing his best for her. The nudge suggested that all would be well because a sum of money would be paid, possibly even a larger sum than was merited. It suggested also that Mrs Malby in the end might find herself doing rather well.

'Compensation?' the teacher said, bending down and scratching at the paint on the sitting-room carpet. 'I'm afraid compensation's out of the question.'

'She's had her carpets ruined,' Mr King snapped quickly. 'This woman's been put about, you know.'

'She got her kitchen done free,' the teacher snapped back at him.

'They released her pets. They got up to tricks in a bed. You'd no damn right –'

'These kids come from broken homes, sir. I'll do my best with your carpets, Mrs Malby.'

'But what about my kitchen?' she whispered. She cleared her throat because her whispering could hardly be heard. 'My kitchen?' she whispered again.

'What about it, Mrs Malby?'

'I didn't want it painted.'

'Oh, don't be silly now.'

The teacher took his jacket off and threw it impatiently on to a chair. He left the sitting-room. Mrs Malby heard him running a tap in the kitchen.

'It was best to finish the painting, Mrs Malby,' Mr King said. 'Otherwise the kitchen would have driven you mad, half done like that. I stood over them till they finished it.'

'You can't take paint off, dear,' Mrs King said, 'once it's on. You've done wonders, Leo,' she said to her husband. 'Young devils.'

'We'd best be getting back,' Mr King said.

'It's quite nice, you know,' his wife added. 'Your kitchen's quite cheerful, dear.'

The Kings went away and the teacher rubbed at the yellow on the carpets with her washing-up brush. The landing carpet was marked anyway, he pointed out, poking a finger at the stains left behind by the paint she'd removed herself with the sponge-cloth from the bathroom. She must be delighted with the kitchen, he said.

She knew she mustn't speak. She'd known she mustn't when the Kings had been there; she knew she mustn't now. She might have reminded the Kings that she'd chosen the original colours in the kitchen herself. She might have complained to the man as he rubbed at her carpets that the carpets would never be the same again. She watched him, not saying anything, not wishing to be regarded as a nuisance. The Kings would have considered her a nuisance too, agreeing to let children into her kitchen to paint it and then making a fuss. If she became a nuisance the teacher and the Kings would drift on to the same side, and the Reverend Bush would somehow be on that side also, and Miss Tingle, and even Mrs Grove and Mrs Halbert. They would agree among themselves that what had happened had to do with her elderliness, with her not understanding that children who brought paint into a kitchen were naturally going to use it.

'I defy anyone to notice that,' the teacher said, standing up, gesturing at the yellow blurs that remained on her carpets. He put his jacket on. He left the washing-up brush and the bowl of water he'd been using on the floor of her sitting-room. 'All's well that ends well,' he said. 'Thanks for your cooperation, Mrs Malby.'

She thought of her two sons, Derek and Roy, not knowing quite why she thought of them now. She descended the stairs with the teacher, who was cheerfully talking about community relations. You had to make allowances, he said, for kids like that; you had to try and understand; you couldn't just walk away.

Quite suddenly she wanted to tell him about Derek and Roy. In the desire to talk about them she imagined their bodies, as she used to in the past, soon after they'd been killed. They lay on desert sand, desert birds swooped down on them. Their four eyes were gone. She wanted to explain to the teacher that they'd been happy, a contented family in Catherine Street, until the war came and smashed everything to pieces. Nothing had been the same afterwards. It hadn't been easy to continue with nothing to continue for. Each room in the house had contained different memories of the two boys growing up. Cooking and cleaning had seemed pointless. The shop which would have been theirs would have to pass to someone else.

And yet time had soothed the awful double wound. The horror of the emptiness had been lived with, and if having the Kings in the shop now wasn't the same as having your sons there at least the Kings were kind. Thirty-four years after the destruction of your family you were happy in your elderliness because time had been merciful. She wanted to tell the teacher that also, she didn't know why, except that in some way it seemed relevant. But she didn't tell him because it would have been difficult to begin, because in the effort there'd be the danger of seeming senile. Instead she said goodbye, concentrating on that. She said she was sorry, saying it just to show she was aware that she hadn't made herself clear to the children. Conversation had broken down between the children and herself, she wanted him to know she knew it had.

He nodded vaguely, not listening to her. He was trying to make the world a better place, he said. 'For kids like that, Mrs Malby. Victims of broken homes.'

On the Zattere

Without meaning to, Verity had taken her mother's place. Six months after her mother's death she had given up her flat and moved back to the house where she and her two brothers – both of them now married – had grown up. She had pretended, even to herself at times, that she was concerned about her father's loneliness, but the true reason was that she wished to make a change on her own account, to break a pattern in her life. She became, as her mother had been, her father's chief companion and was in time exposed to traits in his nature she had not known existed. Preserving within the family the exterior of a bluff and genial man, good-hearted, knowledgeable and wise, her father had successfully disguised the worst of himself; and had been assisted by his wife's loyalty. It was different for a daughter, and Verity found herself watching the old man in a way she would once not have believed possible, impatient with his weaknesses, judging him.

Mr Unwill, unaware of this development in his daughter, was greatly pleased with the turn events had taken. He was touched when Verity gave up her flat and returned to the family home, and he was proud to be seen in her company, believing that strangers might not take her for his daughter but assume instead that he was an older man to whom this beautiful woman was sentimentally attached. He dressed the part when they went on their first holiday together – to Venice, which every autumn in her lifetime he had visited with his wife. In swirls of green and red, a paisley scarf was knotted at his throat and matched the handkerchief that spilt from the top pocket of his navy-blue blazer. There was no reason why they should be taken as father and daughter, he argued to himself, since they were so very different in appearance. Verity, who was neither small nor tall, gave an impression of slightness because she was slim and was delicately made. The nearly perfect features of her face were set on the suspicion of a slant, turning ordinary beauty into the unusual and causing people who saw it for the first time to glance again. Her hair, clinging smoothly around the contours of classically high cheekbones, was the brown of chestnuts; her eyes, almost strangely, matched it. She dressed and made up with care, as if believing that beauty should be honoured.

In contrast, Mr Unwill was a large man in his advanced sixties, with a ruddy complexion and a bald head. People who knew him quite well had difficulty remembering, when no longer in his presence, if he had a moustache or not. The lingering impression of his face – the ruddiness, the tortoiseshell spectacles – seemed somehow to suggest another, taken-for-granted characteristic, and in fact there was one: a grey growth of bristle on his upper lip, unnoticeable because it so easily became one with the similar greyness that flanked the naked dome.

'Well, what shall you do today?' he asked in the pensione dining-room when they had finished breakfast on their third day. 'I'll be all right, you know. Don't spare a worry for me.'

'I thought I'd go to the Church of San Zaccaria.'

'Why not? You trot along, my dear. I'll sit and watch the boats go by.'

They were alone in the dining-room: in early November the pensione was not full. The American family had not come in to breakfast, presumably having it in their rooms. The German girls had been and gone; so had the French threesome and the lone Italian lady in her purple hat.

'Nice, those German girls,' Mr Unwill said. 'The pretty one made a most interesting observation last night.' He paused, tobacco-stained teeth bared, his eyes ruminative behind his spectacles. 'She said she wondered where waiters go between meals. *Most* unGermanic, I thought.'

Verity, who was thirty-eight and had recently come to believe that life was going to pass her by, reached across the table and took one of her father's cigarettes from the packet that was open beside his coffee cup. She acknowledged the observation of the German girl by briefly nodding. She lit her cigarette from the flame of a small, gold lighter, given to her by the man she'd been in Venice with before.

'The pretty one's from Munich,' her father said. 'The other – now, where on earth did they tell me the fat one came from?' Furrows of thought appeared on his forehead, then he gave up. Slowly he removed his spectacles and in the same unhurried manner proceeded to wipe them with his paisley handkerchief. It was a way of his, a hobby almost. The frames were polished first, then each lens; sometimes he went to work with his Swiss penknife, tightening the screws of the hinges with the screwdriver that was incorporated in one of the blades. 'The pretty one's a laboratory assistant,' he said, 'the other one works in a shop or something.'

The penknife had not, this morning, been taken from his blazer pocket. He held the spectacles up to the light. 'I'll probably sit outside at the Cucciolo,' he said.

'The coffee's better at Nico's. And cheaper.'

It was he – years ago, so he said – who had established that, and yesterday it had been confirmed. She'd sat outside the Cucciolo by mistake, forgetting what he'd told her, obliging him to join her when he emerged from the pensione after his afternoon sleep. He'd later pointed out that a cappuccino at the Cucciolo was fifteen hundred but only eleven at Nico's or Aldo's. Her father was mean about spending small sums of money, Verity had discovered since becoming his companion. He didn't like it when she reached out and helped herself to one of his cigarettes, but he hadn't yet learnt to put the packet away quickly.

'Oh, I don't know that I'm up to the walk to Nico's this morning,' he said.

It took less than a minute to stroll along the Zattere to Nico's, and he was never not up to things. She had discovered also that whenever he felt like it he told petty, unimportant lies, and as they left the dining-room she wondered what this latest one was all about.

Straining a white jacket, beads of perspiration glistening on his forehead, the pensione's bearded waiter used a battery-powered gadget to sweep the crumbs from the tablecloths in the dining-room. His colleague, similarly attired and resembling Fred Astaire, laid two tables for the guests who had chosen to have lunch rather than dinner.

The dining-room was low-ceilinged, with mirrors and sideboards set against the fawn silk on the walls, and windows of round green panes. The breathing of the bearded waiter and the slurping of the canal just outside these windows were the only sounds after the crumbs had been cleared and the tables laid. The waiters glanced over their domain and went away to spend their time mysteriously, justifying the German girl's curiosity.

In the hall of the pensione guests who were never seen in the dining-room, choosing to take no meals, awaited the attention of the smart receptionist, this morning all in red. A kitten played on her desk while patiently she gave directions to the Church of the Frari. She told the Italian lady with the purple hat that there was a dry cleaner's less than a minute away. '*Pronto?*' she said, picking up her telephone. The hall, which was not large, featured in the glass door of the telephone-box and the doors that led outside the same round green panes as the dining-room. There were faded prints on the walls, and by the reception desk a map of Venice and a list of the pensione's credit-card facilities. A second cat, grey and gross and bearing the marks of a lifetime's disputes, lay sleeping on the stairs.

'Enjoy yourself, my dear,' Mr Unwill said to his daughter, stepping over this animal. She didn't appear to hear so he said it again when they had passed through the round-paned doors and stood together for a moment on the quayside.

'Yes,' she said. 'I'll probably wander a bit after I've been to San Zaccaria.'

'Why not, old girl? I'll be as happy as a sandboy, you know.'

The fog that had earlier obscured the houses of the Giudecca on the other side of the canal was lifting; already the sun evaporated the dankness in the air. Verity wore a flecked suit of pinkish-orange, with a scarf that matched it loosely tied over a cream blouse. In one lapel there was a tiny pearl brooch, another gift from the man she'd been in Venice with before.

She turned into the *fondamenta* that ran along one side of the pensione. It was cold there, untouched by the November sunshine. She shivered, but felt it was not from this chilliness. She wished she was not alone, for an irony in her present circumstance was that she found the company of other people both tiresome and of use. She walked more quickly, endeavouring to keep certain insistent thoughts out of her mind. At the Accademia she bought her ticket for the vaporetto and waited on the landing-stage. Other people, no matter who they were, disrupted such thoughts, which was something she welcomed. The attention other people demanded, the conversations they began, their faces and their voices, clogged her communication with herself; and yet, so much of the time while in the company of other people, she wished she was not.

Odd, to have taken her mother's place in this old-fashioned way: on the vaporetto she saw again the tortoiseshell spectacles in her father's hands, his square, wide fingers working the paisley silk over the lens. Repetition had etched this image in some corner of her mind: she heard his early-morning cough, and then the lowered tone he used when talking to himself. Had it been panic that had caused her to use his loneliness as an excuse, to break the pattern she found so merciless? Love-making had been easy in the convenient flat, too much had been taken for granted. But even so, giving up the flat might have struck some people as extreme.

On the vaporetto the Italians glanced at her, women assessing her in some Italian way, the men desirous. Venice was different in November, less of a bauble than the summer city she remembered. The tourist crowds had gone, with the mosquitoes and the cruel Italian heat. The orchestras had ceased to play in the Piazza San Marco, the Riva degli Schiavoni was again the property of the Venetians. She imagined her parents walking arm in arm on the Riva, or going to Torcello and Burano. Had the warmth of their companionship been a pretence on his part? For if he'd loved his wife how could he so easily come back to the city he and she had discovered together and had affectionately made their own? Eleven months had passed since her death and already in the pensione they had come to know so well he was striking up acquaintanceships as though nothing of importance had occurred since last he'd been there. There had been a moment in the hall when he mumblingly spoke to the smartly dressed receptionist, who said that everyone at the pensione sympathized. The elderly maid who welcomed him upstairs had murmured in Italian, and in the dining-room the waiters' voices had been low at first. It was he himself who subsequently set the mood, his matter-of-fact manner brushing sentiment aside, summarily dismissing death. Had her mother loved him or had their companionship in this city been, on her part also, a pretence? Marriage was riddled with such falsity, Verity reflected, dressed up as loyalty or keeping faith.

Palaces loomed majestically on either side of her, the lion of St Mark disdainful on his column, St Theodore modest on his. Carpaccio would still have recognized his city in the tranquillity of November, the Virgins of Cima still crossed the city's bridges. It was her mother who had said all that to her, translating emotions she had felt. Verity went on thinking about her parents, not wishing to think about herself, not wishing to catch a glimpse of herself in the summer dresses she had worn when she'd been in Venice before. There had been many weekends spent faithfully with the same companion in many beautiful cities, but Venice that July had left behind a special meaning because hope had died there.

Mr Unwill settled himself on one of the Cucciolo Bar's orange plastic seats. Verity was right: the Cucciolo wasn't a patch on Nico's or Aldo's. Fewer people passed by for a start, and the one cappuccino he'd been served yesterday by the Cucciolo's dour waiter had tasted of the last person's sugar. But the trouble with sitting outside Nico's or Aldo's was that people often turned off the Zattere before they reached them, and he happened to know that the pretty little German girl was still in the pensione because he'd seen the fat one striding off on her own half an hour ago. Of course it could be that the pretty one had preceded her friend, in which case he'd be four hundred lire down, which would be annoying.

'Prego, signore?'

He ordered his coffee. He wished he spoke Italian so that he might draw the waiter's attention to the inadequately washed cup he'd been presented with yesterday. He'd have done so in England: one of the few good things about being old was that you could make a fuss. Another was that you could drop into conversation with people without their thinking it was peculiar of you. Last night he'd wandered in from his stroll after Verity had gone to her room, and had noticed the two girls in the lounge. He'd leafed through a pile of magazines that had to do with the work of the Venetian police, and then the girls had begun to giggle unrestrainedly. By way of a polite explanation, the pretty one had spoken to him in English, explaining that it was the remark about where waiters go between meals which had caused their merriment. After that the conversation had drifted on. He'd told them a thing or two about Venice, which he knew quite well in a professional way.

Mr Unwill was retired, having been employed for all his adult life in a shipping office. Ships and their cargoes, the building, sale and insuring of ships, were what he was most familiar with. It was this interest that had first brought him to Venice, as it had to many other great ports. While his three children were still growing up it had been necessary to limit such travel to the British Isles, but later he and his wife had travelled as far and as adventurously as funds permitted, always economizing so that journeys might be extended or prolonged. Venice had become their favourite.

'Hullo there!' he called out to the German girl as she stepped around the corner, shading her eyes against the sun. She was wearing a short dress that was almost the same colour as her very blonde hair.

'What a day!' Mr Unwill said, standing up so that she could not easily just walk by. 'Now, how about a coffee?'

Her teeth, when she smiled her appreciation of this invitation, glistened damply, large white teeth, each one perfectly shaped. But to his disappointment, while smiling she also shook her head. She was late already, she explained: she was to meet her friend at the Rialto Bridge.

He watched her hurrying along the Zattere, her sturdy legs nicely bronzed, a camera slung across her shoulder. She turned the corner by the Church of the Gesuati and Mr Unwill sighed.

In the Church of San Zaccaria Verity gazed at the Bellini altarpiece her mother had sent her postcards of. Perfectly, she still contained her thoughts, conjecturing again. Had her mother stood on this very spot? Had her father accompanied her to the churches she liked so much or in all their visits had he been concerned only with duller interests? Verity didn't know; it had never seemed important.

The lights that illuminated the picture abruptly went out. Verity felt in her purse for two hundred lire, but before she found the coins a man stepped forward and dropped his through the slot of the little grey box on one side of the altar. The Virgin and her saints, in sacred conversation, were there again. Verity looked for a few moments longer and then moved away.

She hadn't looked at pictures that July. For a second she saw herself and heard her laughter: in a dress with primroses on it, wearing sunglasses and laughing, although she had not felt like laughing. In the church she felt again the effort of that laughter and was angry because for a single second her concentration had faltered. She dropped some money into a poor-box by the door. She hadn't realized how fond she'd been of her mother until the very last moment, until the coffin had soundlessly slipped away behind a beige curtain in the chapel of the crematorium. The soundlessness was eerie and unpleasant; Verity had hated that moment.

She left the church and walked back to the Riva. Metal trestles supported planks of wood, like crude tabletops, on which people might walk if the tides rose and the floods of autumn began. These improvised bridges were called *passerelle*, her father had told her, pointing them out to her on the Zattere. 'Oh heavens, of course I'll manage,' he'd kept repeating on the afternoon of the funeral and all of them, her brothers and her sisters-in-law, she herself, had admired his urbanity and his resolve not to be a nuisance.

She rose and walked slowly along the Riva towards the Arsenale. Already the quayside hotels had a deserted look; the pink Gabrielli-Sandwirth had put up its shutters. 'No, absolutely not,' her father had said on some later occasion. 'You have your own life, Verity.' And of course she had: her own life, her own job, her own flat in which love might be made.

A fun-fair was being erected further along the quay, dodgem cars and a tunnel of fear, swing-boats and fruit machines. 'American Games' a garish announcement read; 'Central Park' proclaimed another. Two bespectacled old women washed down a rifle-range; hobby-horses were unloaded. Outside the Pensione Bucintoro a shirt-sleeved waiter smoked a cigarette and watched.

In the Via Garibaldi children with satchels or school books chased one another on their journey home from morning school; women jostled and pushed at the vegetable stalls. In the public park, tatty and forgotten in the low season, cats swarmed or huddled – mangy tomcats with ravenous eyes, pitiful kittens that seemed resentful of their recent birth, leanly slinking mothers. All of them were dirty; two weakly fought, a hissing, clawing ball of different-coloured fur. Verity bent down and tried to attract a dusty marmalade-coloured kitten, but alarmed by her attentions it darted off. She walked on, still determinedly dwelling upon her father's heartlessness in so casually returning to this city, to the pensione, to the Zattere. She dwelt again upon her mother's misplaced loyalty, which had kept the marriage going. But she herself, in her primrose-yellow dress and her sunglasses, crept through these irrelevant reflections so crudely forced upon her consciousness. Her parents arm-in-arm in Venice, loving or not loving, vanished into wisps of mist, and were replaced by the sound of her own ersatz laughter. There was an image of her face, strained with a smile that choked away the hopelessness she was frightened to surrender to. The ice tinkled in her well-chilled Soave; the orchestras played in the great, romantic square. 'Oh, I am happy!' came the echo of her lying voice, and in the dingy public park her beauty fled as swiftly as the marmalade kitten had leapt from her grasp. She wept, but it did not matter because no one was about.

Mr Unwill, deprived of a conversation with the German girl, left the Cucciolo Bar and strolled down the Zattere in the direction of the western Stazione Marittima. It was an interesting place, this particular Stazione Marittima, and he would like one day to find someone who would show him round it. He often loitered by the bridge that led almost directly into it, hoping to catch the eye of some official with an hour or two on his hands who would welcome the interest of an Englishman who had been concerned with maritime commerce for a lifetime. But the officials were always in a hurry, and usually in groups of three or four, which made matters difficult. Clerks of course they'd be, not quite right anyway. Once he'd noticed a man with gold braid on his cap and his uniform, but when Mr Unwill smilingly approached him the man expostulated wildly, alarmed presumably by the sound of a language he did not understand. Mr Unwill had thought it a strange reaction in a seafaring man, who should surely be used to the world's tongues.

A cargo boat called the *Allemagna Express*, registered in Venice in spite of its German-sounding name, and flying the Italian flag, was being painted. On planks suspended along the side of its hull men dipped long-handled rollers into giant paint-containers which dangled at a convenient drop below each man. A single painter used a brush, touching in the red outline on the letters of *Allemagna Express*. Cautiously he moved back and forth on his plank, often calling up to his colleagues on the deck to work one of the ropes or pulleys. A yellow stripe extended the length of the hull, separating the white of the ship's upper reaches from the brown beneath. The old girl was certainly beginning to look smart, Mr Unwill considered, and wondered if they'd still be in Venice when the job was completed. There was nothing as rewarding as a well-painted ship, nothing as satisfying even if your own contribution had only been to watch the men at work. Mr Unwill sat for a long time on a stone bench on the quayside, content in this unexacting role. He wondered why *Express* was spelt with an 'x' since the vessel was Italian. That morning from his bedroom window he'd noticed the *Espresso Egitto* chugging by.

At half past eleven he rose and walked to Nico's, where he bought a banana ice-cream and ate it sitting on a *passerella*.

'There was a time, you know, when the Venetians could build a warship in a day.'

For dinner they sat at a round table in a corner of the low-ceilinged dining-room of the pensione. The bearded waiter doled out salad on to side plates, and the one who looked like Fred Astaire went round with platters of chicken and fried potatoes.

'I passed near the Arsenale today,' Verity said, remembering that that was where such warships had been built. '*Grazie*.'

'*Prego, signorina*.'

'You called in at the Naval Museum, did you?'

'No, actually I didn't.'

Apart from the German girls, the people who'd been in the dining-room the night before were there again. The American woman, with a blue-and-white bow tie, sat with her husband and her daughter at the table closest to the Unwills'. The two thin Frenchwomen and the frail man were beside the screen that prevented draughts. The solitary Italian woman in the purple hat was by the door. Other Italians, a couple who had not been in the dining-room last night, were at a table next to the German girls.

'I remember going to the Naval Museum,' Mr Unwill said. 'Oh, years ago. When I was first in Venice with your mother.'

'Did she go too?'

'Your mother always liked to accompany me to places. Most interesting she found the Naval Museum. Well, anyone would.'

He went on talking, telling her about the Naval Museum; she didn't listen. That afternoon she'd gone across to the Lido because it was a part of Venice they hadn't visited that July. But instead of the escape she'd hoped for she'd caught a nostalgic mood from its windswept, shuttered emptiness and its dead casino. She'd sat in a bar drinking brandy she didn't like the taste of, and when she returned to the pensione she found herself not wanting to change out of the clothes she'd worn all day. She'd seen her father glancing in surprise at her tired orange suit and she'd felt, ridiculously, that she was letting him down.

'Ah, here they are!' he exclaimed, making a sudden noise as the German girls entered. '*Buona sera!*' he shouted at them eagerly.

The girls smiled, and Verity wondered what on earth they thought of him. One of the Frenchwomen was complaining that her gnocchi was cold. The waiter who resembled Fred Astaire looked worried. She could not eat cold gnocchi, the woman protested, throwing her fork down, marking the white tablecloth.

'Where have you been today?' Mr Unwill called across the dining-room to the German girls. 'Done something nice?'

'*Ja*,' the fat girl replied. 'We have been in a glass factory.'

'Very sensible,' said Mr Unwill.

Another plate of gnocchi replaced the cold one at the French table. The American woman told her daughter that on her wedding day in Nevada she had thrown a cushion out of a window because she'd felt joyful. 'I guess your momma'd been drinking,' the father said, laughing very noisily. The Italian couple talked about the Feast of St Martin.

There had been only one love-making weekend since she'd moved back to the family house: she'd told her father some lie, not caring if he guessed.

'It's an interesting thing,' he was saying to her now, 'this St Martin business. They have a week of it, you know. Old people and children get gifts. Have you seen the confections in the shop windows? San Martino on horseback?'

'Yes, I've noticed them.' Made of biscuit, she had presumed, sometimes chocolate-coated, sometimes not, icing decorated with sweets.

'And *cotognata*,' he went on. 'Have you seen the *cotognata*? Centuries old, that St Martin's sweetmeat is, far nicer than Turkish delight.'

She smiled, and nodded. She'd noticed the *cotognata* also. She often wondered how he came by his information, and guessed he was for ever dropping into conversation with strangers in the hope that they spoke English.

'The first ghetto was in Venice,' he said. 'Did you know that? It's an Italian word, called after the place where the Jewish settlement was.'

'No, I didn't know that.'

'Well, there you are. Something every day.'

The bearded waiter cleared their plates away and brought them each a bowl of fruit.

'I thought we might wander down the Zattere after dinner,' her father suggested, 'and take a glass of mandarinetto and perhaps a slice of cake. Feel up to that, old girl?'

If she didn't accompany him he'd bother the German girls. She said a glass of mandarinetto would be nice.

'They're painting the *Allemagna Express*. Fine-looking vessel.'

In her bedroom she tied a different scarf around her neck, and put her coat on because the nights were cold. When she returned to the hall her father was not there and when he did appear he came from the dining-room, not from upstairs. 'I told them we were going for a drink,' he said. 'They'll join us in a moment. You all right, old girl?'

He was smoking a cigarette and, like her, he had gone to his room for his overcoat. On the Zattere he put his hat on at a jaunty angle. There was a smell of creosote because they'd been repainting the rafts that afternoon. Sheets of newspaper were suspended from strings that were looped along the quayside to draw attention to the newly treated timbers. A terrier settled down for the night among the rubble on a builder's barge. Cats crept about. It was extraordinary, she suddenly thought, that just because she'd given up her flat she should find herself in Venice with this old man.

'Nice here, eh?' he said in the café, surveying the amber-coloured cloths on the tables, the busyness behind the bar. He took his hat and overcoat off, and sat down. He stubbed his cigarette out and lit a fresh one. 'Mandarinetto,' he said to the waiter who came up. '*Due*.'

'*Sì, signore. Subito*.'

She lit a cigarette herself, caressing her lighter with her fingers, then feeling angry and ashamed that she had done so.

'Ah, here they are!' Her father was on his feet, exclaiming like a schoolboy, waving his hat at the German girls. He shouted after the waiter, ordering two more mandarinettos. 'I really recommend it here,' he informed the German girls, flashing his tobacco-stained smile about and offering them cigarettes. He went on talking, telling them about the *Allemagna Express*. He mentioned the Stazione Marittima and asked them if they had noticed the biscuit horsemen and the *cotognata*. 'By the weekend the Votive Bridge will be complete,' he said. 'A temporary timber bridge, you know, erected as a token of thanksgiving. Every year, for three days, Venetians celebrate the passing of the Plague by making a pilgrimage across it, their children waving balloons about. Then it's taken down again.'

Verity smiled at the fatter German, who was receiving less attention than her friend. And a bridge of boats, her father continued, was temporarily established every summer. 'Again to give thanks. Another tradition since the Plague.'

The Americans who had been in the pensione came in and sat not far away. They ordered ice-creams, taking a long time about it, questioning the waiter in English as to whether they would come with added cream.

'Oh, I remember Venice forty years ago,' Mr Unwill said. 'Of course, it's greatly changed. The Yugoslavs come now, you know, in busloads.' He issued a polite little laugh. 'Not to mention the natives of your own fair land.'

'Too many, I think,' the prettier girl responded, grimacing.

'Ah, *ja*, too many,' agreed her companion.

'No, no, no. You Germans travel well, I always say. Besides, to the Venetian a tourist's a tourist, and tourists mean money. The trouble with the Yugoslavs, they apparently won't be parted from it.'

It wasn't usually his opinion that Germans travelled well; rather the opposite. He told the girls that at one time the Venetians had been capable of building a warship in a day. He explained about ghettoes, and said that in Venice it was the cats who feared the pigeons. He laughed in his genial way. He said:

'That was a very clever remark you made last night, Ingrid. About waiters.'

'It was Brigitta who said it first, I think.'

'Oh, was it? Well, it's quite amusing anyway. Now, what we really want to know is how long you're staying at the pensione?'

'*Ja*, just today,' Ingrid said. 'Tomorrow we have gone.'

'Oh dear me, now that's very sad.'

He would not, when the moment came, pay for the mandarinettos or the cake he was now pressing upon his guests. He would discover that he had left his wallet in some other pocket.

'You must not spoil your looks, eh?' he said when Ingrid refused the cake. His smile nudged her in a way he might have thought was intimate, but which Verity observed the girl registering as elderly. Brigitta had already been biting into a slice of cake when the remark was made about the losing of looks. Hastily she put it down. They must go, she said.

'Go? Oh, surely not? No, please don't go.'

But both girls were adamant. They had been too tired last night to see the Bridge of Sighs by lamplight and they must see that before they left. Each held out a hand, to Verity and then to her father. When they had gone Verity realized she hadn't addressed a single word to either of them. A silence followed their departure, then Mr Unwill said in a whisper:

'Those Americans seem rather nice, eh?'

He would hold forth to the Americans, as he had to the German girls, concentrating his attention on the daughter because she was the most attractive of the three. The mother was vulgarly dressed, the father shouted. In the presence of these people everything would be repeated, the painting of the *Allemagna Express*, the St Martin's confections, the temporary bridges.

'No,' Verity said. 'No, I don't want to become involved with those Americans.'

He was taken aback. His mouth remained open after he'd begun to say something. He stared at her, slowly overcoming his bewilderment. For the second time that evening, he asked her if she felt all right. She didn't reply. Time of the month, he supposed, this obvious explanation abruptly dawning on him, wretched for women. And then, to his very great surprise, he was aware that his daughter was talking about her decision, some months ago, to return to the family home.

'"My father's on his own now," I told him, "so I have given up the flat." As soon as I had spoken I felt afraid. "We must be together," is what I thought he'd say. He'd be alarmed and upset, I thought, because I'd broken the pattern of our love affair by causing this hiatus. But all he said was that he understood.'

They'd known, of course, about the wretched affair. Her mother had been depressed by it; so much time passing by, no sign of a resolution in whatever it was, no sign of marriage. Verity had steered all conversation away from it; when the subject was discreetly approached by her mother or her brothers she made it clear that they were trespassing on private property; he himself had made no forays in that direction, it not being his way. Astonishing it was, that she should wish to speak of it now.

'I didn't in the least,' she said, 'feel sorry for your loneliness. I felt sorry for myself. I couldn't bear for a moment longer the routine love-making in that convenient flat.'

Feeling himself becoming hot, Mr Unwill removed his glasses and searched in the pockets of his blazer for his handkerchief. He didn't know what to say, so he said nothing. He listened while Verity more or less repeated what she had said already. There had been sixteen years of routine love-making, ever since she was twenty-two. Her love affair had become her life, the routine punctuated by generous gifts and weekends in beautiful cities.

There was a silence. He polished one lens and then the other. He tightened the screws of the hinges with the useful little screwdriver in his penknife. Since the silence continued, eventually he said:

'If you made an error in coming back to the house it can easily be rectified, old girl.'

'Surely, I thought, those brief weekends would never be enough? Surely we would have to talk about everything again, now that there was no flat to go to?' She spoke of the cities where the weekends had been spent: Bruges, Berlin, Paris, Amsterdam, Venice. Bruges had been the first. In Bruges she had assumed, although he had not said so, that he would leave his wife. They had walked through chilly squares, they had sat for hours over dinner in the Hotel Duc du Bourgogne. In Paris, some time later, she had made the same assumption. He did not love his wife; when the children grew up he would leave her. By the time they visited Venice, the children had grown up. 'Only just grown up,' she said. 'The last one only just, that summer.'

He did not say anything; the conversation was beyond his reach. He saw his daughter as an infant, a nurse holding a bundle towards him, the screwed-up face and tiny hands. She'd been a happy child, happy at school, happy with her friends. Young men had hung about the house; she'd gone to tennis-club dances and winter parties. 'Love's a disease sometimes,' her mother had said, angrily, a year or so ago. Her mother had been cross because Verity always smiled so, pretending the happiness that was no longer there, determinedly optimistic. Because of the love affair, her mother had said also, Verity's beauty had been wasted, seeming to have been uselessly visited upon her.

'It wasn't just a dirty weekend, you know, here in Venice. It's never just that.'

'Please, Verity. Please, now . . .'

'He can't bring himself to be unkind to his wife. He couldn't be bad to a woman if he tried. I promise you, he's a remarkable man.'

He began to expostulate but changed his mind. Everything he tried to say, even everything he felt, seemed clumsy. She stared beyond him, through the smoke from her cigarette, causing him to feel a stranger. Her silliness in love had made her carelessly harsh, selfish and insensitive because she had to think so much about herself. In a daughter who was not naturally silly, who had been gentle as a child, these qualities were painful to observe. Once she could have imagined what it was like for him to hear her refer so casually to dirty weekends; now she didn't care if that hurt him or not. It was insulting to expect him to accept that the man was remarkable. It dismissed his intellect and his sense.

'It was ridiculous,' she said eventually, 'to give up my flat.'

He made some protest when she asked the waiter for the bill, but she didn't listen, paying the bill instead. He felt exhausted. He had sat in this very café with a woman who was dead; the man his daughter spoke of was still alive. It almost seemed the other way round. He would not have claimed a great deal for the marriage there had been: two people rubbing along, forgiving each other for this and that, one left alone to miss the nourishment of affection. Yet when the coffin had slipped away behind the beige curtain his grief had been unbearable and had remained so afterwards, for weeks and months, each day a hell.

'I'm sorry for being a nuisance,' she said before they rose from the table, and he wanted to explain to her that melancholy would have become too much if he allowed a city and its holiday memories to defeat him, that memories were insidious. But he didn't say anything because he knew she would not listen to him properly. She could not help thinking badly of him; the harshness that had been bred in her prevented the allowances that old age demanded. Nor could he, because of anger, make allowances for her.

'Hi!' one of the Americans whom he'd thought it might be quite nice to know called out. They had finished their ice-creams and were preparing to leave also. All of them smiled but it was Verity, not he, who returned their greeting.

'It's I who should be sorry,' he said on the Zattere. He'd been more gently treated than she: you knew where you were with death, in no way was it a confidence trick. He began to say that but changed his mind, knowing she would not wish to hear.

'Heavens, how cold it has become!' She hurried through the gathering fog, and so did he. The conversation was over, its loose ends hanging; each knew they would never be picked up. '*Buona notte*,' the smart receptionist, all in green now, murmured in the hall of the pensione, and they bade her good-night in their different ways.

They lifted their keys from the rack beside the stairs and stepped over the sleeping cat on the bottom step. On the first-floor landing they said good-night, were briefly awkward because of what had passed between them, then entered their separate rooms. Slowly he prepared himself for bed, slowly undressing, slowly washing, folding his clothes with an old man's care. She sat by her window, staring at the lights across the water, until the fog thickened and there was nothing left to see.

Lovers of Their Time

Looking back on it, it seemed to have to do with that particular decade in London. Could it have happened, he wondered, at any other time except the 1960s? That feeling was intensified, perhaps, because the whole thing had begun on New Year's Day, 1963, long before that day became a bank holiday in England. 'That'll be two and nine,' she'd said, smiling at him across her counter, handing him toothpaste and emery boards in a bag. 'Colgate's, remember,' his wife had called out as he was leaving the flat. 'The last stuff we had tasted awful.'

His name was Norman Britt. It said so on a small plastic name-plate in front of his position in the travel agency where he worked, Travel-Wide as it was called. *Marie* a badge on her light-blue shop-coat announced. His wife, who worked at home, assembling jewellery for a firm that paid her on a production basis, was called Hilda.

Green's the Chemist's and Travel-Wide were in Vincent Street, a street that was equidistant from Paddington Station and Edgware Road. The flat where Hilda worked all day was in Putney. Marie lived in Reading with her mother and her mother's friend Mrs Druk, both of them widows. She caught the 8.05 every morning to Paddington and usually the 6.30 back.

He was forty in 1963, as Hilda was; Marie was twenty-eight. He was tall and thin, with a David Niven moustache. Hilda was thin also, her dark hair beginning to grey, her sharply featured face pale. Marie was well-covered, carefully made up, her hair dyed blonde. She smiled a lot, a slack, half-crooked smile that made her eyes screw up and twinkle; she exuded laziness and generosity. She and her friend Mavis went dancing a lot in Reading and had a sizeable collection of men friends. 'Fellas' they called them.

Buying things from her now and again in Green's the Chemist's Norman had come to the conclusion that she was of a tartish disposition, and imagined that if ever he sat with her over a drink in the nearby Drummer Boy the occasion could easily lead to a hug on the street afterwards. He imagined her coral-coloured lips, like two tiny sausages, only softer, pressed upon his moustache and his abbreviated mouth. He imagined the warmth of her hand in his. For all that, she was a little outside reality: she was there to desire, to glow erotically in the heady atmosphere of the Drummer Boy, to light cigarettes for in a fantasy.

'Isn't it cold?' he said as she handed him the emery boards and the toothpaste.

'Shocking,' she agreed, and hesitated, clearly wanting to say something else. 'You're in that Travel-Wide,' she added in the end. 'Me and my friend want to go to Spain this year.'

'It's very popular. The Costa Brava?'

'That's right.' She handed him threepence change. 'In May.'

'Not too hot on the Costa in May. If you need any help –'

'Just the bookings.'

'I'd be happy to make them for you. Look in any time. Britt the name is. I'm on the counter.'

'If I may, Mr Britt. I could slip out maybe at four, or roundabout.'

'Today, you mean?'

'We want to fix it up.'

'Naturally. I'll keep an eye out for you.'

It was hard not to call her madam or miss, the way he'd normally do. He had heard himself saying that he'd be happy to make the bookings for her, knowing that that was business jargon, knowing that the unfussy voice he'd used was a business one also. Her friend was a man, he supposed, some snazzy tough in a car. 'See you later then,' he said, but already she was serving another customer, advising about lipstick refills.

She didn't appear in Travel-Wide at four o'clock; she hadn't come when the doors closed at five-thirty. He was aware of a sense of disappointment, combined with one of anticipation: for if she'd come at four, he reflected as he left the travel agency, their bit of business would be in the past rather than the future. She'd look in some other time and he'd just have to trust to luck that if he happened to be busy with another customer she'd be able to wait. There'd be a further occasion, when she called to collect the tickets themselves.

'Ever so sorry,' she said on the street, her voice coming from behind him. 'Couldn't get away, Mr Britt.'

He turned and smiled at her, feeling the movement of his moustache as he parted his lips. He knew only too well, he said. 'Some other time then?'

'Maybe tomorrow. Maybe lunchtime.'

'I'm off myself from twelve to one. Look, you wouldn't fancy a drink? I could advise you just as easily over a drink.'

'Oh, you wouldn't have the time. No, I mustn't take advantage –'

'You're not at all. If you've got ten minutes?'

'Well, it's awfully good of you, Mr Britt. But I really feel I'm taking advantage, I really do.'

'A New Year's drink.'

He pushed open the doors of the saloon bar of the Drummer Boy, a place he didn't often enter except for office drinks at Christmas or when someone leaving the agency was being given a send-off. Ron Stocks and Mr Blackstaffe were usually there in the evenings: he hoped they'd be there now to see him in the company of the girl from Green's the Chemist's. 'What would you like?' he asked her.

'Gin and peppermint's my poison, only honestly I should pay. No, let me ask you –'

'I wouldn't dream of it. We can sit over there, look.'

The Drummer Boy, so early in the evening, wasn't full. By six o'clock the advertising executives from the firm of Dalton, Dure and Higgins, just round the corner, would have arrived, and the architects from Frine and Knight. Now there was only Mrs Gregan, old and alcoholic, known to everyone, and a man called Bert, with his poodle, Jimmy. It was disappointing that Ron Stocks and Mr Blackstaffe weren't there.

'You were here lunchtime Christmas Eve,' she said.

'Yes, I was.' He paused, placing her gin and peppermint on a cardboard mat that advertised Guinness. 'I saw you too.'

He drank some of his Double Diamond and carefully wiped the traces of foam from his moustache. He realized now that it would, of course, be quite impossible to give her a hug on the street outside. That had been just imagination, wishful thinking as his mother would have said. And yet he knew that when he arrived home twenty-five or so minutes late he would not tell Hilda that he'd been advising an assistant from Green's the Chemist's about a holiday on the Costa Brava. He wouldn't even say he'd been in the Drummer Boy. He'd say Blackstaffe had kept everyone late, going through the new package that Eurotours were offering in Germany and Luxembourg this summer. Hilda wouldn't in a million years suspect that he'd been sitting in a public house with a younger woman who was quite an eyeful. As a kind of joke, she quite regularly suggested that his sexual drive left something to be desired.

'We were thinking about the last two weeks in May,' Marie said. 'It's when Mavis can get off too.'

'Mavis?'

'My friend, Mr Britt.'

Hilda was watching *Z-Cars* in the sitting-room, drinking V.P. wine. His stuff was in the oven, she told him. 'Thanks,' he said.

Sometimes she was out when he returned in the evenings. She went round to friends, a Mr and Mrs Fowler, with whom she drank V.P. and played bridge. On other occasions she went to the Club, which was a place with a licence, for card-players and billiard-players. She quite liked her social life, but always said beforehand when she'd be out and always made arrangements about leaving food in the oven. Often in the daytime she'd go and make jewellery with Violet Parkes, who also went in for this occupation; and often Violet Parkes spent the day with Hilda. The jewellery-making consisted for the most part of threading plastic beads on to a string or arranging plastic pieces in the settings provided. Hilda was quick at it and earned more than she would have if she went out every day, saving the fares for a start. She was better at it than Violet Parkes.

'All right then?' she said when he carried his tray of food into the sitting-room and sat down in front of the television set. 'Want some V.P., eh?'

Her eyes continued to watch the figures on the screen as she spoke. He knew she'd prefer to be in the Fowlers' house or at the Club, although now that they'd acquired a TV set the evenings passed easier when they were alone together.

'No, thanks,' he said in reply to her offer of wine and he began to eat something that appeared to be a rissole. There were two of them, round and brown in a tin-foil container that also contained gravy. He hoped she wasn't going to be demanding in their bedroom. He eyed her, for sometimes he could tell.

'Hi,' she said, noticing the glance. 'Feeling fruity, dear?' She laughed and winked, her suggestive voice seeming odd as it issued from her thin, rather dried-up face. She was always saying things like that, for no reason that Norman could see, always talking about feeling fruity or saying she could see he was keen when he wasn't in the least. Norman considered that she was unduly demanding and often wondered what it would be like to be married to someone who was not. Now and again, fatigued after the intensity of her love-making, he lay staring at the darkness, wondering if her bedroom appetites were related in some way to the fact that she was unable to bear children, if her abandon reflected a maternal frustration. Earlier in their married life she'd gone out every day to an office where she'd been a filing clerk; in the evenings they'd often gone to the cinema.

He lay that night, after she'd gone to sleep, listening to her heavy breathing, thinking of the girl in Green's the Chemist's. He went through the whole day in his mind, seeing himself leaving the flat in Putney, hearing Hilda calling out about the emery boards and the toothpaste, seeing himself reading the *Daily Telegraph* in the Tube. Slowly he went through the morning, deliciously anticipating the moment when she handed him his change. With her smile mistily hovering, he recalled the questions and demands of a number of the morning's customers. 'Fix us up Newcastle and back?' a couple inquired. 'Mid-week's cheaper, is it?' A man with a squashed-up face wanted a week in Holland for himself and his sister and his sister's husband. A woman asked about Greece, another about cruises on the Nile, a third about the Scilly Isles. Then he placed the Closed sign in front of his position at the counter and went out to have lunch in Bette's Sandwiches off the Edgware Road. 'Packet of emery boards,' he said again in Green's the Chemist's, 'and a small Colgate's.' After that there was the conversation they'd had, and then the afternoon with her smile still mistily hovering, as in fact it had, and then her presence beside him in the Drummer Boy. Endlessly she lifted the glass of gin and peppermint to her lips, endlessly she smiled. When he slept he dreamed of her. They were walking in Hyde Park and her shoe fell off. 'I could tell you were a deep one,' she said, and the next thing was Hilda was having one of her early-morning appetites.

'I don't know what it is about that chap,' Marie confided to Mavis. 'Something, though.'

'Married, is he?'

'Oh, he would be, chap like that.'

'Now, you be careful, girl.'

'He has Sinatra's eyes. That blue, you know.'

'Now, Marie –'

'I like an older fella. He's got a nice moustache.'

'So's that fella in the International.'

'Wet behind the ears. And my God, his dandruff!'

They left the train together and parted on the platform, Marie making for the Underground, Mavis hurrying for a bus. It was quite convenient, really, living in Reading and travelling to Paddington every day. It was only half an hour and chatting on the journey passed the time. They didn't travel back together in the evenings because Mavis nearly always did an hour's overtime. She was a computer programmer.

'I talked to Mavis. It's OK about the insurance,' Marie said in Travel-Wide at half past eleven that morning, having slipped out when the shop seemed slack. There'd been some details about insurance which he'd raised the evening before. He always advised insurance, but he'd quite understood when she'd made the point that she'd better discuss the matter with her friend before committing herself to the extra expenditure.

'So I'll go ahead and book you,' he said. 'There'll just be the deposit.'

Mavis wrote the cheque. She pushed the pink slip across the counter to him. 'Payable to Travel-Wide.'

'That's quite correct.' He glanced at it and wrote her a receipt. He said: 'I looked out another brochure or two. I'd quite like to go through them with you. So you can explain what's what to your friend.'

'Oh, that's very nice, Mr Britt. But I got to get back. I mean, I shouldn't be out in the middle of the morning.'

'Any chance of lunchtime?'

His suavity astounded him. He thought of Hilda, deftly working at her jewellery, stringing orange and yellow beads, listening to the Jimmy Young programme.

'Lunchtime, Mr Britt?'

'We'd maybe talk about the brochures.'

He fancied her, she said to herself. He was making a pass, talking about brochures and lunchtime. Well, she wasn't disagreeable. She'd meant what she'd said to Mavis: she liked an older fella and she liked his moustache, so smooth it looked as if he put something on it. She liked the name Norman.

'All right then,' she said.

He couldn't suggest Bette's Sandwiches because you stood up at a shelf on the wall and ate the sandwiches off a cardboard plate.

'We could go to the Drummer Boy,' he suggested instead. 'I'm off at twelve-fifteen.'

'Say half past, Mr Britt.'

'I'll be there with the brochures.'

Again he thought of Hilda. He thought of her wiry, pasty limbs and the way she had of snorting. Sometimes when they were watching the television she'd suddenly want to sit on his knee. She'd get worse as she grew older; she'd get scrawnier; her hair, already coarse, would get dry and grey. He enjoyed the evenings when she went out to the Club or to her friends the Fowlers. And yet he wasn't being fair because in very many ways she did her best. It was just that you didn't always feel like having someone on your knee after a day's work.

'Same?' he said in the Drummer Boy.

'Yes please, Mr Britt.' She'd meant to say that the drinks were definitely on her, after what he'd spent last night. But in her flurry she forgot. She picked up the brochures he'd left on the seat beside her. She pretended to read one, but all the time she was watching him as he stood by the bar. He smiled as he turned and came back with their drinks. He said something about it being a nice way to do business. He was drinking gin and peppermint himself.

'I meant to pay for the drinks. I meant to say I would. I'm sorry, Mr Britt.'

'Norman my name is.' He surprised himself again by the ease with which he was managing the situation. They'd have their drinks and then he'd suggest some of the shepherd's pie, or a ham-and-salad roll if she'd prefer it. He'd buy her another gin and peppermint to get her going. Eighteen years ago he used to buy Hilda further glasses of V.P. wine with the same thought in mind.

They finished with the brochures. She told him she lived in Reading; she talked about the town. She mentioned her mother and her mother's friend Mrs Druk, who lived with them, and Mavis. She told him a lot about Mavis. No man was mentioned, no boyfriend or fiancé.

'Honestly,' she said, 'I'm not hungry.' She couldn't have touched a thing. She just wanted to go on drinking gin with him. She wanted to get slightly squiffy, a thing she'd never done before in the middle of the day. She wanted to put her arm through his.

'It's been nice meeting you,' he said.

'A bit of luck.'

'I think so too, Marie.' He ran his forefinger between the bones on the back of her hand, so gently that it made her want to shiver. She didn't take her hand away, and when she continued not to he took her hand in his.

After that they had lunch together every day, always in the Drummer Boy. People saw them, Ron Stocks and Mr Blackstaffe from Travel-Wide, Mr Fineman, the pharmacist from Green's the Chemist's. Other people from the travel agency and from the chemist's saw them walking about the streets, usually hand in hand. They would look together into the shop windows of Edgware Road, drawn particularly to an antique shop full of brass. In the evenings he would walk with her to Paddington Station and have a drink in one of the bars. They'd embrace on the platform, as other people did.

Mavis continued to disapprove; Marie's mother and Mrs Druk remained ignorant of the affair. The holiday on the Costa Brava that May was not a success because all the time Marie kept wishing Norman Britt was with her. Occasionally, while Mavis read magazines on the beach, Marie wept and Mavis pretended not to notice. She was furious because Marie's low spirits meant that it was impossible for them to get to know fellas. For months they'd been looking forward to the holiday and now, just because of a clerk in a travel agency, it was a flop. 'I'm sorry, dear,' Marie kept saying, trying to smile; but when they returned to London the friendship declined. 'You're making a fool of yourself,' Mavis pronounced harshly, 'and it's dead boring having to hear about it.' After that they ceased to travel together in the mornings.

The affair remained unconsummated. In the hour and a quarter allotted to each of them for lunch there was nowhere they might have gone to let their passion for one another run its course. Everywhere was public: Travel-Wide and the chemist's shop, the Drummer Boy, the streets they walked. Neither could easily spend a night away from home. Her mother and Mrs Druk would guess that something untoward was in the air; Hilda, deprived of her bedroom mating, would no longer be nonchalant in front of the TV. It would all come out if they were rash, and they sensed some danger in that.

'Oh, darling,' she whispered one October evening at Paddington, huddling herself against him. It was foggy and cold. The fog was in her pale hair, tiny droplets that only he, being close to her, could see. People hurried through the lit-up station, weary faces anxious to be home.

'I know,' he said, feeling as inadequate as he always did at the station.

'I lie awake and think of you,' she whispered.

'You've made me live,' he whispered back.

'And you me. Oh, God, and you me.' She was gone before she finished speaking, swinging into the train as it moved away, her bulky red handbag the last thing he saw. It would be eighteen hours before they'd meet again.

He turned his back on her train and slowly made his way through the crowds, his reluctance to start the journey back to the flat in Putney seeming physical, like a pain, inside him. 'Oh, for God's sake!' a woman cried angrily at him, for he had been in her way and had moved in the same direction as she had in seeking to avoid her, causing a second collision. She dropped magazines on to the platform and he helped her to pick them up, vainly apologizing.

It was then, walking away from this woman, that he saw the sign. *Hotel Entrance* it said in red neon letters, beyond the station's main bookstall. It was the back of the Great Western Royal, a short-cut to its comforts for train travellers at the end of their journey. If only, he thought, they could share a room there. If only for one single night they were granted the privilege of being man and wife. People passed through the swing-doors beneath the glowing red sign, people hurrying, with newspapers or suitcases. Without quite knowing why, he passed through the swing-doors himself.

He walked up two brief flights of steps, through another set of doors, and paused in the enormous hall of the Great Western Royal Hotel. Ahead of him, to the left, was the long, curved reception counter and, to the right, the porter's desk. Small tables and armchairs were everywhere; it was carpeted underfoot. There were signs to lifts and to the bar and the restaurant. The stairway, gently rising to his left, was gracious, carpeted also.

They would sit for a moment in this hall, he imagined, as other people were sitting now, a few with drinks, others with pots of tea and plates half empty of assorted biscuits. He stood for a moment, watching these people, and then, as though he possessed a room in the hotel, he mounted the stairs, saying to himself that it must somehow be possible, that surely they could share a single night in the splendour of this place. There was a landing, made into a lounge, with armchairs and tables, as in the hall below. People conversed quietly; a foreign waiter, elderly and limping, collected silver-plated teapots; a Pekinese dog slept on a woman's lap.

The floor above was different. It was a long, wide corridor with bedroom doors on either side of it. Other corridors, exactly similar, led off it. Chambermaids passed him with lowered eyes; someone gently laughed in a room marked *Staff Only*; a waiter wheeled a trolley containing covered dishes, and a bottle of wine wrapped in a napkin. *Bathroom* a sign said, and he looked in, just to see what a bathroom in the Great Western Royal Hotel would be like. 'My God!' he whispered, possessed immediately with the idea that was, for him, to make the decade of the 1960s different. Looking back on it, he was for ever after unable to recall the first moment he beheld the bathroom on the second floor without experiencing the shiver of pleasure he'd experienced at the time. Slowly he entered. He locked the door and slowly sat down on the edge of the bath. The place was huge, as the bath itself was, like somewhere in a palace. The walls were marble, white veined delicately with grey. Two monstrous brass taps, the biggest bath taps he'd ever in his life seen, seemed to know already that he and Marie would come to the bathroom. They seemed almost to wink an invitation to him, to tell him that the bathroom was a comfortable place and not often in use since private bathrooms were now attached to most of the bedrooms. Sitting in his mackintosh coat on the edge of the bath, he wondered what Hilda would say if she could see him now.

He suggested it to Marie in the Drummer Boy. He led up to it slowly, describing the interior of the Great Western Royal Hotel and how he had wandered about it because he hadn't wanted to go home. 'Actually,' he said, 'I ended up in a bathroom.'

'You mean the toilet, dear? Taken short –'

'No, not the toilet. A bathroom on the second floor. Done out in marble, as a matter of fact.'

She replied that honestly he was a one, to go into a bathroom like that when he wasn't even staying in the place! He said:

'What I mean, Marie, it's somewhere we could go.'

'Go, dear?'

'It's empty half the time. Nearly all the time it must be. I mean, we could be there now. This minute if we wanted to.'

'But we're having our lunch, Norman.'

'That's what I mean. We could even be having it there.'

From the saloon bar's juke-box a lugubrious voice pleaded for a hand to be held. *Take my hand,* sang Elvis Presley, *take my whole life too*. The advertising executives from Dalton, Dure and Higgins were loudly talking about their hopes of gaining the Canadian Pacific account. Less noisily the architects from Frine and Knight complained about local planning regulations.

'In a bathroom, Norman? But we couldn't just go into a bathroom.'

'Why not?'

'Well, we couldn't. I mean, we *couldn't*.'

'What I'm saying is we could.'

'I want to marry you, Norman. I want us to be together. I don't want just going to a bathroom in some hotel.'

'I know; I want to marry you too. But we've got to work it out. You know we've got to work it out, Marie – getting married.'

'Yes, I know.'

It was a familiar topic of conversation between them. They took it for granted that one day, somehow, they would be married. They had talked about Hilda. He'd described Hilda to her, he'd drawn a picture in Marie's mind of Hilda bent over her jewellery-making in a Putney flat, or going out to drink V.P. with the Fowlers or at the Club. He hadn't presented a flattering picture of his wife, and when Marie had quite timidly said that she didn't much care for the sound of her he had agreed that naturally she wouldn't. The only aspect of Hilda he didn't touch upon was her bedroom appetite, night starvation as he privately dubbed it. He didn't mention it because he guessed it might be upsetting.

What they had to work out where Hilda was concerned were the economics of the matter. He would never, at Travel-Wide or anywhere else, earn a great deal of money. Familiar with Hilda's nature, he knew that as soon as a divorce was mooted she'd set out to claim as much alimony as she possibly could, which by law he would have to pay. She would state that she only made jewellery for pin-money and increasingly found it difficult to do so due to a developing tendency towards chilblains or arthritis, anything she could think of. She would hate him for rejecting her, for depriving her of a tame companion. Her own resentment at not being able to have children would somehow latch on to his unfaithfulness: she would see a pattern which wasn't really there, bitterness would come into her eyes.

Marie had said that she wanted to give him the children he had never had. She wanted to have children at once and she knew she could. He knew it too: having children was part of her, you'd only to look at her. Yet that would mean she'd have to give up her job, which she wanted to do when she married anyway, which in turn would mean that all three of them would have to subsist on his meagre salary. And not just all three, the children also.

It was a riddle that mocked him: he could find no answer, and yet he believed that the more he and Marie were together, the more they talked to one another and continued to be in love, the more chance there was of suddenly hitting upon a solution. Not that Marie always listened when he went on about it. She agreed they had to solve their problem, but now and again just pretended it wasn't there. She liked to forget about the existence of Hilda. For an hour or so when she was with him she liked to assume that quite soon, in July or even June, they'd be married. He always brought her back to earth.

'Look, let's just have a drink in the hotel,' he urged. 'Tonight, before the train. Instead of having one in the buffet.'

'But it's a hotel, Norman. I mean, it's for people to stay in –'

'Anyone can go into a hotel for a drink.'

That evening, after their drink in the hotel bar, he led her to the first-floor landing that was also a lounge. It was warm in the hotel. She said she'd like to sink down into one of the armchairs and fall asleep. He laughed at that; he didn't suggest an excursion to the bathroom, sensing that he shouldn't rush things. He saw her on to her train, abandoning her to her mother and Mrs Druk and Mavis. He knew that all during the journey she would be mulling over the splendours of the Great Western Royal.

December came. It was no longer foggy, but the weather was colder, with an icy wind. Every evening, before her train, they had their drink in the hotel. 'I'd love to show you that bathroom,' he said once. 'Just for fun.' He hadn't been pressing it in the least; it was the first time he'd mentioned the bathroom since he'd mentioned it originally. She giggled and said he was terrible. She said she'd miss her train if she went looking at bathrooms, but he said there'd easily be time. 'Gosh!' she whispered, standing in the doorway, looking in. He put his arm around her shoulders and drew her inside, fearful in case a chambermaid should see them loitering there. He locked the door and kissed her. In almost twelve months it was their first embrace in private.

They went to the bathroom during the lunch hour on New Year's Day, and he felt it was right that they should celebrate in this way the anniversary of their first real meeting. His early impression of her, that she was of a tartish disposition, had long since been dispelled. Voluptuous she might seem to the eye, but beneath that misleading surface she was prim and proper. It was odd that Hilda, who looked dried-up and wholly uninterested in the sensual life, should also belie her appearance. 'I've never done it before,' Marie confessed in the bathroom, and he loved her the more for that. He loved her simplicity in this matter, her desire to remain a virgin until her wedding. But since she repeatedly swore that she could marry no one else, their anticipating of their wedding-night did not matter. 'Oh, God, I love you,' she whispered, naked for the first time in the bathroom. 'Oh, Norman, you're so good to me.'

After that it became a regular thing. He would saunter from the hotel bar, across the huge entrance lounge, and take a lift to the second floor. Five minutes later she would follow, with a towel brought specially from Reading in her handbag. In the bathroom they always whispered, and would sit together in a warm bath after their love-making, still murmuring about the future, holding hands beneath the surface of the water. No one ever rapped on the door to ask what was going on in there. No one ever questioned them as they returned, separately, to the bar, with the towel they'd shared damping her compact and her handkerchief.

Years instead of months began to go by. On the juke-box in the Drummer Boy the voice of Elvis Presley was no longer heard. '*Why she had to go I don't know*,' sang the Beatles, '*she didn't say ... I believe in yesterday*.' And Eleanor Rigby entered people's lives, and Sergeant Pepper with her. The fantasies of secret agents, more fantastic than ever before, filled the screens of London's cinemas. Carnaby Street, like a jolly trash-can, overflowed with noise and colour. And in the bathroom of the Great Western Royal Hotel the love affair of Norman Britt and Marie was touched with the same preposterousness. They ate sandwiches in the bathroom; they drank wine. He whispered to her of the faraway places he knew about but had never been to: the Bahamas, Brazil, Peru, Seville at Easter, the Greek islands, the Nile, Shiraz, Persepolis, the Rocky Mountains. They should have been saving their money, not spending it on gin and peppermintin the bar of the hotel and in the Drummer Boy. They should have been racking their brains to find a solution to the problem of Hilda, but it was nicer to pretend that one day they would walk together in Venice or Tuscany. It was all so different from the activities that began with Hilda's bedroom appetites, and it was different from the coarseness that invariably surfaced when Mr Blackstaffe got going in the Drummer Boy on an evening when a Travel-Wide employee was being given a send-off. Mr Blackstaffe's great joke on such occasions was that he liked to have sexual intercourse with his wife at night and that she preferred the conjunction in the mornings. He was always going on about how difficult it was in the mornings, what with the children liable to interrupt you, and he usually went into details about certain other, more intimate preferences of his wife's. He had a powerful, waxy guffaw, which he brought regularly into play when he was engaged in this kind of conversation, allying it with a nudging motion of the elbow. Once his wife actually turned up in the Drummer Boy and Norman found it embarrassing even to look at her, knowing as he did so much about her private life. She was a stout middle-aged woman with decorated spectacles: her appearance, too, apparently belied much.

In the bathroom all such considerations, disliked equally by Norman Britt and Marie, were left behind. Romance ruled their brief sojourns, and love sanctified – or so they believed – the passion of their physical intimacy. Love excused their eccentricity, for only love could have found in them a willingness to engage in the deception of a hotel and the courage that went with it: that they believed most of all.

But afterwards, selling tickets to other people or putting Marie on her evening train, Norman sometimes felt depressed. And then gradually, as more time passed, the depression increased and intensified. 'I'm so sad,' he whispered in the bathroom once, 'when I'm not with you. I don't think I can stand it.' She dried herself on the towel brought specially from Reading in her large red handbag. 'You'll have to tell her,' she said, with an edge in her voice that hadn't ever been there before. 'I don't want to leave having babies too late.' She wasn't twenty-eight any more; she was thirty-one. 'I mean, it isn't fair on me,' she said.

He knew it wasn't fair on her, but going over the whole thing yet again in Travel-Wide that afternoon he also knew that poverty would destroy them. He'd never earn much more than he earned now. The babies Marie wanted, and which he wanted too, would soak up what there was like blotting-paper; they'd probably have to look for council accommodation. It made him weary to think about it, it gave him a headache. But he knew she was right: they couldn't go on for ever, living off a passing idyll, in the bathroom of a hotel. He even thought, quite seriously for a moment, of causing Hilda's death.

Instead he told her the truth, one Thursday evening after she'd been watching *The Avengers* on television. He just told her he'd met someone, a girl called Marie, he said, whom he had fallen in love with and wished to marry. 'I was hoping we could have a divorce,' he said.

Hilda turned the sound on the television set down without in any way dimming the picture, which she continued to watch. Her face did not register the hatred he had imagined in it when he rejected her; nor did bitterness suddenly enter her eyes. Instead she shook her head at him, and poured herself some more V.P. She said:

'You've gone barmy, Norman.'

'You can think that if you like.'

'Wherever'd you meet a girl, for God's sake?'

'At work. She's there in Vincent Street. In a shop.'

'And what's she think of you, may I ask?'

'She's in love with me, Hilda.'

She laughed. She told him to pull the other one, adding that it had bells on it.

'Hilda, I'm not making this up. I'm telling you the truth.'

She smiled into her V.P. She watched the screen for a moment, then she said:

'And how long's this charming stuff been going on, may I inquire?'

He didn't want to say for years. Vaguely, he said it had been going on for just a while.

'You're out of your tiny, Norman. Just because you fancy some piece in a shop doesn't mean you go getting hot under the collar. You're no tomcat, you know, old boy.'

'I didn't say I was.'

'You're no sexual mechanic.'

'Hilda –'

'All chaps fancy things in shops: didn't your mother tell you that? D'you think I haven't fancied stuff myself, the chap who came to do the blinds, that randy little postman with his rugby songs?'

'I'm telling you I want a divorce, Hilda.'

She laughed. She drank more V.P. wine. 'You're up a gum tree,' she said, and laughed again.

'Hilda –'

'Oh, for God's sake!' All of a sudden she was angry, but more, he felt, because he was going on, not because of what he was actually demanding. She thought him ridiculous and said so. And then she added all the things he'd thought himself: that people like them didn't get divorces, that unless his girlfriend was well-heeled the whole thing would be a sheer bloody nonsense, with bloody solicitors the only ones to benefit. 'They'll send you to the cleaners, your bloody solicitors will,' she loudly pointed out, anger still trembling in her voice. 'You'd be paying them back for years.'

'I don't care,' he began, although he did. 'I don't care about anything except –'

'Of course you do, you damn fool.'

'Hilda –'

'Look, get over her. Take her into a park after dark or something. It'll make no odds to you and me.'

She turned the sound on the television up and quite quickly finished the V.P. wine. Afterwards, in their bedroom, she turned to him with an excitement that was greater than usual. 'God, that switched me on,' she whispered in the darkness, gripping him with her limbs. 'The stuff we were talking about, that girl.' When she'd finished her love-making she said, 'I had it with that postman, you know. Swear to God. In the kitchen. And since we're on the subject, Fowler looks in here the odd time.'

He lay beside her in silence, not knowing whether or not to believe what she was saying. It seemed at first that she was keeping her end up because he'd mentioned Marie, but then he wasn't so sure. 'We had a foursome once,' she said, 'the Fowlers and me and a chap that used to be in the Club.'

She began to stroke his face with her fingers, the way he hated. She always seemed to think that if she stroked his face it would excite him. She said, 'Tell me more about this piece you fancy.'

He told her to keep her quiet and to make her stop stroking his face. It didn't seem to matter now if he told her how long it had been going on, not since she'd made her revelations about Fowler and the postman. He even enjoyed telling her, about the New Year's Day when he'd bought the emery boards and the Colgate's, and how he'd got to know Marie because she and Mavis were booking a holiday on the Costa Brava.

'But you've never actually?'

'Yes, we have.'

'For God's sake where? Doorways or something? In the park?'

'We go to a hotel.'

'You old devil!'

'Listen, Hilda –'

'For God's sake go on, love. Tell me about it.'

He told her about the bathroom and she kept asking him questions, making him tell her details, asking him to describe Marie to her. Dawn was breaking when they finished talking.

'Forget about the divorce stuff,' she said quite casually at breakfast. 'I wouldn't want to hear no more of that. I wouldn't want you ruined for my sake, dear.'

He didn't want to see Marie that day, although he had to because it was arranged. In any case she knew he'd been going to tell his wife the night before; she'd want to hear the outcome.

'Well?' she said in the Drummer Boy.

He shrugged. He shook his head. He said:

'I told her.'

'And what'd she say, Norman? What'd Hilda say?'

'She said I was barmy to be talking about divorce. She said what I said to you: that we wouldn't manage with the alimony.'

They sat in silence. Eventually Marie said:

'Then can't you leave her? Can't you just not go back? We could get a flat somewhere. We could put off kiddies, darling. Just walk out, couldn't you?'

'They'd find us. They'd make me pay.'

'We could try it. If I keep on working you could pay what they want.'

'It'll never pan out, Marie.'

'Oh, darling, just walk away from her.'

Which is what, to Hilda's astonishment, he did. One evening when she was at the Club he packed his clothes and went to two rooms in Kilburn that he and Marie had found. He didn't tell Hilda where he was going. He just left a note to say he wouldn't be back.

They lived as man and wife in Kilburn, sharing a lavatory and a bathroom with fifteen other people. In time he received a court summons, and in court was informed that he had behaved meanly and despicably to the woman he'd married. He agreed to pay regular maintenance.

The two rooms in Kilburn were dirty and uncomfortable, and life in them was rather different from the life they had known together in the Drummer Boy and the Great Western Royal Hotel. They planned to find somewhere better, but at a reasonable price that wasn't easy to find. A certain melancholy descended on them, for although they were together they seemed as far away as ever from their own small house, their children and their ordinary contentment.

'We could go to Reading,' Marie suggested.

'Reading?'

'To my mum's.'

'But your mum's nearly disowned you. Your mum's livid, you said yourself she was.'

'People come round.'

She was right. One Sunday afternoon they made the journey to Reading to have tea with Marie's mother and her friend Mrs Druk. Neither of these women addressed Norman, and once when he and Marie were in the kitchen he heard Mrs Druk saying it disgusted her, that he was old enough to be Marie's father. 'Don't think much of him,' Marie's mother replied. 'Pipsqueak really.'

Nevertheless, Marie's mother had missed her daughter's contribution to the household finances and before they returned to London that evening it was arranged that Norman and Marie should move in within a month, on the firm understanding that the very second it was feasible their marriage would take place. 'He's a boarder, mind,' Marie's mother warned. 'Nothing but a boarder in this house.' There were neighbours, Mrs Druk added, to be thought of.

Reading was worse than the two rooms in Kilburn. Marie's mother continued to make disparaging remarks about Norman, about the way he left the lavatory, or the thump of his feet on the stair-carpet, or his fingermarks around the light-switches. Marie would deny these accusations and then there'd be a row, with Mrs Druk joining in because she loved a row, and Marie's mother weeping and then Marie weeping. Norman had been to see a solicitor about divorcing Hilda, quoting her unfaithfulness with a postman and with Fowler. 'You have your evidence, Mr Britt?' the solicitor inquired, and pursed his lips when Norman said he hadn't.

He knew it was all going to be too difficult. He knew his instinct had been right: he shouldn't have told Hilda, he shouldn't have just walked out. The whole thing had always been unfair on Marie; it had to be when a girl got mixed up with a married man. 'Should think of things like that,' her mother had a way of saying loudly when he was passing an open door. 'Selfish type he is,' Mrs Druk would loudly add.

Marie argued when he said none of it was going to work. But she wasn't as broken-hearted as she might have been a year or so ago, for the strain had told on Marie too, especially the strain in Reading. She naturally wept when Norman said they'd been defeated, and so for a moment did he. He asked for a transfer to another branch of Travel-Wide and was sent to Ealing, far away from the Great Western Royal Hotel.

Eighteen months later Marie married a man in a brewery. Hilda, hearing on some grapevine that Norman was on his own, wrote to him and suggested that bygones should be allowed to be bygones. Lonely in a bed-sitting-room in Ealing, he agreed to talk the situation over with her and after that he agreed to return to their flat. 'No hard feelings,' Hilda said, 'and no deception: there's been a chap from the Club in here, the Woolworth's manager.' No hard feelings, he agreed.

For Norman Britt, as the decade of the 1960s passed, it trailed behind it the marvels of his love affair with Marie. Hilda's scorn when he had confessed had not devalued them, nor had the two dirty rooms in Kilburn, nor the equally unpleasant experience in Reading. Their walk to the Great Western Royal, the drinks they could not afford in the hotel bar, their studied nonchalance as they made their way separately upstairs, seemed to Norman to be a fantasy that had miraculously become real. The second-floor bathroom belonged in it perfectly, the bathroom full of whispers and caressing, where the faraway places of his daily work acquired a hint of magic when he spoke of them to a girl as voluptuous as any of James Bond's. Sometimes on the Tube he would close his eyes and with the greatest pleasure that remained to him he would recall the delicately veined marble and the great brass taps, and the bath that was big enough for two. And now and again he heard what appeared to be the strum of distant music, and the voices of the Beatles celebrating a bathroom love, as they had celebrated Eleanor Rigby and other people of that time.

Going Home

'Mulligatawny soup,' Carruthers said in the dining-car. 'Roast beef, roast potatoes, Yorkshire pudding, mixed vegetables.'

'And madam?' murmured the waiter.

Miss Fanshawe said she'd have the same. The waiter thanked her. Carruthers said:

'Miss Fanshawe'll take a medium dry sherry. Pale ale for me, please.'

The waiter paused. He glanced at Miss Fanshawe, shaping his lips.

'I'm sixteen and a half,' Carruthers said. 'Oh, and a bottle of Beaune. 1962.'

It was the highlight of every term and every holiday for Carruthers, coming like a no man's land between the two: the journey with Miss Fanshawe to their different homes. Not once had she officially complained, either to his mother or to the school. She wouldn't do that; it wasn't in Miss Fanshawe to complain officially. And as for him, he couldn't help himself.

'Always Beaune on a train,' he said now, 'because of all the burgundies it travels happiest.'

'Thank you, sir,' the waiter said.

'Thank *you*, old chap.'

The waiter went, moving swiftly in the empty dining-car. The train slowed and then gathered speed again. The fields it passed through were bright with sunshine; the water of a stream glittered in the distance.

'You shouldn't lie about your age,' Miss Fanshawe reproved, smiling to show she hadn't been upset by the lie. But lies like that, she explained, could get a waiter into trouble.

Carruthers, a sharp-faced boy of thirteen, laughed a familiar harsh laugh. He said he didn't like the waiter, a remark that Miss Fanshawe ignored.

'What weather!' she remarked instead. 'Just look at those weeping willows!' She hadn't ever noticed them before, she added, but Carruthers contradicted that, reminding her that she had often before remarked on those weeping willows. She smiled, with false vagueness in her face, slightly shaking her head. 'Perhaps it's just that everything looks so different this lovely summer. What will you do, Carruthers? Your mother took you to Greece last year, didn't she? It's almost a shame to leave England, I always think, when the weather's like this. So green in the long warm days –'

'Miss Fanshawe, why are you pretending nothing has happened?'

'Happened? My dear, what has happened?'

Carruthers laughed again, and looked through the window at cows resting in the shade of an oak tree. He said, still watching the cows, craning his neck to keep them in view:

'Your mind is thinking about what has happened and all the time you're attempting to make ridiculous conversation about the long warm days. Your heart is beating fast, Miss Fanshawe; your hands are trembling. There are two little dabs of red high up on your cheeks, just beneath your spectacles. There's a pink flush all over your neck. If you were alone, Miss Fanshawe, you'd be crying your heart out.'

Miss Fanshawe, who was thirty-eight, fair-haired and untouched by beauty, said that she hadn't the foggiest idea what Carruthers was talking about. He shook his head, implying that she lied. He said:

'Why are we being served by a man whom neither of us likes when we should be served by someone else? Just look at those weeping willows, you say.'

'Don't be silly, Carruthers.'

'What has become, Miss Fanshawe, of the other waiter?'

'Now please don't start any nonsense. I'm tired and –'

'It was he who gave me a taste for pale ale, d'you remember that? In your company, Miss Fanshawe, on this train. It was he who told us that Beaune travels best. Have a cig, Miss Fanshawe?'

'No, and I wish you wouldn't either.'

'Actually Mrs Carruthers allows me the odd smoke these days. Ever since my thirteenth birthday, May the 26th. How can she stop me, she says, when day and night she's at it like a factory chimney herself?'

'Your birthday's May the 26th? I never knew. Mine's two days later.' She spoke hastily, and with an eagerness that was as false as the vague expression her face had borne a moment ago.

'Gemini, Miss Fanshawe.'

'Yes: Gemini. Queen Victoria –'

'The sign of passion. Here comes the interloper.'

The waiter placed sherry before Miss Fanshawe and beer in front of Carruthers. He murmured deferentially, inclining his head.

'We've just been saying,' Carruthers remarked, 'that you're a new one on this line.'

'Newish, sir. A month – no, tell a lie, three weeks yesterday.'

'We knew your predecessor.'

'Oh yes, sir?'

'He used to say this line was as dead as a doornail. Actually, he enjoyed not having anything to do. Remember, Miss Fanshawe?'

Miss Fanshawe shook her head. She sipped her sherry, hoping the waiter would have the sense to go away. Carruthers said:

'In all the time Miss Fanshawe and I have been travelling together there hasn't been a solitary soul besides ourselves in this dining-car.'

The waiter said it hardly surprised him. You didn't get many, he agreed, and added, smoothing the tablecloth, that it would just be a minute before the soup was ready.

'Your predecessor,' Carruthers said, 'was a most extraordinary man.'

'Oh yes, sir?'

'He had the gift of tongues. He was covered in freckles.'

'I see, sir.'

'Miss Fanshawe here had a passion for him.'

The waiter laughed. He lingered for a moment and then, since Carruthers was silent, went away.

'Now look here, Carruthers,' Miss Fanshawe began.

'Don't you think Mrs Carruthers is the most vulgar woman you've ever met?'

'I wasn't thinking of your mother. I will not have you talk like this to the waiter. Please now.'

'She wears a scent called "In Love", by Norman Hartnell. A woman of fifty, as thin as fuse wire. My God!'

'Your mother –'

'My mother doesn't concern you – oh, I agree. Still you don't want to deliver me to the female smelling of drink and tobacco smoke. I always brush my teeth in the lavatory, you know. For your sake, Miss Fanshawe.'

'Please don't engage the waiter in conversation. And please don't tell lies about the waiter who was here before. It's ridiculous the way you go on –'

'You're tired, Miss Fanshawe.'

'I'm always tired at the end of term.'

'That waiter used to say –'

'Oh, for heaven's sake, stop about that waiter!'

'I'm sorry.' He seemed to mean it, but she knew he didn't. And even when he spoke again, when his voice was softer, she knew that he was still pretending. 'What shall we talk about?' he asked, and with a weary cheerfulness she reminded him that she'd wondered what he was going to do in the holidays. He didn't reply. His head was bent. She knew that he was smiling.

'I'll walk beside her,' he said. 'In Rimini and Venice. In Zürich maybe.

By Lake Lugano. Or the Black Sea. New faces will greet her in an American Bar in Copenhagen. Or near the Spanish Steps – in Babbington's English Tea-Rooms. Or in Bandol or Cassis, the Ritz, the Hotel Excelsior in old Madrid. What shall we talk about, Miss Fanshawe?'

'You could tell me more. Last year in Greece –'

'I remember once we talked about guinea-pigs. I told you how I killed a guinea-pig that Mrs Carruthers gave me. Another time we talked about Rider Minor. D'you remember that?'

'Yes, but let's not –'

'McGullam was unpleasant to Rider Minor in the changing-room. McGullam and Travers went after Rider Minor with a little piece of wood.'

'You told me, Carruthers.'

He laughed.

'When I first arrived at Ashleigh Court the only person who spoke to me was Rider Minor. And of course the Sergeant-Major. The Sergeant-Major told me never to take to cigs. He described the lungs of a friend of his.'

'He was quite right.'

'Yes, he was. Cigs can give you a nasty disease.'

'I wish you wouldn't smoke.'

'I like your hat.'

'Soup, madam,' the waiter murmured. 'Sir.'

'Don't you like Miss Fanshawe's hat?' Carruthers smiled, pointing at Miss Fanshawe, and when the waiter said that the hat was very nice Carruthers asked him his name.

Miss Fanshawe dipped a spoon into her soup. The waiter offered her a roll. His name, he said, was Atkins.

'Are you wondering about us, Mr Atkins?'

'Sir?'

'Everyone has a natural curiosity, you know.'

'I see a lot of people in my work, sir.'

'Miss Fanshawe's an undermatron at Ashleigh Court Preparatory School for Boys. They use her disgracefully at the end of term – patching up clothes so that the mothers won't complain, packing trunks, sorting out laundry. From dawn till midnight Miss Fanshawe's on the trot. That's why she's tired.'

Miss Fanshawe laughed. 'Take no notice of him,' she said. She broke her roll and buttered a piece of it. She pointed at wheat ripening in a field. The harvest would be good this year, she said.

'At the end of each term,' Carruthers went on, 'she has to sit with me on this train because we travel in the same direction. I'm out of her authority really, since the term is over. Still, she has to keep an eye.'

The waiter, busy with the wine, said he understood. He raised his eyebrows at Miss Fanshawe and winked, but she did not encourage this, pretending not to notice it.

'Imagine, Mr Atkins,' Carruthers said, 'a country house in the mock Tudor style, with bits built on to it: a rackety old gymn and an art-room, and changing-rooms that smell of perspiration. There are a hundred and three boys at Ashleigh Court, in narrow iron beds with blue rugs on them, which Miss Fanshawe has to see are all kept tidy. She does other things as well: she wears a white overall and gives out medicines. She pours out cocoa in the dining-hall and at eleven o'clock every morning she hands each boy four *petit beurre* biscuits. She isn't allowed to say Grace. It has to be a master who says Grace: "For what we're about to receive . . ." Or the Reverend T. L. Edwards, who owns and runs the place, T.L.E., known to generations as a pervert. He pays boys, actually.'

The waiter, having meticulously removed a covering of red foil from the top of the wine bottle, wiped the cork with a napkin before attempting to draw it. He glanced quickly at Miss Fanshawe to see if he could catch her eye in order to put her at her ease with an understanding gesture, but she appeared to be wholly engaged with her soup.

'The Reverend Edwards is a law unto himself,' Carruthers said. 'Your predecessor was intrigued by him.'

'Please take no notice of him.' She tried to sound bracing, looking up suddenly and smiling at the waiter.

'The headmaster accompanied you on the train, did he, sir?'

'No, no, no, no. The Reverend Edwards was never on this train in his life. No, it was simply that your predecessor was interested in life at Ashleigh Court. He would stand there happily listening while we told him the details: you could say he was fascinated.'

At this Miss Fanshawe made a noise that was somewhere between a laugh and a denial.

'You could pour the Beaune now, Mr Atkins,' Carruthers suggested.

The waiter did so, pausing for a moment, in doubt as to which of the two he should offer a little of the wine to taste. Carruthers nodded to him, indicating that it should be he. The waiter complied and when Carruthers had given his approval he filled both their glasses and lifted from before them their empty soup-plates.

'I've asked you not to behave like that,' she said when the waiter had gone.

'Like what, Miss Fanshawe?'

'You know, Carruthers.'

'The waiter and I were having a general conversation. As before, Miss Fanshawe, with the other waiter. Don't you remember? Don't you remember my telling him how I took forty of Hornsby's football cards? And drank the Communion wine in the Reverend's cupboard?'

'I don't believe –'

'And I'll tell you another thing. I excused myself into Rider Minor's gum-boots.'

'Please leave the waiter alone. Please let's have no scenes this time, Carruthers.'

'There weren't scenes with the other waiter. He enjoyed everything we said to him. You could see him quite clearly trying to visualize Ashleigh Court, and Mrs Carruthers in her awful clothes.'

'He visualized nothing of the sort. You gave him drink that I had to pay for. He was obliged to listen to your fantasies.'

'He enjoyed our conversation, Miss Fanshawe. Why is it that people like you and I are so unpopular?'

She didn't answer, but sighed instead. He would go on and on, she knew; and there was nothing she could do. She always meant not to protest, but when it came to the point she found it hard to sit silent, mile after mile.

'You know what I mean, Miss Fanshawe? At Ashleigh Court they say you have an awkward way of walking. And I've got no charm: I think that's why they don't much like me. But how for God's sake could any child of Mrs Carruthers have charm?'

'Please don't speak of your mother like that –'

'And yet men fancy her. Awful men arrive at weekends, as keen for sex as the Reverend Edwards is. "Your mother's a most elegant woman," a hard-eyed lecher remarked to me last summer, in the Palm Court of a Greek hotel.'

'Don't drink too much of that wine. The last time –'

'"You're staggering," she said the last time. I told her I had flu. She's beautiful, I dare say, in her thin way. D'you think she's beautiful?'

'Yes, she is.'

'She has men all over the place. Love flows like honey while you make do with waiters on a train.'

'Oh, don't be so *silly*, Carruthers.'

'She snaps her fingers and people come to comfort her with lust. A woman like that's never alone. While you –'

'Will you please stop talking about me!'

'You have a heart in your breast like anyone else, Miss Fanshawe.'

The waiter, arriving again, coughed. He leaned across the table and placed a warmed plate in front of Miss Fanshawe and a similar one in front of Carruthers. There was a silence while he offered Miss Fanshawe a silver-plated platter with slices of roast beef on it and square pieces of Yorkshire pudding. In the silence she selected what she wanted, a small portion, for her appetite on journeys with Carruthers was never great. Carruthers took the rest. The waiter offered vegetables.

'Miss Fanshawe ironed that blouse at a quarter to five this morning,' Carruthers said. 'She'd have ironed it last night if she hadn't been so tired.'

'A taste more carrots, sir?'

'I don't like carrots, Mr Atkins.'

'Peas, sir?'

'Thank you. She got up from her small bed, Mr Atkins, and her feet were chilly on the linoleum. She shivered, Mr Atkins, as she slipped her night-dress off. She stood there naked, thinking of another person. What became of your predecessor?'

'I don't know, sir. I never knew the man at all. All right for you, madam?'

'Yes, thank you.'

'He used to go back to the kitchen, Mr Atkins, and tell the cook that the couple from Ashleigh Court were on the train again. He'd lean against the sink while the cook poked about among his pieces of meat, trying to find us something to eat. Your predecessor would suck at the butt of a cig and occasionally he'd lift a can of beer to his lips. When the cook asked him what the matter was he'd say it was fascinating, a place like Ashleigh Court with boys running about in grey uniforms and an undermatron watching her life go by.'

'Excuse me, sir.'

The waiter went. Carruthers said:

'"She makes her own clothes," the other waiter told the cook. "She couldn't give a dinner party the way the young lad's mother could. She couldn't chat to this person and that, moving about among *décolletée* women and outshining every one of them." Why is she an undermatron at Ashleigh Court Preparatory School for Boys, owned and run by the Reverend T.L. Edwards, known to generations as a pervert?'

Miss Fanshawe, with an effort, laughed. 'Because she's qualified for nothing else,' she lightly said.

'I think that freckled waiter was sacked because he interfered with the passengers. "Vegetables?" he suggested, and before he could help himself he put the dish of cauliflowers on the table and put his arms around a woman. "All tickets please," cried the ticket-collector and then he saw the waiter and the woman on the floor. You can't run a railway company like that.'

'Carruthers –'

'Was it something like that, Miss Fanshawe? D'you think?'

'Of course it wasn't.'

'Why not?'

'Because you've just made it up. The man was a perfectly ordinary waiter on this train.'

'That's not true.'

'Of course it is.'

'I love this train, Miss Fanshawe.'

'It's a perfectly ordinary –'

'Of course it isn't.'

Carruthers laughed gaily, waiting for the waiter to come back, eating in silence until it was time again for their plates to be cleared away.

'Trifle, madam?' the waiter said. 'Cheese and biscuits?'

'Just coffee, please.'

'Sit down, why don't you, Mr Atkins? Join us for a while.'

'Ah no, sir, no.'

'Miss Fanshawe and I don't have to keep up appearances on your train. D'you understand that? We've been keeping up appearances for three long months at Ashleigh Court and it's time we stopped. Shall I tell you about my mother, Mr Atkins?'

'Your mother, sir?'

'Carruthers –'

'In 1960, when I was three, my father left her for another woman: she found it hard to bear. She had a lover at the time, a Mr Dalacourt, but even so she found it hard to forgive my father for taking himself off.'

'I see, sir.'

'It was my father's intention that I should accompany him to his new life with the other woman, but when it came to the point the other woman decided against that. Why should she be burdened with my mother's child? she wanted to know: you can see her argument, Mr Atkins.'

'I must be getting on now, sir.'

'So my father arranged to pay my mother an annual sum, in return for which she agreed to give me house room. I go with her when she goes on holiday to a smart resort. My father's a thing of the past. What d'you think of all that, Mr Atkins? Can you visualize Mrs Carruthers at a resort? She's not at all like Miss Fanshawe.'

'I'm sure she's not –'

'Not at all.'

'Please let go my sleeve, sir.'

'We want you to sit down.'

'It's not my place, sir, to sit down with the passengers in the dining-car.'

'We want to ask you if you think it's fair that Mrs Carruthers should round up all the men she wants while Miss Fanshawe has only the furtive memory of a waiter on a train, a man who came to a sticky end, God knows.'

'Stop it!' cried Miss Fanshawe. 'Stop it! Stop it! Let go his jacket and let him go away –'

'I have things to do, sir.'

'He smelt of fried eggs, a smell that still comes back to her at night.'

'You're damaging my jacket. I must ask you to release me at once.'

'Are you married, Mr Atkins?'

'Carruthers!' Her face was crimson and her neck blotched with a flushing that Carruthers had seen before. 'Carruthers, for heaven's sake behave yourself!'

'The Reverend Edwards isn't married, as you might guess, Mr Atkins.'

The waiter tried to pull his sleeve out of Carruthers' grasp, panting a little from embarrassment and from the effort. 'Let go my jacket!' he shouted. 'Will you let me go!'

Carruthers laughed, but did not release his grasp. There was a sound of ripping as the jacket tore.

'Miss Fanshawe'll stitch it for you,' Carruthers said at once, and added more sharply when the waiter raised a hand to strike him: 'Don't do that, please. Don't threaten a passenger, Mr Atkins.'

'You've ruined this jacket. You bloody little –'

'Don't use language in front of the lady.' He spoke quietly, and to a stranger entering the dining-car at that moment it might have seemed that the waiter was in the wrong, that the torn sleeve of his jacket was the just result of some attempted insolence on his part.

'You're mad,' the waiter shouted at Carruthers, his face red and sweating in his anger. 'That child's a raving lunatic,' he shouted as noisily at Miss Fanshawe.

Carruthers was humming a hymn. 'Lord, dismiss us,' he softly sang, 'with Thy blessing.'

'Put any expenses on my bill,' whispered Miss Fanshawe. 'I'm very sorry.'

'Ashleigh Court'll pay,' Carruthers said, not smiling now, his face all of a sudden as sombre as the faces of the other two.

No one spoke again in the dining-car. The waiter brought coffee, and later presented a bill.

The train stopped at a small station. Three people got out as Miss Fanshawe and Carruthers moved down the corridor to their compartment. They walked in silence, Miss Fanshawe in front of Carruthers, he drawing his right hand along the glass of the windows. There'd been an elderly man in their compartment when they'd left it: to Miss Fanshawe's relief he was no longer there. Carruthers slid the door across. She found her book and opened it at once.

'I'm sorry,' he said when she'd read a page.

She turned the page, not looking up, not speaking.

'I'm sorry I tormented you,' he said after another pause.

She still did not look up, but spoke while moving her eyes along a line of print. 'You're always sorry,' she said.

Her face and neck were still hot. Her fingers tightly held the paper-backed volume. She felt taut and rigid, as though the unpleasantness in the dining-car had coiled some part of her up. On other journeys she'd experienced a similar feeling, though never as unnervingly as she experienced it now. He had never before torn a waiter's clothing.

'Miss Fanshawe?'

'I want to read.'

'I'm not going back to Ashleigh Court.'

She went on reading and then, when he'd repeated the statement, she slowly raised her head. She looked at him and thought, as she always did when she looked at him, that he was in need of care. There was a barrenness in his sharp face; his eyes reflected the tang of a bitter truth.

'I took the Reverend Edwards' cigarette-lighter. He's told me he won't have me back.'

'That isn't true, Carruthers –'

'At half past eleven yesterday morning I walked into the Reverend's study and lifted it from his desk. Unfortunately he met me on the way out. Ashleigh Court, he said, was no place for a thief.'

'But why? Why did you do such a silly thing?'

'I don't know. I don't know why I do a lot of things. I don't know why I pretend you were in love with a waiter. This is the last horrid journey for you, Miss Fanshawe.'

'So you won't be coming back –'

'The first time I met you I was crying in a dormitory. D'you remember that? Do you, Miss Fanshawe?'

'Yes, I remember.'

'"Are you missing your mummy?" you asked me, and I said no. I was crying because I'd thought I'd like Ashleigh Court. I'd thought it would be heaven, a place without Mrs Carruthers. I didn't say that; not then.'

'No.'

'You brought me to your room and gave me liquorice allsorts. You made me blow my nose. You told me not to cry because the other boys would laugh at me. And yet I went on crying.'

In the fields men were making hay. Children in one field waved at the passing train. The last horrid journey, she thought; she would never see the sharp face again, nor the bitterness reflected in the eyes. He'd wept, as others occasionally had to; she'd been, for a moment, a mother to him. His own mother didn't like him, he'd later said – on a journey – because his features reminded her of his father's features.

'I don't know why I'm so unpleasant, Miss Fanshawe. The Reverend stared at me last night and said he had a feeling in his bones that I'd end up badly. He said I was a useless sort of person, a boy he couldn't ever rely on. I'd let him down, he said, thieving and lying like a common criminal. "I'm chalking you up as a failure for Ashleigh," he said. "I never had much faith in you, Carruthers." '

'He's a most revolting man.' She said it without meaning to, and yet the words came easily from her. She said it because it didn't matter any more, because he wasn't going to return to Ashleigh Court to repeat her words.

'You were kind to me that first day,' Carruthers said. 'I liked that holy picture in your room. You told me to look at it, I remember. Your white overall made a noise when you walked.'

She wanted to say that once she had told lies too, that at St Monica's School for Girls she'd said the King, the late George VI, had spoken to her when she stood in the crowd. She wanted to say that she'd stolen two rubbers from Elsie Grantham and poured ink all over the face of a clock, and had never been found out.

She closed her eyes, longing to speak, longing above all things in the world to fill the compartment with the words that had begun, since he'd told her, to pound in her brain. All he'd ever done on the train was to speak a kind of truth about his mother and the school, to speak in their no man's land, as now and then he'd called it. Tormenting her was incidental; she knew it was. Tormenting her was just by chance, a thing that happened.

His face was like a flint. No love had ever smoothed his face, and while she looked at it she felt, unbearably now, the urge to speak as he had spoken, so many times. He smiled at her. 'Yes,' he said. 'The Reverend's a most revolting man.'

'I'm thirty-eight,' she said and saw him nod as though, precisely, he'd guessed her age a long time ago. 'Tonight we'll sit together in the bungalow by the sea where my parents live and they'll ask me about the term at Ashleigh. "Begin at the beginning, Dora," my mother'll say and my father'll set his deaf-aid. "The first day? What happened the first day, Dora?" And

I shall tell them. "Speak up," they'll say, and in a louder voice I'll tell them about the new boys, and the new members of staff. Tomorrow night I'll tell some more, and on and on until the holidays and the term are over. "Wherever are you going?" my mother'll say when I want to go out for a walk. "Funny time," she'll say, "to go for a walk." No matter what time it is.'

He turned his head away, gazing through the window as earlier she had gazed through the window of the dining-car, in awkwardness.

'I didn't fall in love with a freckled waiter,' he heard her say, 'but God knows the freckled waiter would have done.'

He looked at her again. 'I didn't mean, Miss Fanshawe –'

'If he had suddenly murmured while offering me the vegetables I'd have closed my eyes with joy. To be desired, to be desired in any way at all . . .'

'Miss Fanshawe –'

'Born beneath Gemini, the sign of passion, you said. Yet who wants to know about passion in the heart of an ugly undermatron? Different for your mother, Carruthers: your mother might weep and tear away her hair, and others would weep in pity because of all her beauty. D'you see, Carruthers? D'you understand me?'

'No, Miss Fanshawe. No, I don't think I do. I'm not as –'

'There was a time one Christmas, after a party in the staff-room, when a man who taught algebra took me up to a loft, the place where the Wolf Cubs meet. We lay down on an old tent, and then suddenly this man was sick. That was in 1954. I didn't tell them that in the bungalow: I've never told them the truth. I'll not say tonight, eating cooked ham and salad, that the boy I travelled with created a scene in the dining-car, or that I was obliged to pay for damage to a waiter's clothes.'

'Shall we read now, Miss Fanshawe?'

'How can we read, for God's sake, when we have other things to say? What was it like, d'you think, on all the journeys to see you so unhappy? Yes, you'll probably go to the bad. He's right: you have the look of a boy who'll end like that. The unhappy often do.'

'Unhappy, Miss Fanshawe? Do I seem unhappy?'

'Oh, for God's sake, tell the truth! The truth's been there between us on all our journeys. We've looked at one another and seen it, over and over again.'

'Miss Fanshawe, I don't understand you. I promise you, I don't understand –'

'How could I ever say in that bungalow that the algebra teacher laid me down on a tent and then was sick? Yet I can say it now to you, a thing I've never told another soul.'

The door slid open and a woman wearing a blue hat, a smiling, red-faced woman, asked if the vacant seats were taken. In a voice that amazed Carruthers further Miss Fanshawe told her to go away.

'Well, really!' said the woman.

'Leave us in peace, for God's sake!' shrieked Miss Fanshawe, and the woman, her smile all gone, backed into the corridor. Miss Fanshawe rose and shut the door again.

'It's different in that bungalow by the sea,' she then quite quietly remarked, as though no red-faced woman had backed away astonished. 'Not like an American Bar in Copenhagen or the Hotel Excelsior in Madrid. Along the walls the coloured geese stretch out their necks, the brass is polished and in its place. Inch by inch oppression fills the air. On the chintz covers in the sitting-room there's a pattern of small wild roses, the stair-carpet's full of fading lupins. *To W.J. Fanshawe on the occasion of his retirement*, says the plaque on the clock on the sitting-room mantelpiece, *from his friends in the Prudential*. The clock has a gold-coloured face and four black pillars of ersatz material: it hasn't chimed since 1958. At night, not far away, the sea tumbles about, seeming too real to be true. The seagulls shriek when I walk on the beach, and when I look at them I think they're crying out with happiness.'

He began to speak, only to speak her name, for there was nothing else he could think of to say. He changed his mind and said nothing at all.

'Who would take me from it now? Who, Carruthers? What freckled waiter or teacher of algebra? What assistant in a shop, what bank-clerk, postman, salesman of cosmetics? They see a figure walking in the wind, discs of thick glass on her eyes, breasts as flat as paper. Her movement's awkward, they say, and when she's close enough they raise their hats and turn away: they mean no harm.'

'I see,' he said.

'In the bungalow I'm frightened of both of them: all my life I've been afraid of them. When I was small and wasn't pretty they made the best of things, and longed that I should be clever instead. "Read to us, Dora," my father would say, rubbing his hands together when he came in from his office. And I would try to read. "Spell *merchant*," my father would urge as though his life depended upon it, and the letters would become jumbled in my mind. Can you see it, Carruthers, a child with glasses and an awkward way of walking and two angry figures, like vultures, unforgiving? They'd exchange a glance, turning their eyes away from me as though in shame. "Not bright," they'd think. "Not bright, to make up for the other."'

'How horrid, Miss Fanshawe.'

'No, no. After all, was it nice for them that their single child should be a gawky creature who blushed when people spoke? How could they help themselves, any more than your mother can?'

'Still, my mother –'

' "Going to the pictures?" he said the last time I was home. "What on earth are you doing that for?" And then she got the newspaper which gave the programme that was showing. "*Tarzan and the Apemen*", she read out. "My dear, at your age!" I wanted to sit in the dark for an hour or two, not having to talk about the term at Ashleigh Court. But how could I say that to them? I felt the redness coming in my face. "For children surely," my father said, "a film like that." And then he laughed. "Dora's made a mistake," my mother explained, and she laughed too.'

'And did you go, Miss Fanshawe?'

'Go?'

'To *Tarzan and the Apemen?*'

'No, I didn't go. I don't possess courage like that: as soon as I enter the door of the bungalow I can feel their disappointment and I'm terrified all over again. I've thought of not going back but I haven't even the courage for that: they've sucked everything out of me. D'you understand?'

'Well –'

'Why is God so cruel that we leave the ugly school and travel together to a greater ugliness when we could travel to something nice?'

'Nice, Miss Fanshawe? *Nice?*'

'You know what I mean, Carruthers.'

He shook his head. Again he turned it away from her, looking at the window, wretchedly now.

'Of course you do,' her voice said, 'if you think about it.'

'I really –'

'Funny our birthdays being close together!' Her mood was gayer suddenly. He turned to look at her and saw she was smiling. He smiled also.

'I've dreamed this train went on for ever,' she said, 'on and on until at last you stopped engaging passengers and waiters in fantastic conversation. "I'm better now," you said, and then you went to sleep. And when you woke I gave you liquorice allsorts. "I understand," I said: "it doesn't matter." '

'I know I've been very bad to you, Miss Fanshawe. I'm sorry –'

'I've dreamed of us together in my parents' bungalow, of my parents dead and buried and your thin mother gone too, and Ashleigh Court a thing of the nightmare past. I've seen us walking over the beaches together, you growing up, me cooking for you and mending your clothes and knitting you pullovers. I've brought you fresh brown eggs and made you apple dumplings. I've watched you smile over crispy chops.'

'Miss Fanshawe –'

'I'm telling you about a dream in which ordinary things are marvellous. Tea tastes nicer and the green of the grass is a fresher green than you've ever noticed before, and the air is rosy, and happiness runs about. I would take you to a cinema on a Saturday afternoon and we would buy chips on the way home and no one would mind. We'd sit by the fire and say whatever we liked to one another. And you would no longer steal things or tell lies, because you'd have no need to. Nor would you mock an unpretty undermatron.'

'Miss Fanshawe, I – I'm feeling tired. I think I'd like to read.'

'Why should they have a child and then destroy it? Why should your mother not love you because your face is like your father's face?'

'My mother –'

'Your mother's a disgrace,' she cried in sudden, new emotion. 'What life is it for a child to drag around hotels and lovers, a piece of extra luggage, alone, unloved?'

'It's not too bad. I get quite used to it –'

'Why can He not strike them dead?' she whispered. 'Why can't He make it possible? By some small miracle, surely to God?'

He wasn't looking at her. He heard her weeping and listened to the sound, not knowing what to do.

'You're a sorrowful mess, Carruthers,' she whispered. 'Yet you need not be.'

'Please. Please, Miss Fanshawe –'

'You'd be a different kind of person and so would I. You'd have my love, I'd care about the damage that's been done to you. You wouldn't come to a bad end: I'd see to that.'

He didn't want to turn his head again. He didn't want to see her, but in spite of that he found himself looking at her. She, too, was gazing at him, tears streaming on her cheeks. He spoke slowly and with as much firmness as he could gather together.

'What you're saying doesn't make any sense, Miss Fanshawe.'

'The waiter said that you were mad. Am I crazy too? Can people go mad like that, for a little while, on a train? Out of loneliness and locked-up love? Or desperation?'

'I'm sure it has nothing to do with madness, Miss Fanshawe –'

'The sand blows on to my face, and sometimes into my eyes. In my bedroom I shake it from my sandals. I murmur in the sitting-room. "Really,

Dora," my mother says, and my father sucks his breath in. On Sunday mornings we walk to church, all three of us. I go again, on my own, to Evensong: I find that nice. And yet I'm glad when it's time to go back to Ashleigh Court. Are you ever glad, Carruthers?'

'Sometimes I have been. But not always. Not always at all. I –'

' "Let's go for a stroll," the algebra teacher said. His clothes were stained with beer. "Let's go up there," he said. "It's nice up there." And in the pitch dark we climbed to the loft where the Wolf Cubs meet. He lit his cigarette-lighter and spread the tent out. I don't mind what happens, I thought. Anything is better than nothing happening all my life. And then the man was sick.'

'You told me that, Miss Fanshawe.'

' "You're getting fat," my mother might have said. "Look at Dora, Dad, getting fat." And I would try to laugh. "A drunk has made me pregnant," I might have whispered in the bungalow, suddenly finding the courage for it. And they would look at me and see that I was happy, and I would kneel by my bed and pour my thanks out to God, every night of my life, while waiting for my child.' She paused and gave a little laugh. 'They are waiting for us, those people, Carruthers.'

'Yes.'

'The clock on the mantelpiece still will not chime. "Cocoa," my mother'll say at half past nine. And when they die it'll be too late.'

He could feel the train slowing, and sighed within him, a gesture of thanksgiving. In a moment he would walk away from her: he would never see her again. It didn't matter what had taken place, because he wouldn't ever see her again. It didn't matter, all she had said, or all he had earlier said himself.

He felt sick in his stomach after the beer and the wine and the images she'd created of a life with her in a seaside bungalow. The food she'd raved about would be appalling; she'd never let him smoke. And yet, in the compartment now, while they were still alone, he was unable to prevent himself from feeling sorry for her. She was right when she spoke of her craziness: she wasn't quite sane beneath the surface, she was all twisted up and unwell.

'I'd better go and brush my teeth,' he said. He rose and lifted his overnight case from the rack.

'Don't go,' she whispered.

His hand, within the suitcase, had already grasped a blue sponge-bag. He released it and closed the case. He stood, not wishing to sit down again. She didn't speak. She wasn't looking at him now.

'Will you be all right, Miss Fanshawe?' he said at last, and repeated the question when she didn't reply. 'Miss Fanshawe?'

'I'm sorry you're not coming back to Ashleigh, Carruthers. I hope you have a pleasant holiday abroad.'

'Miss Fanshawe, will you –'

'I'll stay in England, as I always do.'

'We'll be there in a moment,' he said.

'I hope you won't go to the bad, Carruthers.'

They passed by houses now; the backs of houses, suburban gardens. Posters advertised beer and cigarettes and furniture. *Geo. Small. Seeds*, one said.

'I hope not, too,' he said.

'Your mother's on the platform. Where she always stands.'

'Goodbye, Miss Fanshawe.'

'Goodbye, Carruthers. Goodbye.'

Porters stood waiting. Mail-bags were on a trolley. A voice called out, speaking of the train they were on.

She didn't look at him. She wouldn't lift her head: he knew the tears were pouring on her cheeks now, more than before, and he wanted to say, again, that he was sorry. He shivered standing in the doorway, looking at her, and then he closed the door and went away.

She saw his mother greet him, smiling, in red as always she was. They went together to collect his luggage from the van, out of her sight, and when the train pulled away from the station she saw them once again, the mother speaking and Carruthers just as he always was, laughing his harsh laugh.

The Printmaker

In the large room Charlotte hangs her prints to dry, like clothes on clothes lines. Three crows, framed by the legs and belly of a cow, have rested for an instant beneath its udder: all over the room this stark image is multiplied, in black and white and tones of green.

The reality was years ago, in France: Charlotte senses that confidently, without being able to recall the moment of observation. Familiar to her is the feeling that a glance from the window, or from a motor-car, has been retained for half a lifetime. 'This is still the Langevins' land,' Monsieur Langevin said in English, the first time he drove her in his white Citroën the fifteen kilometres from Massuery to St Cérase. Obediently she inspected the fields to her right, treeless and uninteresting, cattle grazing. Perhaps there were three crows also.

In the room the suspended sheets are scrutinized, and one in every seven or eight rejected. Fragile, tapering fingers loosen the tiny, variously coloured pegs that hold the prints in place; each inferior reproduction floats softly to the bare-wood floor. Intent upon her task, Charlotte moves silently in the room, seeming almost a ghost among the ubiquitous repetition of what she has created. At thirty-nine she is as slender as ever, her bones as apparent as her flesh. Bright azure eyes illuminate a face that is still a girl's. Shattered only twice in Charlotte's appearance is the illusion that time has been defeated; grey strands creep through hair that once was as pale as corn, and on the backs of her hands are the reminders that sun and weather do not pass gently by.

One by one, she picks up the rejected prints where they have dropped. She tears each in half and bundles it into the wooden box that is the room's repository for wastepaper. Then she examines one of the suspended sheets, holding it obliquely against the light to see if it has wholly dried. Satisfied that this is so, she releases the pegs and trims the paper in her guillotine. She signs it and writes in pencil *1/50*, then places it in a pale green portfolio. She repeats all this with each remaining print, then loosely ties the folder's tattered ribbons.

'To look at, there is *l'église* St Cérase,' Monsieur Langevin said, that first Wednesday afternoon. He stopped the car in the Place de la Paix and pointed out the way. There was nothing much else in the town, he warned.

A park beside the Maison de la Presse, tea-rooms and cafés, the Hostellerie de la Poste. But the church was quite impressive. 'Well, anyway, the façade,' Monsieur Langevin added.

Charlotte walked to it, admired the façade and went inside. There was a smell of candle grease and perhaps of incense: it was difficult precisely to identify the latter. Charlotte was seventeen then, her presence in the Langevin household arranged by her father, who set great store by what he referred to as 'perfect French'. Some acquaintance of his had a connection with a cousin of Madame Langevin; an arrangement had been made. 'I've been good about your drawing,' her father had earlier claimed, in the parental manner of that time. 'I'm only asking in return that you acquire the usefulness of perfect French.' Her father did not believe in her talent for drawing; a businessman himself, he anticipated for his only child a niche in some international commercial firm, where the French she had perfected would float her to desirable heights. Charlotte's father had her interests – as he divined them – at heart. A prosperous marriage would come latter. He was a conventional man.

In the church of St Cérase she walked by confessionals and the Stations of the Cross, taking no interest at seventeen, only wishing her father hadn't been insistent on sending her to Massuery. She had every Wednesday afternoon to herself, when Madame Langevin took her children riding. She had Sunday afternoons as well, and every evening when the children had gone to bed. But what on earth could she do on Sunday afternoons except go for a walk in the woods? And in the evenings the family seemed surprised if she did not sit with them. There were in all five children, the youngest still an infant. The twins were naughty and, though only six, knew how to tease. Colette sulked. Guy, a dark-haired boy of ten, was Charlotte's favourite.

This family's details were recorded in an unfinished letter in Charlotte's handbag: the sulking, the teasing, Guy's charm, the baby's podginess. Her mother would read between the lines, winkling out an unhappiness that had not been stated; her father would skip a lot. *Madame Langevin's sister is here on a visit. She is tall and languid, an incessant smoker, very painted up, beautifully dressed. Madame Langevin's quite different, smartly dressed too, and just as good-looking in her way, only nicer in the sense that she wants people to be all right. She smiles a lot and worries. Monsieur Langevin does not say much.*

Outside a café in the square she completed the letter, pausing often to make the task last. It was July and necessary to sit in the shade. *There hasn't been a cloud in the sky since I arrived.* She drank tea with lemon and when she'd sealed the envelope and written the address she watched the people going by. But there were few of them because of the heat of the afternoon – a woman in a blue dress, with sunglasses and a poodle, a child on a bicycle, a man delivering shoe-boxes from a van. Charlotte bought a stamp in a *tabac* and found the park by the Maison de la Presse. The seats were dusty, and whitened with bird droppings; sunlight didn't penetrate the foliage of the trees, but at least the place was cool and empty. She read the book she'd brought, *The Beautiful and Damned.*

Twenty-two years later Charlotte sees herself sitting there, and can even recall the illustration on the cover of the novel – a girl with a cigarette, a man in evening dress. *Madame Langevin's conscientious about speaking French to me*, a line in her letter reported. *Monsieur practises his English.* Charlotte was timid then, and innocent of almost all emotion. In her childhood she'd been aware of jealousy, and there'd always been the affection she felt for her father and her mother; but she had no greater experience of the vagaries of her heart, or even of its nature, and only loneliness concerned her at first at Massuery.

In the room set aside for her work Charlotte slips a green Loden overcoat from a coat-hanger and searches for her gloves, the park at St Cérase still vividly recurring. She might have wept that afternoon, protected by the human absence around her; she rather thought she had. After an hour she had gone to the museum, only to find it shut. Beneath a flamboyant female figure representing Eternal Peace she had waited in the Place de la Paix for the bus that would take her back to the gates of Massuery.

'Describe to me England,' Madame Langevin's sister requested that evening, practising her English also. 'Describe to me the house of your father. The food of England is not agreeable, *n'est-ce pas*?'

Replying, Charlotte spoke in French, but the tall, beautifully dressed woman stopped her. She wanted to hear the sound of English, it made a change. She yawned. The country was tedious, but so was Paris in July.

So Charlotte described the house where she lived, and her mother and her father. She explained how toast was made because Madame Langevin's sister particularly wanted to know that, and also how English butchers hung their beef. She wasn't sure herself about the beef and she didn't know the names of the various joints, but she did her best. Madame Langevin's sister lay listening on a sofa, her cigarette in a black holder, her green silk dress clinging to her legs.

'I have heard of Jackson's tea,' she said.

Charlotte had not. She said her parents did not have servants. She did not know much about the Royal Family, she confessed.

'Pimm's Number One,' Madame Langevin's sister prompted. '*Qu'est-ce que c'est que ça?*'

The Massuery estate was extensive. Beyond the gardens there were fields where sheep grazed, and beyond the fields there were plantations of young trees, no more than a foot high. On the slopes beyond them, firs grew in great profusion, and sometimes the chain-saws whirred all day long, an ugly sing-song that grated on Charlotte's nerves.

In front of the house, early every morning, gardeners raked the gravel. An old man and a boy, with rakes wider than Charlotte had ever seen before, worked for an hour, destroying every suspicion of a weed, smoothing away the marks of yesterday's wheels. The same boy brought vegetables to the house an hour or so before lunch, and again in the evening.

Marble nymphs flanked the front door at Massuery. A decorated balustrade accompanied the steps that rose to the left and right before continuing grandly on, as a single flight. The stone of the house was greyish-brown, the slatted shutters of its windows green. Everything at Massuery was well kept up, both inside and out. The silver, the furniture, the chandeliers, the tapestries of hunting scenes, the chessboard marble of the huge entrance hall, were all as lovingly attended to as the gravel. The long, slender stair-rods and the matching brass of the banister were regularly polished, the piano in the larger of the two salons kept tuned, the enamel of the dining-room peacocks never allowed to lose its brilliance. Yet in spite of all its grandeur, Massuery possessed only one telephone. This was in a small room on the ground floor, specially set aside for it. A striped wallpaper in red and blue covered the walls, matching the colours of an ornate ceiling. A blue-shaded light illuminated the telephone table and the chair in front of it. There were writing materials and paper for noting messages on. Madame Langevin's sister, with the door wide open, sat for hours in the telephone room, speaking to people in Paris or to those who, like herself, had left the city for the summer months.

'*Mon Dieu!*' Monsieur Langevin would sometimes murmur, passing the open door. Monsieur Langevin was grey at the temples. He was clean-shaven, of medium height, with brown eyes that became playful and indulgent in his children's presence. But the children, while agreeable to their father's spoiling of them, were equally fond of their mother, even though it was she who always punished them for their misdemeanours. There was the day the twins put the cat in the chimney, and the day the bough of the apricot tree collapsed beneath their weight, and the morning old Jules couldn't find his shoes, not a single pair. There were occasions when Colette refused to speak to anyone, especially to Charlotte, when she lay on her bed, her face turned to the wall, and picked at the wallpaper. Monsieur Langevin was as angry about that as he was about the cat in the chimney, but in each case it was Madame Langevin who arranged for whatever deprivation appeared to her to be just.

Madame Langevin's sister was having an affair. Her husband arrived at the house every Thursday night, long after dinner, close on midnight. He came on the Paris train and remained until Sunday evening, when he took a sleeper back again. He was a vivacious man, not as tall as his wife, with a reddish face and a small black moustache. After his first weekend Madame Langevin told Charlotte that her sister had married beneath her, but even so she spoke affectionately of her brother-in-law, her tone suggesting that she was relaying a simple fact. Madame Langevin would not speak ill of anyone, nor would she seek, maliciously, to wound: she was not that kind of woman. When she mentioned her sister's love affair, she did so with a shrug. On her sister's wedding-day she had guessed that there would be such a development: with some people it was a natural thing. '*Le monde*,' Madame Langevin said, her tone neither condemning her sister nor disparaging her brother-in-law in his cuckold role.

Charlotte descends dimly lit stairs from her flat to the street, the green portfolio under her arm. The chill of a December morning has penetrated the house. The collar of her Loden overcoat is turned up, a black muffler several times wound round her neck. Does it happen, she wonders in other people's lives that a single event influences all subsequent time? When she was five she was gravely ill, and though she easily remembers the drama there was, and how she sensed a closeness to death and was even reconciled to it, the experience did not afterwards pursue her. She left it, snagged in its time and place, belonging there while she herself went lightly on. So, too, she had left behind other circumstances and occurrences, which had seemed as if they must surely cast perpetually haunting shadows: they had not done so. Only that summer at Massuery still insistently accompanies her, established at her very heart as part of her.

'It is the yellow wine of the Jura,' Monsieur Langevin said, in English still. 'Different from the other wines of France.'

From the windows of Massuery you could see the mountains of the Jura. Spring and early summer were sometimes cold because of wind that came from that direction. So they told her: the Jura was often a conversational topic.

'Is there a doctor at hand?' Madame Langevin's sister inquired, quoting from an English phrase-book she had made her husband bring her from Paris. 'What means "at hand"? *Un médicin sur la main? C'est impossible!*' With the precision of the bored, Madame Langevin's sister selected another cigarette and placed it in her holder.

'The lover is a younger man,' Madame Langevin passed on in slowly articulated French. 'Assistant to a pharmacist. One day of course he will wish to marry and that will be that.'

First thing in the morning, as soon as I open my eyes, the smell of coffee being made wafts through my open window. It is the servants' breakfast, I think. Later, at half past eight, ours is served in an arbour in the garden, and lunch is taken there too, though never dinner, no matter how warm the evening. On Sundays Monsieur Langevin's mother comes in a tiny motor-car she can scarcely steer. She lives alone except for a housekeeper, in a village thirty kilometres away. She is small and formidable, and does not address me. Sometimes a man comes with her, a Monsieur Ogé with a beard. He speaks to me in detail about his health, and afterwards I look up the words I do not know. Other relations occasionally come on Sundays also, Madame's cousin from Saulieu and her husband, and the widow of a general.

During the war, when there were only women and children at Massuery, a German soldier was discovered in the grounds. He had made himself a shelter and apparently lived on the remains of food thrown out from the house. He would not have been discovered had he not, in desperation, stolen cheese and bread from a larder. For more than a week the women lived with the knowledge of his presence, catching glimpses of him at night, not knowing what to do. They assumed him to be a deserter and yet were not certain, for he might as easily have been lost. In the end, fearing they were themselves being watched for a purpose they could not fathom, they shot him and buried him in the garden. '*Ici*,' Madame Langevin said, pointing at a spot in the middle of a great oval flowerbed where roses grew. '*C'était moi*,' she added, answering Charlotte's unasked question. On a wet night she and her mother-in-law and a maidservant had waited for the soldier to emerge. Her first two shots had missed him and he'd advanced, walking straight towards them. Her third shot made him stagger, and then she emptied both barrels into his body. She'd only been married a few months, not much older than Charlotte was now. *She seems so very gentle*, Charlotte wrote. *You can't imagine it.*

On 14 August, a date that was to become enshrined in Charlotte's consciousness, she was driven again to her Wednesday-afternoon freedom by Monsieur Langevin. But when they came to the Place de la Paix, instead of opening the car door as usual and driving on to his mid-week appointment, he said:

'I have nothing to do this afternoon.'

He spoke, this time, in French. He smiled. Like her, he said, he had hours on his hands. He had driven her to St Cérase specially, she realized then. On all previous Wednesday afternoons it had been convenient to give her a lift and, now, when it was not, he felt some kind of obligation had been established.

'I could have caught the bus at the gates,' she said.

He smiled again. 'That would have been a pity, Charlotte.'

This was the first intimation of his feelings for her. She didn't know how to reply. She felt confused, and knew that she had flushed. *He's such a charming man*, she'd written. *Both Monsieur and Madame are charming people. There's no other word for it.*

'Let me drive you some place, Charlotte. There's nothing to do here.'

She shook her head. She had a few things to buy, she said, after which she would return to Massuery as usual, on the bus. She would be all right.

'What will you do, Charlotte? Look at the front of the church again? The museum isn't much. It doesn't take long to drink a cup of coffee.'

The French her father wished her to perfect was far from perfect yet. Haltingly, she replied that she enjoyed her Wednesday afternoons. But even as she spoke she knew that what she'd come to enjoy most about them was the drive with Monsieur Langevin. Before, she hadn't dared to allow that thought to form. Now, she could not prevent it.

'I'll wait,' Monsieur Langevin said, 'while you do your shopping.'

When she returned to the car he drove to a country hotel, almost fifty kilometres away. It was ivy-covered, by a river, with doves in the garden and a stream near by. They sat at a table beneath a beech tree, but nobody came hurrying out to ask them what they'd like. The garden was deserted; the hotel seemed so too. Everyone was sleeping, Monsieur Langevin said.

'Are you happy at Massuery, Charlotte?'

She was three feet away from him, yet she could feel a fondness that made her faintly dizzy. Her flesh tingled, as though the tips of his fingers had touched her forearm and were sending reverberations through her body. Yet they hadn't. She tried to think of his children, endeavouring to imagine Colette and the twins at their most tiresome. She tried to think of Madame Langevin, to hear her soft, considerate voice. But nothing happened. All there was was the presence of the man she was with, his white car drawn up in the distance, the small round table at which they sat. A deception was taking place. Already they were sharing a deception.

'Yes, I am happy at Massuery now.'

'You were not at first?'

'I was a little lonely.'

Charlotte walks swiftly through the grey December streets with her portfolio. There was another print, a long time ago, of that round white table, and two faceless figures sitting at it. There was one of three women blurred by heavy rain, waiting among the dripping shrubs. There was one of Massuery caught in dappled sunlight, another of children playing, another of a white Citroën with nobody in it.

'They like you, Charlotte. Guy most of all perhaps.'

'I like them now too.'

They returned to the car when they had talked a while. Only, perhaps, an hour had passed: afterwards she calculated it was about an hour. No one had served them.

'Everyone is still asleep,' he said.

How had it happened that he put his arms around her? Had they stopped in their walk across the grass? Afterwards she realized they must have. But in her memory of the moment she was only aware that she had murmured protests, that the palms of both her hands had pressed against his chest. He hadn't kissed her, but the passion of the kiss was there. Afterwards she knew that too.

'Dear Charlotte,' he said, and then: 'Forgive me.'

She might have fainted and, as though he sensed it, he took her arm, his fingers lightly supporting her elbow, as a stranger on the street might have. He told her, as he drove, about his childhood at Massuery. The old gardener had been there, and nothing much had changed in the house. A forest of birches that had been sold for timber after the war had been replanted. In the fields where sunflowers were grown for their oil now there had been wheat before. He remembered carts and even oxen.

The white Citroën turned in at the gates and glided between the plane trees on the drive, its tyres disturbing the gravel. There'd been an oak close to the house, but its branches had spread too wide and it had been felled. He pointed at the place. They walked up the steps together, and into the hall.

That evening at dinner Madame Langevin's sister tried out a new phrase. 'My friend and I desire to attend a theatre,' she repeated several times, seeking guidance as to emphasis and pronunciation. No one remarked upon the fact that Charlotte had returned in the car with Monsieur Langevin, when always previously on Wednesdays she had arrived back on the bus. No one had noticed; no one was interested. It had been just a moment, she told herself, just the slightest thing. She hadn't been able to reply when he asked her to forgive him. He hadn't even taken her hand.

When Sunday came, Monsieur Langevin's mother brought the bearded Monsieur Ogé who talked about his health, and the widow of the general was there also. The deceived husband was in particularly good spirits that day. '*Mon chéri*,' Madame Langevin's sister murmured on the telephone after he'd left for the railway station in the evening. '*C'est trop cruel.*'

When Wednesday came Madame Langevin asked Charlotte if she'd mind taking the bus to St Cérase today because her husband was not going in that direction. And the following Wednesday, as though a precedent had been set by that, it seemed to be assumed that she would take the bus also. Had Madame Langevin somehow discovered? Her manner did not suggest it, but Charlotte remembered her philosophical tone when she'd first spoken of her sister's relationship with the pharmacist's assistant, her matter-of-fact acceptance of what clearly she considered to be an absurdity.

Sitting at the café where her solitary presence had become a Wednesday-afternoon feature, Charlotte tried to feel relieved that she'd been saved a decision. But would she really have said no if he'd offered, again, to drive her somewhere pleasant, or would her courage have failed her? Alone at the café, Charlotte shook her head. If he'd asked her, her longing to be with him would have quenched her conventional protests: courage did not come into it.

That day, she went again to the museum and sat in the dusty park. She sketched a hobby-horse that lay abandoned by a seat. The deception was still there, even though he'd changed his mind. Nothing could take it from them.

'*Tu es triste*,' Guy said when she bade him good-night that evening. '*Pourquoi es-tu triste, Charlotte?*' Only three weeks were left of her time at Massuery: that was why she was sad, she replied, which was the truth in part. '*Mais tu reviendras*,' Guy comforted, and she believed she would. It was impossible to accept that she would not see Massuery again.

The man nods appreciatively. He knows what he wants and what his clients like. The décor he supplies is enhanced by a pale-framed pleasantry above a minibar or a television set. In the bedrooms of fashionable hotels – and in boardrooms and directors' dining-rooms and the offices of industrial magnates – Charlotte's summer at Massuery hangs.

While her patron examines what she has brought him today, she sees herself walking in the Massuery woods, a lone, slight figure among the trees. What was it about her that had made a man of the world love her? She'd not been without a kind of beauty, she supposes, but often she'd been awkward in her manner and certainly ill-informed in conversation, naïve and credulous, an English schoolgirl whose clothes weren't smart, who hardly knew how to make up her face and sometimes didn't bother. Was it her very artlessness that had attracted his attention? Had he somehow delighted in the alarmed unease that must have been displayed in her face when he said he'd wait for her to finish her shopping? With long hindsight, Charlotte believes she had noticed his attention from the very first day she arrived at Massuery. There was a fondness in the amused glances he cast at her, which she had not understood and had not sought to. Yet as soon as he permitted the *frisson* between them, as soon as his manner and his words created it, she knew that being in his company was in every way different from being in Madame Langevin's, though, before, she had assumed she liked them equally. With that same long hindsight, Charlotte believes she came to love Monsieur Langevin because of his sense of honour and his strength, yet she knows as well that before she was aware of these qualities in him her own first stirrings of emotion had surfaced and, with unconscious propriety, been buried.

Madame Langevin's sister embraced her warmly the day Charlotte left Massuery. 'Farewell,' she wished her, and inquired if that was what was said on such occasions in England. The children gave her presents. Monsieur Langevin thanked her. He stood with his hands on Colette's shoulders, removing one briefly to shake one of Charlotte's. It was Madame Langevin who drove her to the railway station, and when Charlotte looked back from the car she saw in Monsieur Langevin's eyes what had not been there a moment before: the anguish of the sadness that already claimed their clandestine afternoon. His hands remained on his daughter's shoulders but even so it was as if, again, he'd spoken. At the railway station Madame Langevin embraced her, as her sister had.

Journeying through late September sunshine, Charlotte wept in a corner of her compartment. He respected Madame Langevin too much to betray her in the way her sister betrayed the husband she'd once chosen. Nor was he a man to cause his children pain in order to gratify a selfishness in himself. She knew all that, and in turn respected him. Her resignation was melancholy on that train journey, but with the balm of passing time it became more bearable.

'You're miles away, Charlotte,' young men would later amusedly accuse, and she'd apologize, already back at Massuery. Listening to the young men's chatter, she descended again the wide staircase, and walked in the woods. Such memories made it easier when with embarrassed gaucheness the young men seized her hand, or kissed her. When proposals came, her private reply was to see the white car waiting for her in the Place de la Paix, while aloud she apologized to whoever had got it into his head that she was free to love him.

'These'll ring the changes,' the man who has commissioned the new prints says. When a business-room or the bedrooms of a hotel are repainted he always likes to have fresh curtains and fresh prints as well; it's something that's expected. In six months' time, he says, he may be ready for another contribution from her. 'That's something to be thinking about, my love.' He always calls her that. He has mahogany-coloured hair with a spring in it; the stubble on his chin and neck grows so slightly and so softly that he hardly has to shave. 'We'll send a cheque,' he says.

Charlotte thanks him. There are other such men, and women too, who remember her when they want something new and unexacting for their décor. They admire her prints more than Charlotte does herself; for her the prints are by the way. What matters more is the certainty of her faith: even without thinking she knows that time, for her lover also, has failed to absorb the passion that was not allowed. For all the years that have passed she has thought of him as that; and dwelling on the nature of love during all that time she has long ago concluded that it's a mystery, appearing to come from nowhere, no rhyme nor reason to it. The truth will not yield: why did so unsuitably, so cruelly almost, two people love?

Daylight hasn't properly penetrated the December drabness. Fog shrouds the streets; the pavements are dampened by it. Busy with their assets and takeovers, the men of the business-rooms have probably never noticed the prints that hang there. 'How charming that is!' a woman, half-dressed in a hotel bedroom, may have remarked after the scurry of afternoon love or in some idle moment during a weekend's deceit.

Charlotte sits for a while in the corner of a bar, her green portfolio empty beside her. No one else, except two barmen, are there so early in the day. She sips with pleasure the glass of red wine that has been brought to her; she lights a cigarette and with slow deliberation drops the spent match into the discoloured plastic ashtray in front of her. Then idly, on the cover of her folder, she sketches a funeral procession, sombre between two lines of plane trees. When eventually he sees it the man with the mahogany hair will display no curiosity, for he never does; in the rooms destined for her funeral scene no one will wonder either.

She finishes her wine and catches the eye of the taller barman. He brings her another glass. She remembers her father being angry, and her mother frowning in bewilderment. She never told them what she might have; but her father was angry because she had no ambition, because one young man after another was so summarily rejected. 'You're alone so,' her mother sadly observed. Charlotte did not attempt to explain, for how could happily married people understand that such flimsiness could become the heart of a human existence? Ambitions in this direction or that, and would-be husbands keenly persuading, seemed empty of seriousness, ludicrous almost, compared with what she had.

She has never seen Monsieur Langevin's handwriting, but imagines it is large and sloping, a little like Guy's was. She knows she'll never see it, for the thoughts that occur to her from time to time leave no illusions behind them: no letter will ever inform her that Madame Langevin, a month or so ago, was thrown from her horse – as once, unable to help herself, she dreamed. The funeral is not a hope, only another image from her printmaker's stock. Why should an honourable deception end in romance? Rewards for decency are not duly handed out.

Their love affair, for her, is there among the memories of a summer, with the people of a household, the town she visited, Guy saying she will return, the sound of the gravel raked, the early-morning smell of coffee. For Monsieur Langevin, the deception is lived with every day, pain blinked away, words bitten back. For both of them, the pattern of their lives has formed around a moment in an afternoon. It is not often so, her lover tells her in yet another silent conversation. He, too, is grateful.

Raymond Bamber and Mrs Fitch

For fifteen years, ever since he was twenty-seven, Raymond Bamber had attended the Tamberleys' autumn cocktail party. It was a function to which the Tamberleys inclined to invite their acquaintances rather than their friends, so that every year the faces changed a bit: no one except Raymond had been going along to the house in Eaton Square for as long as fifteen years. Raymond, the Tamberleys felt, was a special case, for they had known him since he was a boy, having been close friends of his father's.

Raymond was a tall man, six foot two inches, with spectacles and a small moustache. He was neat in all he did, and he lived what he himself referred to as a tidy life.

'I come here every year,' said Raymond at the Tamberleys', to a woman he had not met before, a woman who was tall too, with a white lean face and lips that were noticeably scarlet. 'It is an occasion for me almost, like Christmas or Easter. To some extent, I guide my life by the Tamberleys' autumn party, remembering on each occasion what has happened in the year gone by.'

'My name is Mrs Fitch,' said the woman, poking a hand out for a drink. 'Is that vermouth and gin?' she inquired of the Tamberleys' Maltese maid, and the maid agreed that it was. 'Good,' said Mrs Fitch.

'Raymond, Raymond,' cried the voice of Mrs Tamberley as Mrs Tamberley materialized suddenly beside them. 'How's Nanny Wilkinson?'

'She died,' murmured Raymond.

'Of course she did,' exclaimed Mrs Tamberley. 'How silly of me!'

'Oh no –'

'You put that sweet notice in *The Times*. His old nurse,' explained Mrs Tamberley to Mrs Fitch. 'Poor Nanny Wilkinson,' she said, and smiled and bustled off.

'What was all that?' asked Mrs Fitch.

'It's one of the things that happened to me during the year. The other was –'

'What's your name, anyway?' the woman interrupted. 'I don't think I ever caught it.'

Raymond told her his name. He saw that she was wearing a black dress with touches of white on it. Her shoulders were bare and bony; she had, Raymond said to himself, an aquiline face.

'The other thing was that an uncle died and left me a business in his will. That happened, actually, before the death of Nanny Wilkinson and to tell you the truth, Mrs Fitch, I just didn't know what to do. "What could I do with a business?" I said to myself. So I made my way to Streatham where the old lady lived. "Run a business, Raymond? You couldn't run a bath," she said.' Raymond laughed, and Mrs Fitch smiled frostily, looking about her for another drink. 'It rankled, that, as you may imagine. Why couldn't I run a business? I thought. And then, less than a week later, I heard that she had died in Streatham. I went to her funeral, and discovered that she'd left me a prayer-book in her will. All that happened in the last year. You see, Mrs Fitch?'

Mrs Fitch, her eyes on her husband, who was talking to a woman in yellow in a distant corner of the room, said vaguely:

'What about the business?'

'I sold the business. I live alone, Mrs Fitch, in a flat in Bayswater; I'm forty-two. I'm telling you that simply because I felt that I could never manage anything like taking on a business so suddenly. That's what I thought when I had considered the matter carefully. No good being emotional, I said to myself.'

'No,' said Mrs Fitch. She watched the woman move quite close to her husband and engage him in speech that had all the air of confidential talk. The woman wasn't young, Mrs Fitch noticed, but had succeeded in giving the impression of youth. She was probably forty-four, she reckoned; she looked thirty.

So Mrs Tamberley had seen the notice in *The Times*, Raymond thought. He had worded it simply and had stated in a straightforward manner the service that Nanny Wilkinson had given over the years to his family. He had felt it her due, a notice in *The Times*, and there was of course only he who might do it. He remembered her sitting regally in his nursery teaching him his tidiness. Orderliness was the most important thing in life, she said, after a belief in the Almighty.

'Get me a drink, dear,' said Mrs Fitch suddenly, holding out an empty glass and causing Raymond to note that this woman was consuming the Tamberleys' liquor at a faster rate than he.

'Gin and vermouth,' ordered Mrs Fitch. 'Dry,' she added. 'Not that red stuff.'

Raymond smiled and took her glass, while Mrs Fitch observed that her husband was listening with rapt care to what the woman in yellow was saying to him. In the taxi-cab on the way to the Tamberleys', he had remarked as usual that he was fatigued after his day's work. 'An early night,' he had suggested. And now he was listening carefully to a female: he wouldn't leave this party for another two hours at least.

'It was quite a blow to me,' said Raymond, handing Mrs Fitch a glass of gin and vermouth, 'hearing that she was dead. Having known her, you see, all my life –'

'Who's dead now?' asked Mrs Fitch, still watching her husband.

'Sorry,' said Raymond. 'How silly of me! No, I meant, you see, this old lady whom I had known as Nanny Wilkinson. I was saying it was a blow to me when she died, although of course I didn't see much of her these last few years. But the memories are there, if you see what I mean; and you cannot of course erase them.'

'No,' said Mrs Fitch.

'I was a particularly tall child, with my spectacles of course, and a longish upper lip. "When you're a big man," I remember her saying to me, "you'll have to grow a little moustache to cover up all that lip." And declare, Mrs Fitch, I did.'

'I never had a nanny,' said Mrs Fitch.

'"He'll be a tennis-player," people used to say – because of my height, you see. But in fact I turned out to be not much good on a tennis court.'

Mrs Fitch nodded. Raymond began to say something else, but Mrs Fitch, her eyes still fixed upon her husband, interrupted him. She said:

'Interesting about your uncle's business.'

'I think I was right. I've thought of it often since, of sitting down in an office and ordering people to do this and that, instead of remaining quietly in my flat in Bayswater. I do all my own cooking, actually, and cleaning and washing up. Well, you can't get people, you know. I couldn't even get a simple char, Mrs Fitch, not for love nor money. Of course it's easy having no coal fires to cope with: the flat is all-electric, which is what, really, I prefer.'

Raymond laughed nervously, having observed that Mrs Fitch was, for the first time since their conversation had commenced, observing him closely. She was looking into his face, at his nose and his moustache and his spectacles. Her eyes passed up to his forehead and down the line of his right cheek, down his neck until they arrived at Raymond's Adam's apple. He continued to speak to her, telling of the manner in which his flat in Bayswater was furnished, how he had visited the Sanderson showrooms in Berners Street to select materials for chair-covers and curtains. 'She made them for me,' said Raymond. 'She was almost ninety then.'

'What's that?' said Mrs Fitch. 'Your nurse made them?'

'I measured up for her and wrote everything down just as she had directed. Then I travelled out to Streatham with my scrap of paper.'

'On a bicycle.'

Raymond shook his head. He thought it odd of Mrs Fitch to suggest, for no logical reason, that he had cycled from Bayswater to Streatham. 'On a bus actually,' he explained. He paused, and then added: 'I could have had them made professionally, of course, but I preferred the other. I thought it would give her an interest, you see.'

'Instead of which it killed her.'

'No, no. No, you've got it confused. It was in 1964 that she made the curtains and the covers for me. As I was saying, she died only a matter of months ago.'

Raymond noticed that Mrs Fitch had ceased her perusal of his features and was again looking vacantly into the distance. He was glad that she had ceased to examine him because had she continued he would have felt obliged to move away from her, being a person who was embarrassed by such intent attention. He said, to make it quite clear about the covers and the curtains:

'She died in fact of pneumonia.'

'Stop,' said Mrs Fitch to the Tamberleys' Maltese maid who happened to be passing with a tray of drinks. She lifted a glass to her lips and consumed its contents while reaching out a hand for another. She repeated the procedure, drinking two glasses of the Tamberleys' liquor in a gulping way and retaining a third in her left hand.

'Nobody can be trusted,' said Mrs Fitch after all that. 'We come to these parties and everything's a sham.'

'What?' said Raymond.

'You know what I mean.'

Raymond laughed, thinking that Mrs Fitch was making some kind of joke. 'Of course,' he said, and laughed again, a noise that was more of a cough.

'You told me you were forty-two,' said Mrs Fitch. 'I in fact am fifty-one, and have been taken for sixty-five.'

Raymond thought he would move away from this woman in a moment. He had a feeling she might be drunk. She had listened pleasantly enough while he told her a thing or two about himself, yet here she was now speaking most peculiarly. He smiled at her and heard her say:

'Look over there, Mr Bamber. That man with the woman in yellow is my husband. We were born in the same year and in the same month, January 1915. Yet he could be in his thirties. That's what he's up to now; pretending the thirties with the female he's talking to. He's praying I'll not approach and give the game away. D'you see, Mr Bamber?'

'That's Mrs Anstey,' said Raymond. 'I've met her here before. The lady in yellow.'

'My husband has eternal youth,' said Mrs Fitch. She took a mouthful of her drink and reached out a hand to pick a fresh one from a passing tray. 'It's hard to bear.'

'You don't look fifty-one,' said Raymond. 'Not at all.'

'Are you mocking me?' cried Mrs Fitch. 'I do not look fifty-one. I've told you so: I've been taken for sixty-five.'

'I didn't mean that. I meant –'

'You were telling a lie, as well you know. My husband is telling lies too. He's all sweetness to that woman, yet it isn't his nature. My husband cares nothing for people, except when they're of use to him. Why do you think, Mr Bamber, he goes to cocktail parties?'

'Well –'

'So that he may make arrangements with other women. He desires their flesh and tells them so by looking at it.'

Raymond looked serious, frowning, thinking that that was expected of him.

'We look ridiculous together, my husband and I. Yet once we were a handsome couple. I am like an old crow while all he has is laughter lines about his eyes. It's an obsession with me.'

Raymond pursed his lips, sighing slightly.

'He's after women in this room,' said Mrs Fitch, eyeing her husband again.

'Oh, no, now –'

'Why not? How can you know better than I, Mr Bamber? I have had plenty of time to think about this matter. Why shouldn't he want to graze where the grass grows greener, or appears to grow greener? That Anstey woman is a walking confidence trick.'

'I think,' said Raymond, 'that I had best be moving on. I have friends to talk to.' He made a motion to go, but Mrs Fitch grasped part of his jacket in her right hand.

'What I say is true,' she said. 'He is practically a maniac. He has propositioned women in this very room before this. I've heard him at it.'

'I'm sure –'

'When I was a raving beauty he looked at me with his gleaming eye. Now he gleams for all the others. I'll tell you something, Mr Bamber.' Mrs Fitch paused. Raymond noticed that her eyes were staring over his shoulder, as though she had no interest in him beyond his being a person to talk at. 'I've gone down on my bended knees, Mr Bamber, in order to have this situation cleared up: I've prayed that that man might look again with tenderness on his elderly wife. But God has gone on,' said Mrs Fitch bitterly, 'in His mysterious way, not bothering Himself.'

Raymond did not reply to these observations. He said instead that he hadn't liked to mention it before but was Mrs Fitch aware that she was clutching in her right hand part of his clothes?

'He shall get to know your Anstey woman,' said Mrs Fitch. 'He shall come to know that her father was a bearlike man with a generous heart and that her mother, still alive in Guildford, is difficult to get on with. My husband shall come to know all the details about your Anstey woman: the plaster chipping in her bathroom, the way she cooks an egg. He shall know what her handbags look like, and how their clasps work – while I continue to wither away in the house we share.'

Raymond asked Mrs Fitch if she knew the Griegons, who were, he said, most pleasant people. He added that the Griegons were present tonight and that, in fact, he would like to introduce them to her.

'You are trying to avoid the facts. What have the Griegons to recommend them that we should move in their direction and end this conversation? Don't you see the situation, Mr Bamber? I am a woman who is obsessed because of the state of her marriage, how I have aged while he has not. I am obsessed by the fact that he is now incapable of love or tenderness. I have failed to keep all that alive because I lost my beauty. There are lines on my body too, Mr Bamber: I would show you if we were somewhere else.'

Raymond protested again, and felt tired of protesting. But Mrs Fitch, hearing him speak and thinking that he was not yet clear in his mind about the situation, supplied him with further details about her marriage and the manner in which, at cocktail parties, her husband made arrangements for the seduction of younger women, or women who on the face of it seemed younger. 'Obsessions are a disease,' said Mrs Fitch, drinking deeply from her glass.

Raymond explained then that he knew nothing whatsoever about marriage difficulties, to which Mrs Fitch replied that she was only telling him the truth. 'I do not for a moment imagine,' she said, 'that you are an angel come from God, Mr Bamber, in order to settle the unfortunateness. I didn't mean to imply that when I said I had prayed. Did you think I thought you were a messenger?' Mrs Fitch, still holding Raymond's jacket and glancing still at her husband and the woman in yellow, laughed shrilly. Raymond said:

'People are looking at us, the way you are pulling at my clothes. I'm a shy man –'

'Tell me about yourself. You know about me by now: how everything that once seemed rosy has worked out miserably.'

'Oh, come now,' said Raymond, causing Mrs Fitch to repeat her laughter and to call out for a further drink. The Tamberleys' maid hastened towards her. 'Now then,' said Mrs Fitch. 'Tell me.'

'What can I tell you?' asked Raymond.

'I drink a lot these days,' said Mrs Fitch, 'to help matters along. Cheers, Mr Bamber.'

'Actually I've told you quite a bit, you know. One thing and another –'

'You told me nothing except some nonsense about an old creature in Streatham. Who wants to hear that, for Christ's sake? Or is it relevant?'

'Well, I mean, it's true, Mrs Fitch. Relevant to what?'

'I remember you, believe it or not, in this very room on this same occasion last year. "Who's that man?" I said to the Tamberley woman and she replied that you were a bore. You were invited, year by year, so the woman said, because of some friendship between the Tamberleys and your father. In the distant past.'

'Look here,' said Raymond, glancing about him and noting to his relief that no one appeared to have heard what Mrs Fitch in her cups had said.

'What's the matter?' demanded Mrs Fitch. Her eyes were again upon her husband and Mrs Anstey. She saw them laugh together, and felt her unhappiness being added to as though it were a commodity within her body. 'Oh yes,' she said to Raymond, attempting to pass a bit of the unhappiness on. 'A grinding bore. Those were the words of Mrs Tamberley.'

Raymond shook his head. 'I've known Mrs Tamberley since I was a child,' he said.

'So the woman said. You were invited because of the old friendship: the Tamberleys and your father. I cannot tell a lie, Mr Bamber: she said you were a pathetic case. She said you hadn't learned how to grow up. I dare say you're a pervert.'

'My God!'

'I'm sorry I cannot tell lies,' said Mrs Fitch, and Raymond felt her grip tighten on his jacket. 'It's something that happens to you when you've been through what I've been through. That man up to his tricks with women while the beauty drains from my face. What's it like, d'you think?'

'I don't know,' said Raymond. 'How on earth could I know? Mrs Fitch, let's get one thing clear: I am not a pervert.'

'Not? Are you sure? They may think you are, you know,' said Mrs Fitch, glancing again at her husband. 'Mrs Tamberley has probably suggested that very thing to everyone in this room. Crueller, though, I would have thought, to say you were a grinding bore.'

'I am not a pervert –'

'I can see them sniggering over that all right. Unmentionable happenings between yourself and others. Elderly newspaper-vendors –'

'Stop!' cried Raymond. 'For God's sake, woman –'

'You're not a Jew, are you?'

Raymond did not reply. He stood beside Mrs Fitch, thinking that the woman appeared to be both drunk and not of her right mind. He did not wish to create a scene in the Tamberleys' drawing-room, and yet he recognized that by the look of her she intended to hold on to his jacket for the remainder of the evening. If he attempted to pull it away from her, she would not let go: she did not, somehow, seem to be the kind of woman who would. She wouldn't mind a scene at all.

'Why,' said Mrs Fitch, 'did you all of a sudden begin to tell me about that woman in Streatham, Mr Bamber, and the details about your chair-covers and curtains? Why did you tell me about your uncle dying and trying to leave you a business and your feeling that in your perverted condition you were unfit to run a business?'

Raymond's hands began to shake. He could feel an extra tug on his jacket, as though Mrs Fitch was now insisting that he stand closer to her. He pressed his teeth together, grinding his molars one upon another, and then opened his mouth and felt his teeth and his lips quivering. He knew that his voice would sound strange when he spoke. He said:

'You are being extremely offensive to me, Mrs Fitch. You are a woman who is a total stranger to me, yet you have seen fit to drive me into a corner at a cocktail party and hold me here by force. I must insist that you let go my jacket and allow me to walk away.'

'What about me, Mr Bamber? What about my husband and your Anstey woman? Already they are immoral on a narrow bed somewhere; in a fifth-class hotel near King's Cross station.'

'Your husband is still in this room, Mrs Fitch. As well you know. What your husband does is not my business.'

'Your business is your flat in Bayswater, is it? And curtains and covers from the Sanderson showrooms in Berners Street. Your world is people dying and leaving you stuff in wills – money and prayer-books and valuable jewellery that you wear when you dress yourself up in a nurse's uniform.'

'I must ask you to stop, Mrs Fitch.'

'I could let you have a few pairs of old stockings if they interest you. Or garments of my husband's.'

Mrs Fitch saw Raymond close his eyes. She watched the flesh on his face redden further and watched it twitch in answer to a pulse that throbbed in his neck. Her husband, a moment before, had reached out a hand and placed it briefly on the female's arm.

'So your nanny was a guide to you,' said Mrs Fitch. 'You hung on all her words, I dare say?'

Raymond did not reply. He turned his head away, trying to control the twitching in his face. Eventually he said, quietly and with the suspicion of a stammer:

'She was a good woman. She was kind in every way.'

'She taught you neatness.'

Raymond was aware, as Mrs Fitch spoke that sentence, that she had moved appreciably closer to him. He could feel her knee pressing against his. He felt a second knee, and felt next that his leg had been cleverly caught by her, between her own legs.

'Look here,' said Raymond.

'Yes?'

'Mrs Fitch, what are you trying to do?'

Mrs Fitch increased the pressure of her knees. Her right hand moved into Raymond's jacket pocket. 'I am a little the worse for wear,' she said, 'but I can still tell the truth.'

'You are embarrassing me.'

'What are your perversions? Tell me, Mr Bamber.'

'I have no perversions of any kind. I live a normal life.'

'Shall I come to you with a pram? I'm an unhappy woman, Mr Bamber. I'll wear black woollen stockings. I'll show you those lines on my body.'

'Please,' said Raymond, thinking he would cry in a moment.

Already people were glancing at Mrs Fitch's legs gripping his so strongly. Her white face and her scarlet lips were close to his eyes. He could see the lines on her cheeks, but he turned his glance away from them in case she mentioned again the lines on her body. She is a mad, drunken nymphomaniac, said Raymond to himself, and thought that never in all his life had anything so upsetting happened to him.

'Embrace me,' said Mrs Fitch.

'Please, I beg you,' said Raymond.

'You are a homosexual. A queer. I had forgotten that.'

'I'm not a homosexual,' shouted Raymond, aware that his voice was piercingly shrill. Heads turned and he felt the eyes of the Tamberleys' guests. He had been heard to cry that he was not a homosexual, and people had wished to see for themselves.

'Excuse me,' said a voice. 'I'm sorry about this.'

Raymond turned his head and saw Mrs Fitch's husband standing behind him. 'Come along now, Adelaide,' said Mrs Fitch's husband. 'I'm sorry,' he said again to Raymond. 'I didn't realize she'd had a tankful before she got here.'

'I've been telling him a thing or two,' said Mrs Fitch. 'We've exchanged life-stories.'

Raymond felt her legs slip away, and he felt her hand withdraw itself from the pocket of his jacket. He nodded in a worldly way at her husband and said in a low voice that he understood how it was.

'He's a most understanding chap,' said Mrs Fitch. 'He has a dead woman in Streatham.'

'Come along now,' ordered her husband in a rough voice, and Raymond saw that the man's hand gripped her arm in a stern manner.

'I was telling that man,' said Mrs Fitch again, seeming to be all of a sudden in an ever greater state of inebriation. Very slowly she said: 'I was telling him what I am and what you are, and what the Tamberleys think about him. It has been home-truths corner here, for the woman with an elderly face and for the chap who likes to dress himself out as a children's nurse and go with women in chauffeur's garb. Actually, my dear, he's a homosexual.'

'Come along now,' said Mrs Fitch's husband. 'I'm truly sorry,' he added to Raymond. 'It's a problem.'

Raymond saw that it was all being conducted in a most civilized manner. Nobody shouted in the Tamberleys' drawing-room, nobody noticed the three of them talking quite quietly in a corner. The Maltese maid in fact, not guessing for a moment that anything was amiss, came up with her tray of drinks and before anyone could prevent it, Mrs Fitch had lifted one to her lips. '*In vino veritas*,' she remarked.

Raymond felt his body cooling down. His shirt was damp with sweat, and he realized that he was panting slightly and he wondered how long that had been going on. He watched Mrs Fitch being aided through the room by her husband. No wonder, he thought, the man had been a little severe with her, if she put up a performance like that very often; no wonder he treated her like an infant. She was little more than an infant, Raymond considered, saying the first thing that came into her head, and going on about sex. He saw her lean form briefly again, through an opening in the crowded room, and he realized without knowing it that he had craned his neck for a last glimpse. She saw him too, as she smiled and bowed at Mrs Tamberley, appearing to be sober and collected. She shook her head at him, deploring him or suggesting, even, that he had been the one who had misbehaved. Her husband raised a hand in the air, thanking Raymond for his understanding.

Raymond edged his way through all the people and went to find a bathroom. He washed his face, taking his spectacles off and placing them beside a piece of lime-green soap. He was thinking that her husband was probably just like any other man at a cocktail party. How could the husband help it, Raymond thought, if he had not aged and if other women found him pleasant to talk to? Did she expect him to have all his hair plucked out and have an expert come to line his face?

Leaning against the wall of the bathroom, Raymond thought about Mrs Fitch. He thought at first that she was a fantastic woman given to fantastic statements, and then he embroidered on the thought and saw her as being more subtle than that. 'By heavens!' said Raymond aloud to himself. She was a woman, he saw, who was pathetic in what she did, transferring the truth about herself to other people. She it was, he guessed, who was the grinding bore, so well known for the fact that she had come to hear the opinion herself and in her unbalanced way sought to pretend that others were bores in order to push the thing away from her. She was probably even, he thought, a little perverted, the way in which she had behaved with her knees, and sought to imbue others with this characteristic too, so that she, for the moment, might feel rid of it: Mrs Fitch was clearly a case for a psychiatrist. She had said that her husband was a maniac where women were concerned; she had said that he had taken Mrs Anstey to a bed in King's Cross when Mrs Anstey was standing only yards away, in front of her eyes. *In vino veritas*, she had said, for no reason at all.

One morning, Raymond imagined, poor Mr Fitch had woken up to find his wife gabbling in that utterly crazy manner about her age and her hair and the lines on her body. Probably the woman was a nuisance with people who came to the door, the deliverers of coal and groceries, the milkman and the postman. He imagined the Express Dairy on the telephone to Mrs Fitch's husband, complaining that the entire milk-round was daily being disorganized because of the antics of Mrs Fitch, who was a bore with everyone.

It accounted for everything, Raymond thought, the simple fact that the woman was a psychological case. He closed his eyes and sighed with relief, and remembered then that he had read in newspapers about women like Mrs Fitch. He opened his eyes again and looked at himself in the mirror of the Tamberleys' smallest bathroom. He touched his neat moustache with his fingers and smiled at himself to ascertain that his teeth were not carrying a piece of cocktail food. 'You have a tea-leaf on your tooth,' said the voice of Nanny Wilkinson, and Raymond smiled, remembering her.

Raymond returned to the party and stood alone watching the people talking and laughing. His eyes passed from face to face, many of which were familiar to him. He looked for the Griegons with whom last year he had spent quite some time, interesting them in a small sideboard that he had just had french polished, having been left the sideboard in the will of a godmother. The man, a Mr French amusingly enough, had come to Raymond's flat to do the job there in the evenings, having explained that he had no real facilities or premises, being a postman during the day. 'Not that he wasn't an expert polisher,' Raymond had said. 'He did a most beautiful job. I heard of him through Mrs Adams who lives in the flat below. I thought it was reasonable, you know: seven guineas plus expenses. The sideboard came up wonderfully.'

'Hullo,' said Raymond to the Griegons.

'How d'you do?' said Mrs Griegon, a pleasant, smiling woman, not at all like Mrs Fitch. Her husband nodded at Raymond, and turned to a man who was talking busily.

'Our name is Griegon,' said Mrs Griegon. 'This is my husband, and this is Dr Oath.'

'I know,' said Raymond, surprised that Mrs Griegon should say who she was since they had all met so pleasantly a year ago. 'How do you do, Dr Oath?' he said, stretching out a hand.

'Yes,' said Dr Oath, shaking the hand rapidly while continuing his conversation.

Mrs Griegon said: 'You haven't told us your name.'

Raymond, puzzled and looking puzzled, said that his name was Raymond Bamber. 'But surely you remember our nice talk last year?' he said. 'I recall it all distinctly: I was telling you about Mr French who came to polish a sideboard, and how he charged only seven guineas.'

'Most reasonable,' said Mrs Griegon. '*Most* reasonable.'

'We stood over there,' explained Raymond, pointing. 'You and I and Mr Griegon. I remember I gave you my address and telephone number in case if you were ever in Bayswater you might like to pop in to see the sideboard. You said to your husband at the time, Mrs Griegon, that you had one or two pieces that could do with stripping down and polishing, and Mr French, who'll travel anywhere in the evenings and being, as you say, so reasonable –'

'Of course,' cried Mrs Griegon. 'Of course I remember you perfectly, and I'm sure Archie does too.' She looked at her husband, but her husband was listening carefully to Dr Oath.

Raymond smiled. 'It looks even better now that the initial shine has gone. I'm terribly pleased with it.' As he spoke, he saw the figure of Mrs Fitch's husband entering the room. He watched him glance about and saw him smile at someone he'd seen. Following the direction of this smile, Raymond saw Mrs Anstey smiling back at Mrs Fitch's husband, who at once made his way to her side.

'French polishing's an art,' said Mrs Griegon.

What on earth, Raymond wondered, was the man doing back at the Tamberleys' party? And where was Mrs Fitch? Nervously, Raymond glanced about the crowded room, looking for the black-and-white dress and the lean aquiline features of the woman who had tormented him. But although, among all the brightly coloured garments that the women wore there were a few that were black and white, none of them contained Mrs Fitch. 'We come to these parties and everything's a sham,' her voice seemed to say, close to him. 'Nobody can be trusted.' The voice came to him in just the same way as Nanny Wilkinson's had a quarter of an hour ago, when she'd been telling him that he had a tea-leaf on his tooth.

'Such jolly parties,' said Mrs Griegon. 'The Tamberleys are wonderful.'

'Do you know a woman called Mrs Fitch?' said Raymond. 'She was here tonight.'

'Mrs Fitch!' exclaimed Mrs Griegon with a laugh.

'D'you know her?'

'She's married to that man there,' said Mrs Griegon. She pointed at Mr Fitch and sniffed.

'Yes,' said Raymond. 'He's talking to Mrs Anstey.'

He was about to add that Mr Fitch was probably of a social inclination. He was thinking already that Mr Fitch probably had a perfectly sound reason for returning to the Tamberleys'. Probably he lived quite near and having seen his wife home had decided to return in order to say goodbye properly to his hosts. Mrs Anstey, Raymond had suddenly thought, was for all he knew Mr Fitch's sister: in her mentally depressed condition it would have been quite like Mrs Fitch to pretend that the woman in yellow was no relation whatsoever, to have invented a fantasy that was greater even than it appeared to be.

'He's always up to that kind of carry-on,' said Mrs Griegon. 'The man's famous for it.'

'Sorry?' said Raymond.

'Fitch. With women.'

'Oh but surely –'

'Really,' said Mrs Griegon.

'I was talking to Mrs Fitch earlier on and she persisted in speaking about her husband. Well, I felt she was going on rather. Exaggerating, you know. A bit of a bore.'

'He has said things to me, Mr Bamber, that would turn your stomach.'

'She has a funny way with her, Mrs Fitch has. She too said the oddest things –'

'She has a reputation,' said Mrs Griegon, 'for getting drunk and coming out with awkward truths. I've heard it said.'

'Not the truth,' Raymond corrected. 'She says things about herself, you see, and pretends she's talking about another person.'

'What?' said Mrs Griegon.

'Like maybe, you see, she was saying that she herself is a bore the way she goes on – well, Mrs Fitch wouldn't say it just like that. What Mrs Fitch would do is pretend some other person is the bore, the person she might be talking to. D'you see? She would transfer all her own qualities to the person she's talking to.'

Mrs Griegon raised her thin eyebrows and inclined her head. She said that what Raymond was saying sounded most interesting.

'An example is,' said Raymond, 'that Mrs Fitch might find herself unsteady on her feet through drink. Instead of saying that she was unsteady she'd say that you, Mrs Griegon, were the unsteady one. There's a name for it, actually. A medical name.'

'Medical?' said Mrs Griegon.

Glancing across the room, Raymond saw that Mr Fitch's right hand gripped Mrs Anstey's elbow. Mr Fitch murmured in her ear and together the two left the room. Raymond saw them wave at Mrs Tamberley, implying thanks with the gesture, implying that they had enjoyed themselves.

'I can't think what it is now,' said Raymond to Mrs Griegon, 'when people transfer the truth about themselves to others. It's some name beginning with an R, I think.'

'How nice of you,' said Mrs Tamberley, gushing up, 'to put that notice in *The Times*.' She turned to Mrs Griegon and said that, as Raymond had probably told her, a lifelong friend of his, old Nanny Wilkinson, had died a few months ago. 'Every year,' said Mrs Tamberley, 'Raymond told us all how she was bearing up. But now, alas, she's died.'

'Indeed,' said Mrs Griegon, and smiled and moved away.

Without any bidding, there arrived in Raymond's mind a picture of Mrs Fitch sitting alone in her house, refilling a glass from a bottle of Gordon's gin. '*In vino veritas*,' said Mrs Fitch, and began to weep.

'I was telling Mrs Griegon that I'd been chatting with Mrs Fitch,' said Raymond, and then he remembered that Mrs Tamberley had very briefly joined in that chat. 'I found her strange,' he added.

'Married to that man,' cried Mrs Tamberley. 'He drove her to it.'

'Her condition?' said Raymond, nodding.

'She ladles it into herself,' said Mrs Tamberley, 'and then tells you what she thinks of you. It can be disconcerting.'

'She really says anything that comes into her head,' said Raymond, and gave a light laugh.

'Not actually,' said Mrs Tamberley. 'She tells the truth.'

'Well, no, you see –'

'You haven't a drink,' cried Mrs Tamberley in alarm, and moved at speed towards her Maltese maid to direct the girl's attention to Raymond's empty glass.

Again the image of Mrs Fitch arrived in Raymond's mind. She sat as before, alone in a room, while her husband made off with a woman in yellow. She drank some gin.

'Sherry, sir?' said the Maltese maid, and Raymond smiled and thanked her, and then, in an eccentric way and entirely on an impulse, he said in a low voice:

'Do you know a woman called Mrs Fitch?'

The girl said that Mrs Fitch had been at the party earlier in the evening, and reminded Raymond that he had in fact been talking to her.

'She has a peculiar way with her,' explained Raymond. 'I just wondered if ever you had talked to her, or had listened to what she herself had to say.' But the Maltese maid shook her head, appearing not to understand.

'Mrs Fitch's a shocker,' said a voice behind Raymond's back, and added: 'That poor man.'

There was a crackle of laughter as a response, and Raymond, sipping his sherry, turned about and moved towards the group that had caused it. The person who had spoken was a small man with shiny grey hair. 'I'm Raymond Bamber,' said Raymond, smiling at him. 'By the sound of things, you saw my predicament earlier on.' He laughed, imitating the laughter that had come from the group. 'Extremely awkward.'

'She gets tight,' said the small man. 'She's liable to tell a home truth or two.' He began to laugh again. '*In vino veritas*,' he said.

Raymond looked at the people and opened his mouth to say that it wasn't quite so simple, the malaise of Mrs Fitch. 'It's all within her,' he wished to say. 'Everything she says is part of Mrs Fitch, since she's unhappy in a marriage and has lost her beauty.' But Raymond checked that speech, uttering in fact not a word of it. The people looked expectantly at him, and after a long pause the small man said:

'Mrs Fitch can be most embarrassing.'

Raymond heard the people laugh again with the same sharpness and saw their teeth for a moment harshly bared and noted that their eyes were like polished ice. They would not understand, he thought, the facts about

Mrs Fitch, any more than Mrs Griegon had seemed to understand, or Mrs Tamberley. It surprised Raymond, and saddened him, that neither Mrs Griegon nor Mrs Tamberley had cared to accept the truth about the woman. It was, he told himself, something of a revelation that Mrs Griegon, who had seemed so pleasant the year before, and Mrs Tamberley whom he had known almost all his life, should turn out to be no better than this group of hard-eyed people. Raymond murmured and walked away, still thinking of Mrs Griegon and Mrs Tamberley. He imagined them laughing with their husbands over Mrs Fitch, repeating that she was a bore and a drunk. Laughter was apparently the thing, a commodity that reflected the shallowness of minds too lazy to establish correctly the facts about people. And they were minds, as had been proved to Raymond, that didn't even bother to survey properly the simple explanations of eccentric conduct – as though even that constituted too much trouble.

Soon afterwards, Raymond left the party and walked through the autumn evening, considering everything. The air was cool on his face as he strode towards Bayswater, thinking that as he continued to live his quiet life Mrs Fitch would be attending parties that were similar to the Tamberleys', and she'd be telling the people she met there that they were grinding bores. The people might be offended, Raymond thought, if they didn't pause to think about it, if they didn't understand that everything was confused in poor Mrs Fitch's mind. And it would serve them right, he reflected, to be offended – a just reward for allowing their minds to become lazy and untidy in this modern manner. 'Orderliness,' said the voice of Nanny Wilkinson, and Raymond paused and smiled, and then walked on.

O Fat White Woman

Relaxing in the garden of her husband's boarding-school, Mrs Digby-Hunter could not help thinking that it was good to be alive. On the short grass of the lawn, tucked out of sight beneath her deck-chair, was a small box of Terry's All Gold chocolates, and on her lap, open at page eight, lay a paper-backed novel by her second-favourite writer of historical fiction. In the garden there was the pleasant sound of insects, and occasionally the buzzing of bees. No sound came from the house: the boys, beneath the alert tutelage of her husband and Mr Beade, were obediently labouring, the maids, Dympna and Barbara, were, Mrs Digby-Hunter hoped, washing themselves.

Not for the moment in the mood for reading, she surveyed the large, tidy garden that was her husband's pride, even though he never had a moment to work in it. Against high stone walls forsythia grew, and honeysuckle and little pear trees, and beneath them in rich, herbaceous borders the garden flowers of summer blossomed now in colourful variety. Four beech trees shaded patches of the lawn, and roses grew, and geraniums, in round beds symmetrically arranged. On either side of an archway in the wall ahead of Mrs Digby-Hunter were two yew trees and beyond the archway, in a wilder part, she could see the blooms of late rhododendrons. She could see as well, near one of the yew trees, the bent figure of Sergeant Wall, an ex-policeman employed on a part-time basis by her husband. He was weeding, his movements slow in the heat of that June afternoon, a stained white hat on his hairless head. It was pleasant to sit in the shade of a beech tree watching someone else working, having worked oneself all morning in a steamy kitchen. Although she always considered herself an easy-going woman, she had been very angry that morning because one of the girls had quite clearly omitted to make use of the deodorant she was at such pains to supply them with. She had accused each in turn and had got nowhere whatsoever, which didn't entirely surprise her. Dympna was just fifteen and Barbara only a month or two older; hardly the age at which to expect responsibility and truthfulness. Yet it was her duty to train them, as it was her husband's duty to train the boys. 'You'll strip wash, both of you,' she'd commanded snappishly in the end, 'immediately you've done the lunch dishes. From top to toe, please, every inch of you.' They had both, naturally, turned sulky.

Mrs Digby-Hunter, wearing that day a blue cotton dress with a pattern of pinkish lupins on it, was fifty-one. She had married her husband twenty-nine years ago, at a time when he'd been at the beginning of a career in the army. Her father, well-to-do and stern, had given her away and she'd been quite happy about his gesture, for love had then possessed her fully. Determined at all costs to make a success of her marriage and to come up to scratch as a wife, she had pursued a policy of agreeableness: she smiled instead of making a fuss, in her easy-going way she accepted what there was to accept, placing her faith in her husband as she believed a good wife should. In her own opinion she was not a clever person, but at least she could offer loyalty and devotion, instead of nagging and arguing. In a bedroom of a Welsh hotel she had disguised, on her wedding night, her puzzled disappointment when her husband had abruptly left her side, having lain there for only a matter of minutes.

Thus a pattern began in their marriage and as a result of it Mrs Digby-Hunter had never borne children although she had, gradually and at an increasing rate, put on weight. At first she had minded about this and had attempted to diet. She had deprived herself of what she most enjoyed until it occurred to her that caring in this way was making her bad-tempered and miserable: it didn't suit her, all the worrying about calories and extra ounces. She weighed now, although she didn't know it, thirteen stone.

Her husband was leaner, a tall man with strong fingers and smooth black hair, and eyes that stared at other people's eyes as if to imply shrewdness. He had a gaunt face and on it a well-kept though not extensive moustache. Shortly after their marriage he had abandoned his career in the army because, he said, he could see no future in it. Mrs Digby-Hunter was surprised but assumed that what was apparent to her husband was not apparent to her. She smiled and did not argue.

After the army her husband became involved with a firm that manufactured a new type of all-purpose, metal step-ladder. He explained to her the mechanism of this article, but it was complicated and she failed to understand: she smiled and nodded, murmuring that the ladder was indeed an ingenious one. Her husband, briskly businesslike in a herring-bone suit, became a director of the step-ladder company on the day before the company ran into financial difficulties and was obliged to cease all production.

'Your father could help,' he murmured, having imparted to her the unfortunate news, but her father, when invited to save the step-ladder firm, closed his eyes in boredom.

'I'm sorry,' she said, rather miserably, feeling she had failed to come up to scratch as a wife. He said it didn't matter, and a few days later he told her he'd become a vending-machine operator. He would have an area, he said, in which he would daily visit schools and swimming-pools, launderettes, factories, offices, wherever the company's vending-machines were sited. He would examine the machines to see that they were in good trim and would fill them full of powdered coffee and powdered milk and a form of tea, and minerals and biscuits and chocolate. She thought the work odd for an ex-army officer, but she did not say so. Instead, she listened while he told her that there was an expanding market for vending-machines, and that in the end they would make a considerable amount of money. His voice went on, quoting percentages and conversion rates. She was knitting him a blue pullover at the time. He held his arms up while she fitted it about his chest; she nodded while he spoke.

Then her father died and left her a sum of money.

'We could buy a country house,' her husband said, 'and open it up as a smart little hotel.' She agreed that that would be nice. She felt that perhaps neither of them was qualified to run an hotel, but it didn't seem worth making a fuss about that, especially since her husband had, without qualifications, joined a step-ladder firm and then, equally unskilled, had gone into the vending-machine business. In fact, their abilities as hoteliers were never put to the test because all of a sudden her husband had a better idea. Idling one evening in a saloon bar, he dropped into conversation with a man who was in a state of depression because his son appeared to be a dunce.

'If I was starting again,' said the man, 'I'd go into the cramming business. My God, you could coin it.' The man talked on, speaking of parents like himself who couldn't hold their heads up because their children's poor performances in the Common Entrance examination deprived them of an association with one of the great public schools of England. The next day Mrs Digby-Hunter's husband scrutinized bound volumes of the Common Entrance examination papers.

'A small boarding-school,' he later said to her, 'for temporarily backward boys; we might do quite nicely.' Mrs Digby-Hunter, who did not immediately take to the notion of being surrounded day and night by temporarily backward boys, said that the idea sounded an interesting one. 'There's a place for sale in Gloucestershire,' her husband said.

The school, begun as a small one, remained so because, as her husband explained, any school of this nature must be small. The turnover in boys was rapid, and it soon became part of the educational policy of Milton Grange to accept not more than twenty boys at any one time, the wisdom of which was reflected in results that parents and headmasters agreed were remarkable: the sons who had idled at the back of their preparatory school classrooms passed into the great public schools of England, and their parents paid the high fees of Milton Grange most gratefully.

At Milton Grange, part ivy-clad, turreted and baronial, Mrs Digby-Hunter was happy. She did not understand the ins and outs of the Common Entrance examination, for her province was the kitchen and the dormitories, but certainly life at Milton Grange as the headmaster's wife was much more like it than occupying half the ground floor of a semi-detached villa in Croydon, as the wife of a vending-machine operator.

'Christ, what a time we're having with that boy for Harrow,' her husband would say, and she would make a sighing noise to match the annoyance he felt, and smile to cheer him up. It was extraordinary what he had achieved with the dullards he took on, and she now and again wondered if one day he might even receive a small recognition, an OBE maybe. As for her, Milton Grange was recognition enough: an apt reward, she felt, for her marital agreeableness, for not being a nuisance, and coming up to scratch as a wife.

Just occasionally Mrs Digby-Hunter wondered what life would have been like if she'd married someone else. She wondered what it would have been like to have had children of her own and to have engaged in the activity that caused, eventually, children to be born. She imagined, once a year or so, as she lay alone in her room in the darkness, what it would be like to share a double bed night after night. She imagined a faceless man, a pale naked body beside hers, hands caressing her flesh. She imagined, occasionally, being married to a clergyman she'd known as a girl, a man who had once embraced her with intense passion, suddenly, after a dance in a church hall. She had experienced the pressure of his body against hers and she could recall still the smell of his clothes and the dampness of his mouth.

But Milton Grange was where she belonged now: she had chosen a man and married him and had ended up, for better or worse, in a turreted house in Gloucestershire. There was give and take in marriage, as always she had known, and where she was concerned there was everything to be thankful for. Once a year, on the last Saturday in July, the gardens of the school were given over to a Conservative fête, and more regularly she and her husband drove to other country houses, for dinner or cocktails. A local Boy Scout group once asked her to present trophies on a sports day because she was her husband's wife and he was well regarded. She had enjoyed the occasion and had bought new clothes specially for it.

In winter she put down bulbs, and in spring she watched the birds collecting twigs and straw for nests. She loved the gardens and often repeated to the maids in the kitchen that one was 'nearer God's Heart in a garden than anywhere else on earth'. It was a beautiful sentiment, she said, and very true.

On that June afternoon, while Mrs Digby-Hunter dropped into a doze beneath the beech trees and Sergeant Wall removed the weeds from a herbaceous border, the bearded Mr Beade walked between two rows of desks in a bare attic room. Six boys bent over the desks, writing speedily. In the room next door six other boys wrote also. They would not be idling, Mr Beade knew, any more than the boys in the room across the corridor would be idling.

'*Amavero*, *amaveris*, *amaverit*,' he said softly, his haired lips close to the ear of a boy called Timpson. '*Amaverimus*, Timpson, *amaveritis*, *amaverint*.' A thumb and forefinger of Mr Beade's seized and turned the flesh on the back of Timpson's left hand. '*Amaveritis*,' he said again, '*amaverint*.' While the flesh was twisted this way and that and while Timpson moaned in the quiet manner that Mr Beade preferred, Dympna and Barbara surveyed the sleeping form of Mrs Digby-Hunter in the garden. They had not washed themselves. They stood in the bedroom they shared, gazing through an open, diamond-paned window, smoking two Embassy tipped cigarettes. 'White fat slug,' said Barbara. 'Look at her.'

They looked a moment longer. Sergeant Wall in the far distance pushed himself from his knees on to his feet. 'He's coming in for his tea,' said Barbara. She held cigarette smoke in her mouth and then released it in short puffs. 'She can't think,' said Dympna. 'She's incapable of mental activity.' 'She's a dead white slug,' said Barbara.

They cupped their cigarettes in their hands for the journey down the back stairs to the kitchen. They both were thinking that the kettle would be boiling on the Aga: it would be pleasant to sit in the cool, big kitchen drinking tea with old Sergeant Wall, who gossiped about the village he lived in. It was Dympna's turn to make his sandwich, turkey paste left over from yesterday, the easy-to-spread margarine that Mrs Digby-Hunter said was better for you than butter. 'Dead white slug,' repeated Barbara, laughing on the stairs. 'Was she human once?'

Sergeant Wall passed by the sleeping Mrs Digby-Hunter and heard, just perceptibly, a soft snoring coming from her partially open mouth. She was tired, he thought; heat made women tired, he'd often heard. He removed his hat and wiped an accumulation of sweat from the crown of his head. He moved towards the house for his tea.

In his study Digby-Hunter sat with one boy, Marshalsea, listening while Marshalsea repeated recently acquired information about triangles.

'Then DEF,' said Marshalsea, 'must be equal in all respects to –'

'Why?' inquired Digby-Hunter.

His voice was dry and slightly high. His bony hands, on the desk between himself and Marshalsea, had minute fingernails.

'Because DEF –'

'Because the triangle DEF, Marshalsea.'

'Because the triangle DEF –'

'Yes, Marshalsea?'

'Because the triangle DEF has the two angles at the base and two sides equal to the two angles at the base and two sides of the triangle ABC –'

'You're talking bloody nonsense,' said Digby-Hunter quietly. 'Think about it, boy.'

He rose from his position behind his desk and crossed the room to the window. He moved quietly, a man with a slight stoop because of his height, a man who went well with the room he occupied, with shelves of textbooks, and an empty mantelpiece, and bare, pale walls. It was simple sense, as he often pointed out to parents, that in rooms where teaching took place there should be no diversions for the roving eyes of students.

Glancing from the window, Digby-Hunter observed his wife in her deck-chair beneath the beeches. He reflected that in their seventeen years at Milton Grange she had become expert at making shepherd's pie. Her bridge, on the other hand, had not improved and she still made tiresome remarks to parents. Once, briefly, he had loved her, a love that had begun to die in a bedroom in a Welsh hotel, on the night of their wedding-day. Her nakedness, which he had daily imagined in lush anticipation, had strangely repelled him. 'I'm sorry,' he'd murmured, and had slipped into the other twin bed, knowing then that this side of marriage was something he was not going to be able to manage. She had not said anything, and between them the matter had never been mentioned again.

It was extraordinary, he thought now, watching her in the garden, that she should lie in a deck-chair like that, unfastidiously asleep. Once at a dinner-party she had described a dream she'd had, and afterwards, in the car on the way back to Milton Grange, he'd had to tell her that no one had been interested in her dream. People had quietly sighed, he'd had to say, because that was the truth.

There was a knock on the door and Digby-Hunter moved from the window and called out peremptorily. A youth with spectacles and long, uncared-for hair entered the sombre room. He was thin, with a slight, thin mouth and a fragile nose; his eyes, magnified behind the tortoiseshell-rimmed discs, were palely nondescript, the colour of water in which vegetables have been boiled. His lengthy hair was lustreless.

'Wraggett,' said Digby-Hunter at once, as though challenging the youth to disclaim this title.

'Sir,' replied Wraggett.

'Why are you moving your head about like that?' Digby-Hunter demanded.

He turned to the other boy. 'Well?' he said.

'If the two angles at the base of DEF,' said Marshalsea, 'are equal to the two angles at the base of –'

'Open the book,' said Digby-Hunter. 'Learn it.'

He left the window and returned to his desk. He sat down. 'What d'you want, Wraggett?' he said.

'I think I'd better go to bed, sir.'

'Bed? What's the matter with you?'

'There's a pain in my neck, sir. At the back, sir. I can't seem to see properly.'

Digby-Hunter regarded Wraggett with irritation and dislike. He made a noise with his lips. He stared at Wraggett. He said:

'So you have lost your sight, Wraggett?'

'No, sir.'

'Why the damn hell are you bellyaching, then?'

'I keep seeing double, sir. I feel a bit sick, sir.'

'Are you malingering, Wraggett?'

'No, sir.'

'Then why are you saying you can't see?'

'Sir –'

'If you're not malingering, get on with the work you've been set, boy. The French verb to drink, the future conditional tense?'

'*Je boive* –'

'You're a cretin,' shouted Digby-Hunter. 'Get out of here at once.'

'I've a pain, sir –'

'Take your pain out with you, for God's sake. Get down to some honest work, Wraggett. Marshalsea?'

'If the two angles at the base of DEF,' said Marshalsea, 'are equal to the two angles at the base of ABC it means that the sides opposite the angles –'

His voice ceased abruptly. He closed his eyes. He felt the small fingers of Digby-Hunter briefly on his scalp before they grasped a clump of hair.

'Open your eyes,' said Digby-Hunter.

Marshalsea did so and saw pleasure in Digby-Hunter's face.

'You haven't listened,' said Digby-Hunter. His left hand pulled the hair, causing the boy to rise from his seat. His right hand moved slowly and then suddenly shot out, completing its journey, striking at Marshalsea's jaw-bone. Digby-Hunter always used the side of his hand, Mr Beade the ball of the thumb.

'Take two triangles, ABC and DEF,' said Digby-Hunter. Again the edge of his right hand struck Marshalsea's face and then, clenched into a fist, the hand struck repeatedly at Marshalsea's stomach.

'Take two triangles,' whispered Marshalsea, 'ABC and DEF.'

'In which the angle ABC equals the angle DEF.'

'In which the angle ABC equals the angle DEF.'

In her sleep Mrs Digby-Hunter heard a voice. She opened her eyes and saw a figure that might have been part of a dream. She closed her eyes again.

'Mrs Digby-Hunter.'

A boy whose name escaped her stood looking down at her. There were so many boys coming and going for a term or two, then passing on: this one was thin and tall, with spectacles. He had an unhealthy look, she thought, and then she remembered his mother, who had an unhealthy look also, a Mrs Wraggett.

'Mrs Digby-Hunter, I have a pain at the back of my neck.'

She blinked, looking at the boy. They'd do anything, her husband often said, in order to escape their studies, and although she sometimes felt sorry for them she quite understood that their studies must be completed since that was reason for their presence at Milton Grange. Still, the amount of work they had to do and their excessively long hours, half past eight until seven at night, caused her just occasionally to consider that she herself had been lucky to escape such pressures in her childhood. Every afternoon, immediately after lunch, all the boys set out with Mr Beade for a brisk walk, which was meant to be, in her husband's parlance, twenty minutes of freshening up. There was naturally no time for games.

'Mrs Digby-Hunter.'

The boy's head was moving about in an eccentric manner. She tried to remember if she had noticed it doing that before, and decided she hadn't. She'd have certainly noticed, for the movement made her dizzy. She reached beneath the deck-chair for the box of All Gold. She smiled at the boy. She said:

'Would you like a chocolate, Wraggett?'

'I feel sick, Mrs Digby-Hunter. I keep seeing double. I can't seem to keep my head steady.'

'You'd better tell the headmaster, old chap.'

He wasn't a boy she'd ever cared for, any more than she'd ever cared for his mother. She smiled at him again, trying to make up for being unable to like either himself or his mother. Again she pushed the box of chocolates at him, nudging a coconut caramel out of its rectangular bed. She always left the coconut caramels and the blackcurrant boats: the boy was more than welcome to them.

'I've told the headmaster, Mrs Digby-Hunter.'

'Have you been studying too hard?'

'No, Mrs Digby-Hunter.'

She withdrew her offer of chocolates, wondering how long he'd stand there waggling his head in the sunshine. He'd get into trouble if the loitering went on too long. She could say that she'd made him remain with her in order to hear further details about his pain, but there was naturally a limit to the amount of time he could hope to waste. She said:

'I think, you know, you should buzz along now, Wraggett –'

'Mrs Digby-Hunter –'

'There's a rule, you know: the headmaster must be informed when a boy is feeling under the weather. The headmaster comes to his own conclusions about who's malingering and who's not. When I was in charge of that side of things, Wraggett, the boys used to pull the wool over my eyes like nobody's business. Well, I didn't blame them, I'd have done the same myself. But the headmaster took another point of view. With a school like Milton Grange, every single second has a value of its own. Naturally, time can't be wasted.'

'They pull the hair out of your head,' Wraggett cried, his voice suddenly shrill. 'They hit you in a special way, so that it doesn't bruise you. They drive their fists into your stomach.'

'I think you should return to your classroom –'

'They enjoy it,' shouted Wraggett.

'Go along now, old chap.'

'Your husband half murdered me, Mrs Digby-Hunter.'

'Now that simply isn't true, Wraggett.'

'Mr Beade hit Mitchell in the groin. With a ruler. He poked the end of the ruler –'

'Be quiet, Wraggett.'

'Mrs Digby-Hunter –'

'Go along now, Wraggett.' She spoke for the first time sharply, but when the boy began to move she changed her mind about her command and called him back. He and all the other boys, she explained with less sharpness in her voice, were at Milton Grange for a purpose. They came because they had idled at their preparatory schools, playing noughts and crosses in the back row of a classroom, giggling and disturbing everyone. They came to Milton Grange so that, after the skilled teaching of the headmaster and

Mr Beade, they might succeed at an examination that would lead them to one of England's great public schools. Corporal punishment was part of the curriculum at Milton Grange, and all parents were apprised of that fact. If boys continued to idle as they had idled in the past they would suffer corporal punishment so that, beneath its influence, they might reconsider their behaviour. 'You understand, Wraggett?' said Mrs Digby-Hunter in the end.

Wraggett went away, and Mrs Digby-Hunter felt pleased. The little speech she had made to him was one she had heard her husband making on other occasions. 'We rap the occasional knuckle,' he said to prospective parents. 'Quite simply, we stand no nonsense.'

She was glad that it had come so easily to her to quote her husband, once again to come up to scratch as a wife. Boys who were malingering must naturally receive the occasional rap on the knuckles and her husband, over seventeen years, had proved that his ways were best. She remembered one time a woman coming and taking her son away on the grounds that the pace was too strenuous for him. As it happened, she had opened the door in answer to the woman's summons and had heard the woman say she'd had a letter from her son and thought it better that he should be taken away. It turned out that the child had written hysterically. He had said that Milton Grange was run by lunatics and criminals. Mrs Digby-Hunter, hearing that, had smiled and had quietly inquired if she herself resembled either a lunatic or a criminal. The woman shook her head, but the boy, who had been placed in Milton Grange so that he might pass on to the King's School in Canterbury, was taken away. 'To stagnate', her husband had predicted and she, knitting another pullover for him, had without much difficulty agreed.

Mrs Digby-Hunter selected a raspberry-and-honey cream. She returned the chocolate-box to the grass beneath her deck-chair and closed her eyes.

'What's the matter, son?' inquired Sergeant Wall on his way back to his weeding.

Wraggett said he had a pain at the back of his neck. He couldn't keep his head still, he said; he kept seeing double; he felt sick in the stomach. 'God almighty,' said Sergeant Wall. He led the boy back to the kitchen, which was the only interior part of Milton Grange that he knew. 'Here,' he said to the two maids, who were still sitting at the kitchen table, drinking tea. 'Here,' said Sergeant Wall, 'have a look at this.'

Wraggett sat down and took off his spectacles. As though seeking to control its wobbling motion, he attempted to shake his head, but the effort, so Barbara and Dympna afterwards said, appeared to be too much for him. His shoulders slipped forward, the side of his face struck the scrubbed surface of the kitchen table, and when the three of them settled him back on his chair in order to give him water in a cup they discovered that he was dead.

When Mrs Digby-Hunter entered the kitchen half an hour later she blinked her eyes several times because the glaring sunshine had affected them. 'Prick the sausages,' she automatically commanded, for today being a Tuesday it would be sausages for tea, a fact of which both Barbara and Dympna would, as always, have to be reminded. She was then aware that something was the matter.

She blinked again. The kitchen contained people other than Barbara and Dympna. Mr Beade, a man who rarely addressed her, was standing by the Aga. Sergeant Wall was endeavouring to comfort Barbara, who was noisily weeping.

'What's the matter, Barbara?' inquired Mrs Digby-Hunter, and she noticed as she spoke that Mr Beade turned more of his back to her. There was a smell of tobacco smoke in the air: Dympna, to Mrs Digby-Hunter's astonishment, was smoking a cigarette.

'There's been a tragedy, Mrs Digby-Hunter,' said Sergeant Wall. 'Young Wraggett.'

'What's the matter with Wraggett?'

'He's dead,' said Dympna. She released smoke through her nose, staring hard at Mrs Digby-Hunter. Barbara, who had looked up on hearing Mrs Digby-Hunter's voice, sobbed more quietly, gazing also, through tears, at Mrs Digby-Hunter.

'Dead?' As she spoke, her husband entered the kitchen. He addressed Mr Beade, who turned to face him. He said he had put the body of Wraggett on a bed in a bedroom that was never used. There was no doubt about it, he said, the boy was dead.

'Dead?' said Mrs Digby-Hunter again. '*Dead?*'

Mr Beade was mumbling by the Aga, asking her husband where Wraggett's parents lived. Barbara was wiping the tears from her face with a handkerchief. Beside her, Sergeant Wall, upright and serious, stood like a statue. 'In Worcestershire,' Mrs Digby-Hunter's husband said. 'A village called Pine.' She was aware that the two maids were still looking at her. She wanted to tell Dympna to stop smoking at once, but the words wouldn't come from her. She was asleep in the garden, she thought: Wraggett had come and stood by her chair, she had offered him a chocolate, now she was dreaming that he was dead, it was all ridiculous. Her husband's voice was quiet, still talking about the village called Pine and about Wraggett's mother and father.

Mr Beade asked a question that she couldn't hear: her husband replied that he didn't think they were that kind of people. He had sent for the school doctor, he told Mr Beade, since the cause of death had naturally to be ascertained as soon as possible.

'A heart attack,' said Mr Beade.

'Dead?' said Mrs Digby-Hunter for the fourth time.

Dympna held towards Barbara her packet of cigarettes. Barbara accepted one, and the eyes of the two girls ceased their observation of Mrs Digby-Hunter's face. Dympna struck a match. Wraggett had been all right earlier, Mr Beade said. Her husband's lips were pursed in a way that was familiar to her; there was anxiety in his eyes.

The kitchen was flagged, large grey flags that made it cool in summer and which sometimes sweated in damp weather. The boys' crockery, of hardened primrose-coloured plastic, was piled on a dresser and on a side table. Through huge, barred windows Mrs Digby-Hunter could see shrubs and a brick wall and an expanse of gravel. Everything was familiar and yet seemed not to be. 'So sudden,' her husband said. 'So wretchedly out of the blue.' He added that after the doctor had given the cause of death he himself would motor over to the village in Worcestershire and break the awful news to the parents.

She moved, and felt again the eyes of the maids following her. She would sack them, she thought, when all this was over. She filled a kettle at the sink, running water into it from the hot tap. Mr Beade remained where he was standing when she approached the Aga, appearing to be unaware that he was in her way. Her husband moved. She wanted to say that soon, at least, there'd be a cup of tea, but again the words failed to come from her. She heard Sergeant Wall asking her husband if there was anything he could do, and then her husband's voice said that he'd like Sergeant Wall to remain in the house until the doctor arrived so that he could repeat to the doctor what Wraggett had said about suddenly feeling unwell. Mr Beade spoke again, muttering to her husband that Wraggett in any case would never have passed into Lancing. 'I shouldn't mention that,' her husband said.

She sat down to wait for the kettle to boil, and Sergeant Wall and the girls sat down also, on chairs near to where they were standing, between the two windows. Her husband spoke in a low voice to Mr Beade, instructing him, it seemed: she couldn't hear the words he spoke. And then, without warning, Barbara cried out loudly. She threw her burning cigarette on the floor and jumped up from her chair. Tears were on her face, her teeth were widely revealed, though not in a smile. 'You're a fat white slug,' she shouted at Mrs Digby-Hunter.

Sergeant Wall attempted to quieten the girl, but her fingernails scratched at his face and her fingers gripped and tore at the beard of Mr Beade, who had come to Sergeant Wall's aid. Dympna did not move from her chair. She was looking at Mrs Digby-Hunter, smoking quietly, as though nothing at all was happening.

'It'll be in the newspapers,' shouted Barbara.

She was taken from the kitchen, and the Digby-Hunters could hear her sobbing in the passage and on the back stairs. 'She'll sell the story,' said Dympna.

Digby-Hunter looked at her. He attempted to smile at her, to suggest by his smile that he had a fondness for her. 'What story?' he said.

'The way the boys are beaten up.'

'Now look here, Dympna, you know nothing whatsoever about it. The boys at Milton Grange are here for a special purpose. They undergo special education – '

'You killed one, Mr Digby-Hunter.' Still puffing at her cigarette, Dympna left the kitchen, and Mrs Digby-Hunter spoke.

'My God,' she said.

'They're upset by death,' said her husband tetchily. 'Naturally enough. They'll both calm down.'

But Mr Beade, hearing those remarks as he returned to the kitchen, said that it was the end of Milton Grange. The girls would definitely pass on their falsehoods to a newspaper. They were telling Sergeant Wall now, he said. They were reminding him of lies they had apparently told him before, and of which he had taken no notice.

'What in the name of heaven,' Digby-Hunter angrily asked his wife, 'did you have to go engaging creatures like that for?'

They hated her, she thought: two girls who day by day had worked beside her in the kitchen, to whom she had taught useful skills. A boy had come and stood beside her in the sunshine and she had offered him a chocolate. He had complained of a pain, and she had pointed out that he must make his complaint to the headmaster, since that was the rule. She had explained as well that corporal punishment was part of the curriculum at Milton Grange. The boy was dead. The girls who hated her would drag her husband's boarding-school through the mud.

She heard the voice of Sergeant Wall saying that the girls, one of them hysterical but calming down, the other insolent, were out to make trouble. He'd tried to reason with them, but they hadn't even listened.

The girls had been in Milton Grange for two and a half months. She remembered the day they had arrived together, carrying cardboard suitcases. They'd come before that to be interviewed, and she'd walked them round the house, explaining about the school. She remembered saying in passing that once a year, at the end of every July, a Conservative fête was held, traditionally now, in the gardens. They hadn't seemed much interested.

'I've built this place up,' she heard her husband say. 'Month by month, year by year. It was a chicken farm when I bought it, Beade, and now I suppose it'll be a chicken farm again.'

She left the kitchen and walked along the kitchen passage and up the uncarpeted back stairs. She knocked on the door of their room. They called out together, saying she should come in. They were both packing their belongings into their cardboard suitcases, smoking fresh cigarettes. Barbara appeared to have recovered.

She tried to explain to them. No one knew yet, she said, why Wraggett had died. He'd had a heart attack most probably, like Mr Beade said. It was a terrible thing to have happened.

The girls continued to pack, not listening to her. They folded garments or pressed them, unfolded, into their suitcases.

'My husband's built the place up. Month by month, year by year, for seventeen years he has built it up.'

'The boys are waiting for their tea,' said Dympna. 'Mrs Digby-Hunter, you'd better prick the sausages.'

'Forget our wages,' said Barbara, and laughed in a way that was not hysterical.

'My husband –'

'Your husband,' said Dympna, 'derives sexual pleasure from inflicting pain on children. So does Beade. They are queer men.'

'Your husband,' said Barbara, 'will be jailed. He'll go to prison with a sack over his head so that he won't have to see the disgust on people's faces. Isn't that true, Mrs Digby-Hunter?'

'My husband –'

'Filth,' said Dympna.

She sat down on the edge of a bed and watched the two girls packing. She imagined the dead body in the bedroom that was never used, and then she imagined Sergeant Wall and Mr Beade and her husband in the kitchen, waiting for the school doctor to arrive, knowing that it didn't much matter what cause he offered for the death if these two girls were allowed to have their way.

'Why do you hate me?' she asked, quite calmly.

Neither replied. They went on packing and while they packed she talked, in desperation. She tried to speak the truth about Milton Grange, as she saw the truth, but they kept interrupting her. The bruises didn't show on the boys because the bruises were inflicted in an expert way, but sometimes hair was actually pulled out of the boys' scalps, small bunches of hair, she must have noticed that. She had noticed no such thing. 'Corporal punishment,' she began to say, but Barbara held out hairs that had been wrenched from the head of a boy called Bridle. She had found them in a wastepaper basket; Bridle had said they were his and had shown her the place they'd come from. She returned the hairs to a plastic bag that once had contained stockings. The hairs would be photographed, Barbara said; they would appear on the front page of a Sunday newspaper. They'd be side by side with the ex-headmaster, his head hidden beneath a sack, and Mr Beade skulking behind his beard. Milton Grange, turreted baronial, part ivy-clad, would be examined by Sunday readers as a torture chamber. And in the garden, beneath the beech trees, a man would photograph the deck-chair where a woman had slept while violence and death occurred. She and her husband might one day appear in a waxworks, and Mr Beade, too; a man who, like her husband, derived sexual pleasure from inflicting pain on children.

'You are doing this for profit,' she protested, trying to smile, to win them from the error of their ways.

'Yes,' they said together, and then confessed, sharing the conversation, that they had often considered telephoning a Sunday newspaper to say they had a story to tell. They had kept the hairs in the plastic bag because they'd had that in mind; in every detail they knew what they were going to say.

'You're making money out of –'

'Yes,' said Dympna. 'You've kept us short, Mrs Digby-Hunter.'

She saw their hatred of her in their faces and heard it in both their voices; like a vapour, it hung about the room.

'Why do you hate me?' she asked again.

They laughed, not answering, as though an answer wasn't necessary.

She remembered, although just now she didn't wish to, the clergyman who had kissed her with passion after a dance in a church hall, the dampness of his lips, his body pressed into hers. The smell of his clothes came back to her, across thirty years, seeming familiar because it had come before. She might have borne his children in some rectory somewhere. Would they have hated her then?

Underclothes, dresses, lipsticks, Woolworth's jewellery, unframed photographs of male singing stars were jumbled together in the two cardboard suitcases. The girls moved about the room, picking up their belongings, while Mrs Digby-Hunter, in greater misery than she had ever before experienced, watched them from the edge of the bed. How could human creatures be so cruel? How could they speak to her about being a figure in a waxworks tableau when she had done nothing at all? How could they so callously propose to tell lies to a newspaper about her husband and Mr Beade when the boy who had so tragically died was still warm with the memory of life?

She watched them, two girls so young that they were not yet fully developed. They had talked about her. In this room, night after night, they had wondered about her, and in the end had hated her. Had they said in their nightly gossiping that since the day of her marriage she had lived like a statue with another statue?

It was all her fault, she suddenly thought: Milton Grange would be a chicken farm again, her husband would be examined by a psychiatrist in a prison, she would live in a single room. It was all her fault. In twenty-nine years it had taken violence and death to make sense of facts that were as terrible.

The girls were saying they'd catch a bus on the main road. Without looking at her or addressing her again they left the bedroom they had shared. She heard their footsteps on the back stairs, and Dympna's voice asking Barbara if she was all right now and Barbara saying she was. A white slug, the girl had called her, a fat white slug.

She did not leave the room. She remained sitting on the edge of the bed, unable to think. Her husband's face appeared in her mind, with its well-kept moustache and shrewd-seeming dark eyes, a face in the bedroom of a Welsh hotel on the night of her wedding-day. She saw herself weeping, as she had not wept then. In a confused way she saw herself on that occasion and on others, protesting, shaking her head, not smiling.

'I'm leaving the army for a step-ladder firm,' he said to her, and she struck his face with her hands, tormented by the absurdity of what he said. She cried out in anger that she had married an army officer, not a step-ladder salesman who was after her father's money. She wept again when ridiculously he told her that he intended to spend his days filling machines full of powdered coffee. He had failed her, she shrilled at him, that night in the Welsh hotel and he had failed her ever since. In front of boys, she accused him of ill-treating those who had been placed in his care. If ever it happened again, she threatened, the police would be sent for. She turned to the boys and ordered them to run about the gardens for a while. It was ludicrous that they should be cooped up while the sun shone, it was ludicrous that they should strive so painfully simply to pass an examination into some school or other. She banged a desk with her hand after the boys had gone, she spat out words at him: they'd all be in the Sunday papers, she said, if he wasn't careful, and she added that she herself would leave Milton Grange for ever unless he pursued a gentler course with the boys who were sent to him, unless he at once dismissed the ill-mannered Mr Beade, who was clearly a sinister man.

In the room that had been the maids' room Mrs Digby-Hunter wept as her mind went back through the years of her marriage and then, still weeping, she left the room and descended the back stairs to the kitchen. To her husband she said that it was all her fault; she said she was sorry. She had knitted and put down bulbs, she said, and in the end a boy had died. Two girls had hated her because in her easy-going way she had held her peace, not wanting to know. Loyalty and devotion, said Mrs Digby-Hunter, and now a boy was dead, and her husband with a sack over his head would be taken from Milton Grange and later would have sessions with a prison psychiatrist. It was all her fault. She would say so to the reporters when they came. She would explain and take the blame, she would come up to scratch as a wife.

Her husband and Sergeant Wall and Mr Beade looked at Mrs Digby-Hunter. She stood in the centre of the kitchen, one hand on the table, a stout woman in a blue-and-pink dress, weeping. The tragedy had temporarily unhinged her, Sergeant Wall thought, and Mr Beade in irritation thought that if she could see herself she'd go somewhere else, and her husband thought that it was typical of her to be tiresomely stupid at a time like this.

She went on talking: you couldn't blame them for hating her, she said, for she might have prevented death and hadn't bothered herself. In a bedroom in Wales she should have wept, she said, or packed a suitcase and gone away. Her voice continued in the kitchen, the words pouring from it, repetitiously and in a hurry. The three men sighed and looked away, all of them thinking the same thing now, that she made no sense at all, with her talk about putting down bulbs and coming up to scratch.

Cocktails at Doney's

'You've forgotten me,' were the first words Mrs Faraday spoke to him in the Albergo San Lorenzo. She was a tall, black-haired woman, wearing a rust-red suede coat cut in an Italian style. She smiled. She had white, even teeth, and the shade of her lipstick appeared subtly to match the colour of her coat. Her accent was American, her voice soft, with a trace of huskiness. She was thirty-five, perhaps thirty-seven, certainly not older. 'We met a long time ago,' she said, smiling a little more. 'I don't know why I never forget a face.'

She was married to a man who managed a business in some town in America he'd never heard of. She was a beautiful woman, but he could remember neither her nor her husband. Her name meant nothing to him and when she prompted him with the information about her husband's business he could not remember any better. Her eyes were brown, dominating her classic features.

'Of course,' he lied politely.

She laughed, clearly guessing it was a lie. 'Well, anyway,' she said, 'hullo to you.'

It was after dinner, almost ten o'clock. They had a drink in the bar since it seemed the natural thing to do. She had to do with fashion; she was in Florence for the Pitti Donna; she always came in February.

'It's nice to see you again. The people at these trade shows can be tacky.'

'Don't you go to the museums as well? The churches?'

'Of course.'

When he asked if her husband accompanied her on her excursions to Florence she explained that the museums, the churches, and the Pitti Donna would tire her husband immensely. He was not a man for Europe, preferring local race-tracks.

'And your wife? Is she here with you?'

'I'm actually not married.'

He wished he had not met Mrs Faraday. He didn't care for being approached in this manner, and her condemnation of the people at the trade exhibitions she spoke of seemed out of place since they were, after all, the people of her business world. And that she was married to a man who preferred race-tracks to culture was hardly of interest to a stranger.

Before their conversation ended he was certain they had not ever met before.

'I have to say good-night,' he said, rising when she finished her drink. 'I tend to get up early.'

'Why, so do I!'

'Good-night, Mrs Faraday.'

In his bedroom he sat on the edge of his bed, thinking about nothing in particular. Then he undressed and brushed his teeth. He examined his face in the slightly tarnished looking-glass above the wash-basin. He was fifty-seven, but according to this reflection older. His face would seem younger if he put on a bit of weight; chubbiness could be made to cover a multitude of sins. But he didn't want that; he liked being thought of as beyond things.

He turned the looking-glass light out and got into bed. He read *Our Mutual Friend* and then lay for a moment in the darkness. He thought of Daphne and of Lucy – dark-haired, tiny Lucy who had said at first it didn't matter, Daphne with her trusting eyes. He had blamed Daphne, not himself, and then had taken that back and asked to be forgiven; they were both of them to blame for the awful mistake of a marriage that should never have taken place, although later he had said that neither of them was, for how could they have guessed they were not suited in that way? It was with Lucy he had begun to know the truth; poor Lucy had suffered more.

He slept, and dreamed he was in Padua with a friend of another time, walking in the Botanical Gardens and explaining to his friend that the tourist guides he composed were short-lived in their usefulness because each reflected a city ephemerally caught. 'You're ashamed of your tourist guides,' his friend of that time interrupted, Jeremy it was. 'Why *are* the impotent so full of shame, my dear? Why *is* it?' Then Rosie was in the dream and Jeremy was laughing, playfully, saying he'd been most amusingly led up the garden path. 'He led me up it too, my God,' Rosie cried out furiously. 'All he could do was weep.'

Linger over the Giambologna birds in the Bargello, and the marble reliefs of Mino da Fiesole. But that's enough for one day; you must return tomorrow.

He liked to lay down the law. He liked to take chances with the facts, and wait for letters of contradiction. *At the height of the season there are twelve times as many strangers as natives in this dusty, littered city. Cascades of graffiti welcome them – the male sexual organ stylized to a Florentine simplicity, belligerent swastikas, hammers and sickles in the streets of gentle Fra Angelico . . .*

At lunchtime on the day after he had met her Mrs Faraday was in Doney's with some other Americans. Seeing her in that smart setting, he was surprised that she stayed in the Albergo San Lorenzo rather than the Savoy or the Excelsior. The San Lorenzo's grandeur all belonged to the past: the old hotel was threadbare now, its curtains creased, its telephones unresponsive. Not many Americans liked it.

'Hi!' she called across the restaurant, and smiled and waved a menu.

He nodded at her, not wishing to seem stand-offish. The people she was with were talking about the merchandise they had been inspecting at the Pitti Donna. Wisps of their conversation drifted from their table, references to profit margins and catching the imagination.

He ordered tagliatelle and the chef's salad, and then looked through the *Nazione*. The body of the missing schoolgirl, Gabriella, had been found in a park in Florence. Youths who'd been terrorizing the neighbourhood of Santa Croce had been identified and arrested. Two German girls, hitchhiking in the south, had been made drunk and raped in a village shed. The *Nazione* suggested that Gabriella – a quiet girl – had by chance been a witness to drug-trafficking in the park.

'I envy you your job,' Mrs Faraday said, pausing at his table as he was finishing his tagliatelle. Her companions had gone on ahead of her. She smiled, as at an old friend, and then sat down. 'I guess I want to lose those two.'

He offered her a glass of wine. She shook her head. 'I'd love another cappuccino.'

The coffee was ordered. He folded the newspaper and placed it on the empty chair beside him. Mrs Faraday, as though she intended to stay a while, had hung her red suede coat over the back of the chair.

'I envy you your job,' she said again. 'I'd love to travel all over.'

She was wearing pearls at her throat, above a black dress. Rings clustered her fingers, earrings made a jangling sound. Her nails were shaped and painted, her face as meticulously made up as it had been the night before.

'Did you mind,' she asked when the waiter had brought their coffee, 'my wondering if you were married?'

He said he hadn't minded.

'Marriage is no great shakes.'

She lit a cigarette. She had only ever been married to the man she was married to now. She had had one child, a daughter who had died after a week. She had not been able to have other children.

'I'm sorry,' he said.

She looked at him closely, cigarette smoke curling between them. The tip of her tongue picked a shred of tobacco from the corner of her mouth.

She said again that marriage was no great shakes. She added, as if to lend greater weight to this:

'I lay awake last night thinking I'd like this city to devour me.'

He did not comment, not knowing what she meant. But quite without wishing to he couldn't help thinking of this beautiful woman lying awake in her bedroom in the Albergo San Lorenzo. He imagined her staring into the darkness, the glow of her cigarette, the sound of her inhaling. She was looking for an affair, he supposed, and hoped she realized he wasn't the man for that.

'I wouldn't mind living the balance of my life here. I like it better every year.'

'Yes, it's a remarkable city.'

'There's a place called the Palazzo Ricasoli where you can hire apartments. I'd settle there.'

'I see.'

'I could tell you a secret about the Palazzo Ricasoli.'

'Mrs Faraday –'

'I spent a naughty week there once.'

He drank some coffee in order to avoid speaking. He sighed without making a sound.

'With a guy I met at the Pitti Donna. A countryman of yours. He came from somewhere called Horsham.'

'I've never been to Horsham.'

'Oh, my God, I'm embarrassing you!'

'No, not at all.'

'Gosh, I'm sorry! I really am! Please say it's all right.'

'I assure you, Mrs Faraday, I'm not easily shocked.'

'I'm an awful shady lady embarrassing a nice Englishman! Please say you forgive me.'

'There is absolutely nothing to forgive.'

'It was a flop, if you want to know.' She paused. 'Say, what do you plan to write in your guidebook about Florence?'

'Banalities mostly.'

'Oh, come *on*!'

He shrugged.

'I'll tell you a nicer kind of secret. You have the cleverest face I've seen in years!'

Still he did not respond. She stubbed her cigarette out and immediately lit another. She took a map out of her handbag and unfolded it. She said:

'Can you show me where Santo Spirito is?'

He pointed out the church and directed her to it, warning her against the motorists' signs which pursued a roundabout one-way route.

'You're very kind.' She smiled at him, lavishly exposing her dazzling, even teeth as if offering a reward for his help. 'You're a kind person,' she said. 'I can tell.'

He walked around the perimeter of the vast Cascine Park, past the funfair and the zoo and the race-track. It was pleasant in the February sunshine, the first green of spring colouring the twiggy hedges, birches delicate by the river. Lovers sprawled on the seats or in motor-cars, children carried balloons. Stalls sold meat and nuts, and Coca-Cola and 7-Up. Runners in training-suits jogged along the bicycle track. *Ho fame* a fat young man had scrawled on a piece of cardboard propped up in front of him, and slept while he waited for charity.

Rosie, when she'd been his friend, had said he wrote about Italian cities so that he could always be a stranger. Well, it was true, he thought in the Cascine Park, and in order to rid himself of a contemplation of his failed relationship with Rosie he allowed the beauty of Mrs Faraday again to invade his mind. Her beauty would have delighted him if her lipstick-stained cigarettes and her silly, repetitious chattering didn't endlessly disfigure it. Her husband was a good man, she had explained, but a good man was not always what a woman wanted. And it had come to seem all of a piece that her daughter had lived for only a week, and all of a piece also that no other children had been born, since her marriage was not worthy of children. It was the Annunciations in Santo Spirito she wanted to see, she had explained, because she loved Annunciations.

'Would it be wrong of me to invite you to dinner?' She rose from a sofa in the hall of the Albergo San Lorenzo as soon as she saw him, making no effort to disguise the fact that she'd been waiting for him. 'I'd really appreciate it if you'd accept.'

He wanted to reply that he would prefer to be left alone. He wanted to state firmly, once and for all, that he had never met her in the past, that she had no claims on him.

'You choose somewhere,' she commanded, with the arrogance of the beautiful.

In the restaurant she ate pasta without ceasing to talk, explaining to him that her boutique had been bought for her by her husband to keep her occupied and happy. It hadn't worked, she said, implying that although her fashion shop had kept her busy it hadn't brought her contentment. Her face, drained of all expression, was lovelier than he had so far seen it, so sad and fragile that it seemed not to belong to the voice that rattled on.

He looked away. The restaurant was decorated with modern paintings and was not completely full. A squat, elderly man sat on his own, conversing occasionally with waiters. A German couple spoke in whispers. Two men and a woman, talking rapidly in Italian, deplored the death of the schoolgirl, Gabriella.

'It must have been extraordinary for the Virgin Mary,' Mrs Faraday was saying. 'One moment she's reading a book and the next there's a figure with wings swooping in on her.' That only made sense, she suggested, when you thought of it as the Virgin's dream. The angel was not really there, the Virgin herself was not really reading in such plush surroundings. 'Later I guess she dreamed another angel came,' Mrs Faraday continued, 'to warn her of her death.'

He didn't listen. The waiter brought them grilled salmon and salad. Mrs Faraday lit a cigarette. She said:

'The guy I shacked up with in the Palazzo Ricasoli was no better than a gigolo. I guess I don't know why I did that.'

He did not reply. She stubbed her cigarette out, appearing at last to notice that food had been placed in front of her. She asked him about the painters of the Florentine Renaissance, and the city's aristocrats and patrons. She asked him why Savonarola had been burnt and he said Savonarola had made people feel afraid. She was silent for a moment, then leaned forward and put a hand on his arm.

'Tell me more about yourself. Please.'

Her voice, eagerly insistent, irritated him more than before. He told her superficial things, about the other Italian cities for which he'd written guidebooks, about the hill towns of Tuscany, and the Cinque Terre. Because of his reticence she said when he ceased to speak:

'I don't entirely make you out.' She added that he was nicer to talk to than anyone she could think of. She might be drunk; it was impossible to say.

'My husband's never heard of the Medicis nor any stuff like this. He's never even heard of Masaccio, you appreciate that?'

'Yes, you've made it clear the kind of man your husband is.'

'I've ruined it, haven't I, telling you about the Palazzo Ricasoli?'

'Ruined what, Mrs Faraday?'

'Oh, I don't know.'

They sat for some time longer, finishing the wine and having coffee. Once she reached across the table and put her hand on one of his. She repeated what she had said before, that he was kind.

'It's late,' he said.

'I know, honey, I know. And you get up early.'

He paid the bill, although she protested that it was she who had invited him. She would insist on their having dinner together again so that she might have her turn. She took his arm on the street.

'Will you come with me to Maiano one day?'

'Maiano?'

'It isn't far. They say it's lovely to walk at Maiano.'

'I'm really rather occupied, you know.'

'Oh, God, I'm bothering you! I'm being a nuisance! Forget Maiano. I'm sorry.'

'I'm just trying to say, Mrs Faraday, that I don't think I can be much use to you.'

He was aware, to his embarrassment, that she was holding his hand. Her arm was entwined with his and the palms of their hands had somehow come together. Her fingers, playing with his now, kept time with her flattery.

'You've got the politest voice I ever heard! Say you'll meet me just once again? Just once? Cocktails tomorrow? Please.'

'Look, Mrs Faraday –'

'Say Doney's at six. I'll promise to say nothing if you like. We'll listen to the music.'

Her palm was cool. A finger made a circular motion on one of his. Rosie had said he limped through life. In the end Jeremy had been sorry for him. Both of them were right; others had said worse. He was a crippled object of pity.

'Well, all right.'

She thanked him in the Albergo San Lorenzo for listening to her, and for the dinner and the wine. 'Every year I hope to meet someone nice in Florence,' she said on the landing outside her bedroom, seeming to mean it. 'This is the first time it has happened.'

She leaned forward and kissed him on the cheek, then closed her door. In his looking-glass he examined the faint smear of lipstick and didn't wipe it off. He woke in the night and lay there thinking about her, wondering if her lipstick was still on his cheek.

Waiting in Doney's, he ordered a glass of chilled Orvieto wine. Someone on a tape, not Judy Garland, sang 'Over the Rainbow'; later there was lightly played Strauss and some rhythms of the thirties. By seven o'clock Mrs Farady had not arrived. He left at a quarter to eight.

*

The next day he wandered through the cloisters of Santa Maria Novella, thinking again about the beauty of Mrs Faraday. He had received no message from her, no note to explain or apologize for her absence in Doney's. Had she simply forgotten? Or had someone better materialized? Some younger man she again hadn't been able to resist, some guy who didn't know any more about Masaccio than her good husband did? She was a woman who was always falling in love, which was what she called it, confusing love with sensuality. Was she, he wondered, what people referred to as a nymphomaniac? Was that what made her unhappy?

He imagined her with some man she'd picked up. He imagined her, satisfied because of the man's attentions, tramping the halls of a gift market, noting which shade of green was to be the new season's excitement. She would be different after her love-making, preoccupied with her business, no time for silliness and Annunciations. Yet it still was odd that she hadn't left a message for him. She had not for a moment seemed as rude as that, or incapable of making up an excuse.

He left the cloisters and walked slowly across the piazza of Santa Maria Novella. In spite of what she'd said and the compliments she'd paid, had she guessed that he hadn't listened properly to her, that he'd been fascinated by her appearance but not by her? Or had she simply guessed the truth about him?

That evening she was not in the bar of the hotel. He looked in at Doney's, thinking he might have misunderstood about the day. He waited for a while, and then ate alone in the restaurant with the modern paintings.

'We pack the clothes, *signore*. Is the carabinieri which can promote the inquiries for *la signora. Mi dispiace, signore.*'

He nodded at the heavily moustached receptionist and made his way to the bar. If she was with some lover she would have surfaced again by now: it was hard to believe that she would so messily leave a hotel bill unpaid, especially since sooner or later she would have to return for her clothes. When she had so dramatically spoken of wishing Florence to devour her she surely hadn't meant something like this? He went back to the receptionist.

'Did Mrs Faraday have her passport?'

'*Sì, signore. La signora* have the passport.'

He couldn't sleep that night. Her smile and her brown, languorous eyes invaded the blur he attempted to induce. She crossed and re-crossed her legs. She lifted another glass. Her ringed fingers stubbed another cigarette. Her earrings lightly jangled.

In the morning he asked again at the reception desk. The hotel bill wasn't important, a different receptionist generously allowed. If someone had to leave Italy in a hurry, because maybe there was sickness, even a deathbed, then a hotel bill might be overlooked for just a little while.

'*La signora* will post to us a cheque from the United States. This the carabinieri say.'

'Yes, I should imagine so.'

He looked up in the telephone directory the flats she had mentioned. The Palazzo Ricasoli was in Via Mantellate. He walked to it, up Borgo San Lorenzo and Via San Gallo. '*No*,' a porter in a glass kiosk said and directed him to the office. '*No*,' a pretty girl in the office said, shaking her head. She turned and asked another girl. '*No*,' this girl repeated.

He walked back through the city, to the American Consulate on the Lungarno Amerigo. He sat in the office of a tall, lean man called Humber, who listened with a detached air and then telephoned the police. After nearly twenty minutes he replaced the receiver. He was dressed entirely in brown – suit, shirt, tie, shoes, handkerchief. He was evenly tanned, another shade of the colour. He drawled when he spoke; he had an old-world manner.

'They suggest she's gone somewhere,' he said. 'On some kind of jaunt.' He paused in order to allow a flicker of amusement to develop in his lean features. 'They think maybe she ran up her hotel bill and skipped it.'

'She's a respectable proprietor of a fashion shop.'

'The carabinieri say the respectable are always surprising them.'

'Can you try to find out if she went back to the States? According to the hotel people, that was another theory of the carabinieri.'

Mr Humber shrugged. 'Since you have told your tale I must try, of course, sir. Would six-thirty be an agreeable hour for you to return?'

He sat outside in the Piazza della Repubblica, eating tortellini and listening to the conversations. A deranged man had gone berserk in a school in Rome, taking children as hostages and killing a janitor; the mayor of Rome had intervened and the madman had given himself up. It was a terrible thing to have happened, the Italians were saying, as bad as the murder of Gabriella.

He paid for his tortellini and went away. He climbed up to the Belvedere, filling in time. Once he thought he saw her, but it was someone else in the same kind of red coat.

'She's not back home,' Mr Humber said with his old-world lack of concern. 'You've started something, sir. Faraday's flying out.'

In a room in a police station he explained that Mrs Faraday had simply been a fellow-guest at the Albergo San Lorenzo. They had had dinner one evening, and Mrs Faraday had not appeared to be dispirited. She knew other people who had come from America, for the same trade exhibitions. He had seen her with them in a restaurant.

'These people, sir, return already to the United States. They answer the American police at this time.'

He was five hours in the room at the police station and the next day he was summoned there again and asked the same questions. On his way out on this occasion he noticed a man who he thought might be her husband, a big blond-haired man, too worried even to glance at him. He was certain he had never met him, or even seen him before, as he'd been certain he'd never met Mrs Faraday before she'd come up to him in the hotel.

The police did not again seek to question him. His passport, which they had held for fifty-six hours, was returned to him. By the end of that week the newspaper references to a missing American woman ceased. He did not see Mr Faraday again.

'The Italian view,' said Mr Humber almost a month later, 'is that she went off on a sexual excursion and found it so much to her liking that she stayed where she was.'

'I thought the Italian view was that she skipped the hotel. Or that someone had fallen ill.'

'They revised their thinking somewhat. In the light of various matters.'

'What matters?'

'From what you said, Mrs Faraday was a gallivanting lady. Our Italian friends find some significance in that.' Mr Humber silently drummed the surface of his desk. 'You don't agree, sir?'

He shook his head. 'There was more to Mrs Faraday than that,' he said.

'Well, of course there was. The carabinieri are educated men, but they don't go in for subtleties, you know.'

'She's not a vulgar woman. From what I said to the police they may imagine she is. Of course she's in a vulgar business. They may have jumped too easily to conclusions.'

Mr Humber said he did not understand. 'Vulgar?' he repeated.

'Like me, she deals in surface dross.'

'You're into fashion yourself, sir?'

'No, I'm not. I write tourist guides.'

'Well, that's most interesting.'

Mr Humber flicked at the surface of his desk with a forefinger. It was clear that he wished his visitor would go. He turned a sheet of paper over.

'I remind sightseers that pictures like Pietro Perugino's *Agony in the Garden* are worth a second glance. I send them to the Boboli Gardens. That kind of thing.'

Mr Humber's bland face twitched with simulated interest. Tourists were a nuisance to him. They lost their passports, they locked their ignition keys into their hired cars, they were stolen from and made a fuss. The city lived off them, but resented them as well. These thoughts were for a moment openly reflected in Mr Humber's pale brown eyes and then were gone. Flicking at his desk again, he said:

'I'm puzzled about one detail in all this. May I ask you, please?'

'Yes, of course.'

'Were you, you know, ah, seeing Mrs Faraday?'

'Was I having an affair, you mean? No, I wasn't.'

'She was a beautiful woman. By all accounts – by yours, I mean – sir, she'd been most friendly.'

'Yes, she was friendly.'

She was naïve for an American, and she was careless. She wasn't fearful of strangers and foolishly she let her riches show. Vulnerability was an enticement.

'I did not mean to pry, sir,' Mr Humber apologized. 'It's simply that Mr Faraday's detectives arrived a while ago and the more they can be told the better.'

'They haven't approached me.'

'No doubt they conclude you cannot help them. Mr Faraday himself has returned to the States: a ransom note would be more likely sent to him there.'

'So Mr Faraday doesn't believe his wife went off on a sexual excursion?'

'No one can ignore the facts, sir. There is indiscriminate kidnapping in Italy.'

'Italians would have known her husband was well-to-do?'

'I guess it's surprising what can be ferreted out.' Mr Humber examined the neat tips of his fingers. He rearranged tranquillity in his face. No matter how the facts he spoke of changed there was not going to be panic in the American Consulate. 'There has been no demand, sir, but we have to bear in mind that kidnap attempts do often nowadays go wrong. In Italy as elsewhere.'

'Does Mr Faraday think it has gone wrong?'

'Faraday is naturally confused. And, of course, troubled.'

'Of course.' He nodded to emphasize his agreement. Her husband was the kind who would be troubled and confused, even though unhappiness had developed in the marriage. Clearly she'd given up on the marriage; more than anything, it was desperation that made her forthright. Without it, she might have been a different woman – and in that case, of course, there would not have been this passing relationship between them: her tiresomeness had cultivated that. 'Tell me more about yourself,' her voice echoed huskily, hungry for friendship. He had told her nothing – nothing of the shattered, destroyed relationships, and the regret and shame; nothing of the pathetic hope in hired rooms, or the anguish turning into bitterness. She had been given beauty, and he a lameness that people laughed at when they knew. Would her tiresomeness have dropped from her at once, like the shedding of a garment she had thought to be attractive, if he'd told her in the restaurant with the modern paintings? Would she, too, have angrily said he'd led her up the garden path?

'There is our own investigation also,' Mr Humber said, 'besides that of Faraday's detectives. Faraday, I assure you, has spared no expense; the carabinieri file is by no means closed. With such a concentration we'll find what there is to find, sir.'

'I'm sure you'll do your best, Mr Humber.'

'Yes, *sir*.'

He rose and Mr Humber rose also, holding out a brown, lean hand. He was glad they had met, Mr Humber said, even in such unhappy circumstances. Diplomacy was like oil in Mr Humber. It eased his movements and his words; his detachment floated in it, perfectly in place.

'Goodbye, Mr Humber.'

Ignoring the lift, he walked down the stairs of the Consulate. He knew that she was dead. He imagined her lying naked in a wood, her even teeth ugly in a rictus, her white flesh as lifeless as the virgin modesty of the schoolgirl in the park. She hadn't been like a nymphomaniac, or even a sophisticated woman, when she'd kissed his cheek good-night. Like a schoolgirl herself, she'd still been blind to the icy coldness that answered her naïveté. Inept and academic, words he had written about the city which had claimed her slipped through his mind. *In the church of Santa Croce you walk on tombs, searching for Giotto's* Life of St Francis. *In Savonarola's own piazza the grey stone features do not forgive the tumbling hair of pretty police girls or the tourists' easy ways*. Injustice and harsh ambition had made her city what it was, the violence of greed for centuries had been its bloodstream; beneath its tinsel skin there was an iron heart. *The Florentines, like true provincials, put work and money first. In the Piazza Signoria the pigeons breakfast off the excrement of the hackney horses: in Florence nothing is wasted.*

He left the American Consulate and slowly walked along the quay. The sun was hot, the traffic noisy. He crossed the street and looked down into the green water of the Arno, wondering if the dark shroud of Mrs Faraday's life had floated away through a night. In the galleries of the Uffizi he would move from Annunciation to Annunciation, Simone Martini's, Baldovinetti's, Lorenzo di Credi's, and all the others. He would catch a glimpse of her red coat in Santa Trinità, but the face would again be someone else's. She would call out from a *gelateria*, but the voice would be an echo in his memory.

He turned away from the river and at the same slow pace walked into the heart of the city. He sat outside a café in the Piazza della Repubblica, imagining her thoughts as she had lain in bed on that last night, smoking her cigarettes in the darkness. She had arrived at the happiest moment of love, when nothing was yet destroyed, when anticipation was a richness in itself. She'd thought about their walk in Maiano, how she'd bring the subject up again, how this time he'd say he'd be delighted. She'd thought about their being together in an apartment in the Palazzo Ricasoli, how this time it would be different. Already she had made up her mind: she would not ever return to the town where her husband managed a business. 'I have never loved anyone like this,' she whispered in the darkness.

In his hotel bedroom he shaved and had a bath and put on a suit that had just been pressed. In a way that had become a ceremony for him since the evening he had first waited for her there, he went at six o'clock to Doney's. He watched the Americans drinking cocktails, knowing it was safe to be there because she would not suddenly arrive. He listened to the music she'd said she liked, and mourned her as a lover might.

Lunch in Winter

Mrs Nancy Simpson – who did not at all care for that name and would have wished to be Nancy le Puys or Nancy du Maurier – awoke on a December morning. She had been dreaming of a time long past in her life, when her name had been Nancy Dawes, before she'd been married to anyone. The band had been playing 'You are my Honeysuckle' and in the wings of the Old Gaiety they had all been in line, smiles ready, waiting to come on. *You are my honey-honeysuckle, I am the bee* ... Was it called something else, known by some other title? 'Smoke Gets in your Eyes' had once been called something else, so Laurie Henderson had said, although, God knows, if Laurie'd said it it probably wasn't true. You could never tell with songs. 'If You were the Only Girl in the World', for instance: was that the full title or was it 'If You were the Only Girl in the World and I was the Only Boy'? She'd had an argument with Laurie about that, a ridiculous all-night argument in Mrs Tomer's digs, Macclesfield, 1949 or '50. '50 probably because soon afterwards Laurie went down to London, doing something – barman probably – for the Festival of Britain thing. He'd walked out of Mrs Tomer's and she hadn't seen him for nine years. '51 actually it must have been. Definitely the Festival had been 1951.

She rose, and before she did anything else applied make-up to her face with very great care. She often thought there was nothing she liked better than sitting in her petticoat in front of a looking-glass, putting another face on. She powdered her lipstick, then smiled at herself. She thought about Fitz because today was Thursday and they'd drifted into the way of having lunch on Thursdays. 'My God, it's Nancy!' he'd said when by extraordinary chance he'd come upon her six months ago gazing into the windows of Peter Jones. They'd had a cup of tea, and had told one another this and that. 'Of course, why ever not?' she'd said when he'd suggested that they might occasionally see one another. 'Old times' sake,' she'd probably said: she couldn't remember now.

Her flat in Putney was high in a red-brick Victorian block, overlooking the river. Near by was the big, old-fashioned Sceptre Hotel, where drinkers from the flats spent a few evening hours, where foreign commercial travellers stayed. During Wimbledon some of the up-and-coming players stayed there also, with the has-beens. She liked to sit in the Bayeux Lounge and watch them passing through the reception area, pausing for their keys. That German who'd got into the final about ten years ago she'd noticed once, and she liked to think that McEnroe had stayed in the Sceptre before he'd got going, but she hadn't actually seen him. Every year from the windows of her tiny flat she watched the Boat Race going by, but really had no interest in it. Nice, though, the way it always brought the crowds to Putney. Nice that Putney in the springtime, one Saturday in the year, was not forgotten.

Fitz would be on his train, she thought as she crossed Putney Bridge on her way to the Underground. The bridge was where Christie, who'd murdered so many prostitutes, had been arrested. He'd just had a meal in the Lacy Dining Rooms and perhaps he'd even been thinking of murdering another that very night when the plain clothes had scooped him up. He'd gone, apparently, without a word of protest.

'My, you're a romantic, Fitz!' she'd said all those years ago, and really he hadn't changed. Typical of him to want to make it a regular Thursday rendezvous. Typical to come up specially from the coast, catching a train and then another train back. During the war they'd been married for four years.

She sang for a moment, remembering that; and then wanting to forget it. His family had thought he was mad, you could see that immediately. He'd led her into a huge drawing-room in Warwickshire, with a grand piano in one corner, and his mother and sister had actually recoiled. 'But for God's sake, you can't!' she'd heard his sister's shrill, unpleasant voice exclaiming in the middle of that same night. 'You can't marry a chorus girl!' But he had married her; they'd had to stomach her in the end.

She'd been a sunflower on the stage of the Old Gaiety when he'd first picked her out; after that he'd come night after night. He'd said she had a flimsy quality and needed looking after. When they met again six months ago in Regent Street he'd said in just the same kind of way that she was far too thin. She'd seen him eyeing her hair, which had been light and fair and was a yellowish colour now, not as pretty as it had been. But he didn't remark on it because he was the kind to remark only on the good things, saying instead she hadn't changed a bit. He seemed boyishly delighted that she still laughed the way she always had, and often remarked that she still held the stem of a glass and her cigarette in her own particular way. 'You're cold,' he'd said a week ago, reminding her of how he'd always gone on in the past about her not wearing enough clothes. He'd never understood that heavy things didn't suit her.

In other ways he hadn't changed, either. Still with a military bearing and hardly grey at all, he had a sunburnt look about the face, as always he'd had. He had not run to fat or slackness, and the sunburnt look extended over his forehead and beyond where his hair had receded. He was all of a piece, his careful suits, his soldier's walk. He'd married someone else, but after twenty-three years she'd gone and died on him.

'Good week?' he inquired in the Trattoria San Michele. 'What have you got up to, Nancy?'

She smiled and shrugged her skimpy shoulders. Nothing much, she didn't say. There'd been a part she'd heard about and had hoped for, but she didn't want to talk about that; it was a long time since she'd had a part.

'The trout with almonds,' he suggested. 'Shall we both have that?'

She smiled again and nodded. She lived on alimony, not his but that of the man she had married last, the one called Simpson. She lit a cigarette; she liked to smoke at meals, sometimes between mouthfuls.

'They've started that thing on the TV again,' she said. 'That *Blankety Blank*. Hilarious.'

She didn't know why she'd been unfaithful to him. She'd thought he wouldn't guess, but when he'd come back on his first leave he'd known at once. She'd promised it would never happen again, swearing it was due to the topsy-turviness of the war, the worry because he was in danger. Several leaves later, when the war was almost over, she promised again. 'I couldn't love anyone else, Fitz,' she'd whimpered, meaning it, really and truly. But at the beginning of 1948 he divorced her.

She hated to remember that time, especially since he was here and being so nice to her. She wanted to pay him back and asked him if he remembered the theme from *State Fair*. 'Marvellous. And then of course "Spring Fever" in the same picture.' She sang for a moment. '... *and it isn't even Spring*. 'Member?'

Eventually she had gone to Canada with a man called Eddie Lush, whom later she had married. She had stayed there, and later in Philadelphia, for thirteen years, but when she returned to England two children who had been born, a boy and a girl, did not accompany her. They'd become more attached to Eddie Lush than to her, which had hurt her at the time, and there'd been accusations of neglect during the court case, which had been hurtful too. Once upon a time they'd written letters to her occasionally, but she wasn't sure now what they were doing.

'And "I'll Be Around". 'Member "I'll Be Around"?' She sang again, very softly. '*No matter how* ... *you treat me now* ... Who was it sang it, d'you 'member?'

He shook his head. The waiter brought their trout and Nancy smiled at him. The tedium that had just begun to creep into these Thursday lunches had evaporated as soon as she'd set eyes on the Trattoria's new waiter six or so weeks ago. On Thursday evenings, in her corner of the Bayeux Lounge, his courtesy and his handsome face haunted her. Yes, he was a little sad, she often said to herself in the Bayeux Lounge. Was there even a hint of pain in those steady Latin eyes?

'Oh, lovely-looking trout,' she said, continuing to smile. 'Thanks ever so, Cesare.'

The man she had been married to was saying something else, but she didn't hear what it was. She remembered a chap like Cesare during the war, an airman from the base whom she'd longed to be taken out by, although in fact he'd never invited her.

'What?' she murmured, becoming aware that she'd been asked a question. But the question, now repeated, was only the familiar one, so often asked on Thursdays: did she intend to remain in her Putney flat, was she quite settled there? It was asked because once she'd said – she didn't know why – that the flat was temporary, that her existence in Putney had a temporary feel to it. She couldn't tell all the truth, she couldn't – to Fitz of all people – reveal the hope that at long last old Mr Robin Right would come bob-bob-bobbing along. She believed in Mr R.R., always had, and for some reason she'd got it into her head that he might quite easily walk into the Bayeux Lounge of the Sceptre Hotel. In the evenings she watched television in her flat or in the Bayeux Lounge, sometimes feeling bored because she had no particular friend or confidante. But then she'd always had an inclination to feel a bit like that. Boredom was the devil in her, Laurie Henderson used to say.

'Thanks ever so,' she said again because Cesare had skilfully placed a little heap of peas beside the trout. Typical of her, of course, to go falling for a restaurant waiter: you set yourself out on a sensible course, all serious and determined, and the next thing was you were half in love with an unsuitable younger man. Not that she looked fifty-nine, of course, more like forty – even thirty-eight, as a chap in the Bayeux Lounge had said when she'd asked him to guess a month ago. Unfortunately the chap had definitely not been Mr R.R.

'I just wondered,' Fitz was saying.

She smiled and nodded. The waiter was aware of her attention, no doubt about it. There was a little wink she was gifted with, a slight little motion of the lids, nothing suggestive about it. 'Makes me laugh, your wink,' Eddie Lush used to say, and it was probably Simpson who had called it a gift. She couldn't think why she'd ever allowed herself to marry Simpson, irritating face he'd had, irritating ways.

'It's been enjoyable, making the garden, building that wall. I never thought I'd be able to build a wall.'

He'd told her a lot about his house by the sea, a perfect picture it sounded, with flowerbeds all around the edge, and rustic trellising with ivy disguising the outside sanitary arrangements. He was terribly proud of what he'd done, and every right he had to be, the way he'd made the garden out of nothing. Won some kind of award the garden had, best on the south coast or the world or something.

'I could sell it very well. I've begun to think of that.'

She nodded. Cesare was expertly gathering up the plates four businessmen had eaten from. The men were stout and flushed, all of them married: you could tell a married look at once. At another table a chap who was married also was taking out a girl less than half his age, and next to them a couple looked as though they were planning a dirty weekend. A party of six, men and women, were at the big central table, just beside where the salads and the bowls of fruit were all laid out and where the dessert trolley was. She'd seen that party here a couple of weeks ago; they'd been talking about *En Tout Cas* tennis courts.

'Once you've made something as you want it,' Fitz was saying, 'you tend to lose interest, I suppose.'

The head-waiter called out to the other, younger Italian, she didn't know what his name was, lumpy-looking boy. But Cesare, because he was less busy, answered. *'Pronto! Pronto!'*

'You're never selling up, Fitz?'

'Well, I'm wondering about it.'

He had told her about the woman he'd married, a responsible type of woman she sounded, but she'd been ill or something and hadn't been able to have children. Twenty-three years was really a very long time for any two people to keep going. But then the woman had died.

'You get itchy feet,' he said. 'Even when you're passing sixty.'

'My, you don't look it.' Automatically she responded, watching the waiter while he served the party at the central table with T-bone steaks, a San Michele speciality. He said something else, but it didn't impinge on her. Then she heard:

'I often think it would be nice to live in London.'

He was eyeing her, to catch her reaction to this. 'You've had a battered life,' he'd said to her, the second time they'd had lunch. He'd looked at her much as he was looking at her now, and had said it twice. That was being an actress, she'd explained: always living on your nerves, hoping for this part or that, the disappointment of don't-call-us. 'Well, I suppose it batters you in the end,' she'd agreed. 'The old Profession.'

He, on the other hand, had appeared to have had quite a cosy time in the intervening years. Certainly, the responsible-sounding woman hadn't battered him, far from it. They'd been as snug as anything in the house by the sea, a heavy type of woman, Nancy imagined she'd been, with this thing wrong with her, whatever it was. It was after she'd dropped off her twig that he'd begun to feel sorry for himself and of course you couldn't blame him, poor Fitz. It had upset him at first that people had led unattached women up to him at cocktail parties, widows and the like, who'd lost their figures or had let their hair go frizzy, or were old. He'd told her all that one lunchtime and on another occasion he'd confessed that after a year or so had passed he'd gone to a bureau place, an introduction agency, where much younger women were fixed up for him. But that hadn't worked either. He had met the first of them for tea in the Ceylon Centre, where she'd told him that her deceased husband had been an important figure in a chemicals firm and that her older daughter was married in Australia, that her son was in the Hong Kong Police and another daughter married to a dentist in Worcester. She had not ceased to talk the entire time she was with him, apparently, telling him that she suffered from the heat, especially her feet. He'd taken another woman to a revival of *Annie Get Your Gun*, and he'd met a third in a bar she had suggested, where she'd begun to slur her speech after half an hour. Poor Fitz! He'd always been a simple soldier. She could have told him a bureau place would be no good, stood to reason you'd only get the down-and-outs.

'Sorry?' she said.

'I don't suppose you'd ever think of giving it another go?'

'Darling Fitz! *Dear* darling Fitz!'

She smiled at him. How typical it was that he didn't know it was impossible to pick up pieces that had been lying about for forty years! The past was full of Simpson and Laurie Henderson and Eddie Lush, and the two children she'd borne, the girl the child of a fertilizer salesman, which was something Eddie Lush had never guessed. You couldn't keep going on journeys down Memory Lane, and the more you did the more you realized that it was just an ugly black tunnel. Time goes by, as the old song had it, a kiss and a sigh and that was that. She smiled again. '*The fundamental things of life*,' she sang softly, smiling again at her ex-husband.

'I just thought –' he began.

'You always said pretty things, Fitz.'

'I always meant them.'

It had been so romantic when he'd said she needed looking after. He'd called her winsome another time. He was far more romantic than any of the others had ever been, but unfortunately when being romantic went on for a while it could become a teeny bit dreary, no other word for it. Not of course that you'd ever call poor Fitz dreary, far from it.

'Where d'you come from, Cesare?' she asked the waiter, thinking it a good idea to cause a diversion – and besides, it was nice to make the waiter linger. He was better looking than the airman from the base. He had a better nose, a nicer chin. She'd never seen such eyes, nor hair she longed so much to touch. Delicate with the coffee flask, his hands were as brown as an Italian fir-cone. She'd been to Italy once, to Sestri Levante with a man called Jacob Fynne who'd said he was going to put on *Lilac Time*. She'd collected fir-cones because she'd been bored, because all Jacob Fynne had wanted was her body. The waiter said he came from somewhere she'd never heard of.

'D'you know Sestri Levante?' she asked in order to keep him at their table.

He said he didn't, so she told him about it. Supposing she ran into him on the street, like she'd run into Fitz six months ago? He'd be alone: restaurant waiters in a city that was foreign to them could not know many people. Would it be so strange to walk together for a little while and then maybe to go in somewhere for a drink? 'Are your lodgings adequate, Cesare?' She would ask the question, and he would reply that his lodgings were not good. He'd say so because it stood to reason that the kind of lodgings an Italian waiter would be put into would of course be abominable. 'I'll look out for somewhere for you': would it be so wrong to say that?

'Would you consider it, Nancy? I mean, is it beyond the pale?'

For a moment it seemed that the hand which had seized one of hers was the waiter's, but then she noticed that Cesare was hurrying away with his flask of coffee. The hand that was paying her attention was marked with age, a bigger, squarer hand than Cesare's.

'Oh Fitz, you are a dear!'

'Well . . .'

'D'you think we might be naughty and go for a brandy today?'

'Of course.'

He signalled the waiter back. She lit another cigarette. When the brandy came and more coffee was being poured she said:

'And how do you like England? London?'

'Very nice, *signora*.'

'When you've tired of London you've tired of life, Cesare. That's a famous saying we have.'

'*Sì, signora*.'

'D'you know Berkeley Square, Cesare? There's a famous song we have about a nightingale in Berkeley Square. Whereabouts d'you live, Cesare?'

'Tooting Bec, *signora*.'

'Good heavens! Tooting's miles away.'

'Not too far, *signora*.'

'I'd rather have Naples any day. See Naples and die, eh?'

She sang a little from the song she'd referred to, and then she laughed and slapped Cesare lightly on the wrist, causing him to laugh also. He said the song was very nice.

'I'm sorry,' Fitz was saying. 'It was a silly thing to say.'

'You've never been silly in your life, Fitz.' She laughed again. 'Except when you married me.'

Gallantly, he shook his head.

'Thanks ever so,' she called after the waiter, who had moved with his coffee flask to the table with the business people. She thought of his being in Putney, in the room she'd found for him, much more convenient than Tooting. She thought of his coming to see her in the flat, of their sitting together with the windows open so that they could look out over the river. It was an unusual relationship, they both knew that, but he confessed that he had always liked the company of older women. He said so very quietly, not looking at her, speaking in a solemn tone. Nothing would change between them, he promised while they drank Campari sodas and she explained about the Boat Race.

'I shouldn't have said it. I'm sorry, Nancy.'

She hummed a snatch of something, smiling at him to show it didn't matter in the least. He'd made another proposal, just like he had when she'd been a sunflower at the Old Gaiety. It was a compliment, but she didn't say so because she was still thinking about sitting with the windows open in Putney.

'I must get back. I'll take an earlier train today,' he said.

'Just a teeny 'nother coffee, Fitz? And perhaps . . .' She lifted her empty brandy glass, her head a little on one side, the way he'd so often said he liked. And when the waiter came again she said:

'And have you always been a waiter, Cesare?'

He said he had, leaving a plate with the bill on it on the table. She tried to think of something else to say to him, but could think of nothing.

When they left the restaurant they walked with a bitter wind in their faces and he didn't take her arm, the way he'd done last week and the week before. On a crowded street the hurrying people jostled them, not apologizing. Once they were separated and for a moment she couldn't see her ex-husband and thought that he had slipped away from her, punishing her because she had been embarrassing with the waiter. But that was not his way. 'I'm here,' his voice said.

His cold lips touched her cheeks, first one, then the other. His large, square fingers gripped her arm for just a moment. 'Well, goodbye, Nancy,' he said, as always he did on Thursday afternoons, but this time he did not mention next week and he was gone before she could remind him.

That evening she sat in her usual corner of the Bayeux Lounge, sipping vodka and tonic and thinking about the day. She'd been terrible; if she knew poor Fitz's number she'd ring him now from the booth in the passage and say she was sorry. 'Wine goes to your head, Nancy,' Laurie Henderson used to say and it was true. A few glasses of red wine in the Trattoria San Michele and she was pawing at a waiter who was young enough to be her son. And Fitz politely sat there, officer and gentleman still written all over him, saying he'd sell his house up and come to London. The waiter'd probably thought she was after his body.

Not that it mattered what he thought, because he and the Trattoria San Michele already belonged in Memory Lane. She'd never been there until that lunchtime six months ago when old Fitz had said, 'Let's turn in here.' No word would come from him, she sensed that also: never again on a Thursday would she hurry along to the Trattoria San Michele and say she was sorry she was late.

I'll be around, no matter how you treat me now ... She'd seen him first when they'd sung that number, the grand finale; she'd suddenly noticed him, three rows from the front. She'd seen him looking at her and had wondered while she danced if he was Mr R.R. Well, of course, he had been in a way. He'd stood up for her to his awful relations, he'd kissed away her tears, saying he would die for her. And then the first thing she'd done when he'd married her after all that fuss, when he'd gone back after his leave, was to imagine that that stupid boy with a tubercular chest was the be-all and end-all. And when the boy had proved beyond a shadow of doubt that he was no such thing there was the new one they'd taken on for his tap-dancing.

She smiled in the Bayeux Lounge, remembering the laughter and the applause when the back legs of Jack and the Beanstalk's Dobbin surprised everyone by breaking into that elegant tap-dance, and how Jack and his mother had stood there with their mouths comically open. She'd told Fitz about it a few lunches ago because, of course, she hadn't been able to tell him at the time on account of the thing she'd had with the back legs. He had nodded solemnly, poor Fitz, not really amused, you could see, but pleased because she was happy to remember. A right little troublemaker that tap-dancer had turned out to be, and a right little scrounge, begging every penny he could lay his hands on, with no intention of paying a farthing back.

If she'd run out of hope, she thought, she could have said yes, let's try again. She could have admitted, because it was only fair to, that she'd never be like the responsible woman who'd gone and died on him. She could have pointed out that she'd never acquire the class of his mother and his sister because she wasn't that sort of person. She'd thought all that out a few weeks ago, knowing what he was getting around to. She'd thought it was awful for him to be going to a bureau place and have women telling him about how the heat affected them. She'd imagined saying yes and then humming something special, probably 'Love is the Sweetest Thing', and leaning her face towards him across the table, waiting for his kiss again. But of course you couldn't live in fantasies, you couldn't just pretend.

'Ready for your second, Nancy?' the barmaid called across the empty lounge, and she said yes, she thought she was.

You gave up hope if you just agreed because it sounded cosy. When he'd swept her off her feet all those years ago everything had sounded lovely: being with him in some nice place when the war was over, never again being short, the flowers he brought her. 'No need to come to London, Fitz,' she might have said today. 'Let's just go and live in your house by the sea.' And he'd have been delighted and relieved, because he'd only mentioned selling up in order to show her that he would if she wanted him to. But all hope would be gone if she'd agreed.

She sighed, sorry for him, imagining him in the house he talked about. He'd have arrived there by now, and she imagined him turning the lights on and everything coming to life. You could tell from the way he talked that there were memories there for him, that the woman he'd married was still all over the place: it wasn't because he'd finished making a stone wall in the garden that he wanted to move on. He'd probably pour himself a drink and sit down to watch the television; he'd open a tin later on. She imagined him putting a match to the fire and pulling over the curtains. Probably in a drawer somewhere he had a photo of her as a sunflower. He'd maybe sit with it in his hand, with his drink and the television. 'Dear, it's a fantasy,' she murmured. 'It couldn't ever have worked second time round, no more'n it did before.'

'Warm your bones, Nancy,' the barmaid said, placing her second vodka and tonic on a cardboard mat on the table where she sat. 'Freeze you tonight, it would.'

'Yes, it's very cold.'

She hadn't returned to the flat after the visit to the Trattoria San Michele;

somehow she hadn't felt like it. She'd walked about during the couple of hours that had to pass before the Bayeux Lounge opened. She'd looked in the shop windows, and looked at the young people with their peculiarly coloured hair. Two boys in eastern robes, with no hair, had tried to sell her a record. She hadn't been keen to go back to the flat because she wanted to save up the hope that something might have come on the second post, an offer of a part. If she saved it up it would still hover in her mind while she sat in the Bayeux Lounge – just a chance in a million but that was how chances always were. It was more likely, when her luck changed, that the telephone would ring, but even so you could never rule out a letter. You never should. You should never rule out anything.

She wished now she'd tried to tell him that, even though he might not ever have understood. She wished she'd explained that it was all to do with not giving up hope. She'd felt the same when Eddie had got the children, even though one of them wasn't his, and when they'd gone on so about neglect. All she'd been doing was hoping then too, not wanting to be defeated, not wanting to give in to what they demanded where the children were concerned. Eddie had married someone else, some woman who probably thought she was an awful kind of person because she'd let her children go. But one day the children would write, she knew that inside her somewhere; one day there'd be that letter waiting for her, too.

She sipped more vodka and tonic. She knew as well that one day Mr R.R. would suddenly be there, to make up for every single thing. He'd make up for all the disappointment, for Simpson and Eddie and Laurie Henderson, for treating badly the one man who'd been good to you. He'd make up for scrounging tap-dancers and waiters you wanted to be with because there was sadness in their faces, and the dear old Trattoria San Michele gone for ever into Memory Lane. You couldn't give up on Mr R.R., might as well walk out and throw yourself down into the river; like giving up on yourself it would be.

'I think of you only,' she murmured in her soft whisper, feeling much better now because of the vodka and tonic, 'only wishing, wishing you were by my side.' When she'd come in at half past five she'd noticed a chap booking in at the reception, some kind of foreign commercial traveller since the tennis people naturally didn't come in winter; fiftyish, handsome-ish, not badly dressed. She was glad they hadn't turned on the television yet. From the corner where she sat she could see the stairs, where sooner or later the chap would appear. He'd buy a drink and then he'd look around and there she'd be.

Coffee with Oliver

That is Deborah, Oliver said to himself: my daughter has come to see me. But at the pavement table of the café where he sat he did not move. He did not even smile. He had, after all, only caught a glimpse of a slight girl in a yellow dress, of fair hair, and sunglasses and a profile: it might not be she at all.

Yet, Oliver insisted to himself, you know a thing like that. You sense your flesh and blood. And why should Deborah be in Perugia unless she planned to visit him? The girl was alone. She had hurried into the hotel next to the café in a businesslike manner, not as a sightseer would.

Oliver was a handsome man of forty-seven, with greying hair, and open, guileless features. This morning he was dressed as always he was when he made the journey to Perugia: in a pale-cream linen suit, a pale shirt with a green stripe in it, and the tie of an English public school. His tan shoes shone; the socks that matched the cream of his suit were taut over his ankles.

'*Signorina!*'

He summoned the waitress who had just finished serving the people at the table next to his and ordered another cappuccino. This particular girl went off duty at eleven and the waitress who replaced her invariably made out the bill for one cappuccino only. It was fair enough, Oliver argued to himself, since he was a regular customer at the café and spent far more there than a tourist would.

'*Sì, signore. Subito.*'

What he had seen in the girl who'd gone into the hotel was a resemblance to Angelica, who was slight and fair-haired also, and had the same quick little walk and rather small face. If the girl had paused and for some reason taken off her dark glasses he would at once, with warm nostalgia, have recognized her mother's deep, dark eyes, of that he was certain. He wouldn't, of course, have been so sure had it not been for the resemblance. Since she'd grown up he'd only seen photographs of his daughter.

It was best to let whatever Deborah had planned just happen, best not to upset the way she wanted it. He could ask for her at the reception desk of the hotel. He could be waiting for her in the hall, and they could lunch together. He could show her about the town, put her into the picture gallery for an hour while he waited at the café across the street; afterwards they could sit over a drink. But that would be all his doing, not Deborah's, and it wouldn't be fair. Such a programme would also be expensive, for Deborah, in spite of being at a smart hotel, might well not be able to offer a contribution: it would not be unlike Angelica to keep her short. Oliver's own purpose in being in Perugia that morning was to visit the Credito Italiano, to make certain that the monthly amount from Angelica had come. He had cashed a cheque, but of course that had to be made to last.

'*Prego, signore*,' the waitress said, placing a fresh cup of coffee in front of him and changing his ashtray for an unused one.

He smiled and thanked her, then blew gently at the foam of his cappuccino and sipped a little of the coffee. He lit a cigarette. You could sit all day here, he reflected, while the red-haired Perugians went by, young men in twos and threes, and the foreign students from the language schools, and the tourists who toiled up, perspiring, from the car parks. Idling time away, just ruminating, was lovely.

Eventually Oliver paid for his coffee and left. He should perhaps buy some meat, in case his daughter arrived at his house at a mealtime. Because it was expensive he rarely did buy meat, once in a blue moon a packet of cooked turkey slices, which lasted for ages. There was a butcher's he often passed in a side street off the via dei Priori, but this morning it was full of women, all of them pressing for attention. Oliver couldn't face the clamour and the long wait he guessed there'd be. The butcher's in Betona might still be open when he arrived off the five past twelve bus. Probably best left till then in any case, meat being tricky in the heat.

He descended from the city centre by a steep short-cut, eventually arriving at the bus stop he favoured. He saved a little by using this particular fare-stage, and though he did not often make the journey to Perugia all such economies added up. What a marvellous thing to happen, that Deborah had come! Oliver smiled as he waited for his bus in the midday sunshine; the best things were always a surprise.

Deborah had a single memory of her father. He'd come to the flat one Sunday afternoon and she'd been at the top of the short flight of stairs that joined the flat's two floors. She hadn't known who he was but had watched and listened, sensing the charged atmosphere. At the door the man was smiling. He said her mother was looking well. He hoped she wouldn't mind, he said. Her mother was cross. Deborah had been five at the time.

'You know I mind,' she'd heard her mother say.

'I was passing. Unfriendly just to pass, I thought. We shouldn't not ever talk to one another again, Angelica.'

Her mother's voice was lowered then. She spoke more than she had already, but Deborah couldn't hear a word.

'Well, no point,' he said. 'No point in keeping you.'

Afterwards, when Deborah asked, her mother told her who the man was. Her mother was truthful and found deception difficult. When two people didn't get on any more, she said, it wasn't a good idea to try to keep some surface going.

He'd lit a cigarette while they'd been talking. Softly, he'd tried to interrupt her mother. He'd wanted to come in, but her mother hadn't permitted that.

'I'm here because of a mistake? Is that it?' Deborah pinned her mother down in a quarrel years after that Sunday afternoon. It was her mother's way of putting it when her marriage came up: two people had made a mistake. Mistakes were best forgotten, her mother said.

The dwelling Oliver occupied, in the hills above the village of Betona, was a stone building of undistinguished shape and proportions. It had once housed sheep during the frozen winter months, and wooden stairs, resembling a heavily constructed ladder, led to a single upstairs room, where shepherds had sought privacy from their animals. Efforts at conversion had been made. Electricity had been brought from the village; a kitchen, and a lavatory with a shower in it, had been fitted into the space below. But the conversion had an arrested air, reflecting a loss of interest on the part of Angelica who, years ago, had bought the place as it stood. At the time of the divorce she had made over to him the ramshackle habitation. She herself had visited it only once; soon after the divorce proceedings began she turned against the enterprise, and work on the conversion ceased. When Oliver returned on his own he found the corrugated roof still letting in rain, no water flowing from either the shower or the lavatory, the kitchen without a sink or a stove, and a cesspit not yet dug. He had come from England with his clothes and four ebony-framed pictures. 'Well, anyway it's somewhere to live,' he said aloud, looking around the downstairs room, which smelt of concrete. He sighed none the less, for he was not deft with his hands.

The place was furnished now, though modestly. Two folding garden chairs did service in the downstairs room. There was a table with a fawn formica surface, and a pitch-pine bookcase. Faded rugs covered most of the concrete floor. The four heavily framed pictures – scenes of Suffolk landscape – adorned the rough stone walls to some effect. Across a corner there was a television set.

The cesspit remained undug, but in other directions Oliver had had a bit of luck. He'd met an Englishman on one of his visits to the Credito Italiano and had helped with a language difficulty. The man, in gratitude, insisted on buying Oliver a cup of coffee and Oliver, sensing a usefulness in this acquaintanceship, suggested that they drive together in the man's car to Betona. In return for a summer's lodging – a sleeping-bag on the concrete floor – the man replaced the damaged corrugated iron of the roof, completed the piping that brought water to the shower and the lavatory, and installed a sink and an antique gas stove that someone had thrown out, adapting the stove to receive bottled gas. He liked to work like this, to keep himself occupied, being in some kind of distress. Whenever Oliver paused in the story of his marriage his companion had a way of starting up about the business world he'd once belonged to, how failure had led to bankruptcy: finding the interruption of his own narration discourteous, Oliver did not listen. Every evening at six o'clock the man walked down to the village and returned with a litre of red wine and whatever groceries he thought necessary. Oliver explained that since he himself would not have made these purchases he did not consider that he should make a contribution to their cost. His visitor was his guest in the matter of accommodation; in fairness, it seemed to follow, he should be his visitor's guest where the odd egg or glass of wine was concerned.

'Angelica was never easy,' Oliver explained, continuing the story of his marriage from one evening to the next. 'There was always jealousy.' His sojourn in the Betona hills was temporary, he stated with confidence. But he did not add that, with his sights fixed on something better, he often dropped into conversation with lone English or American women in the rooms of the picture gallery or at the café next to the hotel. He didn't bore his companion with this information because it didn't appear to have much relevance. He did his best only to be interesting about Angelica, and considered he succeeded. It was a dispute in quite a different area that ended the relationship, as abruptly as it had begun. As well as hospitality, the visitor claimed a sum of money had been agreed upon, but while conceding that a cash payment had indeed been mooted, Oliver was adamant that he had not promised it. He did not greatly care for the man in the end, and was glad to see him go.

When Angelica died two years ago Deborah was twenty. The death was not a shock because her mother had been ill, and increasingly in pain, for many months: death was a mercy. Nonetheless, Deborah felt the loss acutely. Although earlier, in her adolescence, there had been arguments and occasionally rows, she'd known no companion as constant as her mother; and as soon as the death occurred she realized how patient with her and how fond of her Angelica had been. She'd been larky too, amused by unexpected things, given to laughter that Deborah found infectious. In her distress at the time of her mother's death it never occurred to her that the man who'd come to the flat that Sunday afternoon might turn up at the funeral. In fact, he hadn't.

'You'll be all right,' Angelica had said before she died, meaning that there was provision for Deborah to undertake the post-graduate work she planned after she took her degree. 'Don't worry, darling.'

Deborah held her hand, ashamed when she remembered how years ago she'd been so touchy because Angelica once too often repeated that her marriage was a mistake. Her mother had never used the expression again.

'I was a horrid child,' Deborah cried forlornly before her mother died. 'A horrid little bully.'

'Darling, of course you weren't.'

At the funeral people said how much they'd always liked her mother, how nice she'd been. They invited Deborah to visit them at any time, just to turn up when she was feeling low.

When Oliver stepped off the bus in the village the butcher's shop was still open but he decided, after all, not to buy a pork chop, which was the choice he had contemplated when further considering the matter on the bus. A chop was suitable because, although it might cost as much as twenty thousand lire, it could be divided quite easily into two. But supposing it wasn't necessary to offer a meal at all? Supposing Deborah arrived in the early afternoon, which was not unlikely? He bought the bread he needed instead, and a packet of soup, and cigarettes.

He wondered if Deborah had come with a message. He did not know that Angelica had died and wondered if she was hoping he might be persuaded to return to the flat in the square. It was not unlikely. As he ascended the track that led to his property, these thoughts drifted pleasurably through Oliver's mind. 'Deborah, I'll have to think about that.' He saw himself sitting with his daughter in what the man who'd set the place to rights had called the patio – a yard really, with two car seats the man had rescued from a dump somewhere, and an old tabletop laid across concrete blocks. 'We'll see,' he heard himself saying, not wishing to dismiss the idea out of hand.

He had taken his jacket off, and carried it over his arm. '*E caldo!*' the woman he'd bought the bread from had exclaimed, which indicated that the heat was excessive, for in Betona references to the weather were only made when extremes were reached. Sweat gathered on Oliver's forehead and at the back of his neck. He could feel it becoming clammy beneath his shirt. Whatever the reason for Deborah's advent he was glad she had come because company was always cheerful.

In the upstairs room Oliver took his suit off and carefully placed it on a wire coat-hanger on the wall. He hung his tie over one linen shoulder, and changed his shirt. The trousers he put on were old corduroys, too heavy in the heat, but the best he could manage. In the kitchen he made tea and took it out to the patio, with the bread he'd bought and his cigarettes. He waited for his daughter.

After Angelica's death Deborah felt herself to be an orphan. Angelica's brother and his wife, a well-meaning couple she hardly knew, fussed about her a bit; and so did Angelica's friends. But Deborah had her own friends, and she didn't need looking after. She inherited the flat in London and went there in the university holidays. She spent a weekend in Norfolk with her uncle and his wife, but did not do so again. Angelica's brother was quite unlike her, a lumpish man who wore grey, uninteresting suits and had a pipe, and spectacles on a chain. His wife was wan and scatter-brained. They invited Deborah as a duty and were clearly thankful to find her independent.

Going through her mother's possessions, Deborah discovered neither photographs of, nor letters from, her father. She did not know that photographs of herself, unaccompanied by any other form of communication, had been sent to her father every so often, as a record of her growing up. She did not know of the financial agreement that years ago had been entered into. It did not occur to her that no one might have informed the man who'd come that Sunday afternoon of Angelica's death. It didn't occur to her to find some way of doing so herself. None of this entered Deborah's head because the shadowy figure who had smiled and lit a cigarette belonged as deeply in the grave as her mother did.

She had no curiosity about him, and her uncle did not mention him. Nor did any of Angelica's friends on the occasions when they invited Deborah to lunch or drinks, since she had not just turned up as they'd suggested at the funeral. In reply to some casual query by a stranger, she once replied that her father was probably dead. The happiness of her relationship with Angelica was what she thought about and moodily dwelt upon, regretting that she had taken it for granted.

The heat was at its most intense at three o'clock, but afterwards did not lose its fervour. The concrete blocks of Oliver's patio, the metal ribs of the car chairs, the scorching upholstery, the stone of the house itself, all cancelled the lessening of the sun's attack by exuding the heat that had been stored. By half past five a kind of coolness was beginning. By seven it had properly arrived. By half past eight there was pleasure in its relief.

Perhaps he had been wrong, Oliver thought later, not to approach the girl: thoughtfulness sometimes was misplaced. If she had waited for the day to cool she would have found herself too late for the last bus to Betona, and a taxi would have been outrageously expensive. Angelica would have taken a taxi, of course, though in other ways, as he well knew, she could be penny-pinching.

But Deborah didn't come that evening, nor the next day, nor the day after that. So Oliver made the journey into Perugia again, long before it was time for his next visit to the Credito Italiano. The only explanation was that the girl had not been Deborah at all. But he still felt she was, and was bewildered. He even wondered if his daughter was lying low because she'd been sent to spy on him.

'*Sì, signore?*' The clerk in the reception of the hotel smiled at him, and in slow Italian Oliver made his query. He wrote down Deborah's name on a piece of paper so that there could be no confusion. He remembered the date of the day he'd last sat at the café. From the photograph he had of her he described his daughter.

'*Momento, signore. Scusi.*' The clerk entered a small office to one side of the reception desk and returned some minutes later with a registration form. On it were Deborah's name and signature, and the address of the flat in London. She had stayed one night only in the hotel.

'Student,' a girl who had accompanied the clerk from the office said. 'She search a room in Perugia.'

'A room?'

'She ask.' The girl shrugged. 'I no have room.'

'Thank you.' Oliver smiled at both of them in turn. The clerk called after him in Italian. The girl had given Deborah the name of an agency, not twenty metres away, where rooms were rented to students. 'Thank you,' Oliver said again, but did not take the details of the agency. At the café he ordered a cappuccino.

Deborah had enrolled on a course – language or culture, or perhaps a combination. Perugia was famous for its courses; students came from all over the place. Sometimes they spent a year, or even longer, depending on the course they'd chosen. He knew that because now and again he dropped into conversation with one, and in return for a *grappa* or a cappuccino supplied some local information. Once he'd had lunch with a well-to-do young Iranian who'd clearly been grateful for his company.

'*Ecco, signore!*' The waitress who went off duty at eleven placed his coffee in front of him.

'*Grazie.*'

'*Prego, signore.*'

He lit a cigarette. Once he'd had a lighter and a silver cigarette case, given to him by a Mrs Dogsmith, whom he'd met in the Giardini Carducci. For a moment he saw again the slim, faintly embossed case, and the initials curling around one another at the bottom left-hand corner of the lighter. He'd sold both of them years ago.

A woman came out of the hotel and paused idly, glancing at the café tables. She was taller than Mrs Dogsmith and a great deal thinner. A widow or divorcee, Oliver guessed, but then a man came out of the hotel and took her arm.

'Your mother gave you so much.' Angelica's irrational chatter lurched at him suddenly. 'But still you had to steal from her.'

He felt himself broken into, set upon and violated, as he remembered feeling at the time. The unpleasant memory had come because of Deborah, because Deborah's presence put him in mind of Angelica, naturally enough. More agreeably, he recalled that it was he who'd chosen that name for their daughter. 'Deborah,' he'd suggested, and Angelica had not resisted it.

Not wishing to think about Angelica, he watched the waddling movement of a pigeon on the pavement, and then listened to a conversation in Italian between a darkly suited man and his companion, a woman in a striped tan dress. They were talking about swimwear; the man appeared to be the proprietor of a fashion shop. Young people in a group went by, and Oliver glanced swiftly from face to face, but his daughter was not among them. He ordered another cappuccino because in ten minutes or so the early-morning waitress would be going off duty.

It was a silliness of Angelica's to say he'd stolen from his mother. He more than anyone had regretted the sad delusions that had beset his mother. It was he who had watched her becoming vague, he who had suffered when she left all she possessed to a Barnardo's home. Angelica belonged to a later time; she'd hardly known his mother.

Slowly Oliver lit and smoked another cigarette, filling in time while he waited for the new waitress to arrive. As soon as he saw her he crumpled up the little slip that had accompanied his first cup of coffee, and placed on the table the money for the second. But this morning, when he'd gone only a few yards along the street, the waitress came hurrying after him, jabbering in Italian. He smiled and shook his head. She held out the money he'd left.

'Oh! *Mi dispiace!*' he apologized, paying her the extra.

*

'Deborah.'

She heard her name and turned. A middle-aged man was smiling at her. She smiled back, thinking he was one of the tutors whom she couldn't place.

'Don't you recognize me, Deborah?'

They were in the square. He had risen from the edge of a wooden stage that had been erected for some public meeting. The two girls Deborah was with were curious.

'My dear,' the man said, but seventeen years had passed since Deborah had caught her one glimpse of her father that Sunday afternoon. Neither features nor voice were familiar. 'It's really you!' the man said.

Bewildered, Deborah shook her head.

'I'm Oliver,' Oliver said. 'Your father.'

They sat outside, at the nearest café. She didn't take off her sunglasses. She'd spoken to the girls she'd been with and they'd walked on. She had a class at two, she'd said.

'Time at least for a coffee,' Oliver said.

She had a look of him, even though she was more like Angelica. It had been a disappointment, the deduction that she hadn't come here to seek him out. A disappointment that it was no more than a coincidence, her presence in Perugia.

'You knew of course?' he said. 'You did have my address?'

She shook her head. She'd had no idea. She hadn't even been aware that he was not in England.

'But, Deborah, surely Angelica –'

'No, she never did.'

Their coffee came. The waiter was young and unshaven, not neatly in a uniform like the girls at the café by the hotel. He glanced at Deborah with interest. Oliver thought he heard him making a sound with his lips, but he could not be sure.

'I often think of you and your mother in that flat.'

Deborah realized he didn't know Angelica had died, and found it difficult to break the news. She did so clumsily, or so she thought.

'My God!' he said.

Deborah dipped a finger into the foam of her coffee. She didn't like the encounter; she wished it hadn't taken place. She didn't like sitting here with a man she didn't know and didn't want to know. 'Apparently he's my father,' she'd said to her companions, momentarily enjoying the sophistication; but later, of course, all that would have to be explained.

'Poor Angelica!' he said.

Deborah wondered why nobody had warned her. Why hadn't her grey-suited uncle or one of Angelica's friends advised against this particular Italian city? Why hadn't her mother mentioned it?

Presumably they hadn't warned her because they didn't know. Her mother hadn't ever wanted to mention him; it wasn't Angelica's way to warn people against people.

'She used to send me a photograph of you every summer,' he said. 'I wondered why none came these last two years. I never guessed.'

She nodded meaninglessly.

'Why are you learning Italian, Deborah?'

'I took my degree in the history of art. It's necessary to improve my Italian now.'

'You're taking it up? The history of art?'

'Yes, I am.'

'It's lovely you're here.'

'Yes.'

She had chosen Perugia rather than Florence or Rome because the course was better. But if she'd known she wouldn't have.

'Not really a coincidence,' he was saying, very softly. 'These things never are.'

Just for a moment Deborah felt irritated. What had been the use of Angelica's being generous, unwilling to malign, bending over backwards to be decent, when this could happen as a result? What was the good of calling a marriage a mistake, and leaving it at that? But the moment passed; irritation with the dead was shameful.

'Is it far from here, where you live?' she asked, hoping that it was.

Oliver tore a cheque-stub from his cheque-book and wrote his address on it, then tore out another and drew a map. He wrote down the number of the Betona bus.

'It's lovely you're here,' he said again, giving his daughter the cheque-stubs. An excitement had begun in him. If he hadn't been outside the hotel that morning he'd never even have known she was in Perugia. She might have come and gone and he'd have been none the wiser. Angelica had died, the two of them were left; he wouldn't have known that, either.

'If you don't mind,' he heard his daughter saying and felt she was repeating something he hadn't heard the first time, 'I don't think I'll visit you.'

'You've been told unpleasant things, Deborah.'

'No, not at all.'

'We can be frank, you know.'

Angelica had been like that, he knew it to his cost. In his own case, she had laid down harsh conditions, believing that to be his due. The half-converted house and the monthly transfer of money carried the proviso that he should not come to the flat ever again, that he should not live in England. That wasn't pleasant, but since it was what she wanted he'd agreed. At least the money hadn't ceased when the woman died. Oliver smiled, feeling that to be a triumph.

'Angelica was always jealous. It was jealousy that spoilt things.'

'I never noticed that in her.'

He smiled again, knowing better. Heaven alone knew what this girl had been told about him, but today, now that she was here and Angelica was not, it didn't matter.

'A pity you feel you can't come out to Betona. The bus fare's quite a bit, else I'd come in oftener while you're here.'

'Actually, to tell the truth, I'd rather we didn't have to meet.' Deborah's tone was matter of fact and sharp. A note of impatience had entered it, reminding Oliver not of his wife, but strangely of his mother.

'I only come in once a month or so.' He slid a cigarette from his packet of MS. 'Angelica tried to keep us apart,' he said, 'all these years. She made the most elaborate arrangements.'

Deborah rooted in her handbag and found her own cigarettes and matches. Oliver said he'd have offered her one of his if he'd known she smoked. She said it didn't matter.

'I don't want any of this hassle,' she said.

'Hassle, Deborah? A cup of coffee now and again –'

'Look, honestly, not even that.'

Oliver smiled. It was always better not to argue. He'd never argued with Angelica. It was she who'd done the arguing, working herself up, making it sound as though she were angrily talking to herself. Deborah could easily sleep in the downstairs room; there were early-morning buses to Perugia. They could share the expenses of the household: the arrangement there'd been with the bankrupt man had been perfectly satisfactory.

'Sorry,' Deborah said, and to Oliver her voice sounded careless. She blew out smoke, looking over her shoulder, no doubt to see if her friends were still hanging around. He felt a little angry. He might have been just anyone, sitting there. He wanted to remind her that he had given her life.

'It's simple at Betona,' he said instead. 'I'm not well off. But I don't think you'd find it dreadful.'

'I'm sure I wouldn't. All the same –'

'Angelica was well off, you know. She never wanted me to be.'

Deborah missed her two o'clock lesson because it was harder than she'd anticipated to get away. She was told about all sorts of things, none of which she'd known about before. The Sunday afternoon she remembered was mentioned. 'I wasn't very well then,' Oliver said. It was after that occasion that a legal agreement had been drawn up: in return for financial assistance Oliver undertook not to come to the flat again, not ever to attempt to see his child. He was given the house near Betona, no more than a shack really. 'None of it was easy,' he said. He looked away, as if to hide emotion from her. The photographs he annually received were a legality also, the only one he had insisted on himself. Suddenly he stood up and said he had a bus to catch.

'It's understandable,' he said. 'Your not wanting to come to Betona. Of course you have your own life.'

He nodded and went away. Deborah watched him disappearing into the crowd that was again collecting, after the afternoon siesta.

Who on earth would have believed that he'd outlive Angelica? Extraordinary how things happen; though, perhaps, in a sense, there was a fairness in it. Angelica had said he always had to win. In her unpleasant moods she'd said he had to cheat people, that he could not help himself. As a gambler was in thrall to luck, or a dipsomaniac to drink, his flaw was having to show a gain in everything he did.

On the bus journey back to Betona Oliver did not feel angry when he recalled that side of Angelica, and supposed it was because she was dead. Naturally it was a relief to have the weight of anger lifted after all these years, no point in denying it. The trouble had been it wasn't easy to understand what she was getting at. When she'd found the three or four pieces among his things, she'd forgotten that they were his as much as his mother's, and didn't even try to understand that you couldn't have told his mother that, she being like she was. Instead Angelica chose to repeat that he hadn't been able to resist 'getting the better of' his mother. Angelica's favourite theme was that: what she called his pettiness and his meanness left him cruel. He had often thought she didn't care what she said; it never mattered how she hurt.

On the bus Angelica's face lolled about in Oliver's memory, with his mother's and – to Oliver's surprise – his daughter's. Angelica pleaded about something, tears dripped from the old woman's cheeks, Deborah simply shook her head. 'Like cancer in a person', Angelica said. Yet it was Angelica who had died, he thought again.

Deborah would come. She would come because she was his flesh and blood. One day he'd look down and see her on the path, bringing something with her because he wasn't well off. Solicitors had drawn up the stipulations that had kept them apart all these years; in ugly legal jargon all of it was written coldly down. When Deborah considered that, she would begin to understand. He'd sensed, before they parted, a shadow of unease: guilt on Angelica's behalf, which wasn't surprising in the circumstances.

The thought cheered Oliver considerably. In his house, as he changed his clothes, he reflected that it didn't really matter, the waitress running after him for the money. In all, over the months that had passed since this waitress had begun to work at the café, he'd probably had twenty, even thirty, second cups of coffee. He knew it didn't matter because after a little time it hadn't mattered that the bankrupt man had made a scene, since by then the roof was repaired and the plumbing completed. It hadn't mattered when Mrs Dogsmith turned nasty, since already she'd given him the lighter and the cigarette case. That was the kind of thing Angelica simply couldn't understand, any more than she'd understood the confusions of his mother, any more than, probably, she'd understood their daughter. You couldn't keep flesh and blood apart; you actually weren't meant to.

In the kitchen Oliver put the kettle on for tea. When it boiled he poured the water on to a tea-bag he'd already used before setting out for Perugia. He carried the glass out to the patio and lit a cigarette. The car seats were too hot to sit on, so he stood, waiting for them to cool. There'd been no reason why she shouldn't have paid for their coffee since she, after all, had been the cause of their having it. Eighteen thousand lire a cappuccino cost at that particular café, he'd noticed it on the bill.

Torridge

Perhaps nobody ever did wonder what Torridge would be like as a man – or what Wiltshire or Mace-Hamilton or Arrowsmith would be like, come to that. Torridge at thirteen had a face with a pudding look, matching the sound of his name. He had small eyes and short hair like a mouse's. Within the collar of his grey regulation shirt the knot of his House tie was formed with care, a maroon triangle of just the right shape and bulk. His black shoes were always shiny.

Torridge was unique in some way: perhaps only because he was beyond the pale and appeared, irritatingly, to be unaware of it. He wasn't good at games and had difficulty in understanding what was being explained in the classroom. He would sit there frowning, half smiling, his head a little to one side. Occasionally he would ask some question that caused an outburst of groaning. His smile would increase then. He would glance around the classroom, not flustered or embarrassed in the least, seeming to be pleased that he had caused such a response. He was naïve to the point where it was hard to believe he wasn't pretending, but his naïveté was real and was in time universally recognized as such. A master called Buller Yeats reserved his cruellest shafts of scorn for it, sighing whenever his eyes chanced to fall on Torridge, pretending to believe his name was Porridge.

Of the same age as Torridge, but similar in no other way, were Wiltshire, Mace-Hamilton and Arrowsmith. All three of them were blond-haired and thin, with a common sharpness about their features. They wore, untidily, the same clothes as Torridge, their House ties knotted any old how, the laces in their scuffed shoes often tied in several places. They excelled at different games and were quick to sense what was what. Attractive boys, adults had more than once called them.

The friendship among the three of them developed because, in a way, Torridge was what he was. From the first time they were aware of him – on the first night of their first term – he appeared to be special. In the darkness after lights-out someone was trying not to sob and Torridge's voice was piping away, not homesick in the least. His father had a button

Torridge?' Arrowsmith asked at breakfast, and that was the beginning. 'Dad's in the button business,' Torridge beamingly replied. 'Torridge's, you know.' But no one did know.

He didn't, as other new boys did, make a particular friend. For a while he attached himself to a small gang of homesick boys who had only their malady in common, but after a time this gang broke up and Torridge found himself on his own, though it seemed quite happily so. He was often to be found in the room of the kindly housemaster of Junior House, an ageing white-haired figure called Old Frosty, who listened sympathetically to complaints of injustice at the hands of other masters, always ready to agree that the world was a hard place. 'You should hear Buller Yeats on Torridge, sir,' Wiltshire used to say in Torridge's presence. 'You'd think Torridge had no feelings, sir.' Old Frosty would reply that Buller Yeats was a frightful man. 'Take no notice, Torridge,' he'd add in his kindly voice, and Torridge would smile, making it clear that he didn't mind in the least what Buller Yeats said. 'Torridge knows true happiness,' a new young master, known as Mad Wallace, said in an unguarded moment one day, a remark which caused immediate uproar in a geography class. It was afterwards much repeated, like 'Dad's in the button business' and 'Torridge's, you know.' The true happiness of Torridge became a joke, the particular property of Wiltshire and Mace-Hamilton and Arrowsmith. Furthering the joke, they claimed that knowing Torridge was a rare experience, that the private realm of his innocence and his happiness was even exotic. Wiltshire insisted that one day the school would be proud of him. The joke was worked to death.

At the school it was the habit of certain senior boys to 'take an interest in' juniors. This varied from glances and smiles across the dining-hall to written invitations to meet in some secluded spot at a stated time. Friendships, taking a variety of forms, were then initiated. It was flattering, and very often a temporary antidote for homesickness, when a new boy received the agreeable but bewildering attentions of an important fifth-former. A meeting behind Chapel led to the negotiating of a barbed-wire fence on a slope of gorse bushes, the older boy solicitous and knowledgeable. There were well-trodden paths and nooks among the gorse where smoking could take place with comparative safety. Farther afield, in the hills, there were crude shelters composed of stones and corrugated iron. Here, too, the emphasis was on smoking and romance.

New boys very soon became aware of the nature of older boys' interest in them. The flattery changed its shape, an adjustment was made – or the new boys retreated in panic from this area of school life. Andrews and Butler, Webb and Mace-Hamilton, Dillon and Pratt, Tothill and Goldfish

Stewart, Good and Wiltshire, Sainsbury Major and Arrowsmith, Brewitt and Whyte: the liaisons were renowned, the combinations of names sometimes seeming like a music-hall turn, a soft-shoe shuffle of entangled hearts. There was faithlessness, too: the Honourable Anthony Swain made the rounds of the senior boys, a fickle and tartish *bijou*, desired and yet despised.

Torridge's puddingy appearance did not suggest that he had *bijou* qualities, and glances did not readily come his way in the dining-hall. This was often the fate, or good fortune, of new boys and was not regarded as a sign of qualities lacking. Yet quite regularly an ill-endowed child would mysteriously become the object of fifth- and sixth-form desire. This remained a puzzle to the juniors until they themselves became fifth- or sixth-formers and desire was seen to have to do with something deeper than superficial good looks.

It was the apparent evidence of this truth that caused Torridge, first of all, to be aware of the world of *bijou* and protector. He received a note from a boy in the Upper Fifth who had previously eschewed the sexual life offered by the school. He was a big, black-haired youth with glasses and a protruding forehead, called Fisher.

'Hey, what's this mean?' Torridge inquired, finding the note under his pillow, tucked into his pyjamas. 'Here's a bloke wants to go for a walk.'

He read the invitation out: '*If you would like to come for a walk meet me by the electricity plant behind Chapel. Half past four Tuesday afternoon. R.A.J. Fisher.*'

'Jesus Christ!' said Armstrong.

'You've got an admirer, Porridge,' Mace-Hamilton said.

'Admirer?'

'He wants you to be his *bijou*,' Wiltshire explained.

'What's it mean, *bijou*?'

'Tart, it means, Porridge.'

'Tart?'

'Friend. He wants to be your protector.'

'What's it mean, protector?'

'He loves you, Porridge.'

'I don't even know the bloke.'

'He's the one with the big forehead. He's a half-wit actually.'

'Half-wit?'

'His mother let him drop on his head. Like yours did, Porridge.'

'My mum never.'

Everyone was crowding around Torridge's bed. The note was passed from hand to hand. 'What's your dad do, Porridge?' Wiltshire suddenly asked, and Torridge automatically replied that he was in the button business.

'You've got to write a note back to Fisher, you know,' Mace-Hamilton pointed out.

'Dear Fisher,' Wiltshire prompted, 'I love you.'

'But I don't even –'

'It doesn't matter not knowing him. You've got to write a letter and put it in his pyjamas.'

Torridge didn't say anything. He placed the note in the top pocket of his jacket and slowly began to undress. The other boys drifted back to their own beds, still amused by the development. In the wash-room the next morning Torridge said:

'I think he's quite nice, that Fisher.'

'Had a dream about him, did you, Porridge?' Mace-Hamilton inquired. 'Got up to tricks, did he?'

'No harm in going for a walk.'

'No harm at all, Porridge.'

In fact, a mistake had been made. Fisher, in his haste or his excitement, had placed the note under the wrong pillow. It was Arrowsmith, still allied with Sainsbury Major, whom he wished to attract.

That this error had occurred was borne in on Torridge when he turned up at the electricity plant on the following Tuesday. He had not considered it necessary to reply to Fisher's note, but he had, across the dining-hall, essayed a smile or two in the older boy's direction: it had surprised him to meet with no response. It surprised him rather more to meet with no response by the electricity plant. Fisher just looked at him and then turned his back, pretending to whistle.

'Hullo, Fisher,' Torridge said.

'Hop it, look. I'm waiting for someone.'

'I'm Torridge, Fisher.'

'I don't care who you are.'

'You wrote me that letter.' Torridge was still smiling. 'About a walk, Fisher.'

'Walk? What walk?'

'You put the letter under my pillow, Fisher.'

'Jesus!' said Fisher.

The encounter was observed by Arrowsmith, Mace-Hamilton and Wiltshire, who had earlier taken up crouched positions behind one of the chapel buttresses. Torridge heard the familiar hoots of laughter, and because it was his way he joined in. Fisher, white-faced, strode away.

'Poor old Porridge,' Arrowsmith commiserated, gasping and pretending to be contorted with mirth. Mace-Hamilton and Wiltshire were leaning against the buttress, issuing shrill noises.

'Gosh,' Torridge said, 'I don't care.'

He went away, still laughing a bit, and there the matter of Fisher's attempt at communication might have ended. In fact it didn't, because Fisher wrote a second time and this time he made certain that the right boy received his missive. But Arrowsmith, still firmly the property of Sainsbury Major, wished to have nothing to do with R.A.J. Fisher.

When he was told the details of Fisher's error, Torridge said he'd guessed it had been something like that. But Wiltshire, Mace-Hamilton and Arrowsmith claimed that a new sadness had overcome Torridge. Something beautiful had been going to happen to him, Wiltshire said: just as the petals of friendship were opening the flower had been crudely snatched away. Arrowsmith said Torridge reminded him of one of Picasso's sorrowful harlequins. One way or the other, it was agreed that the experience would be beneficial to Torridge's sensitivity. It was seen as his reason for turning to religion, which recently he had done, joining a band of similarly inclined boys who were inspired by the word of the chaplain, a figure known as God Harvey. God Harvey was ascetic, seeming dangerously thin, his face all edge and as pale as milk, his cassock odorous with incense. He conducted readings in his room, offering coffee and biscuits afterwards, though not himself partaking of these refreshments. 'God Harvey's linnets' his acolytes were called, for often a hymn was sung to round things off. Welcomed into this fold, Torridge regained his happiness.

R.A.J. Fisher, on the other hand, sank into greater gloom. Arrowsmith remained elusive, mockingly faithful to Sainsbury Major, haughty when Fisher glanced pleadingly, ignoring all his letters. Fisher developed a look of introspective misery. The notes that Arrowsmith delightedly showed around were full of longing, increasingly tinged with desperation. The following term, unexpectedly, Fisher did not return to the school.

There was a famous Assembly at the beginning of that term, with much speculation beforehand as to the trouble in the air. Rumour had it that once and for all an attempt was to be made to stamp out the smiles and the glances in the dining-hall, the whole business of *bijoux* and protectors, even the faithless behaviour of the Honourable Anthony Swain. The school waited and then the gowned staff arrived in the Assembly Hall and waited also, in grim anticipation on a raised dais. Public beatings for past offenders were scheduled, it was whispered: the Sergeant-major – the school's boxing instructor, who had himself told tales of public beatings in the past – would inflict the punishment at the headmaster's bidding. But that did not happen. Stout and pompous and red-skinned, the headmaster marched to the dais unaccompanied by the Sergeant-major. Twitching with anger that many afterwards declared had been simulated, he spoke at great length of the school's traditions. He stated that for fourteen years he had been proud to be its headmaster. He spoke of decency, and then of his own dismay. The school had been dishonoured; he would wish certain practices to cease. 'I stand before you ashamed,' he added, and paused for a moment. 'Let all this cease,' he commanded. He marched away, tugging at his gown in a familiar manner.

No one understood why the Assembly had taken place at that particular time, on the first day of a summer term. Only the masters looked knowing, as though labouring beneath some secret, but pressed and pleaded with they refused to reveal anything. Even Old Frosty, usually a most reliable source on such occasions, remained awesomely tight-lipped.

But the pronounced dismay and shame of the headmaster changed nothing. That term progressed and the world of *bijoux* and their protectors continued as before, the glances, the meetings, cigarettes and romance in the hillside huts. R.A.J. Fisher was soon forgotten, having never made much of a mark. But the story of his error in placing a note under Torridge's pillow passed into legend, as did the encounter by the electricity plant and Torridge's deprivation of a relationship. The story was repeated as further terms passed by; new boys heard it and viewed Torridge with greater interest, imagining what R.A.J. Fisher had been like. The liaisons of Wiltshire with Good, Mace-Hamilton with Webb, and Arrowsmith with Sainsbury Major continued until the three senior boys left the school. Wiltshire, Mace-Hamilton and Arrowsmith found fresh protectors then, and later these new liaisons came to an end in a similar manner. Later still, Wiltshire, Mace-Hamilton and Arrowsmith ceased to be *bijoux* and became protectors themselves.

Torridge pursued the religious side of things. He continued to be a frequent partaker of God Harvey's biscuits and spiritual uplift, and a useful presence among the chapel pews, where he voluntarily dusted, cleaned brass and kept the hymn-books in a state of repair with Sellotape. Wiltshire, Mace-Hamilton and Arrowsmith continued to circulate stories about him which were not true: that he was the product of virgin birth, that he possessed the gift of tongues but did not care to employ it, that he had three kidneys. In the end there emanated from them the claim that a liaison existed between Torridge and God Harvey. 'Love and the holy spirit', Wiltshire pronounced, suggesting an ambience of chapel fustiness and God Harvey's grey boniness. The swish of his cassock took on a new significance, as did his thin, dry fingers. In a holy way the fingers pressed themselves on to Torridge, and then their holiness became a passion that could not be imagined. It was all a joke because Torridge was Torridge, but the laughter it caused wasn't malicious because no one hated him. He was a figure of fun; no one sought his downfall because there was no downfall to seek.

The friendship between Wiltshire, Mace-Hamilton and Arrowsmith continued after they left the school, after all three had married and had families. Once a year they received the Old Boys' magazine, which told of the achievements of themselves and the more successful of their schoolfellows. There were Old Boys' cocktail parties and Old Boys' Day at the school every June and the Old Boys' cricket match. Some of these occasions, from time to time, they attended. Every so often they received the latest rebuilding programme, with the suggestion that they might like to contribute to the rebuilding fund. Occasionally they did.

As middle age closed in, the three friends met less often. Arrowsmith was an executive with Shell and stationed for longish periods in different countries abroad. Once every two years he brought his family back to England, which provided an opportunity for the three friends to meet. The wives met on these occasions also, and over the years the children. Often the men's distant schooldays were referred to, Buller Yeats and Old Frosty and the Sergeant-major, the stout headmaster, and above all Torridge. Within the three families, in fact, Torridge had become a myth. The joke that had begun when they were all new boys together continued, as if driven by its own impetus. In the minds of the wives and children the innocence of Torridge, his true happiness in the face of mockery and his fondness for the religious side of life all lived on. With some exactitude a physical image of the boy he'd been took root; his neatly knotted maroon House tie, his polished shoes, the hair that resembled a mouse's fur, the pudding face with two small eyes in it. 'My dad's in the button business,' Arrowsmith had only to say to cause instant laughter. 'Torridge's, you know.' The way Torridge ate, the way he ran, the way he smiled back at Buller Yeats, the rumour that he'd been dropped on his head as a baby, that he had three kidneys: all this was considerably appreciated, because Wiltshire and Mace-Hamilton and Arrowsmith related it well.

What was not related was R.A.J. Fisher's error in placing a note beneath Torridge's pillow, or the story that had laughingly been spread about concerning Torridge's relationship with God Harvey. This would have meant revelations that weren't seemly in family circles, the explanation of the world of *bijou* and protector, the romance and cigarettes in the hillside huts, the entangling of hearts. The subject had been touched upon among the three husbands and their wives in the normal course of private conversation, although not everything had been quite recalled. Listening, the wives had formed the impression that the relationships between older and younger boys at their husbands' school were similar to the platonic admiration a junior girl had so often harboured for a senior girl at their own schools. And so the subject had been left.

One evening in June, 1976, Wiltshire and Mace-Hamilton met in a bar called the Vine, in Piccadilly Place. They hadn't seen one another since the summer of 1974, the last time Arrowsmith and his family had been in England. Tonight they were to meet the Arrowsmiths again, for a family dinner in the Woodlands Hotel, Richmond. On the last occasion the three families had celebrated their reunion at the Wiltshires' house in Cobham and the time before with the Mace-Hamiltons in Ealing. Arrowsmith insisted that it was a question of turn and turn about and every third time he arranged for the family dinner to be held at his expense at the Woodlands. It was convenient because, although the Arrowsmiths spent the greater part of each biennial leave with Mrs Arrowsmith's parents in Somerset, they always stayed for a week at the Woodlands in order to see a bit of London life.

In the Vine in Piccadilly Place Wiltshire and Mace-Hamilton hurried over their second drinks. As always, they were pleased to see one another, and both were excited at the prospect of seeing Arrowsmith and his family again. They still looked faintly alike. Both had balded and run to fat. They wore inconspicuous blue suits with a discreet chalk stripe, Wiltshire's a little smarter than Mace-Hamilton's.

'We'll be late,' Wiltshire said, having just related how he'd made a small killing since the last time they'd met. Wiltshire operated in the import-export world; Mace-Hamilton was a chartered accountant.

They finished their drinks. 'Cheerio,' the barman called out to them as they slipped away. His voice was deferentially low, matching the softly lit surroundings. 'Cheerio, Gerry,' Wiltshire said.

They drove in Wiltshire's car to Hammersmith, over the bridge and on to Barnes and Richmond. It was a Friday evening; the traffic was heavy.

'He had a bit of trouble, you know,' Mace-Hamilton said.

'Arrows?'

'She took a shine to some guy in Mombasa.'

Wiltshire nodded, poking the car between a cyclist and a taxi. He wasn't surprised. One night six years ago Arrowsmith's wife and he had committed adultery together at her suggestion. A messy business it had been, and afterwards he'd felt terrible.

In the Woodlands Hotel Arrowsmith, in a grey flannel suit, was not entirely sober. He, too, had run a bit to fat although, unlike Wiltshire and Mace-Hamilton, he hadn't lost any of his hair. Instead, it had dramatically changed colour: what Old Frosty had once called 'Arrows' blond thatch' was grey now. Beneath it his face was pinker than it had been and he had taken to wearing spectacles, heavy and black-rimmed, making him look even more different from the boy he'd been.

In the bar of the Woodlands he drank whisky on his own, smiling occasionally to himself because tonight he had a surprise for everybody. After five weeks of being cooped up with his in-laws in Somerset he was feeling good. 'Have one yourself, dear,' he invited the barmaid, a girl with an excess of lipstick on a podgy mouth. He pushed his own glass towards her while she was saying she didn't mind if she did.

His wife and his three adolescent children, two boys and a girl, entered the bar with Mrs Mace-Hamilton. 'Hi, hi, hi,' Arrowsmith called out to them in a jocular manner, causing his wife and Mrs Mace-Hamilton to note that he was drunk again. They sat down while he quickly finished the whisky that had just been poured for him. 'Put another in that for a start,' he ordered the barmaid, and crossed the floor of the bar to find out what everyone else wanted.

Mrs Wiltshire and her twins, girls of twelve, arrived while drinks were being decided about. Arrowsmith kissed her, as he had kissed Mrs Mace-Hamilton. The barmaid, deciding that the accurate conveying of such a large order was going to be beyond him, came and stood by the two tables that the party now occupied. The order was given; an animated conversation began.

The three women were different in appearance and in manner. Mrs Arrowsmith was thin as a knife, fashionably dressed in a shade of ash-grey that reflected her ash-grey hair. She smoked perpetually, unable to abandon the habit. Mrs Wiltshire was small. Shyness caused her to coil herself up in the presence of other people so that she often resembled a ball. Tonight she was in pink, a faded shade. Mrs Mace-Hamilton was carelessly plump, a large woman attired in a carelessly chosen dress that had begonias on it. She rather frightened Mrs Wiltshire. Mrs Arrowsmith found her trying.

'Oh, heavenly little drink!' Mrs Arrowsmith said, briefly drooping her blue-tinged eyelids as she sipped her gin and tonic.

'It *is* good to see you,' Mrs Mace-Hamilton gushed, beaming at everyone and vaguely raising her glass. 'And how they've all grown!' Mrs Mace-Hamilton had not had children herself.

'Their boobs have grown, by God,' the older Arrowsmith boy murmured to his brother, a reference to the Wiltshire twins. Neither of the two Arrowsmith boys went to their father's school: one was at a preparatory school in Oxford, the other at Charterhouse. Being of an age to do so, they both drank sherry and intended to drink as much of it as they possibly could. They found these family occasions tedious. Their sister, about to go to university, had determined neither to speak nor to smile for the entire evening. The Wiltshire twins were quite looking forward to the food.

Arrowsmith sat beside Mrs Wiltshire. He didn't say anything but after a moment he stretched a hand over her two knees and squeezed them in what he intended to be a brotherly way. He said without conviction that it was great to see her. He didn't look at her while he spoke. He didn't much care for hanging about with the women and children.

In turn Mrs Wiltshire didn't much care for his hand on her knees and was relieved when he drew it away. 'Hi, hi, hi,' he suddenly called out, causing her to jump. Wiltshire and Mace-Hamilton had appeared.

The physical similarity that had been so pronounced when the three men were boys and had been only faintly noticeable between Wiltshire and Mace-Hamilton in the Vine was clearly there again, as if the addition of Arrowsmith had supplied missing reflections. The men had thickened in the same way; the pinkness of Arrowsmith's countenance was a pinkness that tinged the other faces too. Only Arrowsmith's grey thatch of hair seemed out of place, all wrong beside the baldness of the other two: in their presence it might have been a wig, an impression it did not otherwise give. His grey flannel suit, beside their pinstripes, looked like something put on by mistake. 'Hi, hi, hi,' he shouted, thumping their shoulders.

Further rounds of drinks were bought and consumed. The Arrowsmith boys declared to each other that they were drunk and made further *sotto voce* observations about the forming bodies of the Wiltshire twins. Mrs Wiltshire felt the occasion becoming easier as Cinzano Bianco coursed through her bloodstream. Mrs Arrowsmith was aware of a certain familiar edginess within her body, a desire to be elsewhere, alone with a man she did not know. Mrs Mace-Hamilton spoke loudly of her garden.

In time the party moved from the bar to the dining-room. 'Bring us another round at the table,' Arrowsmith commanded the lipsticked barmaid. 'Quick as you can, dear.'

In the large dim dining-room waiters settled them around a table with little vases of carnations on it, a long table beneath the chandelier in the centre of the room. Celery soup arrived at the table, and smoked salmon and pâté, and the extra round of drinks Arrowsmith had ordered, and bottles of Nuits St Georges, and bottles of Vouvray and Anjou Rosé, and sirloin of beef, chicken à la king and veal escalope. The Arrowsmith boys laughed shrilly, openly staring at the tops of the Wiltshire twins' bodies. Potatoes, peas, spinach and carrots were served. Mrs Arrowsmith waved the vegetables away and smoked between courses. It was after this dinner six years ago that she had made her suggestion to Wiltshire, both of them being the worse for wear and it seeming not to matter because of that. 'Oh, *isn't* this jolly?' the voice of Mrs Mace-Hamilton boomed above the general hubbub.

Over Chantilly trifle and Orange Surprise the name of Torridge was heard. The name was always mentioned just about now, though sometimes sooner. 'Poor old bean,' Wiltshire said, and everybody laughed because it was the one subject they all shared. No one really wanted to hear about the Mace-Hamiltons' garden; the comments of the Arrowsmith boys were only for each other; Mrs Arrowsmith's needs could naturally not be voiced; the shyness of Mrs Wiltshire was private too. But Torridge was different. Torridge in a way was like an old friend now, existing in everyone's mind, a family subject. The Wiltshire twins were quite amused to hear of some freshly remembered evidence of Torridge's naïveté; for the Arrowsmith girl it was better at least than being questioned by Mrs Mace-Hamilton; for her brothers it was an excuse to bellow with simulated mirth. Mrs Mace-Hamilton considered that the boy sounded frightful, Mrs Arrowsmith couldn't have cared less. Only Mrs Wiltshire had doubts: she thought the three men were hard on the memory of the boy, but of course had not ever said so. Tonight, after Wiltshire had recalled the time when Torridge had been convinced by Arrowsmith that Buller Yeats had dropped dead in his bath, the younger Arrowsmith boy told of a boy at his own school who'd been convinced that his sister's dog had died.

'Listen,' Arrowsmith suddenly shouted out. 'He's going to join us. Old Torridge.'

There was laughter, no one believing that Torridge was going to arrive, Mrs Arrowsmith saying to herself that her husband was pitiful when he became as drunk as this.

'I thought it would be a gesture,' Arrowsmith said. 'Honestly. He's looking in for coffee.'

'You bloody devil, Arrows,' Wiltshire said, smacking the table with the palm of his hand.

'He's in the button business,' Arrowsmith shouted. 'Torridge's, you know.'

As far as Wiltshire and Mace-Hamilton could remember, Torridge had never featured in an Old Boys' magazine. No news of his career had been printed, and certainly no obituary. It was typical, somehow, of Arrowsmith to have winkled him out. It was part and parcel of him to want to add another dimension to the joke, to recharge its batteries. For the sight of Torridge in middle age would surely make funnier the reported anecdotes.

'After all, what's wrong,' demanded Arrowsmith noisily, 'with old school pals meeting up? The more the merrier.'

He was a bully, Mrs Wiltshire thought: all three of them were bullies.

Torridge arrived at half past nine. The hair that had been like a mouse's fur was still like that. It hadn't greyed any more; the scalp hadn't balded. He hadn't run to fat; in middle age he'd thinned down a bit. There was even a lankiness about him now, which was reflected in his movements. At school he had moved slowly, as though with caution. Jauntily attired in a pale linen suit, he crossed the dining-room of the Woodlands Hotel with a step as nimble as a tap-dancer's.

No one recognized him. To the three men who'd been at school with him the man who approached their dinner table was a different person, quite unlike the figure that existed in the minds of the wives and children.

'My dear Arrows,' he said, smiling at Arrowsmith. The smile was different too, a brittle snap of a smile that came and went in a matter-of-fact way. The eyes that had been small didn't seem so in his thinner face. They flashed with a gleam of some kind, matching the snap of his smile.

'Good God, it's never old Porridge!' Arrowsmith's voice was slurred. His face had acquired the beginnings of an alcoholic crimson, sweat glistened on his forehead.

'Yes, it's old Porridge,' Torridge said quietly. He held his hand out towards Arrowsmith and then shook hands with Wiltshire and Mace-Hamilton. He was introduced to their wives, with whom he shook hands also. He was introduced to the children, which involved further hand-shaking. His hand was cool and rather hard: they felt it should have been damp.

'You're nicely in time for coffee, Mr Torridge,' Mrs Mace-Hamilton said.

'Brandy more like,' Arrowsmith suggested. 'Brandy, old chap?'

'Well, that's awfully kind of you, Arrows. Chartreuse I'd prefer, really.'

A waiter drew up a chair. Room was made for Torridge between Mrs Mace-Hamilton and the Arrowsmith boys. It was a frightful mistake, Wiltshire was thinking. It was mad of Arrowsmith.

Mace-Hamilton examined Torridge across the dinner table. The old Torridge would have said he'd rather not have anything alcoholic, that a cup of tea and a biscuit were more his line in the evenings. It was impossible to imagine this man saying his dad had a button business. There was a suavity about him that made Mace-Hamilton uneasy. Because of what had been related to his wife and the other wives and their children he felt he'd been caught out in a lie, yet in fact that wasn't the case.

The children stole glances at Torridge, trying to see him as the boy who'd been described to them, and failing to. Mrs Arrowsmith said to herself that all this stuff they'd been told over the years had clearly been rubbish. Mrs Mace-Hamilton was bewildered. Mrs Wiltshire was pleased.

'No one ever guessed,' Torridge said, 'what became of R.A.J. Fisher.' He raised the subject suddenly, without introduction.

'Oh God, Fisher,' Mace-Hamilton said.

'Who's Fisher?' the younger of the Arrowsmith boys inquired.

Torridge turned to flash his quick smile at the boy. 'He left,' he said. 'In unfortunate circumstances.'

'You've changed a lot, you know,' Arrowsmith said. 'Don't you think he's changed?' he asked Wiltshire and Mace-Hamilton.

'Out of recognition,' Wiltshire said.

Torridge laughed easily. 'I've become adventurous. I'm a late developer, I suppose.'

'What kind of unfortunate circumstances?' the younger Arrowsmith boy asked. 'Was Fisher expelled?'

'Oh no, not at all,' Mace-Hamilton said hurriedly.

'Actually,' Torridge said, 'Fisher's trouble all began with the writing of a note. Don't you remember? He put it in my pyjamas. But it wasn't for me at all.'

He smiled again. He turned to Mrs Wiltshire in a way that seemed polite, drawing her into the conversation. 'I was an innocent at school. But innocence slips away. I found my way about eventually.'

'Yes, of course,' she murmured. She didn't like him, even though she was glad he wasn't as he might have been. There was malevolence in him, a ruthlessness that seemed like a work of art. He seemed like a work of art himself, as though in losing the innocence he spoke of he had recreated himself.

'I often wonder about Fisher,' he remarked.

The Wiltshire twins giggled. 'What's so great about this bloody Fisher?' the older Arrowsmith boy murmured, nudging his brother with an elbow.

'What're you doing these days?' Wiltshire asked, interrupting Mace-Hamilton, who had also begun to say something.

'I make buttons,' Torridge replied. 'You may recall my father made buttons.'

'Ah, here're the drinks,' Arrowsmith rowdily observed.

'I don't much keep up with the school,' Torridge said as the waiter placed a glass of Chartreuse in front of him. 'I don't so much as think about it except for wondering about poor old Fisher. Our headmaster was a cretin,' he informed Mrs Wiltshire.

Again the Wiltshire twins giggled. The Arrowsmith girl yawned and her brothers giggled also, amused that the name of Fisher had come up again.

'You will have coffee, Mr Torridge?' Mrs Mace-Hamilton offered, for the waiter had brought a fresh pot to the table. She held it poised above a cup. Torridge smiled at her and nodded. She said:

'Pearl buttons d'you make?'

'No, not pearl.'

'Remember those awful packet peas we used to have?' Arrowsmith inquired. Wiltshire said:

'Use plastics at all? In your buttons, Porridge?'

'No, we don't use plastics. Leathers, various leathers. And horn. We specialize.'

'How very interesting!' Mrs Mace-Hamilton exclaimed.

'No, no. It's rather ordinary really.' He paused, and then added, 'Someone once told me that Fisher went into a timber business. But of course that was far from true.'

'A chap was expelled a year ago,' the younger Arrowsmith boy said, contributing this in order to cover up a fresh outburst of sniggering. 'For stealing a transistor.'

Torridge nodded, appearing to be interested. He asked the Arrowsmith boys where they were at school. The older one said Charterhouse and his brother gave the name of his preparatory school. Torridge nodded again and asked their sister and she said she was waiting to go to university. He had quite a chat with the Wiltshire twins about their school. They considered it pleasant the way he bothered, seeming genuinely to want to know. The giggling died away.

'I imagined Fisher wanted me for his *bijou*,' he said when all that was over, still addressing the children. 'Our place was riddled with fancy larks like that. Remember?' he added, turning to Mace-Hamilton.

'*Bijou*?' one of the twins asked before Mace-Hamilton could reply.

'A male tart,' Torridge explained.

The Arrowsmith boys gaped at him, the older one with his mouth actually open. The Wiltshire twins began to giggle again. The Arrowsmith girl frowned, unable to hide her interest.

'The Honourable Anthony Swain,' Torridge said, 'was no better than a whore.'

Mrs Arrowsmith, who for some minutes had been engaged with her own thoughts, was suddenly aware that the man who was in the button business was talking about sex. She gazed diagonally across the table at him, astonished that he should be talking in this way.

'Look here, Torridge,' Wiltshire said, frowning at him and shaking his head. With an almost imperceptible motion he gestured towards the wives and children.

'Andrews and Butler. Dillon and Pratt. Tothill and Goldfish Stewart. Your dad,' Torridge said to the Arrowsmith girl, 'was always very keen. Sainsbury Major in particular.'

'Now look here,' Arrowsmith shouted, beginning to get to his feet and then changing his mind.

'My gosh, how they broke chaps' hearts, those three!'

'Please don't talk like this.' It was Mrs Wiltshire who protested, to everyone's surprise, most of all her own. 'The children are quite young, Mr Torridge.'

Her voice had become a whisper. She could feel herself reddening with embarrassment, and a little twirl of sickness occurred in her stomach. Deferentially, as though appreciating the effort she had made, Torridge apologized.

'I think you'd better go,' Arrowsmith said.

'You were right about God Harvey, Arrows. Gay as a grig he was, beneath that cassock. So was Old Frosty, as a matter of fact.'

'Really!' Mrs Mace-Hamilton cried, her bewilderment turning into outrage. She glared at her husband, demanding with her eyes that instantly something should be done. But her husband and his two friends were briefly stunned by what Torridge had claimed for God Harvey. Their schooldays leapt back at them, possessing them for a vivid moment: the dormitory, the dining-hall, the glances and the invitations, the meetings behind Chapel. It was somehow in keeping with the school's hypocrisy that God Harvey had had inclinations himself, that a rumour begun as an outrageous joke should have contained the truth.

'As a matter of fact,' Torridge went on, 'I wouldn't be what I am if it hadn't been for God Harvey. I'm what they call queer,' he explained to the children. 'I perform sexual acts with men.'

'For God's sake, Torridge,' Arrowsmith shouted, on his feet, his face the colour of ripe strawberry, his watery eyes quivering with rage.

'It was nice of you to invite me tonight, Arrows. Our *alma mater* can't be too proud of chaps like me.'

People spoke at once, Mrs Mace-Hamilton and Mrs Wiltshire, all three men. Mrs Arrowsmith sat still. What she was thinking was that she had become quietly drunk while her husband had more boisterously reached the same condition. She was thinking, as well, that by the sound of things he'd possessed as a boy a sexual urge that was a lot livelier than the one he'd once exposed her to and now hardly ever did. With boys who had grown to be men he had had a whale of a time. Old Frosty had been a kind of Mr Chips, she'd been told. She'd never ever heard of Sainsbury Major or God Harvey.

'It's quite disgusting,' Mrs Mace-Hamilton's voice cried out above the other voices. She said the police should be called. It was scandalous to have to listen to unpleasant conversation like this. She began to say the children should leave the dining-room, but changed her mind because it appeared that Torridge himself was about to go. 'You're a most horrible man,' she cried.

Confusion gathered, like a fog around the table. Mrs Wiltshire, who knew that her husband had committed adultery with Mrs Arrowsmith, felt another bout of nerves in her stomach. 'Because she was starved, that's why,' her husband had almost violently confessed when she'd discovered. 'I was putting her out of her misery.' She had wept then and he had comforted her as best he could. She had not told him that he had never succeeded in arousing in her the desire to make love: she had always assumed that to be a failing in herself, but now for some reason she was not so sure. Nothing had been directly said that might have caused this doubt, but an instinct informed Mrs Wiltshire that the doubt should be there. The man beside her smiled his brittle, malevolent smile at her, as if in sympathy.

With his head bent over the table and his hands half hiding his face, the younger Arrowsmith boy examined his father by glancing through his fingers. There were men whom his parents warned him against, men who would sit beside you in buses or try to give you a lift in a car. This man who had come tonight, who had been such a joke up till now, was apparently one of these, not a joke at all. And the confusion was greater: at one time, it seemed, his father had been like that too.

The Arrowsmith girl considered her father also. Once she had walked into a room in Lagos to find her mother in the arms of an African clerk. Ever since she had felt sorry for her father. There'd been an unpleasant scene at the time, she'd screamed at her mother and later in a fury had told her father what she'd seen. He'd nodded, wearily seeming not to be surprised, while her mother had miserably wept. She'd put her arms around her father, comforting him; she'd felt no mercy for her mother, no sympathy or understanding. The scene formed vividly in her mind as she sat at the dinner table: it appeared to be relevant in the confusion and yet not clearly so. Her parents' marriage was messy, messier than it had looked. Across the table her mother grimly smoked, focusing her eyes with difficulty. She smiled at her daughter, a soft, inebriated smile.

The older Arrowsmith boy was also aware of the confusion. Being at a school where the practice which had been spoken of was common enough, he could easily believe the facts that had been thrown about. Against his will, he was forced to imagine what he had never imagined before: his father and his friends as schoolboys, engaged in passion with other boys. He might have been cynical about this image but he could not. Instead it made him want to gasp. It knocked away the smile that had been on his face all evening.

The Wiltshire twins unhappily stared at the white tablecloth, here and there stained with wine or gravy. They, too, found they'd lost the urge to smile and instead shakily blinked back tears.

'Yes, perhaps I'd better go,' Torridge said.

With impatience Mrs Mace-Hamilton looked at her husband, as if expecting him to hurry Torridge off or at least to say something. But Mace-Hamilton remained silent. Mrs Mace-Hamilton licked her lips, preparing to speak herself. She changed her mind.

'Fisher didn't go into a timber business,' Torridge said, 'because poor old Fisher was dead as a doornail. Which is why our cretin of a headmaster, Mrs Mace-Hamilton, had that Assembly.'

'Assembly?' she said. Her voice was weak, although she'd meant it to sound matter-of-fact and angry.

'There was an Assembly that no one understood. Poor old Fisher had strung himself up in a barn on his father's farm. I discovered that,' Torridge said, turning to Arrowsmith, 'years later: from God Harvey actually. The poor chap left a note but the parents didn't care to pass it on. I mean it was for you, Arrows.'

Arrowsmith was still standing, hanging over the table. 'Note?' he said. 'For me?'

'Another note. Why d'you think he did himself in, Arrows?'

Torridge smiled, at Arrowsmith and then around the table.

'None of that's true,' Wiltshire said.

'As a matter of fact it is.'

He went, and nobody spoke at the dinner table. A body of a schoolboy hung from a beam in a barn, a note on the straw below his dangling feet. It hung in the confusion that had been caused, increasing the confusion. Two waiters hovered by a sideboard, one passing the time by arranging sauce bottles, the other folding napkins into cone shapes. Slowly Arrowsmith sat down again. The silence continued as the conversation of Torridge continued to haunt the dinner table. He haunted it himself, with his brittle smile and his tap-dancer's elegance, still faithful to the past in which he had so signally failed, triumphant in his middle age.

Then Mrs Arrowsmith quite suddenly wept and the Wiltshire twins wept and Mrs Wiltshire comforted them. The Arrowsmith girl got up and walked away, and Mrs Mace-Hamilton turned to the three men and said they should be ashamed of themselves, allowing all this to happen.

Running Away

It is, Henrietta considers, ridiculous. Even so she feels sorry for the girl, that slack, wan face, the whine in her voice. And as if to add insult to injury, Sharon, as a name, is far from attractive.

'Now, I'm sure,' Henrietta says gently, 'you must simply forget all this. Sharon, why not go away for a little? To ... to ...' Where would a girl like Sharon Tamm want to go? Margate? Benidorm? 'I could help you if you'd like me to. We could call it a little loan.'

The girl shakes her head. Hair, in need of washing, flaps. She doesn't want to go away, her whine protests. She wants to stay since she feels she belongs here.

'It's only, Sharon, that I thought it might be easier. A change of scene for a week or two. I know it's hard for you.'

Again the head is shaken, the lank hair flaps. Granny spectacles are removed and wiped carefully on a patchwork skirt, or perhaps a skirt that is simply patched. Sharon's loose, soiled sandals have been kicked off, and she plays with them as she converses. She is sitting on the floor because she never sits on chairs.

'We understand each other, you see,' Henrietta continues softly. 'My dear, I do want you to realize that.'

'It's all over, the thing I had with the Orange People. I'm not like that any more. I'm perfectly responsible.'

'I know the Orange thing is over. I know you've got your feet quite on the ground, Sharon.'

'It was awful, 'smatter of fact, all that.'

The Orange People offer a form of Eastern mysticism about which Henrietta knows very little. Someone once told her that the mysticism is an excuse for sexual licence, but explained no further. The sect is apparently quite different from the Hare Krishna people, who sometimes wear orange also but who eat food of such poor quality that sexual excess is out of the question. The Orange People had camped in a field and upset the locals, but all that was ages ago.

'And I know you're working hard, my dear. I know you've turned over a new leaf.' The trouble is that the leaf has been turned, absurdly, in the direction of Henrietta's husband.

'I just want to stay here,' Sharon repeats. 'Ever since it happened I feel I don't belong anywhere else.'

'Well, strictly speaking, nothing *has* happened, dear.'

'It has to me, though, Henrietta.'

Sharon never smiles. Henrietta can't remember having ever seen a smile enlivening the slack features any more than a hint of make-up has ever freshened the pale skin that stretches over them. Henrietta, who dresses well and maintains with care the considerable good looks she possesses, can understand none of it. Unpresentable Sharon Tamm is certainly no floosie, and hardly a gold-digger. Perhaps such creatures do not exist, Henrietta speculates, one perhaps only reads about them.

'I thought I'd better tell you,' Sharon Tamm says. 'I thought it only fair, Henrietta.'

'Yes, I'm glad you did.'

'*He* never would.'

The girl stands up and puts her sandals on to her grimy feet. There is a little white plastic bow, a kind of clasp, in her hair: Henrietta hasn't noticed it before because the hair has covered it in a way it wasn't meant to. The girl sorts all that out now, shaking her head again, taking the bow out and replacing it.

'He can't hurt people,' she tells Henrietta, speaking of the man to whom Henrietta has been married for more than twenty years.

Sharon Tamm leaves the room then, and Henrietta, who has been sitting in a high-backed chair during the conversation, does not move from it. She is flabbergasted by the last two impertinent statements of the girl's. How dare she say he never would! How dare she imply some knowledge of him by coyly remarking that he cannot hurt people! For a moment she experiences a desire to hurry after the girl, to catch her in the hall and to smack her on the face with the open palm of her hand. But she is so taken aback, so outraged by the whole bizarre conversation, that she cannot move. The girl, at her own request – a whispery whine on the telephone – asked to come to see her 'about something urgent'. And although Henrietta intended to go out that afternoon she at once agreed to remain in, imagining that Sharon Tamm was in some kind of pickle.

The hall door bangs. Henrietta – forty-three last month, dressed now in a blue jersey and skirt, with a necklace of pink corals at her throat and several rings on the fingers of either hand, her hair touched with a preparation that brings out the reddish brown in it – still does not move. She stares at the place on the carpet where the girl has been crouched. There was a time when Sharon Tamm came quite often to the house, when she talked a lot about her family, when Henrietta first felt sorry for her.

She ceased to come rather abruptly, going off to the Orange People instead.

In the garden Henrietta's dog, a cairn called Ka-Ki, touches the glass of the french windows with her nose, asking to be let in. Henrietta's husband, Roy, has trained her to do that, but the training has not been difficult because the dog is intelligent. Henrietta crosses the room to open the french windows, not answering in her usual way the fuss the dog makes of her, scampering at her feet, offering some kind of gratitude. The awful thing is, the girl seemed genuinely to believe in the extraordinary fantasy that possesses her. She would have told Roy of course, and Roy being Roy wouldn't have known what to do.

They had married when Roy was at the very beginning of his career, seven years older than Henrietta, who at the time had been a secretary in the department. She'd been nervous because she didn't belong in the academic world, because she had not had a university education herself. 'Only a typist!' she used bitterly to cry in those early, headstrong quarrels they'd had. 'You can't expect a typist to be bright enough to understand you.' But Roy, urbane and placid even then, had kissed her crossly pouting lips and told her not to be so silly. She was cleverer, and prettier, and more attractive in all sorts of other ways, than one after another of his female colleagues: ever since he has been telling her that, and meaning it. Henrietta cannot accept the 'cleverer', but 'prettier' and 'more attractive' she believes to be true, and isn't ashamed when she admits it to herself. They dress appallingly for a start, most of the women in the department, a kind of arrogance, Henrietta considers.

She clears away the tea things, for she has naturally offered Sharon Tamm tea, and carries them to the kitchen. Only a little less shaky than she was in the sitting-room after the girl's final statements, she prepares a turkey breast for the oven. There isn't much to do to it, but she likes to spike it with herbs and to fold it round a celery heart, a recipe she devised herself. She slices parsnips to roast with it, and peels potatoes to roast also. It isn't a special meal in any way, but somehow she finds herself taking special care because Roy is going to hate it when she mentions the visit of the girl.

She makes a pineapple pudding he likes. He has schoolboy tastes, he says himself, and in Henrietta's view he has too great a fondness for dairy products. She has to watch him where cream is concerned, and she insists he does not take too much salt. Not having children of their own has affected their relationship in ways like this. They look after one another, he in turn insisting that she should not Hoover for too long because Hoovering brings on the strain in her back.

She turns the pudding out into a Pyrex dish, ready to go into the oven in twenty minutes. She hears her husband in the hall, her own name called, the welcoming bark of Ka-Ki. 'Let's have a drink,' she calls back. 'Let's take a drink to the garden.'

He is there, by the summer-house, when she arrives with the tray of sherry and gin and Cinzano. She has done her face again, although she knows it hardly needs it; she has tied a red chiffon scarf into her hair. 'There now,' she says. 'Dinner'll be a while.' He's back earlier than usual.

She pours gin and Cinzano for him, and sherry for herself. 'Well, then?' She smiles at him.

'Oh, nothing much. MacMelanie's being difficult.'

'That man should be shot.'

'I only wish we could find someone to do it.'

There is nothing else to report except that a student called Fosse has been found hallucinating by a park keeper. A pity, apparently, because the boy is bright and has always seemed to be mature and well-balanced.

'Roy, I've something to tell you.'

'Ah?'

He is a man who sprawls over chairs rather than sits in them. He has a sprawling walk, taking up more room than is his due on pavements; he sprawls in cinemas and buses, and over the wheel of his car. His grey hair, of which there is a lot, can never acquire a combed look even though he combs it regularly and in the normal way. His spectacles, thickly rimmed and large, move about on his reddish face and often, in fact, fall off. His suits become tousled as soon as he puts them on, gaps appearing, flesh revealed. The one he wears now is of dark brown corduroy, the suit he likes best. A spotted blue handkerchief cascades out of an upper pocket, matching a loose bow tie.

'Sharon Tamm was here,' Henrietta says.

'Ah.'

She watches while he gulps his gin and vermouth. His eyes behind the pebbly glass of his spectacles are without expression. His mind does not appear to be associated with what she is saying. She wonders if he is thinking that he is not a success in the department, that he should have left the university years ago. She knows he often thinks that when MacMelanie has been troublesome.

'Now, Roy, you have to listen.'

'Well then, I'm listening.'

'It's embarrassing,' she warns.

'What is?'

'This Sharon Tamm thing.'

'She's really pulled herself together, you know. She's very bright. *Really* bright, I mean.'

'She has developed a fantasy about you.'

He says nothing, as if he has not heard, or has heard and not understood.

'She imagines she's in love with you.'

He drinks a mouthful of his drink, and then another. He reaches out to the tray on the table between them and pours himself some more, mostly gin, she notices. He doesn't gesture towards her sherry. He doesn't say anything.

'It was such an awkward conversation.'

All she wants is that it should be known that the girl arrived and said what she did say, that there should be no secret between them about so absurd a matter.

'I had to tell you, Roy. I couldn't not.'

He drinks again, still gulping at the liquid rather than sipping. He is perturbed: knowing him so well she can see that, and she wonders how exactly it is that MacMelanie has been a nuisance again, or if he is depressed because of the boy, Fosse. His eyes have changed behind the glass of his spectacles, something clouds his expression. He is trying not to frown, an effort she is familiar with, a sign of emotion in him. The vein that comes and goes in his forehead will soon appear.

'Roy.'

'I'm sorry Sharon came.'

Attempting to lighten the atmosphere, she laughs slightly. 'She should wear a bra, you know, for a start.'

She pours herself more sherry since he does not intend to. It didn't work, saying the girl should wear a bra: her voice sounded silly. She has a poor head for alcohol of any kind.

'She said you can't hurt people.'

He pulls the spotted handkerchief out of his pocket and wipes sweat from his chin with it. He runs his tongue over his lips. Vaguely, he shakes his head, as if denying that he can't hurt people, but she knows the gesture doesn't mean that. He is upset by what has happened, as she herself has been. He is thinking, as she did, that Sharon Tamm was once taken under their wing. He brought her back with him one evening, encouraging her, as a stray dog might be encouraged into the warmth. Other students, too, have been like daughters or sons to them and have remained their friends, a surrogate family. It was painful when Sharon Tamm left them for the Orange People.

'Of course I know,' Henrietta says, 'that was something we didn't understand.'

Vaguely he offers her more sherry, not noticing that she has had some. He pours more of his mixture for himself.

'Yes, there was something wrong,' he says.

They have been through all that. They talked about it endlessly, sending themselves to sleep with it, lazing with it on a Sunday morning. Henrietta found it hard to forgive the girl for being ungrateful. Both of them, she considered, had helped her in so very many ways.

'Shall we forget it all now?' she suggests, knowing that her voice has become nervous. 'Everything about the wretched girl?'

'Forget?'

That is impossible, his tone suggests. They cannot forget all that Sharon Tamm has told them about her home in Daventry, about her father's mother who lives with the family and stirs up so much trouble, about her overweight sister Diane and her brother Leslie. The world of Sharon Tamm's family has entered theirs. They can see, even now, the grandmother in her special armchair in the kitchen, her face snagged with a sourness that has to do with her wastrel husband, long since dead. They can see the saucepans boiling over on the stove because Mrs Tamm can never catch them in time, and Leslie's motor-cycling gear on the kitchen table, and Diane's bulk. Mr Tamm shouts perpetually, at Leslie to take his motor-cycling clothes away, at Diane for being so fat, at his wife, at Sharon, making her jump. 'You are stupid to an extent,' is the statement he has coined specially for his wife and repeats for her benefit several times every evening. He speaks slowly when he makes this statement, giving the words air, floating them through tired exasperation. His noisy manner leaves him when he dispatches these words, for otherwise – when he tells his wife she is ugly or a bitch – he shouts, and bangs anything he can lay his hand on, a saucepan lid, a tin of mushy peas, a spoon. The only person he doesn't shout at is his mother, for whom he has an exaggerated regard, even, according to Sharon, loves. Every evening he takes her down to the Tapper's Arms, returning at closing time to the house that Sharon has so minutely described: rooms separated by walls through which all quarrels can be heard, cigarette burns on the edge of the bath, a picture of a black girl on the landing, a stair-carpet touched with Leslie's motor-cycling grease and worn away in places. To Henrietta's sitting-room – flowery in summer because the french windows bring the garden in, cheerful with a wood fire when it's cold – these images have been repeatedly conveyed, for Sharon Tamm derived considerable relief from talking.

'Well, she told me and I've told you. Please can we just put it all aside?'

She rises as she speaks and hurries to the kitchen. She opens the oven and places the pineapple pudding on the bottom shelf. She bastes the turkey breast and the potatoes and the parsnips. She washes some broccoli and puts it ready on the draining board. He has not said, as she hoped he would, that Sharon Tamm is really a bit pathetic. Ka-Ki sniffs about the kitchen, excited by the smell that has come from the oven. She trots behind Henrietta, back to the garden.

'She told you too, didn't she, Roy? You knew all this?'

She didn't mean to say that. While washing the broccoli she planned to mention MacMelanie, to change the subject firmly and with deliberation. But the nervousness that Sharon Tamm inspired in her when she said that Roy couldn't hurt people has suddenly returned, and she feels muzzy due to the sherry, not entirely in control of herself.

'Yes, she told me,' he says. 'Well, actually, it isn't quite like that.'

He has begun to sweat again, little beads breaking on his forehead and his chin. He pulls the dotted handkerchief from his pocket and wipes at his face. In a slow, unwilling voice he tells her what some intuition already insists is the unbelievable truth: it is not just that the girl has a silly crush on him but that a relationship of some kind exists between them. Listening, she feels physically sick. She feels she is asleep, trying to wake herself out of a nightmare because the sickness is heaving through her stomach. The face of the girl is vivid, a whitehead in the crease of her chin, the rims of her eyes pink. The girl is an insult to her, with her dirty feet and broken fingernails.

'Let's not mention it ever again,' she hears herself urging repetitiously. 'MacMelanie,' she begins, but does not continue. He is saying something, his voice stumbling, larded with embarrassment. She can't hear him properly.

There has never been an uneasiness about their loyalty to one another, about their love or their companionship. Roy is disappointed because, professionally, he hasn't got on, but that has nothing to do with the marriage. Roy doesn't understand ambition, he doesn't understand that advancement has to be pursued. She knows that but has never said it.

'I'm sorry, Henrietta,' he says, and she wants to laugh. She wants to stare at him in amazement as he sprawls there, sweating and fat. She wants to laugh into his face so that he can see how ridiculous it all is. How can it possibly be that he is telling her he loves an unattractive girl who is thirty years younger than him?

'I feel most awfully dejected,' he mutters, staring down at the paving stones where they sit. Her dog is obedient at his feet. High above them an aeroplane goes over.

Does he want to marry the girl? Will she lead him into the house in

Daventry to meet her family, into the kitchen where the awful grandmother is? Will he shake hands with stupid Mrs Tamm, with Leslie and Diane? Will he go down to the Tapper's Arms with Mr Tamm?

'I can't believe this, Roy.'

'I'm sorry.'

'Do you adore her?'

He doesn't answer.

'Have I been no good to you all these years, Roy?'

'Of course you have.'

They have made love, the girl and he. He tells Henrietta so, confessing awkwardly, mentioning the floor of his room in the department. He would have taken off the girl's granny glasses and put them on the fawn vinyl by the leg of his desk. He would have run his fingers through the lustreless hair.

'How could you do this, Roy?'

'It's a thing that happened. Nobody did anything.' Red-faced, shamefaced, he attempts to shrug, but the effort becomes lost in his sprawling flabbiness. He is as unattractive as the girl, she finds herself reflecting: a stranded jellyfish.

'It's ridiculous, Roy,' she shouts, at last losing control. 'It's madness all this.' They have had quarrels before, ordinary quarrels about ordinary matters. Mild insults were later taken back, apologized for, the heat of the moment blamed.

'Why should it be ridiculous,' he questions now, 'that someone should love me? Why should it be?'

'She's a child, you're a man of fifty. How could there possibly be a normal relationship between you? What have you in common?'

'We fell in love, Henrietta. Love has nothing to do with having things in common or normal relationships. Hesselmann in fact points out –'

'For God's sake, Roy, this is not a time for Hesselmann.'

'He does suggest that love abnormalizes –'

'So you're going to become a middle-aged hippy, are you, Roy? You're going to put on robes and dance and meditate in a field with the Orange People? The Orange People were phony, you said. You said that, Roy.'

'You know as well as I do that Sharon has nothing to do with the Orange People any more.'

'You'll love her grandmother. Not to mention Mr Tamm.'

'Sharon needs to be protected from her family. As a matter of fact, she doesn't want ever to go back to that house. You're being snide, you know.'

'I'm actually suffering from shock.'

'There are things we must work out.'

'Oh, for heaven's sake, Roy, have your menopausal fling with the girl. Take her off to a hotel in Margate or Benidorm.'

She pours herself more sherry, her hands shaking, a harsh fieriness darkening her face, reflecting the fury in her voice. She imagines the pair of them in the places she mentions, people looking at them, he getting to know the girl's intimate habits. He would become familiar with the contents of her handbag, the way she puts on and takes off her clothes, the way she wakes up. Nineteen years ago, on their honeymoon in La Grève, Roy spoke of this aspect of a close relationship. Henrietta's own particular way of doing things, and her possessions – her lipstick, her powder compact, her dark glasses, the leather suitcase with her pre-marriage initials on it, the buttoning of her skirts and dresses – were daily becoming as familiar to him as they had been for so long to her. Her childhood existed for him because of what, in passing, she told him of it.

'D'you remember La Grève?' she asks, her voice calm again. 'The woman who called you Professor, those walks in the snow?'

Impatiently he looks away. La Grève is irrelevant, all of it far too long ago. Again he mentions Hesselmann. Not understanding, she says:

'At least *I* shall not forget La Grève.'

'I've tried to get over her. I've tried not seeing her. None of it works.'

'She said you would not have told me. What did you intend, Roy?'

'I don't know.'

'She said it wasn't fair, did she?'

'Yes, she did.' He pauses. 'She's very fond of you, you know.'

In the oven the breast of turkey would be shrivelling, the pineapple pudding of which he was so boyishly fond would be a burnt mess. She says, and feels ashamed of admitting it: 'I've always had affection for her too, in spite of what I say.'

'I need to talk to her now. I need to tell her we've cleared the air.'

He stands up and drinks what remains of his drink. Tears ooze from beneath his spectacles as he looks down at Henrietta, staring at her. He says nothing else except, yet again, that he is sorry. He shuffles and blows his nose as he speaks. Then he turns and goes away, and a few minutes later she hears the bang of the hall door, as she heard it after Sharon Tamm had left the house also.

Henrietta shops in a greengrocer's that in the Italian small-town manner has no name, just *Fiori e Frutta* above the door. The shy woman who serves there, who has come to know her, adds up the cost of *fagiolini*, pears and spinach on a piece of paper.

'*Mille quattro cento.*' Henrietta counts out the money and gathers up her purchases.

'*Buon giorno, grazie*,' the woman murmurs, and Henrietta wishes her good-day and passes out into the street.

The fat barber sleeps in his customers' chair, his white overall as spotless as a surgeon's before an operation. In the window his wife knits, glancing up now and again at the women who come and go in the Malgri Moda. It is Tuesday and the Jollycaffè is closed. The men who usually sit outside it are nowhere to be seen.

Henrietta buys a slice of beef, enough for one. In the mini-market she buys eggs and a packet of *zuppa di verdura*, and *biscotti strudel 'cocktail di frutta'*, which have become her favourites. She climbs up through the town, to the *appartamento* in the Piazza Santa Lucia. She is dressed less formally than she thought suitable for middle age in England. She wears a denim skirt, blue canvas shoes, a blue shirt which she bought before the weekend from Signora Leici. Her Italian improves a little every day, due mainly to the lessons she has with the girl in the *Informazioni*. They are both determined that by the winter she will know enough to teach English to the youngest children in the orphanage. Sister Maria has said she would welcome that.

It is May. On the verges of the meadows and the wheat fields that stretch below the town pale roses are in bloom. Laburnum blossoms in the vineyards, wires for the vines stretching between the narrow trunks of the trees. It is the season of broom and clover, of poppies, and geraniums forgotten in the grass. Sleepy vipers emerge from crevices, no longer kept down by the animals that once grazed these hillsides. Because of them Henrietta has bought rubber boots for walking in the woods or up Monte Totona.

She is happy because she is alone. She is happy in the small *appartamento* lent to her by friends of her sister, who use it infrequently. She loves the town's steep, cool streets, its quietness, the grey stone of its buildings, quarried from the hill it is built upon. She is happy because the nightmare is distant now, a picture she can illuminate in her mind and calmly survey. She sees her husband sprawling on the chair in the garden, the girl in her granny glasses, and her own weeping face in the bathroom looking-glass. Time shrinks the order of events: she packs her clothes into three suitcases; she is in her sister's house in Hemel Hempstead. That was the worst of all, the passing of the days in Hemel Hempstead, the sympathy of her sister, her generous, patient brother-in-law, their children imagining she was ill. When she thinks of herself now she feels a child herself, not the Henrietta of the suburban sitting-room and the tray of drinks, with chiffon tidily in her hair. Her father makes a swing for her because she has begged so, ropes tied to the bough of an apple tree. Her mother once was cross because she climbed that tree. She cries and her sister comforts her, a sunny afternoon when she got tar on her dress. She skates on an icy pond, a birthday treat before her birthday tea when she was nine. 'I can't stay here,' she said in Hemel Hempstead, and then there was the stroke of good fortune, people she did not even know who had an *appartamento* in a Tuscan hill town.

In the *cantina* of the Contucci family the wine matures in oaken barrels of immense diameter, the iron hoops that bind them stylishly painted red. She has been shown the *cantina* and the palace of the Contucci. She has looked across the slopes of terracotta roof-tiles to Monticchiello and Pienza. She has drunk the water of the nearby spa and has sat in the sun outside the café by the bank, whiling away a morning with an Italian dictionary. *Frusta* means whip, and it's also the word for the bread she has with *Fontina* for lunch.

Her husband pays money into her bank account and she accepts it because she must. There are some investments her father left her: between the two sources there is enough to live on. But one day, when her Italian is good enough, she will reject the money her husband pays her. It is degrading to look for support from someone she no longer respects. And one day, too, she will revert to her maiden name, for why should she carry with her the name of a man who shrugged her off?

In the cool of the *appartamento* she lunches alone. With her *frusta* and *Fontina* she eats peppery radishes and drinks *acqua minerale*. Wine in the daytime makes her sleepy, and she is determined this afternoon to learn another thirty words and to do two exercises for the girl in the *Informazioni*. *Le Chiavi del Regno* by A.J. Cronin is open beside her, but for a moment she does not read it. A week ago, on the telephone to England, she described the four new villas of Signor Falconi to prospective tenants, Signora Falconi having asked her if she would. The Falconis had shown her the villas they had built near their *fattoria* in the hills, and she assured someone in Gloucester that any one of them would perfectly suit her requirements, which were sun and tranquillity and room enough for six.

Guilt once consumed her, Henrietta considers. She continued to be a secretary in the department for six years after her marriage but had given it up because she'd found it awkward, having to work not just for her husband but for his rivals and his enemies. He'd been pleased when she'd done so, and although she'd always intended to find a secretarial post outside the university she never had. She'd felt guilty about that, because she was contributing so little, a childless housewife.

'I want to stay here.' She says it aloud, pouring herself more *acqua minerale*, not eating for a moment. '*Voglio stare qui*.' She has known the worst of last winter's weather; she has watched spring coming; heat will not defeat her. How has she not guessed, through all those years of what seemed like a contented marriage, that solitude suits her better? It only seemed contented, she knows that now: she had talked herself into an artificial contentment, she had allowed herself to become a woman dulled by the monotony of a foolish man, his sprawling bigness and his sense of failure. It is bliss of a kind not to hear his laughter turned on for a television joke, not to look daily at his flamboyant ties and unpolished shoes. *Quella mattina il diario si aprí alla data Ottobre 1917:* how astonished he would be if he could see her now, childishly delighting in *The Keys of the Kingdom* in Italian.

It was her fault, she'd always believed, that they could not have children – yet something informs her now that it was probably more her husband's, that she'd been wrong to feel inadequate. As a vacuum-cleaner sucks in whatever it touches, he had drawn her into a world that was not her own; she had existed on territory where it was natural to be blind – where it was natural, too, to feel she must dutifully console a husband because he was not a success professionally. 'Born with a sense of duty,' her father once said, when she was ten or so. 'A good thing, Henrietta.' She is not so sure: guilt and duty seem now to belong together, different names for a single quality.

Later that day she walks to the Church of San Biagio, among the meadows below the walls of the town. Boys are playing football in the shade, girls lie on the grass. She goes over her vocabulary in her mind, passing by the church. She walks on white, dusty roads, between rows of slender pines. *Solivare* is the word she has invented – to do with wandering alone. *Piantare* means to plant; *piantamento* is planting, *piantagione* plantation. Determinedly she taxes her atrophied memory: *sulla via di casa* and *in modo da; un manovale* and *la briciola*.

In the August of that year, when the heat is at its height, Signora Falconi approaches Henrietta in the *macelleria*. She speaks in Italian, for Henrietta's Italian is better now than Signora Falconi's rudimentary English. There is something, Signora Falconi reveals – a request that has not to do with reassuring a would-be tenant on the telephone. There is some other proposition that Signor Falconi and his wife would like to put to her.

'*Verrò*,' Henrietta agrees. '*Verrò martedí coll'autobus*.'

The Falconis offer her coffee and a little *grappa*. Their four villas, clustered around their *fattoria*, are full of English tenants now. Every fortnight these tenants change, so dirty laundry must be gathered for the *lavanderia*, fresh sheets put on the beds, the villa cleaned. And the newcomers, when they arrive, must be shown where everything is, told about the windows and the shutters, warned about the mosquitoes and requested not to use too much water. They must have many other details explained to them, which the Falconis, up to now, have not quite succeeded in doing. There is a loggia in one of the villas that would be Henrietta's, a single room with a balcony and a bathroom, an outside staircase. And the Falconis would pay just a little for the cleaning and the changing of the sheets, the many details explained. The Falconis are apologetic, fearing that Henrietta may consider the work too humble. They are anxious she should know that women to clean and change sheets are not easy to come by since they find employment in the hotels of the nearby spa, and that there is more than enough for Signora Falconi herself to do at the *fattoria*.

It is not the work Henrietta has imagined when anticipating her future, but her future in her *appartamento* is uncertain, for she cannot live for ever on strangers' charity and one day the strangers will return.

'*Va bene,*' she says to the Falconis. '*Lo faccio.*'

She moves from the Piazza San Lucia. *La governante* Signora Falconi calls her, and the tenants of the villas become her temporary friends. Some take her out to Il Marzucco, the hotel of the town. Others drive her to the sulphur baths or to the abbey at Monte Oliveto, where doves flutter through the cloisters, as white as the dusty roads she loves to walk on. On either side of the pink brick archway are the masterpieces of Luca della Robbia and sometimes the doves alight on them. This abbey on the hill of Oliveto is the most beautiful place she has ever visited: she owes a debt to the girl with the granny glasses.

In the evening she sits on her balcony, drinking a glass of *vino nobile*, hearing the English voices, and the voices of the Italians in and around the *fattoria*. But by October the English voices have dwindled and the only customers of the *fattoria* are the Italians who come traditionally for lunch on Sundays. Henrietta cleans the villas then. She scours the saucepans and puts away the cutlery and the bed linen. The Falconis seem concerned that she should be on her own so much and invite her to their meals occasionally, but she explains that her discovery of solitude has made her happy. Sometimes she watches them making soap and candles, learning how that is done.

The girl, walking up and down the sitting-room that once was Henrietta's, is more matter-of-fact and assured than Henrietta remembers her, though her complexion has not improved. Her clothes – a black jersey and a black leather skirt – are of a better quality. There is a dusting of dandruff on the jersey, her long hair has been cut.

'It's the way things worked out,' she says, which is something she has said repeatedly before, during the time they have had to spend together.

Henrietta does not reply, as she has not on the previous occasions. Upstairs, in blue-and-brown-striped pyjamas, purchased by herself three years ago, the man of whom each has had a share rests. He is out of danger, recovering in an orderly way.

'As Roy himself said,' the girl repeats also, 'we live in a world of mistakes.'

Yet they belong together, he and the girl, with their academic brightness and Hesselmann to talk about. The dog is no longer in the house. Ka-Ki has eaten a plastic bag, attracted by slivers of meat adhering to it, and has died. Henrietta blames herself. No matter how upset she'd felt it had been cruel to walk out and leave that dog.

'I gave Roy up to you,' she says, 'since that was what you and he wanted.'

'Roy is ill.'

'He is ill, but at the same time he is well again. This house is yours and his now. You have changed things. You have let the place get dirty, the windows don't seem ever to have been opened. I gave the house up to you also. I'm not asking you to give it back.'

'Like I say, Henrietta, it was unfortunate about the dog. I'm sorry about that.'

'I chose to leave the dog behind, with everything else.'

'Look, Henrietta –'

'Roy will be able to work again, just as before: we've been quite assured about that. He is to lose some weight, he is to take care of his diet. He is to exercise himself properly, something he never bothered with. It was you, not me, they gave those instructions to.'

'They didn't seem to get the picture, Henrietta. Like I say, we broke up, I wasn't even living here. I've explained that to you, Henrietta. I haven't been here for the past five months, I'm down in London now.'

'Don't you feel you should get Roy on his feet again, since you had last use of him, as it were?'

'That way you're talking is unpleasant, Henrietta. You're getting at me, you're getting at poor Roy. Like you're jealous or something. There was love between us, there really was. Deep love. You know, Henrietta? You understand?'

'Roy explained it to me about the love, that evening.'

'But then it went. It just extinguished itself, like maybe there *was* something in the age-difference bit. I don't know. Perhaps we'll never know, Henrietta.'

'Perhaps not indeed.'

'We were happy for a long time, Roy and me. As happy as any two people could be.'

'I'm sure you were.'

'I'm sorry. I didn't mean to say that. Look, Henrietta, I'm with someone else now. It's different what I've got now. It's going to work out.'

A damp coldness, like the fog that hangs about the garden, touches Henrietta's flesh, insinuating itself beneath her clothes, icy on her stomach and her back. The girl had been at the hospital, called there because Roy had asked for her. She did not say then that she was with someone else.

'May I just, you know, say goodbye to Roy? May I be with him for just five minutes, Henrietta?'

She does not reply. The coldness has spread to her arms and legs. It oozes over her breasts; it reaches for her feet. In blurred vision she sees the steep cool streets of the town, the laburnums and the blaze of clover in the landscape she ran away to.

'I know it's terrible for you, Henrietta.'

Sharon Tamm leaves the room to have her last five minutes. The blur in Henrietta's vision is nothing now. She wonders if they have buried her dog somewhere.

'Goodbye, Henrietta. He's tons better, you know.'

She hears the hall door close as she heard it on the afternoon when the girl came to talk to her, and later when Roy left the house. It's odd, she reflects, that because there has been a marriage and because she bears his name, she should be less free than the girl. Yet is not the life she discovered for herself much the same as finding someone else? Perhaps not.

'I'm sorry,' he says, when she brings him a tray. 'Oh God, I'm sorry about all this mess.'

He cries and is unable to cease. The tears fall on to the egg she has poached for him and into his cup of Bovril. 'Sorry,' he says. 'Oh God, I'm sorry.'

The Penthouse Apartment

'Flowers?' said Mr Runca into his pale blue telephone receiver. 'Shall we order flowers? What's the procedure?' He stared intently at his wife as he spoke, and his wife, eating her breakfast grapefruit, thought that it would seem to be her husband's intention to avoid having to pay for flowers. She had become used to this element in her husband; it hardly ever embarrassed her.

'The procedure's quite simple,' said a soft voice in Mr Runca's ear. 'The magazine naturally supplies the flowers. If we can just agree between us what the flowers should be.'

'Indeed,' said Mr Runca. 'It's to be remembered that not all blooms will go with the apartment. Our fabrics must be allowed to speak for themselves, you know. Well, you've seen. You know what I mean.'

'Indeed I do, Mr Runca –'

'They came from Thailand, in fact. You might like to mention that.'

'So you said, Mr Runca. The fabrics are most beautiful.'

Mr Runca, hearing this statement, nodded. He said, because he was used to saying it when the apartment was discussed:

'It's the best-dressed apartment in London.'

'I'll come myself at three,' said the woman on the magazine. 'Will someone be there at half past two, say, so that the photographers can set up their gear and test the light?'

'We have an Italian servant,' said Mr Runca, 'who opened the door to you before and who'll do the same thing for the photographers.'

'Till this afternoon then,' said the woman on the magazine, speaking lightly and gaily, since that was her manner.

Mr Runca carefully replaced the telephone receiver. His wife, a woman who ran a boutique, drank some coffee and heard her husband say that the magazine would pay for the flowers and would presumably not remove them from the flat after the photography had taken place. Mrs Runca nodded. The magazine was going to devote six pages to the Runcas' flat: a display in full colour of its subtleties and charm, with an article about how the Runcas had between them planned the décor.

'I'd like to arrange the flowers myself,' said Mrs Runca. 'Are they being sent round?'

Mr Runca shook his head. The flowers, he explained, were to be brought to the house by the woman from the magazine at three o'clock, the photographers having already had time to deploy their materials in the manner they favoured.

'But how ridiculous!' cried Mrs Runca. 'That's completely hopeless. The photographers with their cameras poised for three o'clock and the woman arriving then with the flowers. How long does the female imagine it'll take to arrange them? Does she think it can be done in a matter of minutes?'

Mr Runca picked up the telephone and dialled the number of the magazine. He mentioned the name of the woman he had recently been speaking to. He spoke to her again. He said:

'My wife points out that none of this is satisfactory. The flowers will take time to arrange, naturally. What point is there in keeping your photographers waiting? And I myself haven't got all day.'

'It shouldn't take long to arrange the flowers.'

Mrs Runca lit her first cigarette of the day, imagining that the woman on the magazine was saying something like that. She had a long, rather thin face, and pale grey hair that had the glow of aluminium. Her hands were long also, hands that had grown elegant in childhood, with fingernails that now were of a fashionable length, metallically painted, a reflection of her hair. Ten years ago, on money borrowed from her husband, she had opened her boutique. She had called it St Catherine, and had watched it growing into a flourishing business with a staff of five women and a girl messenger.

'Very well then,' said the woman on the magazine, having listened further to Mr Runca. 'I'll have the flowers sent round this morning.'

'They're coming round this morning,' reported Mr Runca to his wife.

'I have to be at St Catherine at twelve,' she said, 'absolutely without fail.'

'My wife has to be at her business at midday,' said Mr Runca, and the woman on the magazine cursed silently. She promised that the flowers would be in the Runcas' penthouse apartment within three-quarters of an hour.

Mr Runca rose to his feet and stood silently for a minute. He was a rich, heavily jowled man, the owner of three publications that appealed to those involved in the clothing trade. He was successful in much the same way as his wife was, and he felt, as she did, that efficiency and a stern outlook were good weapons in the business of accumulating wealth. Once upon a time they had both been poor and had recognized certain similar qualities in one another, had seen the future as a more luxurious time, as in fact it had become. They were proud that once again their penthouse apartment was to be honoured by photographs and a journalist. It was the symbol of their toil; and in a small way it had made them famous.

Mr Runca walked from the spacious room that had one side made entirely of glass, and his feet caused no sound as he crossed a white carpet of Afghanistan wool. He paused in the hall to place a hat on his head and gloves on his hands before departing for a morning's business.

At ten to ten the flowers arrived and by a quarter past eleven Mrs Runca had arranged them to her satisfaction. The Runcas' Italian maid, called Bianca, cleaned the flat most carefully, seeking dust in an expert way, working with method and a conscience, which was why the Runcas employed her. Mrs Runca warned her to be in at half past two because the photographers were coming then. 'I must go out now then,' replied Bianca, 'for shopping. I will make these photographers coffee, I suppose?' Mrs Runca said to give the men coffee in the kitchen, or tea, if they preferred it. 'Don't let them walk about the place with cups in their hands,' she said, and went away.

In another part of the block of flats lived Miss Winton with her Cairn terrier. Her flat was different from the Runcas'; it contained many ornaments that had little artistic value, was in need of redecoration, and had a beige linoleum on the floor of the bathroom. Miss Winton did not notice her surroundings much; she considered the flat pretty in its way, and comfortable to live in. She was prepared to leave it at that.

'Well,' remarked Miss Winton to her dog in the same moment that Mrs Runca was stepping into a taxi-cab, 'what shall we do?'

The dog made no reply beyond wagging its tail. 'I have eggs to buy,' said Miss Winton, 'and honey, and butter. Shall we go and do all that?'

Miss Winton had lived in the block of flats for fifteen years. She had seen many tenants come and go. She had heard about the Runcas and the model place they had made of the penthouse. It was the talk of London, Miss Winton had been told by Mrs Neck, who kept a grocer's shop near by; the Runcas were full of taste, apparently. Miss Winton thought it odd that London should talk about a penthouse flat, but did not ever mention that to Mrs Neck, who didn't seem to think it odd in the least. To Miss Winton the Runcas were like many others who had come to live in the same building: people she saw and did not know. There were no children in the building, that being a rule; but animals, within reason, were permitted.

Miss Winton left her flat and walked with her dog to Mrs Neck's shop. 'Fresh buns,' said Mrs Neck before Miss Winton had made a request. 'Just in, dear.' But Miss Winton shook her head and asked for eggs and honey and butter. 'Seven and ten,' said Mrs Neck, reckoning the cost before reaching a hand out for the articles. She said it was shocking that food should cost so much, but Miss Winton replied that in her opinion two shillings wasn't exorbitant for half a pound of butter. 'I remember it ninepence,' said Mrs Neck, 'and twice the stuff it was. I'd sooner a smear of Stork than what they're turning out today.' Miss Winton smiled, and agreed that the quality of everything had gone down a bit.

Afterwards, for very many years, Miss Winton remembered this conversation with Mrs Neck. She remembered Mrs Neck saying: 'I'd sooner a smear of Stork than what they're turning out today,' and she remembered the rather small, dark-haired girl who entered Mrs Neck's shop at that moment, who smiled at both of them in an innocent way. 'Is that so?' said the Runcas' maid, Bianca. 'Quality has gone down?'

'Lord love you, Miss Winton knows what she's talking about,' said Mrs Neck. 'Quality's gone to pieces.'

Miss Winton might have left the shop then, for her purchasing was over, but the dark-haired young girl had leaned down and was patting the head of Miss Winton's dog. She smiled while doing that. Mrs Neck said:

'Miss Winton's in the flats too.'

'Ah, yes?'

'This young lady,' explained Mrs Neck to Miss Winton, 'works for the Runcas in the penthouse we hear so much about.'

'Today they are coming to photograph,' said Bianca. 'People from a magazine. And they will write down other things about it.'

'Again?' said Mrs Neck, shaking her head in wonderment. 'What can I do for you?'

Bianca asked for coffee beans and a sliced loaf, still stroking the head of the dog.

Miss Winton smiled. 'He has taken to you,' she said to Bianca, speaking timidly because she felt shy of people, especially foreigners. 'He's very good company.'

'Pretty little dog,' said Bianca.

Miss Winton walked with Bianca back to the block of flats, and when they arrived in the large hallway Bianca said:

'Miss Winton, would you like to see the penthouse with all its fresh flowers and fruits about the place? It is at its best in the morning sunlight as Mr Runca was remarking earlier. It is ready for the photographers.'

Miss Winton, touched that the Italian girl should display such thoughtfulness towards an elderly spinster, said that it would be a pleasure to look at the penthouse flat but added that the Runcas might not care to have her walking about their property.

'No, no,' said Bianca, who had not been long in the Runcas' employ.

'Mrs Runca would love you to see it. And him too. "Show anyone you like," they've said to me. Certainly.' Bianca was not telling the truth, but time hung heavily on her hands in the empty penthouse and she knew she would enjoy showing Miss Winton the flowers that Mrs Runca had so tastefully arranged, and the curtains that had been imported specially from Thailand, and the rugs and the chairs and the pictures on the walls.

'Well,' began Miss Winton.

'Yes,' said Bianca and pressed Miss Winton and her dog into the lift.

But when the lift halted at the top and Bianca opened the gates Miss Winton experienced a small shock. 'Mr Morgan is here too,' said Bianca. 'Mending the water.'

Miss Winton felt that she could not now refuse to enter the Runcas' flat, since to do so would be to offend the friendly little Italian girl, yet she really did not wish to find herself face to face with Mr Morgan in somebody else's flat. 'Look here,' she said, but Bianca and the dog were already ahead of her. 'Come on, Miss Winton,' said Bianca.

Miss Winton found herself in the Runcas' small and fastidious hall, and then in the large room that had one side made of glass. She looked around her and noted all the low furniture and the pale Afghanistan carpet and the objects scattered economically about, and the flowers that Mrs Runca had arranged. 'Have coffee,' said Bianca, going quickly off to make some, and the little dog, noting her swift movement and registering it as a form of play, gave a single bark and darted about himself, in a small circle. 'Shh,' whispered Miss Winton. 'Really,' she protested, following Bianca to the kitchen, 'don't bother about coffee.' 'No, no,' said Bianca, pretending not to understand, thinking that there was plenty of time for herself and Miss Winton to have coffee together, sitting in the kitchen, where Mrs Runca had commanded coffee was to be drunk. Miss Winton could hear a light hammering and guessed it was Mr Morgan at work on the water-pipes. She could imagine him coming out of the Runcas' bathroom and stopping quite still as soon as he saw her. He would stand there in his brown overall, large and bulky, peering at her through his spectacles, chewing, probably, a piece of his moustache. His job was to attend to the needs of the tenants when the needs were not complicated, but whenever Miss Winton telephoned down to his basement and asked for his assistance he would sigh loudly into the telephone and say that he mightn't manage to attend to the matter for a day or two. He would come, eventually, late at night but still in his brown overall, his eyes watering, his breath rich with alcohol. He would look at whatever the trouble was and make a swift diagnosis, advising that experts should be summoned the following morning. He didn't much like her, Miss Winton thought; no doubt he considered her a poor creature, unmarried at sixty-four, thin and weak-looking, with little sign that her physical appearance had been attractive in girlhood.

'It's a lovely place,' said Miss Winton to Bianca. 'But I think perhaps we should go now. Please don't bother with coffee; and thank you most awfully.'

'No, no,' said Bianca, and while she was saying it Mr Morgan entered the kitchen in his brown overall.

One day in 1952 Miss Winton had mislaid her bicycle. It had disappeared without trace from the passage in the basement where Mr Morgan had said she might keep it. 'I have not seen it,' he had said slowly and deliberately at that time. 'I know of no cycle.' Miss Winton had reminded him that the bicycle had always had a place in the passage, since he had said she might keep it there. But Mr Morgan, thirteen years younger then, had replied that he could recall none of that. 'Stolen,' he had said. 'I dare say stolen. I should say the coke men carted it away. I cannot always be watching the place, y'know. I have me work, madam.' She had asked him to inquire of the coke men if they had in error removed her bicycle; she had spoken politely and with a smile, but Mr Morgan had repeatedly shaken his head, pointing out that he could not go suggesting that the coke men had made off with a bicycle, saying that the coke men would have the law on him. 'The wife has a cycle,' Mr Morgan had said. 'A Rudge. I could obtain it for you, madam. Fifty shillings?' Miss Winton had smiled again and had walked away, having refused this offer and given thanks for it.

'Was you wanting something, madam?' asked Mr Morgan now, his lower lip pulling a strand of his moustache into his mouth. 'This is the Runcas' flat up here.'

Miss Winton tried to smile at him. She thought that whatever she said he would be sarcastic in a disguised way. He would hide his sarcasm beneath the words he chose, implying it only with the inflection of his voice. Miss Winton said:

'Bianca kindly invited me to see the penthouse.'

'It is a different type of place from yours and mine,' replied Mr Morgan, looking about him. 'I was attending to a tap in the bathroom. Working, Miss Winton.'

'It is to be photographed today,' said Bianca. 'Mr and Mrs Runca will return early from their businesses.'

'Was you up here doing the flowers, madam?'

He had called her madam during all the years they had known one another, pointing up the fact that she had no right to the title.

'A cup of coffee, Mr Morgan?' said Bianca, and Miss Winton hoped he would refuse.

'With two spoons of sugar in it,' said Mr Morgan, nodding his head and adding: 'D'you know what the Irish take in their coffee?' He began to laugh rumbustiously, ignoring Miss Winton and appearing to share a joke with Bianca. 'A tot of the hard stuff,' said Mr Morgan. 'Whisky.'

Bianca laughed too. She left the kitchen, and Miss Winton's dog ran after her. Mr Morgan blew at the surface of his coffee while Miss Winton, wondering what to say to him, stirred hers.

'It's certainly a beautiful flat,' said Miss Winton.

'It would be too large for you, madam. I mean to say, just you and the dog in a place like this. You'd lose one another.'

'Oh, yes, of course. No, I meant –'

'I'll speak to the authorities if you like. I'll speak on your behalf, as a tenant often asks me to do. Put a word in, y'know. I could put a word in if you like, madam.'

Miss Winton frowned, wondering what Mr Morgan was talking about. She smiled uncertainly at him. He said:

'I have a bit of influence, knowing the tenants and that. I got the left-hand ground flat for Mr Webster by moving the Aitchesons up to the third. I got Mrs Bloom out of the back one on the first –'

'Mr Morgan, you've misunderstood me. I wouldn't at all like to move up here.'

Mr Morgan looked at Miss Winton, sucking coffee off his moustache. His eyes were focused on hers. He said:

'You don't have to say nothing outright, madam. I understand a hint.'

Bianca returned with a bottle of whisky. She handed it to Mr Morgan, saying that he had better add it to the coffee since she didn't know how much to put in.

'Oh, a good drop,' said Mr Morgan, splashing the liquor on to his warm coffee. He approached Miss Winton with the neck of the bottle poised towards her cup. He'll be offended, she thought; and because of that she did not, as she wished to, refuse his offering. 'The Irish are heavy drinkers,' said Mr Morgan. 'Cheers.' He drank the mixture and proclaimed it good. 'D'you like that, Miss Winton?' he asked, and Miss Winton tasted it and discovered to her surprise that the beverage was pleasant. 'Yes,' she said. 'I do.'

Mr Morgan held out his cup for more coffee. 'Just a small drop,' he said, and he filled the cup up with whisky. Again he inclined the neck of the bottle towards Miss Winton, who smiled and said she hadn't finished. He held the bottle in the same position, watching her drinking her coffee.

She protested when Bianca poured her more, but she could sense that Bianca was enjoying this giving of hospitality, and for that reason she accepted, knowing that Mr Morgan would pour in more whisky. She felt comfortably warm from the whisky that was already in her body, and she experienced the desire to be agreeable – although she was aware, too, that she would not care for it if the Runcas unexpectedly returned.

'Fair enough,' said Mr Morgan, topping up Bianca's cup and adding a further quantity to his own. He said:

'Miss Winton is thinking of shifting up here, her being the oldest tenant in the building. She's been stuck downstairs for fifteen years.'

Bianca shook her head, saying to Miss Winton: 'What means that?'

'I'm quite happy,' said Miss Winton, 'where I am.' She spoke softly, with a smile on her face, intent upon being agreeable. Mr Morgan was sitting on the edge of the kitchen table. Bianca had turned on the wireless. Mr Morgan said:

'I come to the flats on March the 21st, 1951. Miss Winton here was already in residence. Riding about on a cycle.'

'I was six years old,' said Bianca.

'D'you remember that day, Miss Winton? March the 21st?'

Miss Winton shook her head. She sat down on a chair made of an ersatz material. She said:

'It's a long time ago.'

'I remember the time you lost your cycle, Miss Winton. She come down to me in the basement,' said Mr Morgan to Bianca, 'and told me to tick off the coke deliverers for thieving her bicycle. I never seen no cycle, as I said to Miss Winton. D'you understand, missy?' Bianca smiled, nodding swiftly. She hummed the tune that was coming from the wireless. 'Do you like that Irish drink?' said Mr Morgan. 'Shall we have some more?'

'I must be going,' said Miss Winton. 'It's been terribly kind of you.'

'Are you going, madam?' said Mr Morgan, and there was in his tone a hint of the belligerency that Miss Winton knew his nature was imbued with. In her mind he spoke more harshly to her, saying she was a woman who had never lived. He was saying that she might have been a nun the way she existed, not knowing anything about the world around her; she had never known a man's love, Mr Morgan was saying; she had never borne a child.

'Oh, don't go,' said Bianca. 'Please, I'll make you a cold cocktail, like Mr Runca showed me how. Cinzano with gin in it, and lemon and ice.'

'Oh, no,' said Miss Winton.

Mr Morgan sighed, implying with the intake of his breath that her protest was not unexpected. There were other women in the block of flats,

Miss Winton imagined, who would have a chat with Mr Morgan now and again, who would pass the time of day with him, asking him for racing tips and suggesting that he should let them know when he heard that a flat they coveted was going to be empty. Mr Morgan was probably a man whom people tipped quite lavishly for the performance of services or favours. Miss Winton could imagine people – people like the Runcas maybe – saying to their friends: 'We greased the caretaker's palm. We gave him five pounds.' She thought she'd never be able to do that.

Bianca went away to fetch the ingredients for the drink, and again the dog went with her.

Miss Winton stood still, determined that Mr Morgan should not consider that she did not possess the nerve to receive from the Runcas' Italian maid a midday cocktail. Mr Morgan said:

'You and me has known one another a number of years.'

'Yes, we have.'

'We know what we think of a flat like this, and the type of person. Don't we, Miss Winton?'

'To tell the truth, I don't really know the Runcas.'

'I'll admit it to you: the whisky has loosened my tongue, Miss Winton. You understand what I mean?'

Miss Winton smiled at Mr Morgan. There was sweat, she noticed, on the sides of his face. He said with vehemence: 'Ridiculous, the place being photographed. What do they want to do that for, tell me?'

'Magazines take an interest. It's a contemporary thing. Mrs Neck was saying that this flat is well-known.'

'You can't trust Mrs Neck. I think it's a terrible place. I wouldn't be comfortable in a place like this.'

'Well –'

'You could report me for saying a thing like that. You could do that, Miss Winton. You could tell them I was intoxicated at twelve o'clock in the day, drinking a tenant's liquor and abusing the tenant behind his back. D'you see what I mean, madam?'

'I wouldn't report you, Mr Morgan. It's no business of mine.'

'I'd like to see you up here, madam, getting rid of all this trash and putting in a decent bit of furniture. How's about that?'

'Please, Mr Morgan, I'm perfectly happy –'

'I'll see what I can do,' said Mr Morgan.

Bianca returned with glasses and bottles. Mr Morgan said:

'I was telling Miss Winton here that she could report me to the authorities for misconduct, but she said she never would. We've known one another a longish time. We was never drinking together though.'

Bianca handed Miss Winton a glass that felt cold in Miss Winton's hand. She feared now what Mr Morgan was going to say. He said:

'I intoxicate easily.' Mr Morgan laughed, displaying darkened teeth. He swayed back and forth, looking at Miss Winton. 'I'll put in a word for you,' he said, 'no bother at all.'

She was thinking that she would finish the drink she'd been given and then go away and prepare lunch. She would buy some little present to give Bianca, and she would come up to the Runcas' flat one morning and hand it to her, thanking her for her hospitality and her thoughtfulness.

While Miss Winton was thinking that, Mr Morgan was thinking that he intended to drink at least two more of the drinks that the girl was offering, and Bianca was thinking that it was the first friendly morning she had spent in this flat since her arrival three weeks before. 'I must go to the WC,' said Mr Morgan, and he left the kitchen, saying he would be back. 'It's most kind of you,' said Miss Winton when he had gone. 'I do hope it's all right.' It had occurred to her that Bianca's giving people the Runcas' whisky and gin was rather different from her giving people a cup of coffee, but when she looked at Bianca she saw that she was innocently smiling. She felt light-headed, and smiled herself. She rose from her chair and thanked Bianca again and said that she must be going now. Her dog came to her, wishing to go also. 'Don't you like the drink?' said Bianca, and Miss Winton finished it. She placed the glass on the metal draining-board and as she did so a crash occurred in the Runcas' large sitting-room. 'Heavens!' said Miss Winton, and Bianca raised a hand to her mouth and kept it there. When they entered the room they saw Mr Morgan standing in the centre of it, looking at the floor.

'Heavens!' said Miss Winton, and Bianca widened her eyes and still did not take her hand away from her mouth. On the floor lay the flowers that Mrs Runca had earlier arranged. The huge vase was smashed into many pieces. Water was soaking into the Afghanistan carpet.

'I was looking at it,' explained Mr Morgan. 'I was touching a flower with my fingers. The whole thing gave way.'

'Mrs Runca's flowers,' said Bianca. 'Oh, Mother of God!'

'Mr Morgan,' said Miss Winton.

'Don't look at me, ma'am. Don't blame me for an instant. Them flowers was inadequately balanced. Ridiculous.'

Bianca, on her hands and knees, was picking up the broken stalks. She might have been more upset, Miss Winton thought, and she was glad that she was not. Bianca explained that Mrs Runca had stayed away from her boutique specially to arrange the flowers. 'They'll give me the sack,' she said, and instead of weeping she gave a small giggle.

The gravity of the situation struck Miss Winton forcibly. Hearing Bianca's giggle, Mr Morgan laughed also, and went to the kitchen, where Miss Winton heard him pouring himself some more of the Runcas' gin. Miss Winton realized then that neither Bianca nor Mr Morgan had any sense of responsibility. Bianca was young and did not know any better; Mr Morgan was partly drunk. The Runcas would return with people from a magazine and they would find that their property had been damaged, that a vase had been broken and that a large damp patch in the centre of their Afghanistan carpet would not look good in the photographs. 'Let's have another cocktail,' said Bianca, throwing down the flowers she had collected and giggling again. 'Oh, no,' cried Miss Winton. 'Please, Bianca. We must think what's best to do.' But Bianca was already in the kitchen, and Miss Winton could hear Mr Morgan's rumbustious laugh.

'I tell you what,' said Mr Morgan, coming towards her with a glass in his hand. 'We'll say the dog done it. We'll say the dog jumped at the flowers trying to grip hold of them.'

Miss Winton regarded him with surprise. 'My dog?' she said. 'My dog was nowhere near the flowers.' Her voice was sharp, the first time it had been so that morning.

Mr Morgan sat down in an armchair, and Miss Winton, about to protest about that also, realized in time that she had, of course, no right to protest at all.

'We could say,' said Mr Morgan, 'that the dog went into a hysterical fit and attacked the flowers. How's about that?'

'But that's not true. It's not the truth.'

'I was thinking of me job, madam. And of the young missy's.'

'It was an accident,' said Miss Winton, 'as you have said, Mr Morgan.'

'They'll say what was I doing touching the flowers? They'll say to the young missy what was happening, was you giving a party? I'll have to explain the whole thing to the wife.'

'Your wife?'

'What was I doing in the Runcas' flat with the young one? The wife will see through anything.'

'You were here to mend a water-pipe, Mr Morgan.'

'What's the matter with the water-pipes?'

'Oh really, Mr Morgan. You were repairing a pipe when I came into the flat.'

'There was nothing the matter with the pipes, ma'am. Nor never has been, which is just the point. The young missy telephones down saying the pipes is making a noise. She's anxious for company. She likes to engage in a chat.'

'I shall arrange what flowers we can salvage,' said Miss Winton, 'just as neatly as they were arranged before. And we can explain to the Runcas that you came to the flat to mend a pipe and in passing brushed against Mrs Runca's flowers. The only difficulty is the carpet. The best way to get that damp stain out would be to lift up the carpet and put an electric fire in front of it.'

'Take it easy,' said Mr Morgan. 'Have a drink, Miss Winton.'

'We must repair the damage –'

'Listen, madam,' said Mr Morgan, leaning forward, 'you and I know what we think of a joint like this. Tricked out like they've got it –'

'It's a question of personal taste –'

'Tell them the dog done the damage, Miss Winton, and I'll see you right. A word in the ear of the authorities and them Runcas will be out on the street in a jiffy. Upsetting the neighbours with noise, bringing the flats into disrepute. I'd say it in court, Miss Winton: I seen naked women going in and out of the penthouse.'

Bianca returned, and Miss Winton repeated to her what she had said already to Mr Morgan about the drying of the carpet. Between them, they moved chairs and tables and lifted the carpet from the floor, draping it across two chairs and placing an electric fire in front of it. Mr Morgan moved to a distant sofa and watched them.

'I used not to be bad with flowers,' said Miss Winton to Bianca. 'Are there other vases?' They went together to the kitchen to see what there was. 'Would you like another cocktail?' said Bianca, but Miss Winton said she thought everyone had had enough to drink. 'I like these drinks,' said Bianca, sipping one. 'So cool.'

'You must explain,' said Miss Winton, 'that Mr Morgan had to come in order to repair the gurgling pipe and that he brushed against the flowers on the way across the room. You must tell the truth: that you had invited me to have a look at the beautiful flat. I'm sure they won't be angry when they know it was an accident.'

'What means gurgling?' said Bianca.

'Hey,' shouted Mr Morgan from the other room.

'I think Mr Morgan should go now,' said Miss Winton. 'I wonder if you'd say so, Bianca? He's a very touchy man.' She imagined Mr Runca looking sternly into her face and saying he could not believe his eyes: that she, an elderly spinster, still within her wits, had played a part in the disastrous proceedings in his flat. She had allowed the caretaker to become drunk, she had egged on a young foreign girl. 'Have you no responsibility?' shouted Mr Runca at Miss Winton in her imagination. 'What's the matter with you?'

'Hey,' shouted Mr Morgan. 'That carpet's burning.'

Miss Winton and Bianca sniffed the air and smelt at once the tang of singed wool. They returned at speed to the other room and saw that the carpet was smoking and that Mr Morgan was still on the sofa, watching it. 'How's about that?' said Mr Morgan.

'The fire was too close,' said Bianca, looking at Miss Winton, who frowned and felt afraid. She didn't remember putting the fire so close to the carpet, and then she thought that she was probably as intoxicated as Mr Morgan and didn't really know what she was doing.

'Scrape off the burnt bit,' advised Mr Morgan, 'and tell them the dog ate it.'

They unplugged the fire and laid the carpet flat on the floor again. Much of the damp had disappeared, but the burnt patch, though small, was eye-catching. Miss Winton felt a weakness in her stomach, as though a quantity of jelly were turning rhythmically over and over. The situation now seemed beyond explanation, and she saw herself asking the Runcas to sit down quietly, side by side with the people from the magazine, and she heard herself trying to tell the truth, going into every detail and pleading that Bianca should not be punished. 'Blame me,' she was saying, 'if someone must be blamed, for I have nothing to lose.'

'I'll tell you what,' said Mr Morgan, 'why don't we telephone for Mrs Neck? She done a carpet for her hearth, forty different wools she told me, that she shaped with a little instrument. Ring up Mrs Neck, missy, and say there's a drink for her if she'll oblige Mr Morgan with ten minutes of her time.'

'Do no such thing,' cried Miss Winton. 'There's been enough drinking, Mr Morgan, as well you know. The trouble started with drink, when you lurched against the flowers. There's no point in Mrs Neck adding to the confusion.'

Mr Morgan listened to Miss Winton and then rose from the sofa. He said:

'You have lived in these flats longer than I have, madam. We all know that. But I will not stand here and be insulted by you, just because I am a working man. The day you come after your cycle –'

'I must go away,' cried Bianca in distress. 'I cannot be found with a burnt carpet and the flowers like that.'

'Listen,' said Mr Morgan, coming close to Miss Winton. 'I have a respect for you. I'm surprised to hear myself insulted from your lips.'

'Mr Morgan –'

'You was insulting me, madam.'

'I was not insulting you. Don't go, Bianca. I'll stay here and explain everything to the Runcas. I think, Mr Morgan, it would be best if you went off to your lunch now.'

'How can I?' shouted Mr Morgan very loudly and rudely, sticking his chin out at Miss Winton. 'How the damn hell d'you think I can go down to the wife in the condition I'm in? She'd eat the face off me.'

'Please, Mr Morgan.'

'You and your dog: I have respect for the pair of you. You and me is on the same side of the fence. D'you understand?'

Miss Winton shook her head.

'What d'you think of the Runcas, ma'am?'

'I've said, Mr Morgan: I've never met the Runcas.'

'What d'you think of the joint they've got here?'

'I think it's most impressive.'

'It's laughable. The whole caboodle is laughable. Did you ever see the like?' Mr Morgan pointed at objects in the room. 'They're two tramps,' he shouted, his face purple with rage at the thought of the Runcas. 'They're jumped-up tramps.'

Miss Winton opened her mouth in order to speak soothingly. Mr Morgan said:

'I could put a match to the place and to the Runcas too, with their bloody attitudes. I'm only a simple caretaker, madam, but I'd see their bodies in flames.' He kicked a chair, his boot thudding loudly against pale wood. 'I hate that class of person, they're as crooked as a corkscrew.'

'You're mistaken, Mr Morgan.'

'I'm bloody not mistaken,' shouted Mr Morgan. 'They're full of hate for a man like me. They'd say I was a beast.'

Miss Winton, shocked and perturbed, was also filled with amazement. She couldn't understand why Mr Morgan had said that he and she belonged on the same side of the fence, since for the past fifteen years she had noted the scorn in his eyes.

'We have a thing in common,' said Mr Morgan. 'We have no respect whatever for the jumped-up tramps who occupy this property. I'd like to see you in here, madam, with your bits and pieces. The Runcas can go where they belong.' Mr Morgan spat into the chair which he had struck with his boot.

'Oh, no,' cried Miss Winton, and Mr Morgan laughed. He walked about the room, clearing his throat and spitting carelessly. Eventually he strolled away, into the kitchen. The dog barked, sensing Miss Winton's distress. Bianca began to sob and from the kitchen came the whistling of Mr Morgan, a noise he emitted in order to cover the sound of gin being poured into his glass. Miss Winton knew what had happened: she had read of men who could not resist alcohol and who were maddened by its presence in their bloodstream. She considered that Mr Morgan had gone mad in the Runcas' flat; he was speaking like an insane person, saying he had respect for her dog.

'I am frightened of him,' said Bianca.

'No,' said Miss Winton. 'He's a harmless man, though I wish he'd go away. We can clean up a bit. We can make an effort.'

Mr Morgan returned and took no notice of them. He sat on the sofa while they set to, clearing up the pieces of broken vase and the flowers. They placed a chair over the burnt area of carpet so that the Runcas would not notice it as soon as they entered the room. Miss Winton arranged the flowers in a vase and placed it where the other one had been placed by Mrs Runca. She surveyed the room and noticed that, apart from the presence of Mr Morgan, it wasn't so bad. Perhaps, she thought, the explanation could be unfolded gradually. She saw no reason why the room shouldn't be photographed as it was now, with the nicely arranged flowers and the chair over the burnt patch of carpeting. The damp area, greater in size, was still a little noticeable, but she imagined that in a photograph it mightn't show up too badly.

'You have let me get into this condition,' said Mr Morgan in an aggressive way. 'It was your place to say that the Runcas' whisky shouldn't be touched, nor their gin neither. You're a fellow-tenant, Miss Winton. The girl and I are servants, madam. We was doing what came naturally.'

'I'll take the responsibility,' said Miss Winton.

'Say the dog done it,' urged Mr Morgan again. 'The other will go against the girl and myself.'

'I'll tell the truth,' said Miss Winton. 'The Runcas will understand. They're not monsters that they won't forgive an accident. Mrs Runca –'

'That thin bitch,' shouted Mr Morgan, and added more quietly: 'Runca's illegitimate.'

'Mr Morgan –'

'Tell them the bloody dog done it. Tell them the dog ran about like a mad thing. How d'you know they're not monsters? How d'you know they'll understand, may I ask? "The three of us was boozing in the kitchen," are you going to say? "Mr Morgan took more than his share of the intoxicant. All hell broke loose." Are you going to say that, Miss Winton?'

'The truth is better than lies.'

'What's the matter with saying the dog done it?'

'You would be far better off out of this flat, Mr Morgan. No good will come of your raving on like that.'

'You have always respected me, madam. You have never been familiar.'

'Well –'

'I might strike them dead. They might enter that door and I might hit them with a hammer.'

Miss Winton began to protest, but Mr Morgan waved a hand at her. He sniffed and said: 'A caretaker sees a lot, I'll tell you that. Fellows bringing women in, hypocrisy all over the place. There's those that slips me a coin, madam, and those that doesn't bother, and I'm not to know which is the worse. Some of them's miserable and some's boozing all night, having sex and laughing their heads off. The Runcas isn't human in any way whatsoever. The Runcas is saying I was a beast that might offend their eyes.' Mr Morgan ceased to speak, and glared angrily at Miss Winton.

'Come now,' she said.

'A dirty caretaker, they've said, who's not fit to be alive –'

'They've never said any such thing, Mr Morgan. I'm sure of it.'

'They should have moved away from the flats if they hated the caretaker. They're a psychological case.'

There was a silence in the room, while Miss Winton trembled and tried not to show it, aware that Mr Morgan had reached a condition in which he was capable of all he mentioned.

'What I need,' he said after a time, speaking more calmly from the sofa on which he was relaxing, 'is a cold bath.'

'Mr Morgan,' said Miss Winton. She thought that he was at last about to go away, down to his basement and his angry wife, in order to immerse his large body in cold water. 'Mr Morgan, I'm sorry that you should think badly of me –'

'I'll have a quick one,' said Mr Morgan, walking towards the Runcas' bathroom. 'Who'll know the difference?'

'No,' cried Miss Winton. 'No, please, Mr Morgan.'

But with his glass in his hand Mr Morgan entered the bathroom and locked the door.

When the photographers arrived at half past two to prepare their apparatus Mr Morgan was still in the bathroom. Miss Winton waited with Bianca, reassuring her from time to time, repeating that she would not leave until she herself had explained to the Runcas what had happened. The photographers worked silently, moving none of the furniture because they had been told that the furniture was on no account to be displaced.

For an hour and twenty minutes Mr Morgan had been in the bathroom. It was clear to Miss Winton that he had thrown the vase of flowers to the ground deliberately and in anger, and that he had placed the fire closer to the carpet. In his crazy and spiteful condition Miss Winton imagined that he was capable of anything: of drowning himself in the bath maybe, so that the Runcas' penthouse might sordidly feature in the newspapers. Bianca had been concerned about his continued presence in the bathroom, but Miss Winton had explained that Mr Morgan was simply being unpleasant since he was made like that. 'It is quite disgraceful,' she said, well aware that Mr Morgan realized she was the kind of woman who would not report him to the authorities, and was taking advantage of her nature while involving her in his own. She felt that the Runcas were the victims of circumstance, and thought that she might use that very expression when she made her explanation to them. She would speak slowly and quietly, breaking it to them in the end that Mr Morgan was still in the bathroom and had probably fallen asleep. 'It is not his fault,' she heard herself saying. 'We must try to understand.' And she felt that the Runcas would nod their heads in agreement and would know what to do next.

'Will they sack me?' said Bianca, and Miss Winton shook her head, repeating again that nothing that had happened had been Bianca's fault.

At three o'clock the Runcas arrived. They came together, having met in the hallway downstairs. 'The flowers came, did they?' Mr Runca had inquired of his wife in the lift, and she had replied that the flowers had safely been delivered and that she had arranged them to her satisfaction. 'Good,' said Mr Runca, and reported to his wife some facts about the morning he had spent.

When they entered their penthouse apartment the Runcas noted the presence of the photographers and the photographers' apparatus. They saw as well that an elderly woman with a dog was there, standing beside Bianca, that a chair had been moved, that the Afghanistan carpet was stained, and that some flowers had been loosely thrust into a vase. Mr Runca wondered about the latter because his wife had just informed him that she herself had arranged the flowers; Mrs Runca thought that something peculiar was going on. The elderly woman stepped forward to greet them, announcing that her name was Miss Winton, and at that moment a man in a brown overall whom the Runcas recognized as a Mr Morgan, caretaker and odd-job man, entered the room from the direction of the bathroom. He strode towards them and coughed.

'You had trouble with the pipes,' said Mr Morgan. He spoke urgently and it seemed to Mr and Mrs Runca that the elderly woman with the dog was affected by his speaking. Her mouth was actually open, as though she had been about to speak herself. Hearing Mr Morgan's voice, she closed it.

'What has happened here?' said Mrs Runca, moving forward from her husband's side. 'Has there been an accident?'

'I was called up to the flat,' said Mr Morgan, 'on account of noise in the pipes. Clogged pipes was on the point of bursting, a trouble I've been dealing with since eleven-thirty. You'll discover the bath is full of water. Release it, sir, at five o'clock tonight, and then I think you'll find everything OK. Your drain-away was out of order.'

Mrs Runca removed her gaze from Mr Morgan's face and passed it on to the face of Miss Winton and then on to the bowed head of Bianca. Her husband examined the silent photographers, sensing something in the atmosphere. He said to himself that he did not yet know the full story: what, for instance, was this woman with a dog doing there? A bell rang, and Bianca moved automatically from Miss Winton's side to answer the door. She admitted the woman from the magazine, the woman who was in charge of everything and was to write the article.

'Miss Winton,' said Mr Morgan, indicating Miss Winton, 'occupies a flat lower down in the building.' Mr Morgan blew his nose. 'Miss Winton wished,' he said, 'to see the penthouse, and knowing that I was coming here she came up too and got into conversation with the maid on the doorstep. The dog dashed in, in a hysterical fit, knocking down a bowl of flowers and upsetting an electric fire on the carpet. Did you notice this?' said Mr Morgan, striding forward to display the burnt patch. 'The girl had the fire on,' added Mr Morgan, 'because she felt the cold, coming from a warmer clime.'

Miss Winton heard the words of Mr Morgan and said nothing. He had stood in the bathroom, she reckoned, for an hour and twenty minutes, planning to say that the girl had put on the fire because, being Italian, she had suddenly felt the cold.

'Well?' said Mr Runca, looking at Miss Winton.

She saw his eyes, dark and intent, anxious to draw a response from her, wishing to watch the opening and closing of her lips while his ears listened to the words that relayed the explanation.

'I regret the inconvenience,' she said. 'I'll pay for the damage.'

'Damage?' cried Mrs Runca, moving forward and pushing the chair further away from the burnt area of carpet. 'Damage?' she said again, looking at the flowers in the vase.

'So a dog had a fit in here,' said Mr Runca.

The woman from the magazine looked from Mr Morgan to Bianca and then to Miss Winton. She surveyed the faces of Mr and Mrs Runca and glanced last of all at the passive countenances of her photographers. It seemed, she reflected, that an incident had occurred; it seemed that a dog had gone berserk. 'Well now,' she said briskly. 'Surely it's not as bad as all that? If we put that chair back who'll notice the carpet? And the flowers look most becoming.'

'The flowers are a total mess,' said Mrs Runca. 'An animal might have arranged them.'

Mr Morgan was discreetly silent, and Miss Winton's face turned scarlet.

'We had better put the whole thing off,' said Mr Runca meditatively. 'It'll take a day or two to put everything back to rights. We are sorry,' he said, addressing himself to the woman from the magazine. 'But no doubt you see that no pictures can be taken?'

The woman, swearing most violently within her mind, smiled at Mr Runca and said it was obvious, of course. Mr Morgan said:

'I'm sorry, sir, about this.' He stood there, serious and unemotional, as though he had never suggested that Mrs Neck might be invited up to the Runcas' penthouse apartment, as though hatred and drink had not rendered him insane. 'I'm sorry, sir,' said Mr Morgan. 'I should not have permitted a dog to enter your quarters, sir. I was unaware of the dog until it was too late.'

Listening to Mr Morgan laboriously telling his lies, Miss Winton was visited by the thought that there was something else she could do. For fifteen years she had lived lonesomely in the building, her shyness causing her to keep herself to herself. She possessed enough money to exist quite comfortably; she didn't do much as the days went by.

'Excuse me,' said Miss Winton, not at all knowing how she was going to proceed. She felt her face becoming red again, and she felt the eyes of everyone on her. She wanted to explain at length, to go on talking in a manner that was quite unusual for her, weaving together the threads of an argument. It seemed to Miss Winton that she would have to remind the Runcas of the life of Mr Morgan, how he daily climbed from his deep basement, attired invariably in his long brown overall. 'He has a right to his resentment,' was what she might say; 'he has a right to demand more of the tenants of these flats. His palm is greased, he is handed a cup of tea in exchange for a racing tip; the tenants keep him sweet.' He had come to consider that some of the tenants were absurd, or stupid, and that others were hypocritical. For Miss Winton he had reserved his scorn, for the Runcas a share of his hatred. Miss Winton had accepted the scorn, and understood why it was there; they must seek to understand the other. 'The ball is in your court,' said Miss Winton in her imagination, addressing the Runcas and pleased that she had thought of a breezy expression that they would at once appreciate.

'What about Wednesday next?' said Mr Runca to the woman from the magazine. 'All this should be sorted out by then, I imagine.'

'Wednesday would be lovely,' said the woman.

Miss Winton wanted to let Mr Morgan see that he was wrong about these people. She wanted to have it proved here and now that the Runcas were human and would understand an accident, that they, like anyone else, were capable of respecting a touchy caretaker. She wished to speak the truth, to lead the truth into the open and let it act for itself between Mr Morgan and the Runcas.

'We'll make a note of everything,' Mrs Runca said to her, 'and let you have the list of the damage and the cost of it.'

'I'd like to talk to you,' said Miss Winton. 'I'd like to explain if I may.'

'Explain?' said Mrs Runca. 'Explain?'

'Could we perhaps sit down? I'd like you to understand. I've been in these flats for fifteen years. Mr Morgan came a year later. Perhaps I can help. It's difficult for me to explain to you.' Miss Winton paused, in some confusion.

'Is she ill?' inquired the steely voice of Mrs Runca, and Miss Winton was aware of the woman's metallic hair, and fingernails that matched it, and the four shrewd eyes of a man and a woman who were successful in all their transactions. 'I might hit them with a hammer,' said the voice of Mr Morgan in Miss Winton's memory. 'I might strike them dead.'

'We must try to understand,' cried Miss Winton, her face burning with embarrassment. 'A man like Mr Morgan and people like you and an old spinster like myself. We must relax and attempt to understand.' Miss Winton wondered if the words that she forced from her were making sense; she was aware that she was not being eloquent. 'Don't you see?' cried Miss Winton with the businesslike stare of the Runcas fixed harshly upon her.

'What's this?' demanded Mrs Runca. 'What's all this about understanding? Understanding what?'

'Yes,' said her husband.

'Mr Morgan comes up from his basement every day of his life. The tenants grease his palm. He sees the tenants in his own way. He has a right to do that; he has a right to his touchiness –'

Mr Morgan coughed explosively, interrupting the flow of words. 'What are you talking about?' cried Mrs Runca. 'It's enough that damage has been done without all this.'

'I'm trying to begin at the beginning.' Ahead of her Miss Winton sensed a great mound of words and complication before she could lay bare the final truth: that Mr Morgan regarded the Runcas as people who had been in some way devoured. She knew that she would have to progress slowly, until they began to guess what she was trying to put to them. Accepting that they had failed the caretaker, as she had failed him too, they would understand the reason for his small revenge. They would nod their heads guiltily while she related how Mr Morgan, unhinged by alcohol, had spat at their furniture and had afterwards pretended to be drowned.

'We belong to different worlds,' said Miss Winton, wishing the ground would open beneath her, 'you and I and Mr Morgan. Mr Morgan sees your penthouse flat in a different way. What I am trying to say is that you are not just people to whom only lies can be told.'

'We have a lot to do,' said Mrs Runca, lighting a cigarette. She was smiling slightly, seeming amused.

'The bill for damage must be paid,' added Mr Runca firmly. 'You understand, Miss Winter? There can be no shelving of that responsibility.'

'I don't do much,' cried Miss Winton, moving beyond embarrassment now. 'I sit with my dog. I go to the shops. I watch the television. I don't do much, but I am trying to do something now. I am trying to promote understanding.'

The photographers began to dismantle their apparatus. Mr Runca spoke in a whisper to the woman from the magazine, making some final arrangement for the following Wednesday. He turned to Miss Winton and said more loudly: 'Perhaps you had better return to your apartment, Miss Winter. Who knows, that little dog may have another fit.'

'He didn't have a fit,' cried Miss Winton. 'He never had a fit in the whole of his life.'

There was a silence in the room then, before Mr Runca said:

'You've forgotten, Miss Winter, that your little dog had a bout of hysteria and caused a lot of trouble. Come now, Miss Winter.'

'My name is not Miss Winter. Why do you call me a name that isn't correct?'

Mr Runca threw his eyes upwards, implying that Miss Winton was getting completely out of hand and would next be denying her very existence. 'She's the Queen Mother,' whispered Mrs Runca to one of the photographers, and the photographer sniggered lightly. Miss Winton said:

'My dog did not have a fit. I am trying to tell you, but no one bothers to listen. I am trying to go back to the beginning, to the day that Mr Morgan first became caretaker of these flats –'

'Now, madam,' said Mr Morgan, stepping forward.

'I am going to tell the truth,' cried Miss Winton shrilly. Her dog began to bark, and she felt, closer to her now, the presence of Mr Morgan. 'Shall we be going, madam?' said Mr Morgan, and she was aware that she was being moved towards the door. 'No,' she cried while the movement continued. 'No,' whispered Miss Winton again, but already she was on the landing and Mr Morgan was saying that there was no point whatsoever in attempting to tell people like the Runcas the truth. 'That type of person,' said Mr Morgan, descending the stairs with Miss Winton, his hand beneath her left elbow as though she required aid, 'that type of person wouldn't know the meaning of the word.'

I have failed, said Miss Winton to herself; I have failed to do something that might have been good in its small way. She found herself at the door of her flat, feeling tired, and heard Mr Morgan saying: 'Will you be all right, madam?' She reflected that he was speaking to her as though she were the one who had been mad, soothing her in his scorn. Mr Morgan began to laugh. 'Runca slipped me a quid,' he said. 'Our own Runca.' He laughed again, and Miss Winton felt wearier. She would write a cheque for the amount of the damage, and that would be that. She would often in the future pass Mr Morgan on the stairs and there would be a confused memory between them. The Runcas would tell their friends, saying there was a peculiar woman in one of the flats. 'Did you see their faces,' said Mr Morgan, 'when I mentioned about the dog in a fit?' He threw his head back, displaying all his teeth. 'It was that amusing,' said Mr Morgan. 'I nearly smiled.' He went away, and Miss Winton stood by the door of her flat, listening to his footsteps on the stairs. She heard him on the next floor, summoning the lift that would carry him smoothly to the basement, where he would tell his wife about Miss Winton's dog having a fit in the Runcas' penthouse, and how Miss Winton had made a ridiculous fuss that no one had bothered to listen to.

A Trinity

Their first holiday since their honeymoon was paid for by the elderly man they both called Uncle. In fact, he was related to neither of them: for eleven years he had been Dawne's employer, but the relationship was more truly that of benefactor and dependants. They lived with him and looked after him, but in another sense it was he who looked after them, demonstrating regularly that they required such care. 'What you need is a touch of the autumn sun,' he had said, ordering Keith to acquire as many holiday brochures as he could lay his hands on. 'The pair of you're as white as bedsheets.'

The old man lived vicariously through aspects of their lives, and listened carefully to all they said. Sharing their anticipation, he browsed delightedly through the pages of the colourful brochures and opened out on the kitchen table one glossy folder after another. He marvelled over the blue of the Aegean Sea and the flower markets of San Remo, over the Nile and the pyramids, the Costa del Sol, the treasures of Bavaria. But it was Venice that most instantly caught his imagination, and again and again he returned to the wonder of its bridges and canals, and the majesty of the Piazza San Marco.

'I am too old for Venice,' he remarked a little sadly. 'I am too old for anywhere now.'

They protested. They pressed him to accompany them. But as well as being old he had his paper-shop to think about. He could not leave Mrs Withers to cope on her own; it would not be fair.

'Send me one or two postcards,' he said. 'That will be sufficient.'

He chose for them a package holiday at a very reasonable price: an air flight from Gatwick Airport, twelve nights in the fairyland city, in the Pensione Concordia. When Keith and Dawne went together to the travel agency to make the booking the counter clerk explained that the other members of that particular package were an Italian class from Windsor, all of them learning the language under the tutelage of a Signor Bancini. 'It is up to you if you wish to take the guided tours of Signor Bancini,' the counter clerk explained. 'And naturally you have your own table for breakfast and for dinner.'

The old man, on being told about the party from Windsor, was well pleased. Mixing with such people and, for just a little extra, being able to avail themselves of the expertise of an Italian language teacher amounted to a bonus, he pointed out. 'Travel widens the mind,' he said. 'I deplore I never had the opportunity.'

But something went wrong. Either in the travel agency or at Gatwick Airport, or in some anonymous computer, a small calamity was conceived. Dawne and Keith ended up in a hotel called the Edelweiss, in Room 212, in Switzerland. At Gatwick they had handed their tickets to a girl in the yellow-and-red Your-Kind-of-Holiday uniform. She'd addressed them by name, had checked the details on their tickets and said that that was lovely. An hour later it had surprised them to hear elderly people on the plane talking in North of England accents when the counter clerk at the travel agency had so specifically stated that Signor Bancini's Italian class came from Windsor. Dawne had even remarked on it, but Keith said there must have been a cancellation, or possibly the Italian class was on a second plane. 'That'll be the name of the airport,' he confidently explained when the pilot referred over the communications system to a destination that didn't sound like Venice. 'Same as he'd say Gatwick. Or Heathrow.' They ordered two Drambuies, Dawne's favourite drink, and then two more. 'The coach'll take us on,' a stout woman with spectacles announced when the plane landed. 'Keep all together now.' There'd been no mention of an overnight stop in the brochure, but when the coach drew in at the Edelweiss Hotel Keith explained that that was clearly what this was. By air and then by coach was how these package firms kept the prices down, a colleague at work had told him. As they stepped out of the coach it was close on midnight: fatigued and travel-stained, they did not feel like questioning their right to the beds they were offered. But the next morning, when it became apparent that they were being offered them for the duration of their holiday, they became alarmed.

'We have the lake, and the water-birds,' the receptionist smilingly explained. 'And we may take the steamer to Interlaken.'

'An error has been made,' Keith informed the man, keeping the register of his voice even, for it was essential to be calm. He was aware of his wife's agitated breathing close beside him. She'd had to sit down when they realized that something was wrong, but now she was standing up again.

'We cannot change the room, sir,' the clerk swiftly countered. 'Each has been given a room. You accompany the group, sir?'

Keith shook his head. Not this group, he said, a different group; a group that was travelling on to another destination. Keith was not a tall man, and often suffered from what he considered to be arrogance in other people, from officials of one kind or another, and shop-assistants with a tendency to assume that his lack of stature reflected a diminutive personality. In a way Keith didn't care for, the receptionist repeated:

'This is the Edelweiss Hotel, sir.'

'We were meant to be in Venice. In the Pensione Concordia.'

'I do not know the name, sir. Here we have Switzerland.'

'A coach is to take us on. An official said so on the plane. She was here last night, that woman.'

'Tomorrow we have the *fondue* party,' the receptionist went on, having listened politely to this information about an official. 'On Tuesday there is the visit to a chocolate factory. On other days we may take the steamer to Interlaken, where we have teashops. In Interlaken mementoes may be bought at fair prices.'

Dawne had still not spoken. She, too, was a slight figure, her features pale beneath orange-ish powder. 'Mingy', the old man had a way of saying in his joky voice, and sometimes told her to lie down.

'Eeh, idn't it luvely?' a voice behind Keith enthused. 'Been out to feed them ducks, 'ave you?'

Keith did not turn round. Speaking slowly, giving each word space, he said to the receptionist: 'We have been booked on to the wrong holiday.'

'Your group is booked twelve nights in the Edelweiss Hotel. To make an alteration now, sir, if you have changed your minds –'

'We haven't changed our minds. There's been a mistake.'

The receptionist shook his head. He did not know about a mistake. He had not been told that. He would help if he could, but he did not see how help might best be offered.

'The man who made the booking,' Dawne interrupted, 'was bald, with glasses and a moustache.' She gave the name of the travel agency in London.

In reply, the receptionist smiled with professional sympathy. He fingered the edge of his register. 'Moustache?' he said.

Three aged women who had been on the plane passed through the reception area. Had anyone noticed, one of them remarked, that there were rubber linings under the sheets? Well, you couldn't be too careful, another agreeably responded, if you were running a hotel.

'Some problem, have we?' another woman said, beaming at Keith. She was the stout woman he had referred to as an official, flamboyantly attired this morning in a two-tone trouser-suit, green and blue. Her flesh-coloured spectacles were decorated with swirls of metal made to seem like gold; her grey hair was carefully waved. They'd seen her talking to the yellow-and-red girl at Gatwick. On the plane she'd walked up and down the aisle, smiling at people.

'My name is Franks,' she was saying now. 'I'm married to the man with the bad leg.'

'Are you in charge, Mrs Franks?' Dawne inquired. 'Only we're in the wrong hotel.' Again she gave the name of the travel agency and described the bald-headed counter clerk, mentioning his spectacles and his moustache. Keith interrupted her.

'It seems we got into the wrong group. We reported to the Your-Kind-of-Holiday girl and left it all to her.'

'We should have known when they weren't from Windsor,' Dawne contributed. 'We heard them talking about Darlington.'

Keith made an impatient sound. He wished she'd leave the talking to him. It was no good whatsoever going on about Darlington and the counter clerk's moustache, confusing everything even more.

'We noticed you at Gatwick,' he said to the stout woman. 'We knew you were in charge of things.'

'I noticed *you*. Well, of course I did, naturally I did. I counted you, although I dare say you didn't see me doing that. Monica checked the tickets and I did the counting. That's how I know everything's OK. Now, let me explain to you. There are many places Your-Kind-of-Holiday sends its clients to, many tours, many different holidays at different prices. You follow me? Something to suit every pocket, something for every taste. There are, for instance, villa holidays for the adventurous under-thirty-fives. There are treks to Turkey, and treks for singles to the Himalayas. There is self-catering in Portugal, November reductions in Casablanca, February in Biarritz. There's Culture-in-Tuscany and Sunshine-in-Sorrento. There's the Nile. There's Your-Kind-of-Safari in Kenya. Now, what I am endeavouring to say to you good people is that all tickets and labels are naturally similar, the yellow with the two red bands.' Mrs Franks suddenly laughed. 'So if you simply followed other people with the yellow-and-red label you might imagine you could end up in a wildlife park!' Mrs Franks' speech came hurriedly from her, the words tumbling over one another, gushing through her teeth. 'But of course,' she added soothingly, 'that couldn't happen in a million years.'

'We're not meant to be in Switzerland,' Keith doggedly persisted.

'Well, let's just see, shall we?'

Unexpectedly, Mrs Franks turned and went away, leaving them standing. The receptionist was no longer behind the reception desk. The sound of typing could be heard.

'She seems quite kind,' Dawne whispered, 'that woman.'

To Keith it seemed unnecessary to say that. Any consideration of Mrs Franks was, in the circumstances, as irrelevant as a description of the man in the travel agent's. He tried to go over in his mind every single thing that had occurred: handing the girl the tickets, sitting down to wait, and then the girl leading the way to the plane, and then the pilot's voice welcoming them aboard, and the air hostess with the smooth black hair going round to see that everyone's seat-belt was fastened.

'Snaith his name was,' Dawne was saying. 'It said *Snaith* on a plastic thing in front of him.'

'What are you talking about?'

'The man in the travel place was called Snaith. *G. Snaith* it said.'

'The man was just a clerk.'

'He booked us wrong, though. That man's responsible, Keith.'

'Be that as it may.'

Sooner or later, Dawne had guessed, he'd say 'Be that as it may'. He put her in her place with the phrase; he always had. You'd make an innocent remark, doing your best to be helpful, and out he'd come with 'Be that as it may'. You expected him to go on, to finish the sentence, but he never did. The phrase just hung there, making him sound uneducated.

'Are you going to phone up that man, Keith?'

'Which man is this?'

She didn't reply. He knew perfectly well which man she meant. All he had to do was to get through to Directory Inquiries and find out the number of the travel agency. It was no good complaining to a hotel receptionist who had nothing to do with it, nor to a woman in charge of a totally different package tour. No good putting the blame where it didn't belong.

'Nice to have some young people along,' an elderly man said. 'Nottage the name is.'

Dawne smiled, the way she did in the shop when someone was trying to be agreeable, but Keith didn't acknowledge the greeting because he didn't want to become involved.

'Seen the ducks, 'ave you? Right champion them ducks are.'

The old man's wife was with him, both of them looking as if they were in their eighties. She nodded when he said the ducks were right champion. They'd slept like logs, she said, best night's sleep they'd had for years, which of course would be due to the lakeside air.

'That's nice,' Dawne said.

Keith walked out of the reception area and Dawne followed him. On the gravel forecourt of the hotel they didn't say to one another that there was an irony in the catastrophe that had occurred. On their first holiday since their honeymoon they'd landed themselves in a package tour of elderly people when the whole point of the holiday was to escape the needs and demands of the elderly. In his bossy way Uncle had said so himself when they'd tried to persuade him to accompany them.

'You'll have to phone up Snaith,' Dawne repeated, irritating Keith further. What she did not understand was that if the error had occurred with the man she spoke of it would since have become compounded to such a degree that the man would claim to be able to do nothing about their immediate predicament. Keith, who sold insurance over the counter for the General Accident insurance company, knew something of the complications that followed when even the slightest uncertainty in a requirement was passed into the programme of a computer. Somewhere along the line that was what had happened, but to explain it to Dawne would take a very long time. Dawne could work a till as well as anyone; in the shop she knew by heart the price of Mars bars and the different kinds of cigarettes and tobacco, and the prices of all the newspapers and magazines, but otherwise Keith considered her slow on the uptake, often unable to follow simple argument.

'Hi, there!' Mrs Franks called out, and they turned and saw her picking her way across the gravel towards them. She had a piece of pink paper in her hand. 'I've been doing my homework!' she cried when she was a little closer. She waved the pink paper. 'Take a look at this.'

It was a list of names, a computer print-out, each name a series of tiny dots. *K. and H. Beale*, they read, *T. and G. Craven, P. and R. Feinman.* There were many others, including *B. and Y. Nottage*. In the correct alphabetical position they were there themselves, between *J. and A. Hines* and *C. and L. Mace*.

'The thing is,' Dawne began, and Keith looked away. His wife's voice quietly continued, telling Mrs Franks that their holiday had been very kindly paid for by the old man whom they lived with, who had been her employer before they ever moved in to live with him, who still was. They called him Uncle but he wasn't a relation, a friend really – well, more than that. The thing was, he would be angry because they were not in Venice, he having said it should be Venice. He'd be angry because they were in a package for the elderly when he wanted them to have a rest from the elderly, not that she minded looking after Uncle herself, not that she ever would. The person in the travel agency had said the Windsor people were quite young. 'I always remember things like that,' Dawne finished up. 'Snaith he was called. G. Snaith.'

'Well, that's most interesting,' Mrs Franks commented, and added after a pause: 'As a matter of fact, Dawne, Mr Franks and myself are still in our fifties.'

'Be that as it may,' Keith said. 'At no time did we book a holiday in Switzerland.'

'Well, there you are, you see. The ticket you handed to me at Gatwick is as clear as daylight, exactly the same as the Beales' and the Maces', the same as our own, come to that. Not a tither of difference, Keith.'

'We need to be conveyed to our correct destination. An arrangement has to be made.'

'The trouble is, Keith, I don't know if you know it but you're half a continent away from Venice. Another thing is, I'm not employed by Your-Kind, nothing like that. They just reduce our ticket a bit if I agree to keep an eye. On location we call it.' Mrs Franks went on to say that her husband had also scrutinized the piece of pink paper and was in complete agreement with her. She asked Keith if he had met her husband, and said again that he was the man with the bad leg. He'd been an accountant and still did a lot of accountancy work one way or another, in a private capacity. The Edelweiss Hotel was excellent, she said. Your-Kind would never choose an indifferent hotel.

'We are asking you to get in touch with your firm in London,' Keith said. 'We do not belong with your group.'

In silence, though smiling, Mrs Franks held out the pink list. Her expression insisted that it spoke for itself. No one could gainsay the dotted identification among the others.

'Our name is there by mistake.'

A man limped across the gravel towards them. He was a large man of shambling appearance, his navy-blue pin-striped jacket and waistcoat at odds with his brown trousers, his spectacles repaired with Sellotape. The sound of his breath could be heard as he approached. He blew it through half-pursed lips in a vague rendition of a Gilbert and Sullivan melody.

'These are the poor lost lambs,' Mrs Franks said. 'Keith and Dawne.'

'How do?' Mr Franks held a hand out. 'Silly thing to happen, eh?'

It was Mr Franks who eventually suggested that Keith should telephone Your-Kind-of-Holiday himself, and to Keith's surprise he got through to a number in Croydon without any difficulty. 'Excuse me a minute,' a girl said when he finished. He heard her talking to someone else and he heard the other person laughing. There was a trace of laughter in the girl's voice when she spoke again. You couldn't change your mind, she said, in the middle of a package. In no circumstances whatsoever could that be permitted. 'We're not changing our minds,' Keith protested, but while he was explaining all over again he was cut off because he hadn't any more coins. He cashed a traveller's cheque with the receptionist and was supplied with a number of five-franc pieces, but when he re-dialled the number the girl he'd spoken to couldn't be located so he explained everything to another girl. 'I'm sorry, sir,' this girl said, 'but if we allowed people to change their minds on account of they didn't like the look of a place we'd be out of business in no time.' Keith began to shout into the telephone, and Dawne rapped on the glass of the booth, holding up a piece of paper on which she'd written *G. Snaith the name was*. 'Some sort of loony,' Keith heard the girl say in Croydon, the mouthpiece being inadequately muffled. There was an outburst of giggling before he was cut off.

It was not the first time that Keith and Dawne had suffered in this way: they were familiar with defeat. There'd been the time, a couple of years after their marriage, when Keith had got into debt through purchasing materials for making ships in bottles; earlier – before they'd even met – there was the occasion when the Lamb and Flag had had to let Dawne go because she'd taken tips although the rules categorically forbade it. Once Keith had sawn through the wrong water pipe and the landlords had come along with a bill for nearly two hundred pounds when the ceiling of the flat below collapsed. It was Uncle who had given Dawne a job in his shop after the Lamb and Flag episode and who had put them on their feet by paying off the arrears of the handicraft debt. In the end he persuaded them to come and live with him, pointing out that the arrangement would suit all three of them. Since his sister's death he had found it troublesome, managing on his own.

In Interlaken they selected a postcard to send him: of a mountain that had featured in a James Bond film. But they didn't know what to write on it: if they told the truth they would receive the old man's unspoken scorn when they returned – a look that came into his eyes while he silently regarded them. Years ago he had openly said – once only – that they were accident-prone. They were unfortunate in their dealings with the world, he had explained when Dawne asked him; lame ducks, he supposed you could say, if they'd forgive the expression, victims by nature, no fault of their own. Ever since, such judgements had been expressed only through his eyes.

'You choose your piece of gâteau,' Dawne said, 'up at the counter. They put it on a plate for you. Then the waitress comes along and you order the tea. I've been watching how it's done.'

Keith chose a slice of glazed greengage cake and Dawne a portion of strawberry flan. As soon as they sat down a waitress came and stood smiling in front of them. 'Tea with milk in it,' Dawne ordered, because when she'd said they were going abroad someone who'd come into the shop had warned her that you had to ask for milk, otherwise the tea came just as it was, sometimes no more than a tea-bag and a glass of hot water.

'A strike?' Dawne suggested. 'You're always hearing of strikes in airports.'

But Keith continued to gaze at the blank postcard, not persuaded that an attempt at falsehood was wise. It wasn't easy to tell the old man a lie. He had a way of making such attempts feel clumsy, and in the end of winkling out the truth. Yet his scorn would continue for many months, especially since he had paid out what he would call – a couple of hundred times at least – 'good money' for their tickets. 'That's typical of Keith, that is,' he'd repeatedly inform his customers in Dawne's hearing, and she'd pass it on that night in bed, the way she always passed his comments on.

Keith ate his greengage slice, Dawne her strawberry flan. They did not share their thoughts, although their thoughts were similar. 'You've neither of you a head for business,' he'd said after the ships-in-bottles calamity, and again when Dawne unsuccessfully attempted to make a go of dressmaking alterations. 'You wouldn't last a week in charge of things downstairs.' He always referred to the shop as 'downstairs'. Every day of his life he rose at five o'clock in order to be downstairs for the newspapers when they arrived. He'd done so for fifty-three years.

The plane couldn't land at the Italian airport, Keith wrote, *owing to a strike. So it had to come down here instead. It's good in a way because we're seeing another country as well! Hope your cold's cleared up*, Dawne added. *It's really lovely here!* XXX

They imagined him showing the postcard to Mrs Withers. 'That's typical, that is,' they imagined him saying and Mrs Withers jollying him along, telling him not to be sarky. Mrs Withers was pleased about earning the extra; she'd been as keen as anything when he'd asked her to come in fulltime for a fortnight.

'Could happen to anyone, a strike,' Dawne said, voicing Mrs Withers' response.

Keith finished his greengage slice. 'Call in to Smith's for a will form,' he imagined the cross, tetchy voice instructing Mrs Withers, the postcard already tucked away on the Embassy Tipped shelf. And when she arrived with the will form the next morning he'd let it lie around all day but have it in his hand when she left, before he locked the shop door behind her. 'Silly really,' Mrs Withers would say when eventually she told Dawne about it.

'I'd just as soon be here,' Dawne whispered, leaning forward a bit, daring at last to say that. 'I'd just as soon be in Switzerland, Keithie.'

He didn't reply, but looked around the teashop: at the display of cake in the long glass cabinet that served also as a counter – apricot and plum and apple, carrot-cake and Black Forest gâteau, richly glazed fruitcake, marzipan slices, small lemon tarts, orange éclairs, coffee fondants. Irritated because his wife had made that statement and wishing to be unpleasant to her by not responding, he allowed his gaze to slip over the faces of the couples who sat sedately at round, prettily arranged tables. In a leisurely manner he examined the smiling waitresses, their crimson aprons matching the crimson of the frilled tablecloths. He endeavoured to give the impression that the waitresses attracted him.

'It's really nice,' Dawne said, her voice still shyly low.

He didn't disagree; there was nothing wrong with the place. People were speaking in German, but when you spoke in English they understood you. Enoch Melchor, in Claims, had gone to somewhere in Italy last year and had got into all sorts of difficulties with the language, including being given the head of a fish when he thought he'd ordered peas.

'We could say we liked it so much we decided to stay on,' Dawne suggested.

She didn't seem to understand that it wasn't up to them to decide anything. Twelve days in Venice had been chosen for them; twelve days in Venice had been paid for. 'No better'n a sewer,' Enoch Melchor had said, not that he'd ever been there. 'Stinks to high heaven,' he'd said, but that wasn't the point either. Memories of Venice had been ordered, memories that were to be transported back to London, with glass figurines for the mantelpiece because Venice was famous for its glass. The menus at the Pensione Concordia and the tunes played by the café orchestras were to be noted in Dawne's day-to-day diary. Venice was bathed in sunshine, its best autumn for years, according to the newspapers.

They left the teashop and walked about the streets, their eyes stinging at first, until they became used to the bitter breeze that had got up. They examined windows full of watches, and went from one to another of the souvenir shops because notices said that entrance was free. There was a clock that had a girl swinging on a swing every hour, and another that had a man and a woman employing a cross-saw, another that had a cow being milked. All sorts of tunes came out of different-shaped musical boxes: 'Lily Marlene', 'The Blue Danube', 'Lara's Theme' from *Doctor Zhivago*, the 'Destiny Waltz'. There were oven gloves with next year's calendar printed on them in English, and miniature arrangements of dried flowers, framed, on velvet. In the chocolate shops there were all the different brands, Lindt, Suchard, Nestlé, Cailler, and dozens of others. There was chocolate with nuts, and chocolate with raisins, with nougat and honey, white chocolate, milk or plain, chocolate with fudge filling, with cognac or whisky or chartreuse, chocolate mice and chocolate windmills.

'It's ever so enjoyable here,' Dawne remarked, with genuine enthusiasm. They went into another teashop, and this time Keith had a chestnut slice and Dawne a blackcurrant one, both with cream.

At dinner, in a dining-room tastefully panelled in grey-painted wood, they sat among the people from Darlington, at a table for two, as the clerk in the travel agency had promised. The chicken-noodle soup was quite what they were used to, and so was the pork chop that followed, with apple sauce and chipped potatoes. 'They know what we like,' the woman called Mrs Franks said, making a round of all the tables, saying the same thing at each.

'Really lovely,' Dawne agreed. She'd felt sick in her stomach when they'd first realized about the error; she'd wanted to go to the lavatory and just sit there, hoping it was all a nightmare. She'd blamed herself because it was she who'd wondered about so many elderly people on the plane after the man in the travel place had given the impression of young people, from Windsor. It was she who had frowned, just for a moment, when the name of the airport was mentioned. Keith had a habit of pooh-poohing her doubts, like when she'd been doubtful about the men who'd come to the door selling mattresses and he'd been persuaded to make a down-payment. The trouble with Keith was, he always sounded confident, as though he knew something she didn't, as though someone had told him. 'We'll just be here for the night,' he'd said, and she'd thought that was something he must have read in the brochure or that the clerk in the travel place had said. He couldn't help himself, of course; it was the way he was made. 'Cotton-wool in your brain-box, have you?' Uncle had rudely remarked, the August Bank Holiday poor Keith had got them on to the slow train to Brighton, the one that took an hour longer.

'Silver lining, Keithie.' She put her head on one side, her small features softening into a smile. They'd walked by the lakeside before dinner. Just by stooping down, she'd attracted the birds that were swimming on the water. Afterwards she'd changed into her new fawn dress, bought specially for the holiday.

'I'll try that number again tomorrow,' Keith said.

She could see he was still worried. He was terribly subdued, even though he was able to eat his food. It made him cross when she mentioned the place they'd bought the tickets, so she didn't do so, although she wanted to. Time enough to face the music when they got back, better to make the best of things really: she didn't say that either.

'If you want to, Keithie,' she said instead. 'You try it if you've a call to.'

Naturally he'd feel it more than she would; he'd get more of the blame, being a man. But in the end it mightn't be too bad, in the end the storm would be weathered. There'd be the *fondue* party to talk about, and the visit to the chocolate factory. There'd be the swimming birds, and the teashops, and the railway journey they'd seen advertised, up to the top of an alp.

'Banana split?' the waiter offered. 'You prefer meringue Williams?'

They hesitated. Meringue Williams was meringue with pears and ice-cream, the waiter explained. Very good. He himself would recommend the meringue Williams.

'Sounds lovely,' Dawne said, and Keith had it too. She thought of pointing out that everyone was being nice to them, that Mrs Franks was ever so sympathetic, that the man who came round to ask them if the dinner was all right had been ever so pleasant, and the waiter too. But she decided not to because often Keith just didn't want to cheer up. 'Droopy Drawers', Uncle sometimes called him, or 'Down-in-the-Dumps Donald'.

All around them the old people were chattering. They were older than Uncle, Dawne could see; some of them were ten years older, fifteen even. She wondered if Keith had noticed that, if it had added to his gloom. She could hear them talking about the mementoes they'd bought and the teashops they'd been to; hale and hearty they looked, still as full of vim as Uncle. 'Any day now I'll be dropping off my twig,' he had a way of saying, which was nonsense of course. Dawne watched the elderly mouths receiving spoonfuls of banana or meringue, the slow chewing, the savouring of the sweetness. A good twenty years Uncle could go on for, she suddenly thought.

'It's just bad luck,' she said.

'Be that as it may.'

'Don't say that, Keithie.'

'Say what?'

'Don't say "Be that as it may".'

'Why not?'

'Oh just because, Keithie.'

They had in common an institution background: they had not known their parents. Dawne could remember Keith when he was eleven and she was nine, although at that time they had not been drawn to one another. They'd met again later, revisiting their children's home for the annual dance, disco as it was called these days. 'I got work in this shop,' she'd said, not mentioning Uncle because he was only her employer then, in the days when his sister was alive. They'd been married for a while before he became an influence in their lives. Now they could anticipate, without thinking, his changes of heart and his whims, and see a mile off another quarrel with the Reverend Simms, whose church occasionally he attended. Once they'd tried to divert such quarrels, to brace themselves for changes of heart, to counter the whims that were troublesome. They no longer did so. Although he listened carefully, he took no notice of what they said because he held the upper hand. The Smith's will forms and an old billiard-room – 'the happiest place a man could spend an hour in' – were what he threatened them with. He met his friends in the billiard-room; he read the *Daily Express* there, drinking bottles of Double Diamond, which he said was the best bottled beer in the world. It would be a terrible thing if men of all ages could no longer play billiards in that room, terrible if funds weren't available to keep it going for ever.

Mrs Franks made an announcement. She called for silence, and then gave particulars of the next day's programme. There was to be a visit to the James Bond mountain, everyone to assemble on the forecourt at half past ten. Anyone who didn't want to go should please tell her tonight.

'We don't have to, Keithie,' Dawne whispered when Mrs Franks sat down. 'Not if we don't want to.'

The chatter began again, spoons excitedly waved in the air. False teeth, grey hair, glasses; Uncle might have been among them except that Uncle never would because he claimed to despise the elderly. 'You're telling *me*, are you? You're telling *me* you got yourselves entangled with a bunch of O.A.P's?' As clearly as if he were beside her Dawne could hear his voice, enriched with the pretence of amazement. 'You landed up in the wrong country and spent your holiday with a crowd of geriatrics! You're never telling me that?'

Sympathetic as she was, Mrs Franks had played it down. She knew that a young couple in their thirties weren't meant to be on a package with the elderly; she knew the error was not theirs. But it wouldn't be any use mentioning Mrs Franks to Uncle. It wouldn't be any use saying that Keith had got cross with the receptionist and with the people in Croydon. He'd listen and then there'd be a silence. After that he'd begin to talk about the billiard-room.

'Had a great day, did you?' Mrs Franks said on her way out of the dining-room. 'All's well that ends well, eh?'

Keith continued to eat his meringue Williams as if he had not been addressed. Mr Franks remarked on the meringue Williams, laughing about it, saying they'd all have to watch their figures. 'I must say,' Mrs Franks said, 'we're lucky with the weather. At least it isn't raining.' She was dressed in the same flamboyant clothes. She'd been able to buy some Madame Rochas, she said, awfully good value.

'We don't have to say about the old people,' Dawne whispered when the Frankses had passed on. 'We needn't mention that.'

Dawne dug into the deep glass for the ice-cream that lay beneath the slices of pear. She knew he was thinking she would let it slip about the old people. Every Saturday she washed Uncle's hair for him since he found it difficult to do it himself. Because he grumbled so about the tepid rinse that was necessary in case he caught a cold afterwards, she had to jolly him along. She'd always found it difficult to do two things at once, and it was while washing his hair that occasionally she'd forgotten what she was saying. But she was determined not to make that mistake again, just as she had ages ago resolved not to get into a flap if he suddenly asked her a question when she was in the middle of counting the newspapers that hadn't been sold.

'Did you find your friends from Windsor then?' an old woman with a walking frame inquired. 'Eeh, it were bad you lost your friends.'

Dawne explained, since no harm was meant. Other old people stood by to hear, but a few of them were deaf and asked to have what was being said repeated. Keith continued to eat his meringue Williams.

'Keithie, it isn't their fault,' she tentatively began when the people had passed on. '*They* can't help it, Keithie.'

'Be that as it may. No need to go attracting them.'

'I didn't attract them. They stopped by. Same as Mrs Franks.'

'Who's Mrs Franks?'

'You know who she is. That big woman. She gave us her name this morning, Keithie.'

'When I get back I'll institute proceedings.'

She could tell from his tone that that was what he'd been thinking about. All the time on the steamer they'd taken to Interlaken, all the time in the teashop, and on the cold streets and in the souvenir shops, all the time they'd been looking at the watch displays and the chocolate displays, all the time in the grey-panelled dining-room, he had been planning what he'd say, what he'd probably write on the very next postcard: that he intended to take legal proceedings. When they returned he would stand in the kitchen and state what he intended, very matter of fact. First thing on Monday he'd arrange to see a solicitor, he'd state, an appointment for his lunch hour. And Uncle would remain silent, not even occasionally inclining his head, or shaking it, knowing that solicitors cost money.

'They're liable for the full amount. Every penny of it.'

'Let's try to enjoy ourselves, Keithie. Why don't I tell Mrs Franks we'll go up the mountain?'

'What mountain's that?'

'The one she was on about, the one we sent him a postcard of.'

'I need to phone up Croydon in the morning.'

'You can do it before ten-thirty, Keithie.'

The last of the elderly people slowly made their way from the dining-room, saying good-night as they went. A day would come, Dawne thought, when they would go to Venice on their own initiative, with people like the Windsor people. She imagined the Windsor people in the Pensione Concordia, not one of them a day older than themselves. She imagined Signor Bancini passing among them, translating a word or two of Italian as he went. There was laughter in the dining-room of the Pensione Concordia, and bottles of red wine on the tables. The young people's names were Désirée and Rob, and Luke and Angélique, and Sean and Aimée. 'Uncle we used to call him,' her own voice said. 'He died a while back.'

Keith stood up. Skilful with the tablecloths, the waiter wished them good-night. In the reception area a different receptionist, a girl, smiled at them. Some of the old people were standing around, saying it was too cold to go for a walk. You'd miss the television, one of them remarked.

The warmth of their bodies was a familiar comfort. They had not had children because the rooms above the shop weren't suitable for children. The crying at night would have driven Uncle mad, and naturally you could see his point of view. There'd been an error when first they'd lived with him; they'd had to spend a bit terminating it.

They refrained from saying that their bodies were a comfort. They had never said so. What they said in their lives had to do with Keith's hoping for promotion, and the clothes Dawne coveted. What they said had to do with their efforts to make a little extra money, or paying their way by washing the woodwork of an old man's house and tacking down his threadbare carpets.

When he heard their news he would mention the savings in the Halifax Building Society and the goodwill of the shop and the valuation that had been carried out four years ago. He would mention again that men of all ages should have somewhere to go of an evening, or in the afternoons or the morning, a place to be at peace. He would remind them that a man who had benefited could not pass on without making provision for the rent and the heating and for the replacing of the billiard tables when the moment came. 'Memorial to a humble man', he would repeat. 'Shopkeeper of this neighbourhood'.

In the darkness they did not say to one another that if he hadn't insisted they needed a touch of the autumn sun they wouldn't again have been exposed to humiliation. It was as though, through knowing them, he had arranged their failure in order to indulge his scorn. Creatures of a shabby institution, his eyes had so often said, they could not manage on their own: they were not even capable of supplying one another's needs.

In the darkness they did not say that their greed for his money was much the same as his greed for their obedience, that greed nourished the trinity they had become. They did not say that the money, and the freedom it promised, was the galaxy in their lives, as his cruelty was the last pleasure in his. Scarcely aware that they held on to one another beneath the bedclothes, they heard his teasing little laugh while they were still awake, and again when they slept.

BY THE SAME AUTHOR

Felicia's Journey

Winner of the 1994 Whitbread Book of the Year Award and the *Sunday Express* Book of the Year Award.

'A book so brilliant that it compels you to stay up all night galloping through to the end ... exquisitely crafted' – Val Hennessy in the *Daily Mail*

'Immensely readable ... The plot twist – a characteristic mix – is both sinister and affecting, and so skilfully done that you remember why authors had plot twists in the first place' – Philip Hensher in the *Guardian*

Two Lives

'*Two Lives* offers two superb novels in one volume ... as rich and moving as anything I have read in years ... When I had reached the ends of both these marvellous novels, I wanted to start right again at the beginning' – Glyn Hughes in the *Guardian*

Two Lives comprises the novels *Reading Turgenev* and *My House in Umbria*.

Fools of Fortune

Willie Quinton lived a pleasant, cossetted life in County Cork, untouched by the troubles ... until the soldiers came and took a terrible revenge ... Spanning sixty years, William Trevor's tender and beautiful love story has at its centre a dark and violent act that spills over into the mutilated lives of generations to come.

'To my mind William Trevor's best novel and a very fine one' – Graham Greene

Also published:

The Old Boys
The Love Department
The Children of Dynmouth
Elizabeth Alone
Mrs Eckdorf in O'Neill's Hotel
The Collected Stories
The Boarding House
The Silence in the Garden
Excursions in the Real World
Ireland: Selected Stories
Other People's Worlds